BY

GEORGE HILL

Published by White Feather Press. (www.whitefeatherpress.com)

ISBN 978-1-61808-025-7

Printed in the United States of America

Cover design created by Ron Bell of AdVision Design Group
(www.advisiondesigngroup.com)

Interior Castle photo ©iStockphoto.com/ Emmanouil Filippou
Interior battle sketches by Zack Hill (AKA-Zulu)

White Feather Press

Reaffirming Faith in God, Family, and Country!

**Fifty Caliber Endorsements to Die For!**

I can think of no other human being on Earth capable of mixing raw patriotism and humor with an unbridled knowledge of the mechanisms and machinery necessary to create the perfect cocktail of zombie apocalyptic action. George Hill writes as he is, incredibly knowledgeable, witty and above all, intense. I have known George for a long time and *Uprising USA* is evidence of why I will call on George when the outbreak begins!

*Mark Walters*
*Nationally Syndicated Talk Radio Host-Armed American Radio*
*Concealed Carry Magazine Columnist and Author*

George Hill has long been known as a talented blogger and journalist. Now his first novel, *Uprising USA*, shows readers he has a bright future in dramatic fiction as well. George's vivid writing takes readers on a fast-paced journey through a zombie apocalypse with enough detail to make you feel like a part of the human resistance. The narration is heavy with technical details that will entertain savvy readers, without bogging down the action. More than just an empty page-turner, *Uprising USA* revolves around important themes of family, responsibility, government, politics and freedom. At the same time, readers get a glimpse into the life and philosophy of George Hill, a man affectionately known to his friends as the "Mad Ogre." This is a good read for anyone, but particularly for freedom-loving Americans and fellow gun enthusiasts!

*– Duane Diaker –*
*Gun Writer and Journalist*

This is what you want to be a part of when the Zed outbreak begins. Every page erupts with relentless action as the story's vibrant characters fight for much more than their own survival. As I read, I felt like I was there, like I had my own place in this story and I could almost smell the smoke, the rot, the sweat, and the tyranny. *Uprising USA* is what zombie fans have been missing and it's chock-full of special delights that any gun lover will appreciate. 100% pure win!

*– Daniel Shaw –*
*Host of Gunfighter Cast*
*US Marine Infantryman*
*Weapons and Tactics Instructor*

Move over, *Zombieland*! The Mad Ogre has arrived with the ultimate post-zombie-apocalyptic gore and gun fest. Funny, demented, and right on target – like the author – *Uprising USA* is the latest and greatest addition to the zombie apocalypse canon. Read it now or face the wrath of Mad Ogre!

*– Marcus Wynne –*
*Author of Warrior in the Shadows & Brother in Arms*

# UPRISING
# UK

# Dedication

To my beloved bride, for always backing me up.

Special thanks to the members of WeTheArmed.com.

## The Ogre has Landed

We had been in the air for fourteen hours straight, so when the pilot called back that we were approaching Scotland, I was happy to make my way up to the cockpit. Below us, the clouds were a thick blanket over the country. When we started to descend, we had no idea where the ceiling was.

"Just keep going down until we break through." I urged.

"This is Scotland, we might not break out of it until we auger into the ground." The pilot said as he pushed the nose of our C-17 down.

"That's not going to happen. I have too much to do today and crashing isn't on the list. Don't have time for it."

The pilot cautiously pulled back on the throttles and slowed the plane as clouds completely enveloped us. "Five thousand feet."

Water condensed on the windows, turning into rivulets, making visibility all the harder. "Four thousand feet."

I noticed the pilot pulling back slightly, "Give me some flaps." The Co-Pilot nodded and lowered the flaps slightly. I could feel the increased drag pulling the aircraft and the nose coming up, but we continued to descend. Suddenly the clouds gave away and the ground was visible below us.

"There it is." The pilot said.

"I told you. Don't have time to crash."

We flew low and slow over Inverness, Scotland. The sky was heavy and we had a low 3500-foot ceiling. We didn't have a lot of visibility, only a couple miles, but we saw enough. The city was completely lifeless as far as normal life goes, but the streets were filled with shambling undead. "Sir, with all due respect, you are freaking crazy."

I nodded. I was sure he was right. "Thanks for the support there, appreciate that."

"Okay, there is the Inverness Castle." The pilot pointed to a large squarish stone building coming up on the right. "There is no landing near here." The pilot announced what I was thinking.

"That's fine. We can fight our way in. They always want to do it the hard way." I looked as far ahead as I could see through the cockpit. "Bank right a bit. Take a heading more to the south. Leys Castle should be that way." I pointed and the pilot banked the aircraft. I got lay of the land in my mind as we flew over. Off in the distance, back northwards I saw a wisp of smoke from a chimney. Someone was left alive here.

"There it is." The pilot said as we passed over the small castle. From the air, Leys looked tiny. It was nothing compared to Inverness Castle, but the fact that there was little more around it than trees was a good thing. It would make a great base of operations until we found or had taken better. I looked at it as Leys passed below us. It would do just fine for now.

"Can you set it down in that field over there?" I pointed to the north east, and the pilot craned his neck to see.

"I don't know." The pilot sounded doubtful.

"Damn it, I knew I should have gotten Navy pilots to fly us." I pushed his buttons on purpose. I saw the pilot stiffen at the insult.

"Yeah, I can set her down there."

The pilot circled around and dropped his gear and flaps. Then he hit the intercom. "Landing on an unprepared surface. Everyone buckle up. This is going to get a bit bumpy."

Everyone in the plane buckled into their seats and got ready. Thankfully, the landing was smooth. The pilot had done a good job of handling his large aircraft. We hurried and unloaded the vehicles quickly. We rolled them off the field as the huge aircraft taxied around and took off the way it had come in. Moments later the second plane came in, unloaded, and took off. The third aircraft, did the same, but clipped the treetops coming in.

I took a deep breath as it climbed back up into the clouds and disappeared. *Well*, I thought, *this is it. We're in Scotland.* Green below and grey above. Just as I thought it would be. I had never been to Scotland before, but something about it felt like coming home. The unfamiliar was familiar, and, while I was a stranger in a strange land, I didn't feel out of place. I pulled up the Blue Force Tracker and plotted out where we needed to go. I had a feeling I could have driven there in the dark without any navigational help.

"Sir. Over there." The driver of the Expedition pointed. Across the field was a trio of zombies. They had been shambling in our direction. As I looked, they recognized us a possible food source and broke out into a run.

"They are fast." The driver observed.

He was right. These zombies were easily twice as fast as the zombies back in the US. They were covering the distance like Olympic Sprinters. I only said one word. "Guns." Several of my Crimson Guard brought up their weapons and fired. Rounds lanced out and tore into the zombies. Chunks of dead flesh were blasted off them. A couple of them stumbled, but picked themselves back up and kept running. Then the shooters found their range and head shots came next.

"Judas Priest." I looked at where the zombies fell and where they started running. "These zombies are different. Everyone, keep a sharp eye out."

The Girl Squad, my female bodyguard team, were intensely covering the terrain, weapons at ready, watching the treeline as everyone else got the vehicles ready to roll. Some trucks, such as the M-ATV needed air in the tires, and others were getting their weapons mounted. My bride, Debbie, also stood watch with her Remington shotgun. She was guarding the truck that had our children, as I got the other trucks lined out. We were alone, and we had no support of any kind. Even though we saw no more signs of undead near Leys from the air, we had to be careful.

It didn't take long to get everything organized. Isabella drove the lead in the M-ATV, following the course I plotted for her in the Blue Force Tracker. I followed, driving my heavily modified Ford Raptor. We crossed the fields and found a gap between some trees and passed through a wood line into another field and were soon in front of Leys Castle.

## Leys Castle

Leys Castle is small, and stretches the definition of Castle, but its solid stone construction and high windows and heavy doors make for a good fortification against the undead. I had wanted to take Leys eventually, but now was as good of a time as any since it makes for a good starting point into Inverness.

"CONTACT LEFT!" April was up top in the turret with her .50 BMG, but she used her ACR instead. Good girl, I thought. The ACR was suppressed, and the reduced sound signature would attract fewer zombies. I heard firing before I saw the threat.

Zombies were coming out of they wood line across the field. They were fast. Very fast. Ruth, in the M-ATV's turret opened up with her M-4. About forty Zeds were racing at us. I picked my 930 SPX out of the rack and stepped out of the truck. The Crimson Guard were firing at the zombies from the other vehicles with suppressed weapons. All that firepower against only forty zombies was not much of a concern to me. I turned my back on the incoming zeds and looked at the castle. The doors were shut. Knocking would probably yield no results.

I turned around and saw only a few zombies left. They had crossed most of the field in no time. I raised my shotgun and aimed at the one closest to me. 35 yards, 25 yards. April's last shots killed it, and I didn't have to fire. I was grateful for that, as I didn't have a suppressor for a shotgun. Standing orders were to use suppressed unless otherwise ordered. Gunshots could bring zombies from miles around. The other general order was to aim, make shots count, conserve ammo as much as possible. We only had as much ammunition as we had brought with us.

The area was quiet again, and no more zombies were in view. Into my radio, "Secure the area around the castle. Let's not be taken surprised by anything." Men jumped out of the trucks and started patrolling around the castle.

The only men that had come with me were completely loyal and sworn members of the Crimson Guard. Each one well armed with 5.56mm suppressed weapon, side arms, and large knives. All wore multicam BDU's and jungle boots.

As small as Leys was, it was still impressive. I was looking up at the windows, and all of them seemed shut tight. The front doors had a covered entrance, like a car port that you could drive under. Above that, large windows. I couldn't tell if they were open or not. Just for fun, I checked the front doors. Locked, of course. The doors were built of heavy timbers. The wood was torn up with deep scratches and smeared with now dried blood. A fingernail was embedded in the wood. Zombies wanted to get in, but the doors held.

"Looks like we're going to go up stairs." I looked at Isabella, "Izzy, drive the M-ATV half under this thing so I can climb up."

Izzy looked at me, looked at the castle and nodded. She jogged back to the M-ATV and pulled it up. When she stopped, I climbed up on top of the truck's roof. I had to jump, but caught the upper edge and pulled myself up. Joy followed me. From up here, I looked at the convoy and the surrounding area. I nudged Joy and pointed out a zombie that was shambling up the road. Joy raised her ACR, took careful aim, and fired a single round that popped the zombie through the head. It fell backwards and was still. "Good shot." Joy smiled and flicked her weapon back to safe.

I turned to the window. It was locked, but I didn't want to break the glass. I examined the window and saw that it wasn't the most secure. I pulled one of my blades out. With shockingly little effort, I slipped my Becker Companion into the frame and popped the latch. With relative ease, I pushed the window in to open it all the way. The wood was softer than it should be. Then again, this was an old castle. Not old by castle standards. By castle standards, this one was brand new. It was built in 1833.

I pushed aside the curtain and went in. I had just entered a castle using a knife to break in. I almost laughed out loud at that. It was dark inside. The radio crackled in my ear piece. "You okay?" It was Debbie. I clicked my mic key twice to acknowledge affirmative. There was an electric lamp on a stand near the window. I flicked the switch, but it didn't come on. There was no power. I didn't think there would be, but it would have been nice. The tactical light on my shotgun, however, worked just fine. When I flipped the light's toggle, the powerful beam lit up the room. The room was decorated with ornate art work and gilding. Gaudy. Taking up most of the room was a huge bed with a canopy. Leys was nothing more than a hotel for tourists. A fancy bed and breakfast. But it would serve our purposes just fine for the time being.

We cleared the room, finding dried blood streaks in the bathroom, but nothing else. We went to the door and I decided to transition to my handgun. It had a can on it and the shotgun didn't. Joy slowly pulled the door open. In the hallway I saw a zombie; it was tall and gaunt, leaning against the wall, its head against a portrait. It was just standing there, breathing heavily.

"Psst." I whispered. "Hey you."

The zombie turned its head and milky eyes to me. Its lips pulled back over yellow teeth and blackened gums. As it turned, I saw the other half of its head, bare skull bone. The creature was emaciated, completely skeletal. It's clothes, while stained and filthy, were at one point probably very nice. It was a wool suit that now hung off of him like clothes on a hanger. The zombie took steps in my direction but it was slow and awkward. The expression on its face was almost a pleading, like it was begging to eat. A single shot dropped him and he fell like a sack of laundry. I approached the corpse and looked at the painting. Then I looked back at the zombie's face. Strangely, the man in the painting looked like the zombie, if you put about forty pounds back onto him and gave him blue eyes again.

This made me wonder if the zombie was staring at the picture trying to remember what he was. The thought gave me a chill, but I had no time to dwell on it. I motioned for Joy to come on and she entered the hall like a member of FBI's HRT, smooth, quick, and with her weapon up.

We went down the hallway to the stairs and started down. Zombies had gathered by the front door, hearing the vehicles outside had attracted them. These zombies were much like the first. Well dressed skeletons that still moved. The flesh on the bones was dry and brittle. We saved our ammo and used our big knives to hack the dead back to death. The Becker Bowie made easy work of the fragile zombies.

"They didn't even moan." Joy said. "It was like they wanted us to end them."

"Look at the door." I said.

The heavy wooden doors were barred from the inside. The zombies had forgotten how to unbolt it. Instead they had clawed at it, worse than on the outside. I unbolted the doors and pulled. Izzy and Ruth were outside, one kneeling facing the doors, the other facing out for security. "I want a full sweep of the building, clear every closet, under every bed. And pull every corpse outside and stack the bodies out back, out of sight for the time being." It took only 20 minutes before the Crimson Guard had the building cleared and the dead dragged out. The castle was now deemed safe.

I walked over to the Raptor and opened the passenger door. "My Lady, your castle awaits you." I took Debbie's hand as I led her to the entrance. We were almost knocked down as my boys rushed in. The twins had their P-90's and Kilo had an AUG, all with suppressors. The younger boys ran in full of excitement. I nodded to Ruth who looked worried about them and she chased off after them.

"Sir." One of the Crimson Guard approached me. His name was Alan, and he was a former member of the 19th SF group. He volunteered to join us as he had family in the UK. "This area is secure, we have a 150-meter perimeter around the castle grounds. Up the road," Alan pointed, "we have walking dead... only a few of them though and they are not coming this way at this time."

"Excellent. Have those zeds cleaned off when someone gets the chance or they get bored."

"Of course." Alan said. "Sir, I request a couple of men for a recon into Inverness."

"That's fine, Alan. But be extremely careful."

"Yes, Sir."

"Alan..."

"Yes, Sir?"

"You can call me Ogre."

"Yes, Ogre, Sir." He snapped a salute and jogged off. I shook my head. The Crimson Guard had unstrapped the KLR-650 off the back of the Deuce and rolled it up near the door. There was no way I was going to leave my bike behind.

"George," April called as she climbed out of the truck. "Message." I went over to the Raptor and looked in at the computer.

"If you can take Duart castle without knocking it down, I'd consider it a favor. - MacLean."

I had to laugh. I suspected that our friend from Seattle would show up eventually. I sent the following message back.

"If I take it, I'm putting my clan's tartan all over it."

I turned back to the castle and smiled. Small, but solid. A good little castle. It would be the first of many.

## Clearing our New Home

One of the priorities for us was getting our communications set up. And that meant power. We had several portable generators which we had brought with us. These were placed up on the roof. Fuel tanks were placed on ground level with lines going up to the generators. This way they could be refueled without carting diesel fuel up stairs. With power for the coms systems, we had our radio and satellite systems online.

We sent reports back to the States, reporting our position and status. Moments later we received conformation that our message was received.

"Any local traffic?" I asked.

Our radio operator listened in on all frequencies for any other radio signal. He shook his head, there was no other signals. At least not now.

"Well, keep trying. If we have survivors in the area, we'll want to help them as soon as possible."

The RO nodded and turned back to his equipment.

My boys were kicking back, stretching out their legs and getting drowsy, snacking on some dried fruit leather and beef jerky. I was with them when we kept hearing a low thump. At first I thought it was someone up stairs or in another room setting up some equipment. But it never stopped.

*Thump.*

I got up and started trying to located the sound.

*Thump.*

I walked into another room.

*Thump.* The sound came from a closet.

I found a hidden door in the closet below some dresses and knelt down. I pulled an Energizer Hardcase tactical light off my vest and turned it on. The LED beam was plenty bright enough and I shined it on the door. It was partially hidden as the seams matched the wallpaper.

*Thump.*

The sound was coming from behind this hidden door. Carefully I pulled the door open and let the beam shine in. It was pitch black in the small passageway.

From deep within the passage, I saw a pair of eyes. There was a rush of rotten air that almost made me gag if I had not been used to it. I put the Hardcase light down and had just put my hand to the grip of my suppressed pistol when something crashed into me. It was a small boy at one point. Its arms were grey and mottled with black streaks and decayed flesh, but it was strong. The thing had pushed me over backwards and I was lucky to grab the zombie boy by the throat and kept it from biting me.

It was grunting and shrieking at the same time, frantic and frustrated that it couldn't get its teeth on me. What it could do though was slash at me. It no longer had fingernails, but the bones in the tips served just fine as weapons. I had been in this situation before, but before the zombie was much larger and heavier. This time I was able to hold it away from me while I pulled my knife out.

"Sorry kid."

The Becker knife slide through the brittle skull like it was a crusty old pumpkin. The zombie still thrashed until I gave the blade a twist. When I did, the zombie boy was turned off like a switch. It just went limp and I stayed their holding the blade's handle in one hand, and the throat in the other. I looked at the kid and recognized that he was probably about ten years old when he had been bitten. Bitten and hurt, then ran and hid in the secret passageway. He had blonde hair at one point and the realization made me fear for my own boys. What if this was one of my own kids?

I rolled the kid off to the side, pulled my knife out, and stood up as Joy and April came running into the room.

"We had this room cleared!"

"Where did he come from?"

I pointed. "Secret passageway. There are probably more of them. Have them searched out. We can't have anymore surprises."

I went back to the other room and just sat and held my youngest boy.

"What's wrong, Dad?" One of my boys asked.

"Nothing... nothing now." I lied.

It was getting late in the evening and everyone was settling in when our recon team called in.

"Recon One to Leys Actual."

"Leys Actual, Go ahead Recon One."

"We have a Sit-Rep for the Ogre."

"Roger that, Recon One, hold on a second."

One of the Coms guys, Martin, I think his name was, came running downstairs to get me. I was playing poker with some of the men and Caroline. Caroline and Mike were doing too well and I was beginning to suspect an alliance. But I was confident that I had the upper hand this time.

"Sir, Recon One is on the radio."

I looked up at Martin and then back at my cards. "Bad hand anyways. I fold." I tossed my pair of eights and pair of queens on the table and stood up. Mike looked at my cards and groaned. *Damn it*, I thought to myself. *I would have had him.* I went upstairs to the coms room, which was set up in the top floor and took the radio.

"Go for Ogre, Recon One."

"Recon One has entered Inverness. Take away the zombies, this place would be a ghost town, Over."

"Roger that, how many zombies are there?"

"A lot, Sir. More than I care to count. Almost the whole population of the city, or so it seems."

"Understood. I saw some smoke to the north east of the city, looks like it was coming from a chimney. How about you take a look, Over."

"Will do. Recon one, Out!"

Torching a Prius

Alan sat in the LAV-25 and looked out his view port. Hundreds of zombies surrounded his vehicle. Shoulder to shoulder they reached, they scratched, and they moaned. Alan ignored them. An LAV-25 is a large armored fighting vehicle that can shrug off small arms fire. Teeth and fingernails were little concern. The moaning was annoying, but he could push that out of his mind.

He turned his eyes to the buildings, the windows, and searched for signs of actual human life. The city was full of houses that stood together as tight as the zombies. Most of the windows were dark and empty. Others had curtains or shutters drawn tight. Some windows had blood streaks here and there. If anyone was still human, they were not making themselves known.

The one thing that was alive though, were the crows. It seemed that there were no crows over Inverness when they first got there, but now they were plentiful.

"Hey, Richards." Alan said.

"Yeah?"

"What do you call a bunch of crows?"

"A flock?"

"A murder. You have a flock of birds, but it's a murder of crows."

"Don't be melodramatic." Richards guffawed.

"No, he's right." Barnes said. "It's called a murder." Barnes was the gunner, who normally kept his own council but liked seeing Richards get his feathers ruffled.

Alan nodded, "Goes back to the black plague days."

Richards turned back and glared at Alan. "That's some unnecessarily grim shit right there." Richards turned back through his open hatch and looked up at the crows that lined the tops of the buildings, cawing down at them. Others circled overhead. The whole sky was grey and flecked with black swirling spots. "Let's get moving please."

Alan nodded "Yeah, there's nothing here." Richards put the LAV into gear and rolled forward at a slow, easy pace. Zombies fell under the LAV and got flattened. Driving through the sea of undead was no more difficult for the big 8 wheeled vehicle than driving up hill. What was difficult was the sensation, even just the imaginary sensation, of rolling over human bodies. Alan could just feel the wheels of the LAV crushing the heads of what used to be humans. It made him sick.

Recon One turned and headed north east and sped up. They saw a wisp of smoke and followed it out of the Inverness city proper. As they left the city, zombies followed, running hard with no sign of slowing down. Alan turned the turret around and had the gunner fire along the road they had just come down. The pack of undead running after them didn't seem be bothered by the large weapon, they just kept running and shrieking and moaning. 25mm HEAP rounds splattered the zombies in long streaks, each round blasting apart several dozen at a time. Suddenly the LAV was no longer being followed. Alan sighed as he looked at the darkening grey sky. He had yet to see any blue overhead and it looked like he wouldn't for a while yet. He turned the turret back to face forward.

When they found the smoke they also found a little house behind some trees in the middle of a thick garden. Smoke was indeed coming up through the chimney, but there was not much left of the house. Fire had gutted the home and was still burning. The question came to his mind as to how the fire started. There was no electrical power in the area for poor wiring to ignite it.

There were few zombies around here, so Alan jumped up out of the commander's hatch and looked around. Much of the garden was scorched, but the lush greens and rain held the fire. Alan jumped off the LAV and walked around the house. WWII style Jerry Cans lay on the stone walkway that connected the house to the street. As Alan searched the grounds, he found a partially fallen wall that allowed an easy entrance into the house. Alan checked his MP5SD and flicked the safety off before he ducked inside the small house. Inside he found two charred corpses tethered to the remains of a heavy wooden table with chains. He knelt down and took a closer look. The chains were around the legs of each of the bodies. The smell of the burned meat was still strong, so this had happened very recently. Everything in the house was overdone barbecue.

Alan keyed the radio. "Coming out."

"Did you find anything?"

"Well, this was no accident." Alan said into the radio to the Gunner who was now sitting in the Commander's seat.

"What did you find?"

"Gas cans, three of them. Bodies, two of them. Someone wanted this place to go up."

"So what? Who cares? Come on, let's go."

"Well, it tells us something."

"And that is?"

"Someone is alive around here." Alan said as he jumped back up to the turret using the tires as steps. Back in the vehicle, Alan marked the location on the BFT and made a note.

"Can I make a request?" The gunner asked.

"Sure. What is it?"

"Can we take a closer look at that big castle we saw."

"Why not? Oh, wait a second." Alan popped up out of the turret's commander hatch and looked at the small red car parked across the street, half through a hedge. It was a Toyota Prius. "I'll just be a second."

Alan jumped out of the big armored fighting vehicle and jogged across the street to the car. Yup, it was a Prius. Alan pulled something off his tactical vest, pulled the pin, and jogged back to the LAV. As he climbed in, there was a dull "Thump" and the interior of the Prius was instantly engulfed in flames that licked the sky from the partially opened windows.

"What was that about?" Richards asked.

"Standing orders for Crimson Guard. Toyota Priuses get burned on sight."

"Ah…" Richards thought about it for a moment. "All of them?"

"All of them."

"Why?"

"Because they're a lie. They're supposed be good for the planet and make baby seals smile as they drive past. But in reality they are worse for the environment because of what goes into building them."

Richards considered it. "Not because they are slow and ugly and get worse gas mileage than any car with a diesel engine?"

"Now you are hitting all the high notes. Lets get rolling."

The LAV turned back around and reentered Inverness.

They drove around the famous Inverness Castle. The castle itself was sound, but the signs of battle surrounded it. Bodies of the dead lay strewn around, in some places in thick piles. They drove up to the entrance and stopped. The doors of the castle had been crushed inwards. The doors were not all that heavy or strong, but solid enough that whatever crushed them had to have been massive.

"Let's dismount and check this out." Alan grabbed his M4 and climbed out. He looked up at the tall castle walls. Already the crows were landing and crying at them. Alan had the thought that they were watching them for reasons other than hoping they might drop some crumbs. "Richards, come on. Barnes, man the turret and keep watch."

Alan jumped off the LAV and shouldered his M4. As he approached the doors he was almost overwhelmed by the putrid smell of decay coming out.

"Oh my God!" Richards turned from the door and retched.

Alan went inside and found the scene of a horror show. Gallons of blood and chunks of meat covered the floor. Large smears of blood tracked deeper into the castle. It looked like bodies had been dragged.

On the walls were writing, in blood, and pentagrams. The writing was in another language and Alan couldn't read it, but he knew what a pentagram was.

"I don't like this one bit." Alan whispered. "We should report this."

"What? To the Ogre? What's he going to do? Who the hell is he anyway?"

Alan turned to Richardson. "He's the guy that's given you a purpose. Would you rather be back home in Detroit starving to death hiding from the zeds?"

"Hell no! Detroit was a shit hole even before the uprising."

"Then remember that and show some respect." Alan sighed heavily.

"I heard he was some sort of tactical trainer before he was a politician. How does a politician know how to shoot?"

"The Ogre was a grunt when he was younger."

"Bullshit."

"You know where I first met him?"

"Some fundraiser?"

"Fort Benning, the ITC. He was the NCOIC at Malone 18. He was my ARM Instructor. Mean as hell too."

"You're kidding me."

Alan looked at Richardson, "No, I'm not kidding. I remember I complained about my rifle one time. He said to sit there while he shot the course. He goes and grabs an old Winchester .30-30 and shoots the course standing. He shot the whole course clean. Perfect expert score. And do you know what he said?"

Richardson just looked at Alan. "He said nothing. He just looked at me like he was disappointed. Then he walked away shaking his head. I was 18 years old and I still remember that like it was this morning."

"His shooting?"

"That look." Alan glanced up at the sky again. It was almost completely dark. He keyed his radio to call Leys Actual.

## Fried Fish and Eels

Debbie was busy cleaning out Leys and had several people running buckets of soapy water and rags over the messy bits. In the kitchen was a large fridge filled with rotten foods. The power had been out for some time. The pantry held dried and canned goods, which were all still fine. None of the labels she read were anything she recognized. VAW Special Batter Flour, Dri-Fri Gold, canned haddock, jellied eels, and pickled fish. The stuff she found the most of was tea and biscuits. Bags and bags of dried teas of all sorts and biscuits, small dried cookies and crackers.

"I guess we could fry up the fish and eels?" I tried to be helpful.

"That sounds disgusting." Debbie said.

"I'm sure it's not that bad." I took a jar of pickled fish and opened it. Debbie wrinkled her nose.

When I pulled out a large fish and ate it, I suddenly wish I hadn't. I only chewed it a few times and swallowed the rest down. The flavor was strong. "I'm sure it would be pretty good on a cracker with some cheese."

"Fine you eat it."

"Naw, I'm good. Save it for the boys."

Suddenly the radio crackled. "Recon One to Ogre."

"Go for Ogre, Recon One."

"We're at Inverness Castle. There was a huge battle here."

"Not unexpected, Recon One."

"Looks like the defenders lost, Sir. Castle doors are breached. We can't see anything alive inside now, but you should see this."

"What is it, Recon One?"

"Writing on the walls, Sir. And I don't mean figuratively. You need to see this."

"Roger that. I'm coming to take a look."

"We'll be here waiting for you, Sir. Out."

"Oh man, we have to sit here and wait?" Richards said in disgust. "This place gives me the creeps, and it smells."

"You got some place else to go?"

"Any place but here."

"You mean like someplace that hasn't been checked out yet?"

"No, but..."

"Then shut the hell up. Your making Barnes twitchy. Just keep an eye out." Alan said and turned his eyes to the large statue of Flora MacDonald.

I walked outside. Uncle Musket was sitting in the back of a Deuce and a Half and he had the stock off the action of one of the many old fine shotguns and double rifles we had found in Leys, wiping it down with an oily cloth. I had claimed a beautiful Holland and Holland for myself and let the men have the rest. "The weather here will tarnish even gold." Musket was grumbling.

I cleared my throat loudly to get his attention but he kept on muttering to himself.

"No wonder our kinfolk left this place. I feel moss in my bones already."

"Musket!" I yelled at him.

My brother finally looked up and saw me. "Aye lad, I am here. You don't have to shout so."

"I'm going to Inverness Castle to check it out. Recon says that the defenses were breached and that there is some strange writing on the walls. I'm going to see if the Castle is a viable point of defense. You want to come?"

"Sounds good! If I stay here much longer I'll grow roots. Let me get this old smoke pole back together first!"

"I'll bring the ride around."

April and Joy came with me.

I jumped into the LAV and fired it up. "Hey, I'm the designated driver for all cool cars." Joy insisted. "Do you know how to even drive one of these?" I asked.

"Sure I do. I had a Marine show me back in Utah after your brother Josh got there."

I climbed up to the Commander's seat, while April took the Gunner's seat.

"Do you know how to use the…"

"Marines at Ogre Ranch taught me." She beamed at me.

"Well, then. Driver, take us to the front of the castle to pick up our Musket." The LAV lurched forward and we drove around the castle wide and a bit too quickly. "Easy, driver."

The rear hatch lowered and three Crimson Guards jumped in, armed with suppressed M-4s. Musket climbed in with two long guns and two pistols in his belt along with a wicked looking bowie and a tomahawk. "Let's go get us a bigger castle!"

# Evil at Inverness

Joy rolled the LAV through the thickest groups of the mob, gunning the engine and laughing the whole way. The LAV's lights shown harsh against the dead faces before they went under the wheels. I was slightly disturbed to find that I was chuckling too. April fired a couple rounds from the 25mm Bushmaster chain gun with the results of almost clearing a street as the projectiles caused a wake of gore like a speed boat skimming across the top of red water.

It didn't take long before we pulled up to the front of castle Inverness, where the other LAV was waiting. I looked at the castle and saw how the door was crushed in like it was made of balsa wood. The shape of Inverness was impressive. It truly looked like a castle that could withstand a siege. Until you looked at the bottom level and saw that it was much like a hospital or school building, and I knew it would be a difficult position to defend. But not impossible. I was still hopeful.

Alan climbed out of his LAV as did I. From the darkness a fog was forming, coming off the river Ness. This gave our lights distinct beams like spotlights, and made the area around the front of Inverness Castle seem to glow.

"Have you gone in yet?" I asked.

"You said to wait."

"I did, didn't I? Did you spot any survivors?"

"No, Sir. Some signs that there was some, but nothing that looked recent but one thing. That smoke you wanted me to look at. The house had been burned. Gas cans were out in front of it. Torched the place on purpose. Couldn't have been more than a couple days at most."

"No clues as to who or why?"

"No, Sir. There were a couple bodies chained inside, charred beyond recognition. Could be that they were burned on purpose. Maybe whoever lit it used the house as a funeral pyre."

I caught a glimpse of a zombie that was coming up the road to the castle and considered the new information. While thinking, I raised my handgun and put the glowing tritium front dot on the zombie's head and let the trigger break. The zombie fell backwards like a sack of wet laundry without a twitch.

I looked at the Castle door and the blackness inside. I felt cold all of the sudden, but I was determined. "Well then… Let's do this."

We went inside moving quickly, tac-lights searching. I was pleased with how well April and Joy moved compared to the guys from the 19th. Since I first met them, the girls had become very good at running and gunning. Jen was getting very good too, before she died. I had to turn my thoughts away from that painful memory… and the shame that came after it. I looked away from April and looked at the writing on the wall, illuminating it with a hand-held Surefire Executive light. The writing wasn't any script I knew, but I thought I recognized it from somewhere. Just couldn't place it.

"Do you know what it says?" Alan asked.

"I think it's a warning. I've seen that writing before, but I don't know what it says. We'll find someone who knows what this is."

Alan nodded.

I took some photos with a small digital camera. The flash from the camera bathed everything in reflected red.

"No survivors, huh?"

Alan shook his head. "None yet. Maybe they're hiding."

"We'll find them."

## Catching the Red Eye

Uncle Musket stayed with the vehicles, sitting on top of one with his musket in one hand and a suppressed 1911 in the other because of my insistence. Until he could fit a gun muffler to the old muzzle loader, it was an operational necessity. Begrudgingly, he accepted that. He flicked the safety on and off. Click. Click. Click. Click. Click. "Huh?" Musket stopped and listened, tilting his head. There was something out there in the fog. He could hear shuffling off in the distance, but he couldn't tell where it came from. He stared into the swirling mist, looking through the light and dark and not seeing anything. But he could feel it. He left the pistol off safe.

The entrance was a vast wide space, but the whole thing felt less castle and more office space or hotel. It was no longer a fortress. However its excellent position still made it valuable. As we searched we found everything that you would find an average visitor center, but something wasn't right. I stopped and signaled everyone to halt and be quiet. We listened, and I closed my eyes and felt the air. This place was dark and not just for the lack of light. Something happened here beyond just a swarm of hungry zombies. For one, the door was crushed in by something large, and it didn't have the markings of undead scratching at the door and pressing in on it.

The blood on the floor and the drag marks through it, smearing the blood down hallways. It dawned on me what was missing. Footprints. Bloody tracks. I didn't mention it to the others, but this was not right. I motioned everyone to start searching again and we went deeper into the castle.

We cleared room after room, finding nothing. When I turned down a hallway near the rear of the castle, my light panned over dark streaks on the floors again.

We moved forward, following the dried blood and we found them. Behind a closed door in the upper floor of the large tower overlooking the river, we discovered a room with bodies stacked like cord wood. Methodically and uniformly all the way to the ceiling. The builder stacked the bodies alternating heads and feet so the stack didn't want to lean and risk a collapse.

Each body was whole, and killed in the same way. Their throats were slit. Men, women, children, each one executed then brought here. They were probably killed near the entrance.

We didn't step into the room to look closer. None of us wanted to. It was once inches deep in blood. From evaporation or leakage what remained was a thick sticky coating that looked like black fruit leather. The whole place was ridden with flies and maggots and the smell was enough to knock you over. Here we finally found foot prints. Bloody prints lead to and from the room. More than one set of prints. I studied the prints and noted at least three sets going in and out. The steps leading away from the room were straight, like a man walking normally. Not the staggering, shuffling steps of the mindless undead.

Alan was thinking the same thing I was. From behind me as I knelt to look at the prints, he said "This wasn't zombies." His voice was just above a whisper. I only nodded before I stood back up and looked at him.

"Who did this or why, we don't know yet. But we will find out. Justice will be served."

Alan nodded and I saw his grip tighten on his rifle.

My impulse was to purge the castle, cleanse it with fire, and leave this place in ashes. We left the tower and finished clearing the castle. There were no survivors anywhere.

"Musket to Ogre... are you there, Master Ogre?"

"Ogre here, go ahead Musket."

"I could hear zombie moans all around... a great lot of undead. But then they all suddenly stopped. Something is about to happen, Brother! Get out here!"

Musket very rarely ever calls for help. We ran back to the main entrance and saw why. As a small breeze picked up, some of the fog was pushed away, revealing Musket's cause for alarm. He was right. Zombies were shoulder to shoulder at the base of the hill and were poised like sprinters waiting for the starter's gun. But they were holding their ground. Waiting. I could think of only one reason. A Red Eye was out there.

"Get in the LAV's!"

We ran to our respective vehicles and climbed in. The zombies, at least a thousand of them at the base of the hill.

Alan came over the radio. "Why are they just standing there? What in the hell is going on?"

"They are being held back. There's a Red Eye in the area." I answered. "Scan the crowd, look for something different."

Alan's LAV pivoted and pulled up alongside mine. I glanced over and saw his turret slowly move back and forth. At the back of my mind I had a distinct feeling that something filled with malice was watching us. I looked up and noticed the crows. What had been a few dozen was now hundreds. I turned my attention back to the zombies and looked at the mass of grinning undead.

"Gunners, use your IR." as soon as I said it, I saw him. Front center of the undead, one in particular stood out. He wasn't swaying or jerking back and forth like the others. He stood stone cold still. He was tall and thin and wore a leather jacket. Sunglasses covered his eyes. I noticed his hands were fists and he wore a sly half grin.

Through the IR view the gunners both recognized the Red Eye due to the enormous heat bloom. "Red Eye! Dead center!" Both gunners called out. "Engaging."

"Stop! Hold on a sec." I said.

"Why do you insist on talking to them?" Joy asked.

"Morbid curiosity." I said as I picked up the mic for the PA system. The turrets slowly rotated to train on the unmistakable target. The Red Eye seemed to be nonplussed by the cannons.

"Hello there, you in the black jacket with the red eyes behind those Ray-bans."

The Red Eye smiled and raised his head. "Hello back to you, American. Always a pleasure to have a visit from the colonies." It said in a whisper but I heard him clearly even across the distance and through the hull of the armored vehicle. "This is especially delightful. We've been waiting for you to come into town, George." His voice was like cold water down my back and I felt nauseous.

I turned to April. "Love, I think I've changed my mind." "

April looked at me with a raised eyebrow.

"Shoot the bastard."

"On the way." April opened up. Wham! Wham! Wham! Wham! Wham!

The Red Eye exploded and as soon as he did, the flood gates opened. Recon One opened up with the Bushmaster and the Coax. Alan had the Commander's gun rocking and rolling as well. The push of the zombies in the face of the firepower we were unleashing was impressive. The surge took them half way up the hill.

I was firing the Commander's M-240 unbuttoned, sweeping my gun back and forth. I glanced over at the other rig and saw Alan was doing the same. In a few minutes we stopped the surge, and then we were pushing them back. Musket opened the rear hatch and ran between the LAVs. He started hurling fragmentation grenades like they were baseballs. He let them cook off in his hand for a couple seconds before pitching them, so the grenades were airbursting over the heads of the zombies, blasting them apart and making holes in their lines, in spite of this, they still tried to run at us with coordination. I started looking for another Red Eye.

I saw a figure in a window to my left. It was standing in the window, close to the glass and I could have sworn I saw a glimpse of a red flash the instant I saw it. I swung my 240 over and hosed the window. Glass shattered and looked like glitter. I watched my rounds impacting the dark figure, knocking it back into the room and out of sight. I continued sending rounds into the window and then along the walls for good measure before I pulled the weapon back to the meat grinder in front of us. Soon we had the zombies running out of numbers and no more came at us. Instead of running at us, they were piled up in front of us, like a levy made up of bodies.

In the back of my mind, I heard a voice. Soft and familiar. "Return to Leys." I looked around and, for a moment, thought I didn't really hear anything. But I had the feeling that returning to Leys was the right thing to do. The Red Eyes facing us here… there was no point to it. Unless they wanted to hold us here. They could have attacked while we were still in Inverness Castle. They could have stopped us from getting into the LAVs. They didn't want to. They only wanted to delay us, to keep us from getting back. This was a diversion. Shit!

"Let's get back to Leys! Alan, move out - you got point! Rikki Tikki! Don't slow down for nothing!"

I heard two clicks on the radio and saw Alan drop into this vehicle, button up and the LAV jumped forward. "Joy, stay right on his ass."

I started to change the belt of ammo in my M-240 as the LAV surged forward and climbed over the mound of zombie corpses. I could hear the crunching and squishing sounds of the 8x8's tires as it churned through blood, meat and bone. In the distance I could have sworn I had heard the sound of a woman laughing, but as soon as I recognized it, it was gone. No bother. I had other things to worry about. Like Joy's driving. In a lesser vehicle, we might have not made it, but the LAV plowed over and through. Alan's LAV was kicking up a rooster tail of gore as one tire spun as it nosed down the other side of the corpse levy, and it was soon charging down the road. We were right behind it a moment later. I knew why Alan had dropped down inside Recon One. Being up in the turret trying to reload wasn't a good thing. I was bashed back and forth in the hatch. Even in body armor, I had taken a beating. Now that we were on level pavement, I was able to get the belt changed and the weapon cocked and ready.

We found the main road to the south and we drove out from under the fog. Thankfully. With a clear night, we could see what was ahead before we bashed through it. The ride back to Leys castle was fast and brutal. The streets were filled with the undead and we rolled over them without slowing, then just before we left the city, the zombies thinned out and we were past them.

"What was that? April asked.

"That was a welcoming party" I said. "They knew we were there. We have to assume they know where we're staying."

It was starting to get dark out. We were fast approaching Leys when we heard the radio chatter. "Contact Front!"

"Contact Rear!"

"They're coming through the trees!"

"There's hundreds of them!"

We could hear gunfire on the channel. Up ahead, over the trees we could see flashes of light and an occasional tracer zip up into the air. I didn't have to say anything to the drivers, we sped up.

"Ogre to Leys, Two friendlies coming in. Me and Recon One."

"Roger that, Ogre, you are just in time for the party. Over."

We raced to the front of Leys castle and added our guns to the fray. I could see some of my men running, but the zombies were on top of them. They were pulled down and we watched them get pulled apart. "NO!" My shouts changed nothing. The zombies jumped back up and ran for Leys as soon as the men were dead. Instead of feeding, they just killed and went hunting for new victims.

The undead had the castle surrounded, but not for long. Between two running LAVs with their 25mm chain guns, riflemen on the roof who were taking aimed shots while grenadiers and machine gunners pounding nonstop, we made short work of invaders.

"That was too easy." I said.

Alan nodded "There was probably only two hundred or so."

"They were scouts, probing us, testing our defenses."

"If that's true, they're going to come at us again. More of them. A lot more."

"Then we had best get ready for them."

We strengthened our defenses, brought people inside and up on the roof. The doors were barred. The LAV's Commander's M-240's were mounted on tripods on the roof, all three of them. We had a couple .50 caliber M2s as well. The preparations were done quickly, but no other assault came.

Finally, we tucked in for the night, with Debbie checking on the boys by the light of a candle. The Crimson Guard wore NVGs as did the Girls and I. Fatigue swept me an hour later. It had been a long day. I had Debbie and the boys safe in an inner bedroom with a heavy door. If trouble started, they would be as safe as possible. I was in the room I had first broken into when I entered Leys. My eyes were heavy. I pulled up a small couch facing the window.

Joy paced the room, occasionally looking out the windows. Set up in front of the window was an M-249 on a tall tripod mount. If the undead tried to climb up, they would not make it into the room.

April curled up on another couch next to mine, her head on a pillow of kevlar armor. Everything was quiet. My fatigue became stronger, like a weight on me, pressing me down, hanging anchors on my eyelids. I fell asleep and dreamed of the Inverness Castle.

I was a guest in the rooms when the outbreak happened. People were in total panic. The castle's staff barred the doors and we could hear screams outside. Once again I heard the laughter of a woman… a woman I had never met before, but the laugh was familiar and it sent a chill up my spine because the laugh was full of malice.

Suddenly there were screams inside. A tall man in Ray-Bans and a black leather motorcycle jacket grinned at me. He lifted his sunglasses and all I could see under them was red light. He had a metal rod in one hand. He turned to the person next to me and swung the rod. The weighted end of it crushed the man's head like it was a soft-boiled egg and he dropped to the floor. The man in leather bent down and pulled back the fallen man's head. He used a long thin straight razor and pulled it through the man's neck, cutting deeply. I could hear the blade crunch through windpipe. Then the man with the red eyes said "It's so good that you've come, George."

## Sons of the Hounds

Suddenly I felt hands on my shoulders, giving me a light jostle, "Wake up, George! Wake up! You have to get up!" I opened my eyes and I thought I saw Jen standing there, smiling at me, her hand on my shoulders. I blinked and she was gone. I shook it off. It was part of the dream. But I was wide awake.

I stood up and saw that April was still asleep. Joy was slumped against the couch, also sleeping. I was angry at first and then realized that Joy had been through everything that I had gone through and I couldn't be mad at her.

When I called a radio check, there was no answer. I ran from the room, up the stairs to the ladder that lead to the roof. Everyone was asleep up here too. Everyone in the house was asleep. This wasn't a good thing. The night was almost completely black save for a point of light high above. I heard movement behind me and spun with my hand on the grip of my rifle. Uncle Musket came up the ladder, his head slowly rising above the hatch until his eyes peeked over the edge. He looked surprised to see me. He climbed the rest of the way up, a Brown Bess over one shoulder and a flintlock pistol in one hand.

"What is it, Musket?"

"I had a dream, your girl Jen, the little busty blond one. She was waking me up like it was urgent. Told me to come up here, she did."

I turned my face up to the sky. There was a part in the clouds and I could see only a few stars. One of them was very bright, but not enough to shed any light on the darkness below. "I had the same dream."

Musket looked around. "Shiat! You know I don't like spirits… you are fooling with me. What's all this?"

I looked down across the grounds. "They're here."

"Where?" Musket asked, looking into the dark.

"Everywhere." I picked up a flare launcher and popped it. The flare shot up into the air and deployed a small chute to let it drift slowly back to earth. The harsh light it cast penetrated into the trees. Strange shadows moved inside the treeline in front of us. I knew it would be the same all around.
I raised my M-14 over my head and yelled out my Clan's battle cry as loud as I could, "SONS OF THE HOUNDS! COME HITHER AND GET FLESH!"

Two things happened at the same time. All my sleeping men were instantly wide awake and scrambling. The zombies in trees rushed forward. Musket raised his rifle and shouted as well, "Chlanna nan con thigibh a so's gheib sibh feail!" It was the same thing I said but in the original language. For a moment I wondered where he had learned that, but was too busy to give it much consideration. I leveled my rifle and started firing.

Musket fired as well, his rifle ten times louder and sounding like a truck backfiring. Soon every gun on the roof was firing, in all directions. Tracers lanced out, the flashes connecting with lurching bodies in the flickering light of the flare. In the trees I saw the glow of red eyes, glaring at me. My Trijicon ACOG made it easy to put the chevron right between the eyes, raised it slightly for range, then I let the gun buck. The glowing red eyes looked for a second that they shot out in two different directions. Just like late night coyote hunting back in Utah.

"Look for the red eyes in the trees. They have to be watching what's going on."

"I keen see that for myself, laddy! Glad you're catching on!" Musket said and fired his huge muzzle loader. Ka-pow-Boom! Out in the field, a zombie was blown open from head to his navel.

What the hell is he loading in those muskets? I shook my head and tucked back into my rifle. The zombies had reached the castle and were pounding on the doors and lower windows, trying to climb the walls. The more we fired, the more zombies came out of the trees. I concentrated on looking for any Red Eye that could be controlling the numbers. Every time I saw a pair of red eyes I took aim and fired, the eyes went out.

The horde of undead washed over our vehicles outside of the castle. They crawled over them, looking for ways to rip their way in and they screamed when they couldn't. We shot them off as fast as we could aim and fire and reload and fire again. We fought all night.

The sun came up and everything was quiet and still. The doors and windows had not been breached. Bodies piled up in the fields and near the castle. We were already smelling the decay and sickness. "Let's get the bodies carted out of here. If we don't, the stink will drive us out."

"Where do we take them?"

"Send them to France."

"Huh?"

"Throw them into the sea."

"Aye," Musket growled and went out about it. He grabbed several men for the task.

"Everyone, listen up." The Crimson Guard assembled around me. "I don't know what happened last night but everyone, myself included, fell asleep." I paced back and forth. "This can't happen again. I don't know if it was just that everyone was tired… I don't know if this was some supernatural influence. But this is unacceptable. It will not happen again. If you are on watch and you get feeling like you are about to nod off - call someone. This isn't Ogre Ranch. There is no Safe Zone here. Not yet. Probably not for a while. We're in hostile territory. Behind enemy lines. You must be vigilant. We must all be vigilant."

I looked over the field. "Rest in shifts. Count off in threes, every third man, or woman, rests. The second helps Musket with the corpse removal, the rest of you rearm and reload magazines! Am I clear?"

"Crystal!" They shouted.

The men were dismissed and went about their business. Alan stayed for a moment. "There is another castle we found. Not far. Castle Stewart. A little bigger than Leys and more defensible."

"Stewart is a fancy archaic hotel like Leys is. But it's a good idea. They know we're here. But I think a little bigger and somewhat more defensible isn't good enough. We're going to need a lot bigger and a lot more defensible. Widen your search. The Inverness Airport needs to be checked out, so head that way."

"Yes sir."

"Alan."

"Yes, Sir?"

"I'm glad to see your shooting has improved."

"Thank you, Sergeant, Sir." Alan grinned, saluted and headed to his LAV.

I went back upstairs to the room with the covered bed and big windows. I threw myself onto the bed and closed my eyes. The battle had exhausted much of our ammunition. I hadn't expected so much resistance, and I had expected more survivors. This place was almost completely depopulated.

Then it hit me. Gun Control. The UK had strict Gun Control. People couldn't defend themselves. The whole culture was against even the concept of self defense. Even this place. They had guns here at Leys. But they were all locked up in the gun cabinets in the study. Not one was used to defend the castle. They probably hadn't even thought about it. They just locked the doors and tried to call for help, expecting some sort of authorities to come save them.

April came into the room and fell down into the bed. "We're supposed to be your body guards." April started snoring. Joy had already sprawled across the couch and was out.

Debbie walked in, Remington in her hand. "It's over? The shooting went on all night."

I opened an eye. "I don't know how many, but I counted seventeen Red

Eyes."

"Seventeen? So many? There weren't even seventeen in the States." Debbie looked concerned. "And what exactly is a Red Eye?"

"At first, we thought they were just a kind of zombie." I rolled over and looked up at her. "But we soon found that they can be something more. They control other zombies. They have powers. Telekinetic powers. Cause pain. I think they can influence the living as well, put thoughts in people's head. Whisper to them. And I think they can cause people to sleep. Jen was killed by one of them. It flipped our car while we passed it. It swept his hands and it felt like a cement truck hit us." I had never told Debbie what had happened.

"How can a zombie do all that?"

"I don't know, but I think it's demonic, honestly. A possession. Their eyes are not just blood shot, but they can glow red when it's using its powers. When I killed Shannon, I saw the red eyes change to white, because the demon had left. I think it's a demon. I don't know. It's not natural." I didn't tell Debbie of what they had been saying.

"How do you fight them?"

I yawned, "We put a bullet in their head. That seems to work." I don't know what happened after I said that because I fell asleep.

Some time later, I woke up and stretched. Debbie was gone. April and Joy were still asleep, weapons in their hands, cuddled like stuffed bears.

I walked downstairs. Musket was melting metal in the fireplace, pouring it into molds, then after a moment, opening the molds and dumping the balls into a bucket of water. "I'll be needing more powder soon. And flints." There were MREs on the table and bottles of water. I grabbed one and a bottle.

"How many did you count, my Brother?" I asked as I sat down on an ornate over stuffed chair.

"Two thousand one hundred forty seven zeds. Twenty three Red Eyes total."

"I counted seventeen."

"Aye, you got seventeen... you got them... I got a few of me own. Thank you very much."

I opened my MRE pouch and pulled out chicken stew with cheese and crackers. Not an ideal breakfast, but it would do. "That's a lot of Red Eyes in one area. We've not seen that before. There's a reason for that. We never saw more than one at a time in the States, did we?"

"Aye, but you are forgetting. It's an old country here, Brother. Old stones, old bones. The adversary has had more time to sink his roots into the very rock here."

"And they are faster. They made it from the trees across the field to our walls in seconds. Zombies just aren't this fast. We've lost four men. Pulled apart and torn to shreds, then the zombies would take after someone else. They don't stop to eat like normal zombies."

"Brother Ogre, the fact that you are talking about zombies and normality in the same breath is a wee bit disturbing. Nothing is ever going to be normal again, I can promise you that, Sir. We just get accustomed to a new strangeness. Aye, they be faster here than back home across the pond. They seem more urgent, they do. Frantic, I'd say. I think it has to do with the same reason we've seen more of the bloody Red Eyes too. There's a connection. I know there is."

I looked at Musket and considered his words. He was right. "A more urgent task, with more effort put to the task. So many Red Eyes in one spot. I don't like this."

"You don't have to like them, Brother. You just have to end them."

"How do we do that? We're getting low on ammunition. Very low. We've only been here a couple days and we've used up most of it. We'll be depleted by the end of the week."

"We need to use more blades for one. That and we'll find a good ammo supply. The British Isles are not without their means. This was one of the greatest empires in the history of the world. They didn't get there by playing nice. They have ammo somewhere."

I nodded as I slurped gelatinous cold chicken stew from a bag. The wisdom of the musket, you can't argue with it.

*Engines. Aircraft engines.* "What the?"

Musket and I ran outside and looked up into the sky. Up above I saw a Globemaster. I could see it had its cargo ramp was down and a drogue chute was streaming out behind. The drogue pulled out a larger chute, which in turn started pulling pallets out the back of the plane. Each pallet fell, then parachutes opened up, leaving the cargo to float to the ground. Before the first pallet landed, the Globemaster was already banking and heading east.

"What the hell?"

"Don't look it in the mouth, Master Ogre."

"What?"

"The Gift Horse."

We watched as a huge crate landed in the field in front of the castle, its parachute fell on top of it. More landed in the field, some in the trees.

"Of course not, but who in the hell is up there?" I asked, but didn't expect an answer. Musket and I walked over to the crate. I pulled the chute away. Musket pulled out his bowie knife. "No, be careful with it. Might need it."

He sheathed his knife and helped me roll of the chute. "Fine, waste not want not."

The crate was massive and I could tell it was heavy. I looked around the crate and found how to open it. I used my Becker to pop the latch and the crate fell open.

It was ammunition. Cases and cases of 5.56, 7.62, .50 BMG, and 25mm. Others reported the same thing in the other crates that had dropped on us. I couldn't help it, I fell to one knee and gave a prayer of thanks.

"Where do you want all of this?" One of the Crimson Guards asked.

"Take it all inside Leys, and make sure everyone is reloaded and topped off. And make sure there is plenty in each vehicle."

"Yes, Sir."

I laughed as I patted Musket on the back. "Look at this!" It was a case of black powder, with a bag of new flints. His eyes went wide. "Glory!" Then Musket dropped to his knees and prayed his thanks.

## Unexpected Visitor Drops In

The next day I had just finished stoking the fire in and set the spit for a good roasting. One of the patrols found another welcomed surprise. Near by Leys, one of the farms had pigs. We took one, then fed and watered the others. I tasked one of the men to keep an eye on the farm. Someone had been caring for them until recently, but there was no sign of the owner or caretaker now. Perhaps they were hiding from us. Perhaps they had left. Or perhaps they had died for some reason.

Rosa had volunteered to turn the spit, and Caroline had to keep telling her, "Slowly, but not so slow that the juice drips off too quick."

While it was only lunch time, if they kept this up, come dinner time it would be perfect. Caroline was a fair hand with a gun, but she was even better in the kitchen, helping Rosa.

The smell of the roasting pig was keeping me from leaving. Along with a lot of the men too. Musket sat on a chair backwards, resting his chin on the back while he stared at the turning pig.

My radio crackled to life. "Captain Alan to Ogre."

"Go for Ogre."

"Check the Blue Force Tracker for my location. If you can, meet me here as soon as possible."

"Roger that, what's up?"

"Have something for you. You're going to like this."

"10-4, 10-17. Out." I walked outside to the Raptor, grateful to get away from the roasting pork. It was driving me mad. Inside the Raptor, I turned on the Blue Force Tracker. Looking at Alan's position I saw that it was in the city, across the Ness river, not too far from the Castle Inverness. I didn't think I wanted to drive the Raptor in there.

"What's going on?" April walked out of Leys Castle and came up to me.

"Just got a call from Alan. He's in the city and wants to show me something."

"Sounds good. Let's go. Just give me a second." April ran back inside.

I looked at my M-14 and decided that I might want something a little different for this run. I opened the back of the Raptor and pulled out the Truck Vault's drawer. I put the M-14 Sage into the fitted foam slot and pulled out the Crusader Broadsword Carbine. It was a .308 like the M-14, but in a smaller, lighter package. I checked the AAC Cyclone suppressor to make sure it was tight, then switched all the mags on my tactical vest. The optic was a Night Force 2.5-10 scope with a Trijicon RMR mounted at a 45-degree angle for close in work. It was a bit techy, but I felt the need to modernize.

April came out with Jen and Izzy. "Uh oh. You know something we don't?"

"Naw... just wanted some variety."

"Oh?" Joy raised an eyebrow. "Does that mean I get you under my sheets tonight?"

I winked at her and laughed. "You wish." I put on more bravado than I felt. I could feel my face flush and turned away. I shut the Truck Vault drawer and closed the Raptor's tail gate. With a quick glance at April, I saw her lower her eyes as she adjusted her ACR. Joy didn't catch anything and I hoped no one else did either.

"We're taking the Mat-Vee this time. Saddle up."

We drove the M-ATV for it's greater protection, but I was already missing the Raptor's agility and speed. As good of a rig as the M-ATV was, it just wasn't spry. What the M-ATV had though, was the ability to roll over the walking dead almost as easily as an LAV. The resistance the undead were offering us was troublesome to say the least. Normally, a zombie wouldn't pay a lot attention to a moving vehicle. They mostly reacted to the sight of people. Here, they would fling themselves at the M-ATV, frantic to grab us. I turned the corner extra wide, making sure I clipped a zombie and ran a wheel over it. As I came through the turn, I saw the LAV-25 parked in the middle of the street with dead zombies laying around it. I pulled up and saw that Alan had gone inside one of the buildings. One of Alan's team, sitting up in the LAV's turret. He was wearing a ball cap and a set of Impact Sport earmuffs. He nodded and pointed to a door.

As I approached the door, I called out, "Ogre coming in."

From inside, I heard "Roger that, watch your step."

Entering the building, I stepped over several dead zeds. As I looked around I was starting to get the meaning of Alan's message. "This is awesome." I looked around and I liked everything I was seeing.

The shop was half store, half museum. They had made armor here. Real armor. Chain. Plate. Footsoldier's to Knight's. Helms. Gauntlets. Grieves. Everything. I looked in a back room. It was stockpiled. A brochure on the counter explained that they provided armor for TV and Films.

An hour later I looked like I was off the set of *Excalibur*. I had my tactical vest over the breast plate. The vest was too small and wouldn't close over the larger steel plate so it was secured with zip ties. It was ghetto, but functional for now.

The girls had a harder time getting fitted. There was no plate mail fitted for women here, but we found chain mail, gauntlets and grieves that worked quite well for them. They wore their tactical gear over their chain mail with no problem.

I found a helmet I liked, a dark Great Helm with brass trim and the shape of a cross on the face of it. I'd have to get a set of ear-pro built in to it, but it would work.

"I want every one of my fighters geared up. No more bites!" We had lost too many men to zombie bites since we arrived. This was a casualty rate that was too high. These UK zombies were faster than the zombies back in the US. Probably because of the greater number of Red Eyes.

I looked at Alan as he came out from the back room. Like me, he retained his combat boots, but wore the plate metal shin guards. Everything else was covered in burnished steel. He looked like a Space Marine from *Warhammer 40,000*. I grinned. "Absolutely badass."

"I thought you would like this," He said with a grin.

"Hell yeah." I gave him a fist bump. "This is going to even the odds."

I moved and turned, surprised how agile one can be in armor. And how quiet it was. Under the joints of the plate was heavy leather, which kept it from clanking as I moved. "I don't know about the bright polish though." I checked the feeling of shouldering my rifle in the Armor, then adjusted the stock. At the shortest position, it worked just fine. I put on the helmet and found that I could still see through the scope. The single point sling, adjusted out to the max held the rifle just right.

"Now I just have to pick out a sword." Alan said.

"Ooh... good idea. I want a mace too." I ended up with a nice long bastard sword with a wide blade and a heavy-headed mace. The mace was carried off the belt, and the sword had a carrier that allowed it to be carried across the back. That worked. The girls picked shorter Scottish broadswords and dirks. I looked at them up and down. "Add a short Kilt and you girls would be a D&D player's fantasy."

"With automatic weapons." April said as she hoisted her ACR.

Alan's team was fully kitted out as well. "We're going to get everyone here, including my boys and their girl friends." I announced.

It was getting late, so we went back outside just in time to hear something strange.

Engines.

Aircraft engines, but they sounded wrong. "What the hell?" We looked up into the sky. A C-130 Hercules was trailing smoke and banking sharply. There was a flash and we could see flames. A moment later we saw a parachute fall out of it, then another one. Then the plane disappeared out of view and a few seconds later we heard the crash.

No orders were necessary, everyone jumped into the vehicles with a lot of banging and crashing. Getting in and out would take a little getting used to, especially into the LAV. I watched as Alan tried to jump in with his sword still across his back. The hilt caught the top of the rear hatch and it flipped backwards. He was shaken, but scrambled inside as the LAV started moving.

"Where did it look like it went down?" April asked.

I scanned around the map in the BFT. "It looked like it could have come down in Bellfield Park... let's see... we're on Crown..." I plotted the course and sent Alan the information. Without waiting for Alan's confirmation, I spun the M-ATV and raced for the park. On Southside road I looked back in the rear view and saw the coolest thing I'd ever seen before. The LAV-25 8-wheel drifting around the curve with the four front tires turned, all the wheels spinning. I envisioned Jeremy Clarkson inviting soldiers to take a lap around the track in a reasonably priced APC. Which reminded me, I wanted to find that track. I knew I could beat his time.

Idle imaginations were quickly discarded as up ahead I could see flames rising above the treeline. Once we got to the park, we could see that the Herc was completely destroyed. It had augered in upside down, nose first. Fire engulfed the bird with most of the flame shooting out of the cargo bay. The fire had spread to the trees, the whole area around the plane was also burning. The only survivors were the ones that jumped before the crash.

"Ogre to Alan."

"Alan."

"Look for chutes."

"Roger."

The LAV started to circle the park, with Alan riding unbuttoned, his armor reflecting the fire light. If we had rolled into Iraq like that, I think even France would have surrendered to us... again.

"Could the parachutes have drifted very far?" April asked.

"No. The plane was too low. Those guys would have really burned in. The chutes would barely have had time to slow them down." *If at all*, I thought. I had horrid memories of an officer in the 19th SF group that burned in like that. He suffered spiral fractures up both legs and had been unconscious from the pain and loss of blood. "We gotta find these guys before the zeds do."

I don't know why, but for some reason I went to the Ness River and looked down stream. I saw a chute, billowed with air under it, drifting out of view. "Shit."

"Ogre to Alan... I think they went in the river. I saw a chute in the water."

We heard moaning and knew that time was running out for the guys that jumped out. We searched the bank of the Ness river but didn't see anyone.

"Alan, run up to the bridge, just under the castle Inverness. Take a look from there. Might see them floating down river." At this point in my estimation we were looking for bodies. You had to be really lucky to survive a jump from 500 feet. Looking at the Herc... luck wasn't a lady for them.

"On the way, Ogre. A helicopter would be real handy about now."

I went back to the M-ATV and climbed in. I decided to drive up to the castle and maybe get a better view of the area from up there. "Ogre to Leys."

"Leys Control, go ahead Master Ogre." It was Musket.

"It's dark and the zeds are coming out to play. We have a C-130 down with two chutes observed. We have to find them before the zeds do."

"Aye, and we better do it quickly."

"Saddle up the other two LAV-25's. We could use the thermal sights to help search."

"They'll be coming along shortly, Master Ogre. Musket out."

I was almost to the castle when Isabella noticed something. She was up in the turret and had her NVGs on. "Boss, there's something up by the castle."

"What is it?"

"Can't make it out from here."

"Okay, let's roll. Joy, get us to Inverness Castle, Rikki Tikki." Joy had become an adept M-ATV driver and we were soon racing up the hill to the castle. A work detail had taken the bodies of the dead and thrown them into the river Ness to be taken out to sea. "Sent to France" as has become the phrase, even if the currents would more likely take the bodies to the Netherlands.

As we pulled up I saw the large parachute that Isabella had seen It must have been dropped before the plane was going down. The chute was draped over something large. I jumped out of the M-ATV and walked over to the chute. I grabbed it with a gauntlet covered hand and pulled the chute off. "Oh shit!"

It was a Jeep secured to a pallet. It took me a moment to recognize just what I was seeing. This rig was familiar. I'd seen it before. All of a sudden my blood ran cold as the connection was made. The Jeep belonged to our friend Louis Quarleno from back in the USA. This meant that Q either died in the crash, or he was hanging off one of those two chutes we saw.

Izzy jumped out of the turret and ran over. "Is this..." She covered her mouth with her hands, "No!"

Isabella," I said with a hand on her shoulder. "We'll find him. I'm sure he's okay." *He damn well better be okay.* Something caught my eye. A green star cluster flare. I let Izzy go and ran to the back of the M-ATV and reached in. I had a green star cluster as well. I popped it on back bumper of the M-ATV and watched the flare go up. "He's alive, Izzy. And I bet he's coming this way."

"Alan to Ogre, we've got movement."

"Roger that, Alan. I think it's our missing bird droppings."

"Ah, that's a negative, Sir. We've got incoming zeds. I'm moving back off the bridge."

I pulled my rifle out of the rack and grabbed an ammo can. "Come on, we've got to cover the bridge."

The location of the castle Inverness was a perfect position to overwatch the bridge across the Ness River. I watched the LAV backing up and off the bridge to get to a good firing position. Even in the dark I could see Alan in the commander's seat behind the M-240.

The zombies reached the far end of the bridge and started crossing it. They moved in mass, as a unit. "When they reach the half way mark, let them have it." I said to everyone. I adjusted my optic, turned on the illumination for the reticle, and took my weapon off Safe. The girls were ready as well.

"There are a lot of them." Joy said.

"Get ready, Girls. Three... two... one!"

The fight didn't last long. We were able to pick out the Red Eyes from a distance and end them before the fight really even began. The other two LAVs showed up, and the combination of all three 25mm Bushmasters made short work of the zombie mob as it tried to cross the narrow bridge. It seemed the zombies numbers in Inverness were dropping. This was a good thing. Less undead meant better odds for Q, or whoever jumped out of the Herc.

After the fight was over, we waited for an hour with no sign of Q or anyone else. I sent the LAVs around town on the far side of the bridge to search with their IR systems, but no sign was found. After another hour of searching, we called it quits. Whoever jumped was either already dead, or didn't want to be found. Which made me curious. We got the Jeep ready to drive. Keys were in the ignition and the rig started right up. It also had a full tank of gas.

If Q had made it, I suspected that he would, when able to, make it to the castle. So under the windshield wiper, I left a note.

"Sorry we missed you. Had a little party in your absence, celebrating your arrival. Bon Fire, Fire Works. Sorry you missed that. Hope you had a good swim. We'll have to do it again sometime. - G."

Fearing a Red Eye that might be able to read, I left GPS coordinates of the Castle Leys. I also left him some water bottles and some MREs, and a radio on the driver's seat. On a second thought, I left a loaded rifle and some spare magazines with the little four by four, just in case.

If Q didn't make it, or if the Jeep went unclaimed, I'd have it taken back to Leys and we'd put it to good use.

"Ogre to Alan."

"Alan here."

"I want one LAV on the bridge to provide security and support to Q as soon as he shows himself. Let him know his Jeep is at the Castle Inverness with snacks and drinks for him."

"How will we know Q?"

"He'll be the guy that is soggy, angry, hungry, and hopefully he wont be a zombie."

"How long are we going to wait?"

"Let's give him twenty four hours. Wait in rotations. If he doesn't show up within twenty hours, we can assume he's KIA."

Alan paused. "Got it." He said, quietly. The rest of us went back to Leys.

We had another mission to plan out. We had to retake the Clan's strongholds.

An hour later, Alan was sitting in the back of the LAV with his feet up on some ammo crates. He was eating a jar of pickled herring with some crackers and washing them down with some Guinness. Richards tapped on the hull, "Hey Alan, we've got some movement up ahead."

Alan dropped another chunk of fish into his mouth. "So."

"It's one guy and he's alone. Might be our man."

Alan climbed up into the Commander's hatch and pulled up his NVGs. Someone was running in a crouch up the street, keeping to the sides, ducking behind steps, mailboxes and parked cars. He took his time, working his way up the street. When a zombie appeared, the man quickly dispatched it with a suppressed rifle then moved to the next spot. When the man reached the bridge he stopped, seeing the LAV parked in the middle of the street just opposite. Alan smiled and reached down for his Surefire G2X and pulled it out. Using his hand to cover the bezel, Alan gave three quick flashes, waited a moment, and sent three more. He watched as the guy stood up and walked out of the shadows into the middle of the street and walked straight to the armored fighting vehicle.

Alan looked down at the man. "Pickled Herring?" He held out the half empty jar.

"I'd rather have some of that." The man nodded to the can of Guinness.

Alan chuckled and pulled a new can out of the box and tossed it to the stranger. "I'm hoping you are Louis Quarleno."

The man popped open the brew and drank deeply. When the can was empty, he looked up at Alan. "Call me 'Q'."

## Good Night Ogre Father

I didn't sleep well that night. Things bothered me. There were too many thoughts clouding my mind, and I was restless because of it. When I dreamed, I saw a beautiful woman across the field. She started walking to me, laughing as she came. It was a hateful laugh with no joy in it. As she walked, I looked at her. She had long straight hair, shiny black with feathers tied into it. As she got closer, I saw her face. Young and beautiful. She looked Native American. Suddenly a crow flew between us, and, after it passed, the face was dead and dried out, mostly just a skull. The laughter turned into the cawing of a crow.

I suddenly bolted awake and sat up with the sound of crows ringing in my ears. But there were no crows, no skeletal woman. I looked around with my hand on the stock of my rifle. Laying next to me, Debbie was tossing and turning. It was 4:30AM local time. I thought about laying back down, but I knew there was no more sleep for me tonight. Might as well just get up.

I swung my legs out of bed and looked over at the chair that held my armor. Cold and unforgiving, the helm glared at me like I owed it money. I stood up and walked over to the window. Moonlight illuminated the field in front of Leys and I could clearly see the men who patrolled the perimeter and I knew there was also men up on the roof with belted machine guns. Assorted military trucks and Humvees, LAV's, a Raptor, an Excursion, a M-ATV, a bunch of Toyota Hiluxs, and Q's Jeep were all parked out front.

I'd been relieved when Q got in last night. He rolled in like it was just a Sunday drive. No one was more relieved than Izzy. When Q got out of the Jeep, Izzy jumped him so hard and fast that she was wrapped around him before he hit the ground. Louis was a large man, strongly built, dark hair, dark eyes, dark stache and beard. Seeing him knocked to his butt by the little brunette that was all curly hair and attitude was one of the funniest things that any of us had seen in a long time. The laughter was just the tension release that we all needed. I was pleased to see it for another reason. Not only was it funny, but healthy relationships between the survivors were important. And I knew that Izzy needed Q as much as he needed her even if he wouldn't admit it.

Q's arrival was a huge addition to our overall strength and now we could extend ourselves a bit further. I had just the plan for that, after making a certain logistical stop.

Debbie and my littlest one slept soundly. At least they had some peace. Scotland agreed with Debbie, as I knew it would. I felt that if I could answer the questions in my head, I could find that peace as well. I was wearing sweats, and had my pistol belt over my shoulder, with my bare feet on the cold floor. It was fall and the temperatures were dropping, but we still had good weather for the most part, if you didn't mind a lack of direct sunlight. We've still not seen blue sky yet.

I peeked into the room with my boys. They were sprawled out on the wide beds, sleeping soundly.

The guard at the door was wide awake and gave me a quiet nod. He was one of the first men to join the Crimson Order. Mike was his name. He was built of muscle and sinew and wore his body armor like most guys would just wear a T-shirt. Safariland Cover-6. He was armed with a Para-FAL and a Glock 20. He had a chair to sit in, but chose to stand.

I walked around the corner. Our adopted Japanese girls were in this room. I peeked in on them. Two of them were curled up next to each other, but the third was awake. She was reading by candle light at the table in the center of the room. She was dismissive of my presence until she looked at me and recognized me. Then she sat up bolt straight and apologized for being awake like she was doing something wrong. She was frightened of me.

"No, no... your fine. You're okay." I whispered. I sat down on one of the wood chairs and smiled at her. She seemed to relax, relieved that she wasn't in trouble. She had been reading a book, and I pointed at it.

"What are you reading?" I asked.

"Oliver Twist." She said as she held it up for me to see as she smiled meekly, seeking approval.

"Ah... that's a good one." I nodded.

"You have read Oliver Twist?"

"Yes, when I was your age. I read it for school." I've not really spent much time with these girls, and I couldn't remember their names yet, or ages, or anything. But I did know that they were smart and they really liked to play pranks on everyone, but they had never pranked me. They didn't dare. Having some common ground to talk about that wasn't involving death and destruction, was a good thing. She was excited to talk about the book with someone else who had read it. We talked for few minutes about the characters and the troubles that they had. After a few minutes, I patted her head with a smile and stood up to leave the room as I heard the still timid voice. "Good night, Ogre Father." I looked back and looked at the girl's face. Innocent and full of hope, she smiled sheepishly.

"Good night, Chosen Daughter."

She beamed as I left the room. I told myself that I'd get to know these kids better. My family was growing and I had to make sure I looked out for all of them.

The guard at this door was one of the women who joined the Crimson Order after the initial group of hirelings. A former dancer and a friend of my In-Laws back in Utah. She was loyal to my family, having lost hers in Salt Lake. She had really taken to the young girls and enjoyed their company during the day. You would often find them running or dancing together. It brightened the atmosphere. I smiled at her. "Does she read a lot?" I asked with a tilt of my head to the door I had just closed.

"All night... every night. She has nightmares when she doesn't."

I went down stairs to the kitchen. Fire was roaring in the fire place, with something in the pot above it, simmering. I peeked in and found it was beans. As usual. Rosa was planning ahead for breakfast. Musket had put up a hammock again, of course, near food. He was snoring like a grizzly bear. Everything seemed fine. But I couldn't shake the itch. I went back upstairs, cleaned up, and got back into my armor.

## I Get a Bad Feeling

Something was coming. I felt it. This false sense of security was a temporary illusion. On the roof I watched the eastern horizon start to brighten. The East. That's where the trouble was. I looked at it with suspicion.

As the sun crested the horizon, the impression that we needed to get out of here was overwhelming to me. I still didn't know why, but I just knew that we needed to go really soon. Everyone. I just didn't know where. I knelt on the roof, and, while on one knee, I closed my eyes and stilled my mind. I didn't pray. I didn't ask for anything. In matters of faith, I am faithful in that I know that God is there. I just don't know if he listens to me. So I just try to listen for him.

We had to go now.

We had to go north.

North? But I wanted to go South.

*North.*

Today?

*Now*!

We've got to go now. That thought, "*we've got to go now*" felt right.

It felt urgent too.

I thought about going south. But as I did, I forgot what I was thinking about, and my thoughts became cloudy. I thought about north and it became sharp and clear. I could feel it.

I went down stairs.

"Pack everything up. We're leaving."

"What?" The guards at the kids rooms looked surprise.

"Get the kids out into the Excursion. You two are driving it."

I popped into Debbie's room. "Deb, get everything together - get out to a vehicle, we're moving."

Q was walking down the hallway, looking better than he did last night. "Pack your kit back up. We're pulling back to a different location."

"Huh?" He seemed confused.

"We've got to relocate, ASAP."

"Right." He jogged up the hall back to his room. A moment later, Izzy came dashing out with an arm full of clothes, wearing panties and a short silk top with nothing underneath it. She grinned at me as she ran past. I just shook my head. In April's and Joy's room I peeked in. Joy was polishing her new armor with a rag and April was pulling a bore snake through her ACR. They looked up as I came in.

"We've got to leave this place... we're relocating now."

"What? Why? I love this place."

"It's not secure enough. Hurry, we don't have much time. Come on. Grab your gear, throw it into the back of the Raptor. April, grab mine too."

She nodded and started scrambling. Joy always stayed in a state of near readiness so she was quick. I ran downstairs and got everyone ready to leave.

In ten minutes time, everyone was out by the vehicles. The biggest issue was with Rosa, who was in the middle of breakfast preparations.

"Put a lid on the pots. We'll take them with us". Her response was to unleash long and passionate strings of Spanish at me as she stomped back inside. The wood piles that had been cut were loaded in the back of the Toyotas. No sense in leaving them. The KLR-650 and a couple Triumphs that somehow got picked up were ridden by one of the Guards.

Sheepishly, Izzy asked to ride with Q. "Yeah, that's a good idea." I said, with a straight face. "He gets in trouble a lot, Iz. I think he could really use some help. Why don't you watch him for me. You would be doing me a big favor."

Q overheard that and gave me a shot of raised brow. "Hey, don't look at me like that, Louis... She's your new Battle Buddy. I can't have you getting your ass lost again. You don't like it, I'll assign Musket on you."

Suddenly I looked around. "Where's Musket?"

Q shrugged. April shrugged. Joy shook her head. I looked up and saw Musket up on the roof pulling down a flag I never noticed before. A minute later he was back and climbed up into the M-ATV, and soon every vehicle was rolling. We went cross country heading North East till we hit the A9 and turned north.

As soon as we had everyone going, I started to feel relaxed, like a burden was lifted. Then I noticed two things. First, we had blue skies. Bright blue, clear of clouds. Then I noticed the second thing. Leys castle had thousands of crows circling over it.

North bound lanes were relatively clear of stopped vehicles, but the south-bound lanes were clogged with abandoned cars of odd makes and models that I had heard of but wasn't familiar with. We turned east onto the A96, followed that until we turned north at Newton. I'd never been here before, so I didn't know where I was going, but I knew I was going in the right direction. A sign said that another castle was up ahead. Castle Stuart. The castle that Alan had mentioned. It didn't feel right. I kept going. We passed the airport. As we drove past it, I saw that the runways were clogged with emergency vehicles and burnt airliners. Looks like a crash between two jets on the ground as both plane had landing gear down. We passed the airport and continued north.

After awhile of driving, we came to the place I was drawn to. "This is it", I said. It certainly looked defensible. It had to be.

It was called "Fort George". I couldn't help but smile as we approached. The place was massive with barracks, a church, and all the comforts of home; which was perfect, because it *was* our new home. Fort George was old, built to suppress any Jacobite uprising, it would protect us through the zombie uprising. It was perfect to fend off zombies. Mote and walls, it even had cannons.

As we pulled in, we found bodies. British Soldiers, some civilians. All torn up. I got out and walked over to one of the bodies. They had a single Land Rover and it looked like they'd tried to make a stand. My men fanned out and searched for survivors. "Sir, All their rifles were run dry. Not a single round left."

I could see it for myself. Empty brass was all around.

"This isn't a good sign." Joy muttered.

"It's not a sign. It just means they were too few and didn't have enough ammo. We have more people, more guns, and for the time being, plenty of ammo. Besides. They didn't have Joy. We do." I smiled at her and nodded to the Fort. "Come on. We need to get moved in."

We made ourselves at home. In a couple hours, everyone was settled in. People had staked claims and we had a lot more room than at Leys or what was possible at Inverness.

"Musket, Q." I got their attention. "Organize our defenses and make a rotation schedule for sentries. With the fortifications, we can go with fewer people on if people can respond to an alarm. I want the Machine guns up, and I think here we can break out the Mark Nineteens. With that, we can rest more guys and maybe take it a little easy." The MK-19 was a belt fed, full auto, 40mm Grenade Launcher. With two of them, and with plenty of ammo, they could hold off all the zombies in England.

Q looked at Musket and both said "We're on it!"

April came up behind me. "I want to show you something, come on." She took me into one of the buildings, which served as a museum. It was filled with muskets and swords and pikes. "We can arm survivors." She said.

"If we can find any." I shrugged.

"We will. I know it." She seemed optimistic and then smiled. It was the first time that we had been alone together in some time, since... and here she was, optimistic and smiling.

"This is good. Very good." I nodded.

"Hey, uh..." April wanted to say something but I could tell she didn't know what to say. I didn't know what to say either. But I was pretty sure that I didn't want to say it. I looked down at the wooden floor and didn't say anything. I felt a swirl of emotions, all shouting at me and guilt was the loudest.

"April..." I shook my head. "I'm sorry about what happened."

"But I'm not."

"We can't..."

"George, I'm... I'm pregnant."

"Uh..." I felt like my world was caving in. April was special to me, and I cared for her. But not this.

"You're the only man I've been with in a long, long time." She said softly as she stepped to me and put a hand on my arm. "And I love you."

"April..." I felt dizzy and sick to my stomach. "I..."

"Stop. Don't say anything. I know you love me too." She wrapped her arms around me. "I know it. You just can't say it because you're married and you love your wife too."

She looked me in the eyes. "You don't have to say anything. This isn't a problem you have to deal with. No one else has to know right now, just you and me."

I looked at her. She was beautiful, and she loved me, and she was having my baby... any man would be proud. I felt like I wanted to die.

"April, I need to process this." Somehow, I already knew. When we fought the Shannon Demon. Her powers couldn't touch April, because of what was inside her, growing.

"Of course you do. It's okay. I'm going to go find our quarters." April left and I was still standing there, looking at a Pike and wondering how I could run myself through with it. That was when he came out from around a display panel. He just stood there, looking me in the eye. I couldn't return the gaze.

"It's okay, Dad. I'll keep this a secret." Kilo said as he walked out. "I don't want Mom to go to hell too... for killing you."

"Shit."

It was a mistake. I had been drunk, and I don't drink. But after Jen's funeral I'd drank a lot. And April came to find me at the Pub since I had turned my radio off. I was in one of the rooms that one of the Bar Wenches had taken me to (more like threw me in to) so I could sleep it off. April came in, wearing an LA Raiders shirt and those cargo shorts of hers. She'd had a little to drink as well. It's no excuse. But it's what happened. If I could take it back. Good God, if I could take it back!

I walked back outside some time later. Alan and Q had done a sweep of the grounds.

"Find anything?"

Q threw his rifle up casually over his shoulder. "This is a good location, Ogre. We had a couple zeds in one of the buildings, and one in the chapel, but other than that everything is clear now. We checked everything twice, under ever bed, behind every door. The fort is secure. We have a good base of operations now."

"That's great. I wish we had seen this when we came in. But at least we are here now."

## Fort George

We had finally had Inverness cleared out of usable food stuffs. Gathering teams had been thorough and scored us a mountain of supplies. Another team carefully looted all the gold, silver and gems to be found in the city and surrounding area. Wealth collection didn't mean much to us now, but it would in the future. Fuel was a bigger concern. Filling stations around the area had underground tanks full of diesel and we marked each location on our GPS systems. After locating several tanker trucks, we had pumped them full of diesel fuel and had them at Fort George so we could easily refuel our vehicles there. Military trucks drank fuel at an impressive rate, so we tried to limit running their engines. Regular gas-powered vehicles were also used when we could, such as the Toyota Hilux trucks and Land Rovers. They were more efficient, but offered less protection. Because of that, we used them mostly in areas that were more cleared than others. These areas were getting wider all the time, but they still had to be patrolled. A normal patrol consisted of teams of four armored men in a pair of Hilux trucks. Redundancy was key. If there was a problem, one truck could pull the other. And sometimes there were problems. We had a couple mechanics, but most of the time a vehicle with some sort of problem was just parked and replaced with another vehicle. We had no shortage of usable vehicles. These patrols were sent out in all directions mapping out locations of useful supplies and searching for survivors, and putting down zombies as they were found. If a large group of undead was found, they would call in more firepower if it was needed.

Other than some Catholics, a Priest and a couple Nuns, and their special needs charges, we found only a small number of survivors, nine in total. The tenth had been bitten and we were forced to put her down. This was hard on the other survivors as she was a grandmother to some, and a well known woman in the community. I was glad to see that these survivors were strong, they new it was necessary and while it was a horrible emotional crisis, they accepted it and buried the woman outside of the Fort near the woods to the east.

B9092 is a small rural highway that connects just south of Fort George back to the A92 near Nairn. Nairn was completely destroyed. Not only was the population infected, but much of the city burned to the ground. Looks like it had been burned some time ago. Probably during the opening days of the uprising. The fires contributed a lesser number of zombies and breaking our way through was not a problem. One building that wasn't scorched was a small grocery store. I was directing the loading of food supplies into the back of a truck, when I noticed a sign.

"Forres is the next town, then RAF Kinloss. Not too far either. Kilo, come with us." I turned to the senior Guard nearest to me. "I want the rest of the freight taken back to the Fort."

"Yes, Sir." the Crimson Guard said. He turned and yelled to the others. "Alright boys, let's get this food back to Fort George! We've got people to feed!"

"Kilo, come on, saddle up."

I climbed into the Raptor with Kilo riding shotgun and April taking up her usual gunner's seat and Joy riding behind me. When we started rolling, Joy did something that surprised me. She pulled out Jen's old boom-box. I had forgotten that we still had it. Joy selected a CD and popped it in. Guns & Roses filled my ears. We've not had music in some time, so it was a welcome change. Most music players require batteries, and most vehicles don't have a stereo. Batteries have become a precious commodity and are reserved for use in lights, red dots, NVGs and the like... less mission-critical devices like Jen's boom-box were almost wasteful uses of those batteries. The Raptor has a stereo, but it's behind the mounting hardware for the Blue Force Tracker.

We cruised along the A96 through Forres, weaving in and out of abandoned cars. The zombies we passed charged after us. We ignored them and let them run after us.

We reached RAF Kinloss without much incident, but did have to run through a few mags worth of rounds. At the base, we were able to roll in and straight onto the tarmac. Corpses littered the area around the hangers. Lots of spent brass. Lots of dried blood splatter and streaks.

"What are those?" Kilo asked.

I looked at the aircraft Kilo was eyeballing. There were a half dozen of them. Large aircraft, like jetliners, but swollen like they had eaten something they were allergic to. "I think those are called Nimrods. They are an Anti-Submarine aircraft."

"Can we use them?"

"I don't know. Do zombies drive subs?"

"Probably not then." Kilo admitted.

"Well, they do have long range. Just not a lot of carry capacity. But we could use those." I pointed across the runway to another set of hangers. Parked outside of those were some long, skinny, goofy-looking planes.

"What are they?"

"Those are Vigilant T-1s. Motor gliders. We can use them for observation, scouting and recon."

"Oh, that's cool, because I thought you were going to say they could bore the zombies to death."

"Not everything needs guns on it."

"Yes, I think they do. That's why you put guns on that little plane you brought to Ogre Ranch."

"I didn't put guns on it."

"Oh, sorry. Hydra Rockets."

"That's right... some things need rocket pods."

"Your truck doesn't have rockets."

"No," I said, pointing up and back at April. "This one has a machine gun. But a rocket launcher is a good idea."

"I like rockets." Joy yelled from the back seat, giving us a thumbs up. She was wearing headphones now and didn't realize she was almost shouting.

Kilo chuckled.

## Ogre Ammos Up

We drove around the runway, looking at different buildings. I wasn't sure what I was looking for, but when I spotted it, I knew.

"There we go." I said, and headed to a couple small bunker-like buildings. These buildings had a few military trucks around it, and lots of rotting bodies. "I think what we want is in there."

We pulled up and got out. The men here had fought a defensive battle and lost. The door was opened, and inside the little bunkers were a few more bodies. Ammunition. We started loading the back of the Raptor, but I knew we would have to come back with the trucks for the rest of it all.

Suddenly a truck pulled up outside. Two men from the RAF climbed out, both armed with L-85's.

"Just what the hell do you blokes think you're doing?"

I set the two heavy ammo crates down as Kilo positioned them in the back of the Raptor. "Well, if it looks like we're stealing ammo so that we can keep fighting zombies... that's just what we are doing."

The men were wearing berets on their heads and held HK MP5SDs. Luckily for them, the guns were not aimed at any of us. Joy was in a position behind them, sitting in the back seat of the Raptor with her ACR rifle up and ready. I gave her a subtle hold on look and she gave me a slight nod in return.

The first man cocked his head slightly and squinted. "You're from the Colonies?"

"Yes, we are."

"You think we are going to let you take our ammunition?"

"Yes, you are." I said.

"Why would we do that?"

"Because we're going to use it to make all of the undead very dead." I walked over and held my hand out. "I'm George Hill, from Utah."

"Oh really? The President of the United Fooking States, George Hill? The Ogre himself? Right, and I'm King Henry fooking the Eighth." He looked back at his partner and laughed then picked up his foot, "Here, pull the other one."

I nodded. "Yeah, I'm that George 'fooking' Hill. We've taken over Fort George and cleared out most of Inverness." My patience was started to wear thin. "And we've taken over your little base here too."

"What? You, a girl and a long-haired boy? Wearing armor doesn't make you an army."

I nodded and Joy quickly pushed open the door and clicked her weapon from "safe" to "kill". It was a very distinct and loud click. Both the Airmen froze.

"Well, I suppose I could have been more hospitable." The taller Airman gulped.

The other guy looked at me and leaned over to the taller guy.

"I think he really is the Ogre."

"How would you know?" The taller Airman said.

"Facebook friends." He said.

"I'm sorry, I've not been on Facebook for awhile." I said with a shrug.

"Nelson, Jory Nelson." He held out his hand. "It's good to finally meet you, Sir, er, Mister President."

I had to laugh. "Just call me Ogre, that will be fine. I'm not the President of the US anymore."

Kilo offered his insight, "But former Presidents are still given the honorific of President when addressed."

"Guys, this is my eldest son, he goes by the name Kilo. This is April, one of my bodyguards. And the gal that got the drop on you is Joy. Say hello, Joy."

Joy flicked her weapon back to safe and grinned, "hello."

"How many of you guys are left?" I asked the Airmen, looking at Jory.

"It's just us, now. We were hiding out in the control tower when we saw you driving around. Had to come check you out. What's with the armor?"

"Zombies can't bite through it. The extra protection has really helped out." I looked around at the dead bodies laying around. They looked like they had been here for a long time. "Too late for these guys, but we can get you guys some if you want to come with us. We have food, security, water, a small army... and your ammunition."

The RAF Airmen looked at each other. "Yeah, if you're sure you don't mind us tagging along. We'd hate to be a bother." The taller one said.

"Excellent! We can use the man power. We've taken some casualties since we landed. But that was before we got the armor and took Fort George."

"You said you had food?" Jory asked, hesitantly.

I looked at him and his companion. They had been here for a long time, by themselves. They were gaunt and they looked dehydrated. I put my hand on his shoulder and felt the bones under his shirt. "Yeah, we have plenty of food, my friends." I looked at April, "grab them both an MRE and something to drink, some Gatorade." The Airmen's eyes lit up. I didn't want to ask when they had eaten last.

The Airmen tore into the MREs like wolves on a kill, while the rest of us loaded more ammo into the back of their truck and they followed us back to Fort George.

I had my armor laid out in pieces in the grass besides the fort's chapel. One of the places we raided was a hardware store. They had a full section of spray paints, including flats and camo colors. We took them, just for fun. But this morning I had felt like using them. With the help of some sandpaper, I roughed up the burnished steel and then used an automotive primer as a base coat. On top of that, I laid down multiple layers of muted earth tone colors. The result was a nice Multicam pattern on all the armor and great helm. I painted all the edging in flat black, including the cross on the face of the helm. Inside the helm, I fixed the earpro using the muffs and internals from a set of Impact Sports and through them, ran the radio. The mic for the VOX, I wired in to the front of the helm. When I tested it out, I could hear and communicate just fine.

When others saw what I was doing with my Armor, everyone else did the same. Soon, no one had shiny silver armor anymore. April and Joy did theirs in a more simple striped camo that reminded me of Nam Era Tiger Striped camo. Musket's was simply all flat black. My three eldest boys had armor and wanted theirs to look just like mine. I helped them with the Multicam and after they learned out to do it, finished it with no problems. Kilo trimmed his armor in desert tan. Bravo's in OD, and Echo in black like mine. They looked great.

Debbie's armor was very different. I painted it all grey with white shoulder pauldrons and gold trim. Across the breastplate, I painted an eagle, with outspread wings holding a pair of crossed rifles. Her head protection was a gold-colored mail coif, long in the back. Covering the back was a short cape of crimson. I stepped back and looked at it, tilting my head one way and then the other.

"What do you think?" I asked, as I knew who was standing behind me.

"Warhammer much?" Q said while looking at my artwork.

"Not really, but I thought Debbie's armor could use some decoration."

"She's going to look like a Goddess."

I smiled. "She is my Goddess." I said quietly.

"Really? Because I was thinking maybe April was."

I dropped the cloth I was holding and couldn't help but to ball up my fists. Before I could say anything, Q's next question cut me to the core. "She's pregnant, isn't she?"

I froze. "How did you know?" I turned and look him in his eyes, nose to nose.

"Izzy noticed that April hasn't been using any, uh, feminine napkins and she had been getting morning sick... but that's passed now. Don't worry, I told Izzy to keep it to herself. Only we know. It's yours isn't it?"

"Yes." I looked down at the grass. "I made a mistake, and it's going haunt me for the rest of my life."

"Debbie doesn't know does she?"

"No. Not yet."

"Well, you won't have to worry. The rest of your life won't be that long as soon as Debbie finds out. This armor some sort of apology?"

"No," I shook my head. "I just want her protected. How can a man apologize for that? There is nothing he can say or do."

"No, there isn't. And this isn't going to help that. But it will help if any zeds get in the fort."

Q nodded as he walked away. I could tell he had something on his mind. I turned my attention back to the armor. But I ended up just staring into the grass. After awhile I shook it off and checked on my own armor again. It was dry so I started putting it on. Plate armor was restrictive, but not too much so. I could still move and fight in it. Probably wouldn't win any judo match while wearing it, but the protection was important. After seeing how easily zombies ripped through soft armor, this hard armor was an advantage, a huge advantage. Sure, a zed could grab an edge of the plate, but at least it gave you protection and time to lop the hand off that was grabbing you. Q eventually showed up later that evening in some Roman styled armor, Lorica Segmentata, just to be different. His arms were protected with chainmail and he had steel gauntlets. The chest plate was hammered to look like muscles and across the shoulders he had large wings painted. Not eagle, different. Angelic. I didn't think much about it. The Lorica Segmentata provided enough protection, and still allowed him to move how he wanted. I had to give it a nod of approval and kind of wished I had found some of that stuff first. Oh well, mine was certainly good enough for zombie killing.

The rest of the Crimson Order's armor fell in a random pattern of all sorts of camo styles. The one constant however, was given by the use of a stencil: a simple red thistle with crossed swords behind it. This was also painted on the doors of all our vehicles. Someone even tagged my motorcycle and Raptor.

The plumbing in the Fort worked. We just didn't have hot water. Some of the men promised to work on that. So while the showers were cold, at least we had them.

Dinner at the Fort was spaghetti. The first time we had pasta in some time. The two RAF airmen, having their first hot meal in over a month, were very happy. They could hardly stop smiling even while shoveling coiled noodles and sauce into their maws.

Debbie was not happy about the boy's armor. With them in wargear, she felt they were more likely to get into trouble, like I was putting the boys at risk. This was a bad time to point out the armor we had for her. I had it taken to our quarters. She could wear it or not, but she had it. Since dinner, she tended to stay away from me. Something had changed in her. She wouldn't even look at me. And when she did, it was with eyes like daggers. This wasn't just about the boy's armor. It was then I realized she knew about April.

After dinner I walked around the Fort. Guns were in place, .50 cals, M-240s, MK-19s. Q's defense strategy was sound. It would take a flood of zombies to get through.

I wanted to go back to my quarters and go to sleep, but I couldn't face Debbie right now. Instead I took a room in another building. As I walked across the courtyard, I was aware of my two shadows. Joy behind me, and April flanking her. Rifles held low, with the stocks up in their shoulders. They were quiet and didn't say anything. Joy would look at me and wink. April wouldn't look directly at me. When I went into my room, I whispered

"Good night" and shut the door. Outside the door, I only heard one set of footsteps walking away.

The beds at the Fort were small and less than comfortable, unlike at Leys Castle. Military style bunks were no comparison. Maybe I could run back to Leys and snag those awesome beds. I fell asleep to unsettling dreams.

The next morning I woke up sore and stiff. In spite of the last evening's happenings, I was determined to carry on as normal. I couldn't mope about, and I didn't have the luxury of feeling sorry for myself. I talked with some of the Guardsmen and visited with the survivors we had found. I smiled and shook hands and showed everyone that I was still in control. The Airmen from Kinsloss were both drinking canned sodas and eating burritos of some sort.

I started thinking about those beds again. It was late afternoon, but I could get to Leys and back again before dark.

"I think we left something back at Leys." I said to April. She was so surprised that I had spoken directly to her that she didn't say anything.

Joy looked at her, then at me. "No, we got all our stuff. We double checked." Joy said.

"Nope, we left the beds."

April's face showed the marked enthusiasm for my idea. "We did, didn't we?"

"I think we need to go get them."

"Let's do it." She said.

"After we get the good beds again." Joy said with a sly look and a wink.

I just shook my head and grabbed my rifle.

Caroline met us out at the Raptor. "What's going on?" She asked.

"We're going back to Leys to grab those big feather beds." April said cheerfully.

Caroline grinned, "I'm coming too! I want to sleep good tonight. Those bunks suck."

We fired up the Raptor and I called into the new Command Center. "Ogre to F.G. Actual."

"Go ahead, Ogre. We read you."

"Making a run back to Leys Castle. Forgot something there."

"Roger that, Ogre. Be Careful. Units will be standing by for support if needed."

The Command Center had a Blue Force Tracker and SincGars, Sat-Phones, CB, and Ham Radio. They were picking up some chatter from civilian and military survivors. The guys were setting up a second antenna outside of the Fort to allow some direction finding so we could locate signal sources better. There was a brief conversation with some survivors from an RAF Airbase called Lossiemouth. They were curt and unfriendly at first, but had quickly warmed up to the idea of an actual secured base with plenty of food.

Unfortunately they were unable to move. They wouldn't say why. We offered to come get them, but were refused. I put Lossiemouth on the ever growing "To Do" list.

Messages were sent back to the States requesting a full Stryker Platoon and a team of Engineers, per Q's request. No answer yet. I think Harm was still pissed at me for dropping the ball on him... the Football. He had every right to be angry with me, I pretty much just bailed out on him. I grinned just imagining what his face looked like when he was handed the presidency.

We hit the highway with music playing and I was feeling optimistic about a great many things. We cut though fields and crossed our first landing zone. I didn't notice until later that the sky over Leys was filled with large black birds, crows again. When we passed through the last line of trees I slammed on the brakes and the Raptor slid to a stop.

Leys was gone.

## Great Balls of Fire!

There were lots of zombies around the ruins of the castle. Hundreds of them. The Castle was still being torn down. Zeds were crawling all over it, and I watched as some were throwing chunks of stone and brick, scattering them. A single zombie stood out from the chaos. He was watching the turmoil then slowly turned his head to us. He grinned through a lipless mouth.

April scrambled from the back seat up into the turret ring. I heard the action of the M2 being racked back and then the thunder started. I barely had time to put in my Surefire EP3 earpro. Zombies started popping like prairie dogs from the big fifty's slugs. The Red Eye rolled over to the side, dodging the rounds. Then he did something I've never seen before. He threw his head back and raised his arms. Flames suddenly, out of nowhere, leapt from the ground and engulfed him completely. He looked at us again, with his grin of teeth and bone. This time his eyes were dark, black, and they seemed to suck in the light. I had the feeling that we needed to get the hell away. The Red started walking towards us. "SHOOT HIM!" I yelled as I threw the truck into reverse and spun the wheels. I executed a "*Rockford Files*" turn and sent the Raptor on a ballistic course back to the highway. April's butt was on my shoulder as she fired backwards. In the rear view mirror I saw a giant fireball coming at us and I swerved the truck away from it. A tree besides the truck erupted, exploding, and igniting other trees around it. We made our escape and got back to the highway with no further drama.

April dropped back into the truck. "What the hell was that!?"

"I don't know. Why didn't you shoot it?"

"Are you kidding me? He was the only thing I was aiming at! I emptied the belt on him!"

"Shit." I slammed the steering wheel.

"What can we do about that thing?" Joy's eyes were big.

"I don't even know what that thing was." I said as I sent the message back to FG Actual. "Leys Destroyed. 10-17 RTB."

It was late when we got back. Dinner was still being served in the Mess Hall. I found a spread of rice and fish with some vegetables.

"Caught this morning, Sir. They are delicious." I nodded and took my tray of food and sat down at a long table. The Girl Squad took their food as well and sat on either side of me.

It didn't take long before Musket, Alan, and Q were there too, as well as platoon leaders and other members of the Crimson Guard. Everyone wanted to know what happened.

I told the others of what we saw. How the Red Eye changed at will. The fire. The total destruction of Leys Castle.

"Have we ever seen zombies tear down a building before?" I asked and looked around the room as I ate my fish. Everyone shook their heads. At most, zombies have battered down barricades, but they've never leveled a building before. Especially not a castle.

A lot of people were muttering that April can't shoot. April slammed her tray at this and stormed out of the room.

"She's been running guns since I found her and she was good then and has only gotten better."

It's possible that maybe she missed. The thing freaked me out enough that I couldn't dismiss it. However something told me she didn't miss. The bullets either didn't have an effect on it, or they went around it. I think the bullets were somehow deflected. Either way, it was still out there. Whatever it was.

This brings up a question, Q had said. "If the Red Eyes control the Zombies, who controls them?"

"I think we may have found the answer." I grumbled, but I had a feeling that it was much worse.

# A Wandering Spirit

After a cold shower, I put my armor back on instead of getting ready for bed. I went and made sure my family was okay, then went up to the ramparts. Debbie's dismissal "I'm fine" still rang in my ears. As I walked the Fort, I noticed some changes.

Musket had taken twenty four of the old cannons from the water side of the fort, cleaned them, and readied them and moved to the front.

The next morning, Musket tested them and demonstrated their old school power. It was an impressive demonstration. He had been training some of the Crimson Guard and some of the survivors to be gun crews. He then set the cannons for overlapping and layered fields of fire. Everything was covered.

The only problem, we had more cannons than we had men to run them. So the guns were preset. All that had to be done was to fuse them and ignite them. To protect the fuse holes from the weather, Leather straps were used, just like back in the old days. "All is ready Sar!" Musket barked and saluted. I was satisfied. And I was even more convinced my younger brother was born in the wrong time era... or maybe it was exactly the right one.

Our backs were to the water now, the only safe direction. Zombies don't swim or boat, so it was our escape plan. We were gathering some boats for that purpose. Just in case. We had over a dozen at the ready, and some were frequently used for fishing. I didn't mind that at all. It helped with the food situation. Fresh protein is a good thing.

The night sky was dark and overcast. No stars, no moon, no light. Since we ran all the electrics off of generators, we spared no energy for lighting unless it was an emergency. Some of the sentries used NVGs to watch the approaches to the fort. Out past the walls, through the fields and trees, we had placed flares and tripwires. Inside the flares we had claymore mines set in a layered pattern.

The clouds hung low and heavy, promising rain but didn't give us any. The weather we have found to be typical. The air was cooler tonight, with a slight chill. I watched the men go about their watches, and then I looked up into the ramparts and saw someone walking along them, watching the ocean side.

"You see him do you?" It was one of the RAF Airmen. Reggie, he was called.

"Yeah, who is that?" I asked.

"It's not a who, but a what."

"What?"

"Precisely."

I looked back at the ramparts and the man was no longer in view. Probably because it was so dark. I turned back to the Airman. "Who was that?"

"He's a ghost, Mister Ogre. A wandering spirit. Keeping watch for another Jacobite uprising."

"Not much of a chance for that now."

"No, perhaps not. But you can't tell him that." The Airman walked away and I looked back at where the phantom had been. I shrugged it off. Ghosts were not a concern. They were already dead. It was the undead that concerned me. And other matters... I thought as I looked back at April who was standing a few yards away. She was armed with guns and blades. On top of her mail coif, she had a pair of NVGs ready for use. She had pulled the chainmail and hood up over her head to keep off the chill of the night. April was always there, watching my back. As I looked at her, she turned her head to me. From under the chain mail, her hair hung in framing strands. She had a sad look on her face, until she saw me looking at her and her eyes brightened. She smiled, slightly. She looked elegant standing there. I smiled back and nodded towards the steps back down to the Fort's courtyards. I was heading to bed.

## The Black-eyed One

The next morning I was eating a breakfast burrito while I walked amongst the cannons and guns of the Fort's defenses. Burrito in one hand, a can of Mt Dew in the other. It was a beautiful morning.

My boys, Bravo and Kilo, were outside of the Fort, hunting with Big Mike of the Crimson Guard. The boys were armed with their P-90's as usual, but these were carried across their backs and in their hands were Browning T-Bolts in .17HMR. It's a lot of rifle for the harvesting of rabbit, as a direct hit would ruin much of the meat, so they had been popping them with head shots. Big Mike was carrying the kills. Bravo had five rabbits, Kilo had seven. Bravo was boasting that his rabbits were larger and were the equal if not better than Echo's smaller bunnies. They were walking back to the Fort when they heard the moaning. The three of them stopped in their tracks. "Where did that come from?" Echo whispered. The moaning was louder. "Everywhere." Big Mike hissed as his eyes scanned the trees behind them.

"Run to the Fort. NOW! RUN!"

The boys broke out in a dead run from the trees, sprinting as fast as they could. Big Mike was right behind them.

"OGRE!" April pointed. "There!" Her voice was shrill.

I turned and looked and saw my boys running hell bent for leather across the field. I instantly dropped my breakfast, all thoughts of food forgotten, I swung my rifle up and braced on the ramparts. I could see movement in the trees. Flying above the trees were thousands of crows. I could hear their calling. What is it with these damned birds and the zombies? My attention on the big, black birds was torn away as suddenly tripwire flares shot up into the sky, scattering the murder of crows. A second later, I saw the flash inside the tree line from some of the Claymore Mines. Moments later I could here the cracking of the high explosives.

Oh God. "CANNONS READY!" I shouted. April ran to the nearest .50 cal machine gun and pulled back the charging handle. The guards on duty started uncovering the flash holes and inserting the fuses. Each guard had four cannons. More were coming, but the alert was just getting to the barracks.

The first zombie broke from the trees and hit the field in front of the fort. I set my ACOG on him and fired. The boys were ahead of Big Mike. A strange looking zombie was right behind him. I didn't have a clear shot, but if I didn't take it, it wouldn't matter if I hit Mike or the zombie. I let my breath out and held it as I put pressure on the trigger. Big Mike moved slightly to left, just enough to open up more of the target. I couldn't go for a clean kill, so I took the next best thing. The Crusader Broadsword bucked against my shoulder, but was instantly back on target. The .308 round shattered the zombie's pelvis and it went down. The zombie right behind it tripped and tumbled and Mike pulled away from the undead.

More zombies busted out of the trees and my rifle started feeling like a jackhammer against my shoulder. There were hundreds of them. The boys and their guard reached the safe zone so I pulled back from the ACOG. "ALL GUNS, FIRE!"

The cannons started firing, belching great clouds of smoke. The .50BMGs opened up, with April's firing first. Then the stuttering fire of the MK-19s added to the beat. The field was boiling from high explosives. The gun crews manning the cannons were reloading the cannons with grape shot now. Each time one fired, whole swaths of running undead were cut down.

I looked below at my boys as they charged through the fort's entrance. As soon as they were across the bridge, Musket rolled one of his volley guns into the entrance way and waited until he saw the first zombie. The zombie was shrieking as it ran, tearing the ground as it charged like a wild beast. Nothing about it seemed human anymore. Its jaws were distended, and the fingers on its hands long and claw-like. Its shriek filled the entrance. Behind it, three more zombies appeared, much like the first, they too were misshapen and feral.

Musket clenched his teeth, letting all of them into the entrance tunnel. "Back to hell with thee!" He fired the gun by pulling hard on the lanyard.

Twenty barrels fired one at a time in the space of one second. A wall of lead filled the entrance way. The zombies were instantly turned into what looked like ground meat. The recoil rolled the volley gun backwards on its wheels, which helped Musket push it out of the way, so he could roll the next volley gun into place. Guardsmen started reloading the multiple barrels as Musket placed the next gun and aimed it, waiting for more zombies to show themselves. None did. He looked up at the sky, listening. The cannons stopped. The grenade launchers stopped. The rifle fire stopped. After a moment the call went out. "Cease Fire!" Musket patted the big volley gun and nodded. He turned back to the boys who were behind wooden ammo crates, with their P-90's aimed and ready.

"You did fine, boys. You brought me something to test my new hardware on! Thank you for that!"

Echo and Bravo looked at each other, and just started to laugh from the relief of having escaped death. Big Mike was still breathing hard. He was clutching the stringers of rabbits and his chest was heaving.

"That..." He breathed, "was the best hunt I've ever been on."

I watched the field as the smoke cleared and the dust settled.
A lone zombie walked out from the trees. He was naked. He had a full beard

with long black hair and tattoos over much of his pot bellied body. He was laughing.

"Impressive show, I'll give you that." It said from a distance across the field, but it sounded like he was right in front of me. "But your pathetic attempts are just a delay of the inevitable. Lighting candles to fight off the coming night!"

I sighted the man through the ACOG. His bare flesh was grey and mottled with what looked like a crosshatching of cuts. I fired a round and the man-creature-zombie made a motion like he was batting away a fly and there was a flash of red from the eyes. I saw a tuft of dirt kick up fifteen feet behind and to the right of him. "You'll have to do better than that!"

I fired a whole magazine of 7.62 ammunition. None of the rounds hit. The thing started to growl, then it roared, "I'm done toying with my food. I'm going to eat your souls!"

The zombie lifted its arms and head and instantly burst into flames. He reached for me and I felt hands on me, grabbing my arms, holding me and lifting me up off the ground. I didn't know it could throw its power this far! More hands were around my neck, cutting off my air. It felt like I was being grabbed by a hundred hands. I struggled to free myself, and my feet kicked helplessly in the air.

I heard a buzz zip passed me, over my shoulder and recognized the sound as that of a rifle bullet. I opened my eyes and looked in time to watch the zombie's head explode and the body fall to the ground as I was released. April ran to me.

"I'm alright." I croaked. I looked back up at the ramparts behind me. Izzy lifted her rifle with a grin.

"Nice shot, Izzy!" I said into the radio. She gave me a thumbs up.

"I had a theory. I didn't think he could lift you and deflect bullets at the same time. It worked." She explained.

## The Bloody Runes

Battlefield assessment showed a hole in our defenses, that was cleared up with an adjustment of the cannons and a relocation of an M2. I showed the gunners how to draw range cards and get better use of the T&E mechanism for when the cannons obscure the field with the smoke. Overall, I was very pleased with the defense. Anything coming across that field had better be in a tank if they hoped to get across in one piece.

I went down to the courtyard and found my boys. They had quite the fright. I grabbed them around their heads and held them tight. "I didn't know you boys could move so fast!"

"That was awesome! Those cannons were shooting right over our heads!"

"We heard that zombie moan, then another one from the other side, and we just Jet-Moto'd."

"Yeah, Mike yelled run for it and we just took off."

"At first, I was like 'WTF?' and just started running after Echo."

They were still breathing hard.

"I'm just glad you boys are alright." I said.

"Was that you shooting over our heads at the beginning?" Bravo asked.

"Yeah. They were right behind you." I explained.

"Kinda close."

"So were about a hundred zombies."

I let the boys go after my eyes dried a little more, then I clanked them on their armored shoulders.

"From now on, any hunting out there and you have a squad of Guards and a support vehicle." I was looking at Mike, who nodded.

"Thank you." I looked at the big Guardsman, who just nodded. Mike ran behind the boys. If the zombies caught up to them, Mike would have been pulled down first, giving my boys time to put more distance on them and reach the Fort.

"Thank you, Sir. I could feel their breath on the back of my neck."

I nodded, then Mike continued. "It was my hope that if they did get me, you would have ended me quickly rather than... let them..."

I held out my hand and we shook, grabbing each other by the wrist.

"And I'd hope the same for me and my own."

I dismissed Big Mike who went off to his quarters.

"Take a look at this, Brother." Musket said, pointing at one of the dead zombies that had made it into the Fort's entrance. "You need to see this."

I walked over to the corpse. What I saw actually surprised me. The Volley Gun had delivered massive damage to the body, but some things were still clear. The face was distorted and its jaws stretched, misshapen and wrong. One hand was still intact. The fingers, to the first and second knuckles were also stretched out. The nails on the fingers were thickened, long and pointed. The hand reminded me more of raptor talons than a hand. It wasn't human anymore. It was something else, like something had taken the flesh and remolded it. I looked around, the parts of the other bodies here were also wrong, no longer the parts of bodies of humans.

"You!" I snapped at one of the Guardsmen. "Clean up this filth. Get it out of here. This one though, take this to the clinic." I left Musket to his volley guns and headed back into the Fort.

I needed to talk to someone about this. This transformation of the body. There was something decidedly unclean about this. I watched as men carried the remains off. Time to go find Father Mulcahy.

We were standing around the gurney with the body laid out, what was left of it. One arm was missing, as were the legs. The remaining arm, however, was the interesting part, as was the jaw. Then Q rolled the body over. "Look at this."

On the corpse's back were deep cuts from a blade that wasn't quiet sharp. The cuts formed symbols. Q pointed to the one in the center. An upturned horseshoe with a star in it. The cuts went to bone in a lot of places, dried blood indicated that the body was alive when these cuts were made.

Q looked at us then closed his eyes as he started to speak. "I was a rookie cop back in '98. Carolina Beach, the "Redneck Riviera" we called it. I'd been on the job all of seven months. A number of us were called into the Duty Sergeant's office to meet a Detective Wade, who had a search warrant he was going to serve. It was supposed to be for some stolen goods. Some druggies around town had been boosting cars and unattended summer homes. I wasn't on the entry team that night, not at first, that came later. I posted out back to catch any runners when we knocked. Wade and a couple of officers made the entry, then I heard yelling, then screams. I ran around front, the door was open, and into the living room. The folks inside had been playing with a Ouija board and some paints, candles lit the room.

There were three of them. Wade was fighting a skinny junkie, who took Wade's arm in one hand and wrenched it, the bones snapped and they jutted out his bicep. As I watched Wade shoved his service pistol under his chin, blowing his brains on the ceiling. Buckethead, a monster of an officer was wrestling with two tweekers not much bigger than my Izzy, they were tossing him around the room like a ragdoll, laughing. I grabbed one and she pitched me through the wall into a bedroom, stepping after me. I didn't even have time to draw my weapon before she was on me, her face in mine. Her breath smelled like something dead left out in the sun too long. She grabbed my left arm and made a wish, separating the shoulder. I remember screaming as I fell, drawing my weapon and firing, the holes traveled up her body, striking her in the neck and face, her body falling on top of me.

I made it back into the living room and saw Buckethead grab the last one head and twist it to the side. She was trying to bite his face. Her neck snapped and that one too fell.

"I radioed for back-up as Buckethead saw to Detective Wade. After we got his arm stabilized we found Grey, the other officer, unconscious in a heap in the corner. We found out later when the SBI did their investigation they found a bunch of occult manuals and stuff. They each had this rune painted on their chest, and the last one I swear had red eyes as her neck was snapped."

I looked at Q "What happened to the investigation?"

"Swept under the rug, the official release was that we found a PCP lab and they jumped us, hyped up as they were, we had no other option but for deadly force.

"Wade medically retired and Buckethead went on to become a fitness trainer and bodybuilder. Grey stayed on the PD. I left and went into freelance close-protection for a couple of movie studios."

Father Mulcahy cleared his throat from behind me. He looked small in his black and white cassock, his fingers playing with his rosary. "I was an initiate some years ago before I took my vows in the Dominican Order. I was a clerk in the Paras and I went to work in one of the Jesuit libraries in Vatican City. I was helping one of the priests catalog some of the older volumes when I found a book listing the names and sigils of the demons. This was in it." he said pointing at the mark on the body. But I don't remember the name that went with it. I tried to forget all of that. But I guess you can't. Not all of it."

Father Mulcahy shook off a thought and continued. "I showed it to Father Matias who explained that it was used in rituals to allow a demon entrance into a willing host. The deeper the mark, the more power the demon was able to exert on the waking world."

"Well judging by the way that Black-eyed one threw fireballs around, it must have been pretty damn deep." I said. "And these cuts. These are to the bone."

"Alan take this body outside the walls and burn it then salt the ashes. We don't want to take any chances on this, thing, getting a foothold here." Q ordered. Alan looked at me and I nodded. I walked out knowing I needed more help than just firepower.

Why, I wasn't sure. But I needed to think things through clearly and the garrison chapel was the least used, quietest place in the whole fort. Especially on a Friday. This was the first time I'd stepped foot in a church in some time, but I felt no trepidation as I marched in. "Wait here." I said to April and Joy, who obediently took up positions at the door.

I walked up the center isle and knelt in front of the center of the chapel, kneeling before the stained glass visage of the Savior. Demons. Demonic possessions. Undead... the Dead walking the earth. Things were getting stranger and stranger, and the evil … it was getting stronger. I turned off my radio and I started to pray.

When I came out of the chapel it was dark and quiet. I felt a fatigue so deep that I could hardly stand. But I knew what I had to do. Some of the members of the CG were outside, waiting for me. April and Joy stood before the door of the chapel, they had prevented people from coming in and disturbing me.

"Thank you, Girls." I whispered as I walked past. The girls fell into step behind me.

"Ogre, we've had calls from RAF Lossiemouth. They need help, the last call was an hour ago."

"What was their situation last time we had contact?"

"They were surrounded... said the base was being over run. The transmission was cut off, Sir... Uh... in the transmission... it sounded weird... there was a distortion." Jared was a solid radio guy and knew what he was doing. Special Forces had trained him very well.

"Distortion? Signal interference? How? Do you have a cause?"

"Uh, no. You have to hear it for yourself." Jared looked uncomfortable.

"Do you have a recording?"

"That I have." He held up an iPod and handed me the earphones. I held the buds to my ears and nodded. Jared pressed play. I closed my eyes and listened.

The voice was someone with a thick, British accent, and it sounded panicked. "*We've pulled back to.... Overrun... Requesting support! Please GOD! Ven aquí, Fillos de Cameron. Estamos esperando.*"

"Again."

"*We've pulled back to.... Overrun... Requesting support! Please GOD! Ven aquí, Fillos de Cameron. Estamos esperando.*"

I looked up at Jared. "Two voices?" He nodded.

"Q, listen to this." I held out the ear bud. "I think we've been called out."

Louis closed his eyes and listened. "Sounds like Latin, but it isn't. Father?" He handed the earbuds to Father Mulcahy who listened to the recording. "I don't know... but it sounds familiar. I've heard it before."

Uncle Musket took the earbuds and listened twice. "It's Galician." I looked at him, the father looked at him, Q looked at him. He shrugged. "Been there... went to Spain on a beer tour."

"What did it say?"

"I don't know. I don't speak it, but I remember a bit... a phrase... the last part. It said 'we're waiting.'"

I felt anger inside, like a burning coal in my gut. "Okay, saddle up the LAVs. I want a fire team in each unit. Q, you take one, Alan the other one and I've got the third. Alan, you're going to take point. We're rolling in five minutes."

## Son of Cameron - We're Waiting

Five minutes later, I was sitting in the commander's seat of the second LAV. Behind the three armored fighting vehicles we had supporting vehicles. A Deuce, driven by Musket with a load of Guardsmen and the two Airmen. The M-ATV was driven by Caroline with more Guardsmen. Then we had a fuel truck and an ambulance. Pulling up the rear we had our up armored Ford Excursion. We drove best speed on the highways, snaking our convoy through the long abandoned traffic and desiccated corpses on the road.

Joy had wanted to play some music, but I vetoed that, listening instead to the engine. I had too much to think about to be entertained.

We left the Fuel truck a mile away, on the highway. This was our Objective Rally Point. Louis came over while the LAVs were refueling. "Hey, I was thinking."

"Oh? Something on your mind?."

"Yeah, there is. George, what clan are you?"

"Cameron, why?"

"They're calling you out. The middle part of the message is archaic Latin, it means 'Son of Cameron.'"

"Too late to worry about that now, we're almost there."

"I'm getting Izzy and some snipers to higher ground. I'll join you when we get set-up.

"Roger that Q, keep frosty."

We topped off the fuel tanks and checked our ammo. When we were ready, we rolled on for the RAF base, and the fuel truck headed home to Fort George.

We approached the base at highway speed. The gate was blocked with burnt out vehicles, so we crashed through the fence. The big armored vehicles had no problem rolling over the chain link and razor-wire. The other vehicles followed us close. The base was quiet, and we drove around the buildings once quick and came to a stop in the middle of the airfield. I unbuttoned and stood in the hatch. It was quiet. There was nothing I saw that indicated where anyone else could be, save for the one tell-tale sign I had learned to hate. The crows were flying over the main terminal building, circling and landing and screaming their calls. Whatever was here, was over there.

I heard the sound of an approaching LAV and knew Q's snipers were ready. I climbed out of my vehicle and stood on the tarmac, rifle in hand. Q unbuttoned and jumped down.

"Anything?" Q asked.

"Nothing but the wind and those crows" said George.

Alan walked up, in his hand was his M-4, "Zip." He nodded to Q.

Q took up his pair of Pentax binos and looked around the flight line. "Tornado jets, some Merlin helos, and a Blackhawk. Probably a NATO cross trainer."

"How do they look?"

"Intact."

"Movement!" Alan shouted. I turned and looked. A bunch of kids, teen-agers and some women were running in our direction. Soldiers were with them, firing back into the terminal they had come from. Zombies followed them outside. We could hear the gunfire, from here it sounded like crackling and popping.

"Covering Fire!" The turrets of the LAVs swung around facing the terminal. The gunners opened up with the Bushmasters and the COAX M240s. "Victor One, Move over to those helicopters and take up a flanking position!"

The Excursion's engine roared and the heavy SUV surged forward as the roof opened up. A huge gun emerged from the top and spun around. It was a Dillon mini-gun. A perfect anti-zombie horde weapon. Unfortunately it wasn't exactly a precision weapon, it needed a clear line of fire.

Q yelled into his radio "Eagle teams take out any Zeroes getting too close to the civvies." I could hear the pops of a large caliber rifle.

The Excursion got into position and its big Dillon opened up, sounding like a motorcycle. The crossfire of heavy weapons cut down the zombie horde like a scythe.

Finally, the first of the civilians reached us. "Get into the APCs!" I directed them inside for safety. They would fill all three, leaving no room for us or our Guardsmen. That's okay, we could ride on top and we had guns and armor. The Civvies didn't.

"Color Sergeant Urqhart Sir!" I turned and looked. Standing before me, was a grim faced soldier with a beret on his head and a salute. He was breathing hard, but he stood tall and proud. "Her Majesty's Marines."

"Good to have you, Sergeant. Get your people on the LAVs. What's happened here? Last I had heard, you guys were holding and didn't want any assistance."

"We were secure until this morning, sir. Then a whole mob of them showed up, a bunch of them with red eyes and one with black ones. They looked like those monsters on the telly."

"Huh? You mean Supernatural?" Q said, he looked at me. Black and Red eyes. Not good."

"That's the one. All emo and gothic like." The Color Sergeant nodded.

Q slotted a new mag, hitting the bolt release. "I hate Emo."

"Anyway, we gathered up the kids and civilians into the terminal. They just stood outside as we called you for help. Then they started trying to get in. The Colonel and some of the others held them off while we got out to the fields."

"Ogre, we can't fit all these people. There's too many!" one of the drivers radioed.

"Shit." I grumbled.

Q grabbed one of the RAF squaddies, "Are those Helo's ready to go?" He asked.

"Take a few minutes, but they're sitting on Go." He answered.

"LAV One, get over to the flight line and prep those birds. We'll fall back and load them up." George ordered as a bunch of RAF climbed on top and they headed to the helos.

"We have more incoming Sir!" one of the troopers yelled.

In the windows of the terminal, I could see people, half-naked with red eyes glowing.

"Reds in the windows!" Q said, flipping his weapons selector to full auto. He unleashed a long burst into the windows and some of the zeds fell, hit. The rest just stood there, staring at us.

I took a knee, then got lower, into a sitting position with my Crusader Broadsword nested in the crook of my left arm. It wasn't the most stable of positions, but it worked better than kneeling.

"Ogre engaging." I said, squeezing off a round. I watched through the ACOG as a Red Eye's head exploded.

"Hit." Q said, squeezing off another burst, catching another Red in the throat and face. The others retreated inside the building and out of our line of sight and we began firing on the mass crossing the field at us.

I was on my fifth magazine when my radio crackled. "Ogre, the flying sergeants have the Merlins prepped and ready to go. The Blackhawk's up as well." Alan radioed.

"Eagle teams, engage the Reds at the terminal, spike any leakers as we fall back to the flight line." I ordered.

"Eagle One copies." I heard Izzy say, the toneless voice letting me know she had her "A" game running.

"Eagle Two wilco." acknowledged Thomerson.

"Fall back by LAVs to the flight line! LAV two, let's go." I said as I got back up on my feet. "Q watch your ass, we've got you on the backside."

"And here I thought it was my charming personality. Get going." Q said, reloading his ACR.

The first of the Merlins took off heading back to Fort Ogre, full of civilians and some of the Royal Marines. The second Merlin took off, flew low over the flight line, over our heads, its side mounted 20mm cannon blasting holes in the terminal.

Suddenly a great fountain of flame erupted from a terminal window catching the Merlin broadside as it passed too close. The Merlin flared back and started spinning out of control, the pilots were roasted in their seats but the engines still roared with the throttles wide open. It headed back towards us, full of fuel and completely engulfed in flame. The way the helicopter moved through the air, it seemed that it was being pushed and not under its own aerodynamic ability.

I grabbed Q's arm and pulled him as I ran. I'd been in a helicopter crash before, and I didn't want to be in another one. Especially when I was outside of it. We ran and hit the deck as the Merlin came crashing to the ground between us and my LAV. The flames spread and grew in height, cutting us off from my Armored Vehicle. I looked for another route of retreat as the Black Eye stepped from the terminal, zombies streaming around him. I would have to hitch a ride with Q, who motioned for me to come his way.

"George!" April screamed over the radio.

"I'm alright girl, get out of here!" I yelled.

"Not without you!" April was hysterical.

"Joy get her and you out of here, get back to the Fort!"

"George come back to us. Roger your last, out." she said. I could hear the sounds of scuffling in the background and I knew April was being held back.

I looked over the flames and could see the Merlins streaming back to Fort

Ogre. I saw the LAVs trying to get around the flames, to no avail. Good, they were getting away clean.

"Eagle Teams bug out. LAVs pick up and get back to the Fort." Q ordered over the radio. "HALO has the package."

"Fuck you, Q!" April screamed over the radio, cutting off as Joy took the mike.

"Girls acknowledge. Get home safe, George. Out."

"I'll see you Girls back at the Fort soon." George said, determination in his voice.

"Eagle One to HALO6, Louie come back to me." Izzy radioed.

"I will Iz, promise. Eagle Three get her out of here."

"Eagle Three copies, Godspeed guys." Paul radioed.

"Well, looks like it's just us." Q said, as I was watching the horde came closer.

"Damn, I guess it is. Hold the line!" he said, kneeling next to me.

"Hold the line!" echoed through the men as they readied their weapons. The MG teams linking together the belts.

"There are too few of us." I thought as I reloaded my rifle. The Black Eye strode forward, the zombies and Red Eyes arrayed behind him. The black eyed man was thin and shirtless, with the flesh of his chest torn away exposing his rib cage and the organs pulsing inside. He wore ragged jeans and his hair was hanging in long, thick dreadlocks.

"*Son of Cameron, oh how sweet this will be. And what's this? Gabriel's chosen! A twofer!" he laughed. "The tortures I have in store for you, you've made my Master very angry. Maybe I'll have one of my lesser Daemons inhabit you while you're still alive and have you feast on your own blood and kin.*"

"Jeez, I think this guy is going to talk us to death." Q quipped.

"No doubt. I'm bored already. Fire!" I yelled, raising my rifle.

The heavy volume of fire from our guns tore into the lines of the undead, dropping many of them. Several of the Red Eyes fell too. The Black Eye reached out with one hand and made a backhanded gesture. I could hear screams as half the men were knocked down. The zombies crashed into us.

Some of us drew blades as weapons ran dry. I turned my head, and, as I did, I saw the black-eyed zombie make another gesture and I was suddenly knocked backwards.

## Fighting for Survival

We were being pushed into the flames. Guardsmen, Royal Marines and Airmen started to fall. When I emptied my last magazine for my rifle, I let it drop to the ground instantly forgotten. One zombie lunched at me and I grabbed its throat in my steel-clad fist. It flailed at me with its hands as I crushed its throat. Brains, you have to destroy the brain. I pulled my side-arm and fired a single round through its forehead. I dropped that zed and started firing headshots into more zombies. I could hear clashing of bone and steel as my pistol quickly ran dry.

As I was reloading, a Red Eye crashed into me from the side and I was knocked hard to the ground. Over the din of battle, I heard the sighing of long steel from oiled leather, then the sound of steel ripping through the air, then through flesh and bone. I turned and saw the Red Eye cleaved through. Q was carrying his long Katana in follow through from the stroke. The red-eyed woman fell to the ground, to her knees first. The red in her eyes faded white, just as Shannon's did back in the States. Then part of her shoulders fell off. As her mouth opened, I dropped the slide on a fresh magazine and fired a round into her teeth. She fell off, letting go of my shoulder plate. From the ground, I pumped a couple more rounds into her head for good measure, then dropped two more zombies that were grappling beside me. My pistol slide was locked back on an empty magazine. I stood back up and look around.

We had our backs against a wall of flame and wreckage. I looked over at the others with me. Q was bloodied, angry, and determined. He looked down at his rifle and tossed it aside. He rolled his head, popping his neck and drew his katana again.

The Royal Marine, was also without rifle or sidearm. Instead in his hands were a pair of wicked looking long knives. The remaining Crimson Guard was letting a zombie slide off of him, having just pulled a Ka-Bar knife from its skull. He looked at me and nodded, unclipping a tomahawk. He was alright.

I reached up over my shoulder and slowly drew my sword. The steel rang as it pulled free. I held it with two hands before me and pointed the tip at the enemy in front of us.

"*Tsk, Tsk, Tsk, what a waste.*" Black Eyed monster said, "*I had hoped to have you join our ranks, but I see that won't be happening.*" The litch pointed a finger at me, and it felt as if I had been stabbed through the heart. I fell to my knees, but kept hold of my sword.

Louis let out a roar and charged, but the litch swatted him down. Q hit the ground so hard his armor crunched and he didn't move.

"*Such a determined one. All for naught.*"

I couldn't move. All I could do was watch the other two men as they fought the swarm. The Marine was pulled down instantly, but the Guard stood his ground longer. The tomahawk was a blur of motion, leaving trails of blood and gore in the air. Then a zombie got a grip on his armor and the hawk stopped swinging. I could hear the man scream as he fought. He took several Reds down with him, but then his head was pulled from his shoulders and it was over.

Then they were on me. I was pulled up by my armpits by a zombie dressed in a military uniform, it had red eyes and its breath smelled like rot. I wasn't going to go down like this. I pushed one of the Reds off me and spun, bringing my sword up as I turned. I swung for a home run. The Red that had hold of my left arm was cleaved from hip to shoulder. I turned to face another when the litch grabbed me around my neck. Its hands felt cold on me as if I wasn't wearing any armor at all. My arms and legs were pinned. I was held by my throat and pulled towards the litch with the black eyes, my heels dragged the ground. The vile thing chuckled casually as I choked, unable to breath. All I could fight for was to get air, but the grip around my throat was too strong.

I saw the litch make a gesture and my helmet was torn off my head and flung aside.

"*Watch as I devour your friend.*"

The litch reached down and picked up Louis. Louis opened his eyes and they went wide. My eyes were closing and I could feel myself blacking out.

Then I heard a voice, deep, clear and powerful. "*Not this time Mammon.*" The voice was not any of my men, but it sounded familiar. There was a flash of light and suddenly I was released from the force that was holding me. I fell to my knees and filled my lungs with air. As I got oxygen back into my bloodstream, I could see again, but blearily.

Q was laying on the ground and I pulled myself to him. He was dizzy and disorientated, blood was coming from his mouth. But he was still with me.

Smoke and light was obscuring everything. Through the light, I heard voices again.

"*We will have this world Gabriel!*" The litch screamed. "*This world and all in it*!"

There was another flash of light, and then everything was quiet save for the sound of the fire. I knew the undead around us were gone.

"*You will survive Louis.*" The voice said. At that, Q breathed deep and his eyes came into focus.

"*George, take heed, you must find a way to close the gate. If you can do that, their powers will be lessened.*"

"How? Where?" I said.

"*Have faith.*" The voice said and the world seemed to go dim again. Back to normal.

It was just the two of us now. I looked down at Louis who was getting reoriented. He blinked then coughed as he sat up. "Thanks, Gabe."

"Gabe?"

"Yeah, we're cool like that."

I went over to where I had dropped my sword. It hurt to bend down and pick it up. I didn't realize how tired I was until I lifted it up and slid it into the scabbard across my back.

Q handed me my helmet, but I didn't put it on. We gathered our weapons and looked at the bodies of our fallen brethren.

"How are we getting home?" Louis asked as we walked across the field. I looked around and saw the Blackhawk was still sitting at the other end of the runway.

"We can take that." I said and headed towards it.

"Oh great, a lawn dart." Q sighed.

"It'll be fine. It's either that or we walk."

"Just don't hit any power lines."

"Smart ass." We laughed as we limped to the helicopter. Q found an SA-80 rifle with a full magazine, laying in the grass. He picked it up and checked it. "This will have to do for now."

We climbed into the helicopter, me into the cockpit and Q in the back scanning the area with his weapon ready. I starting going over the gauges and saw that everything looked good. When I grabbed hold of the cyclic and collective, the Blackhawk suddenly shut down.

"What did you do?" Q asked, "What happened?"

"I don..." suddenly movement caught my eye. Up on the roof the hanger, I saw a figure crouching. "There." I pointed.

"I got him." Q swung his rifle and started firing. His rounds impacted the roof where the figure was just an instant before. The creature had leaped and rolled off the sloped hanger roof, landing on its feet. It spun behind a trailer as more rounds impacted.

"*We didn't say you can leave yet!*" The voice was everywhere and the sound of it was painful, like it was crushing my head.

"*We've been patient.*" Q grabbed his head with one hand.

"*We've been tolerant.*" Suddenly Q was lifted abruptly and slammed into the ceiling, then back down onto the deck. The pain the voice delivered almost made me black out, but I held on.

"*But we are no longer amused.*" Q was jerked like a rag doll out of the helicopter.

The Red walked with confidence, taking large strides as it approached the Blackhawk. As its power wrapped around my throat, choking me, I heard another voice. It filled my chest with warmth and dispelled the pain. "*He has no power over you, George. Unless you let him.*"

Suddenly, my sight and my thoughts were clear again. I lowered my head back down and took in a full breath of air. I knew the Red was trying to crush my windpipe, and it glared at me with the most exquisite hatred I had ever seen, but I felt nothing of it. I stepped out of the helicopter onto the tarmac, and the Red smiled its predatory smile. In my heart, I prayed for strength and for faith. I saw Q out of the corner of my left eye, picking himself back up. He was pissed off.

The red laughed as I walked to it, meeting it face to face. It laughed, "*You think you have FAITH? God doesn't listen to you! The Father spares none of His light for you. You are pathetic!*"

When the Red saw that its powers and words had no effect on me, its eyes widened and it knew fear. It was about to turn, but it was too late. I reached out an armored left hand and grabbed the Red by the collar of its black shirt. With my right fist, I pulled back and punched the Red right in the face as hard as I could. The smack sound was punctuated by the crack of bone and cartilage breaking. I heard screaming. I punched again, sending teeth and blood flying. Its eyes rolled up as I punched again. Even through the armored gauntlet, I could feel bone giving away. The next blow avulsed the Red's left eye and the body went limp, but I held it up and struck again and again, caving in the head before I let the body fall to the ground. I came down on it with another blow with my blood-washed gauntlet.

Q came up from behind as I punched the tarmac where the Red's head used to be. "You got him!" I punched again. "He's down!" In my mind's eye I could still see that smug grinning face, so I punched again. Q grabbed my arm and I shrugged him off and punched again.

"George." He said in a simple calm tone of voice. The pile driver I was putting on the Red stopped. I stood up over the corpse and breathed deeply, realizing that the screaming was my own voice.

Q almost stammered, not knowing what to say. The zombie's head was nothing but pulp. "Come on, let's get home."

*Home...* I thought of family. I thought of the reason I came here. *Debbie's Sister and her family.* In my mind I pictured them, clearly. I could see them, moss-covered stones behind them. Familiar stones in some way. Then suddenly I knew where they were.

"Where's my helmet?" I wanted the radio in it.

Q pointed and I saw the Great Helm sitting on the co-pilot's seat. It looked like it was scowling at me. I went over and picked it up. For the first time I noticed all the blood on me. "Ogre to base." I said as I motioned Q to head back to the bird.

"Fort George Actual copies, go ahead, Ogre."

"Halo 6 and I are going to be home late. Taking a little detour, over."

Protests erupted on the radio from April and Izzy, with some degree of cursing.

"That's a negative. We've got some survivors to pick up."

I turned off the radio as I restarted the Blackhawk and checked gauges again.

"We're not going home yet?" Q said loudly over the sound of the turbine engine.

"Not yet." The rotors overhead started turning.

"So where are we heading?" Q buckled himself in the back seat and checked his rifle.

The Blackhawk lifted off the ground, and I turned it heading south west. "Skipness."

## Family Reunion

I knew the UH-60 had long enough legs to make it to Skipness. What I didn't tell Q was that we didn't have enough juice to make it back. I remembered there was a Royal Navy base that would be in range, but just where that was, I wasn't exactly sure. At first I was enjoying flying low and fast, following the contour of the Earth, letting Scotland roll past beneath us. It gave a sense of speed that matched my sense of urgency. Soon the ground gave way to water.

"Loch Ness." Q said.

The sense of speed gave way to some tedium as we followed the long lake, flying at only a thousand feet and 175 miles an hour.

"There, Urquhart Castle." I said, pointing to the right. "Debbie's clan."

The castle wasn't in the best of shape, but it did look like someone was there as a tendril of smoke snaked out of it. "Someone's home." Q remarked.

As we flew past, a couple people ran out and waved. "Can you do another flyby over them?" Q had an idea.

"Yeah, sure."

Q used the sharpie that was hanging from a string off the door and used it to write on the only thing he had, which was an empty pistol magazine. "*We'll be back as soon as possible. If you can, make it to Fort George, near Inverness. We have Safety, Medics and Food.*"

I came around and made a slow, level pass at a low altitude. Q tossed the magazine down and watched it land in the visitor parking lot. "They got it." He said, as he watched the kid dart out, grab the magazine, and run back. The people waved again as I tucked the nose of the chopper down and increased the throttle again, accelerating our way.

We flew the rest of the way with no more signs of human life. Below us on occasion we saw a zombie or two standing in a field or road. We saw wildlife, and I had a feeling that survivors would be able to maintain and thrive if we could just get things together again.

I looked over at Q and saw that his head was down to his chest, for a split second I was worried until I heard a slight snore. I looked back at the horizon and cruised in silence. As I approached Skipness, I let the helicopter drift lower as I lined up on the castle. More like the ruins of a small Keep than an actual castle. There was a car, children in the courtyard, and that was all I made out as we flashed by. I brought the chopper around, passing over the ruins of the old church and graveyard. Fairly fresh dirt marked a new grave to the ancient resting place. I set the chopper down gently and shut it down. Q woke up.

"We there yet?"

"Yeah man. We made it."

A woman and a young girl were running out from the castle. I recognized them both! It was Cathy. I jumped out of the helicopter and started to walk to her. A look of horror came across her face and she screamed. She didn't recognize me. How could she? I was wearing dark bloodied armor, I had blood spattered on my face. Cathy's girl screamed too and fell down.

I held out my hands, "CATHY! It's me! George!" I realized from the sound of my voice I was wearing my helmet. I pulled it off and let it fall to the ground. "Cathy! It's George! I'm here to take you back to Debbie. We're here!"

Cathy was in the middle of grabbing her daughter, turning and about to run. My voice sunk in and she stopped. She slowly turned, a look of confusion and fear still on her face. "George?"

"Its me, Cathy. It's okay."

She finally recognized me and started sobbing. "Debbie's here?" She started looking back at the helicopter.

"She's back at the Fort, but she's here in Scotland, with the boys. I'm going to take you to her."

Cathy fell against my armor, crying. "I've prayed... so hard. I thought..."

"It's okay, Cathy. It's okay."

"Uncle George?" Cathy's girl, "Little Princess" looked up at me.

"Hey Sunshine!"

She ran up to me and threw her arms around my waist.

"Who's he?" Cathy was looking over my shoulder.

"That's Louis Q. Call him Q. He's one of my Generals." I looked back at Q who smirked back at me.

"Your Generals?"

"You've been out of contact for a long time."

"Well, I heard you were Governor of Utah."

I laughed. "I was also the President."

She looked confused. "Debbie can fill you in when we get you back..." I almost said home. "... to the fort."

I saw all the kids, plus a couple more. "Uh... Cathy... Where's Mark?" I looked back to the graveyard, suddenly worried.

"He's in the Castle."

"What's wrong with him?"

She didn't say anything. "Cathy?"

"He'll need help getting to the helicopter."

"Mark got into a couple zombies three days ago. He got bit on the ankle."

"He turned?"

"No, he cut off his leg."

I ran into the castle tower. Mark was on a couch running a fever. The bloody rags started below his left knee and didn't go much further down.

"Mark, how you doing, brother?"

"George... was that you making so much noise?"

"No... that was my ride. Dude, you cut off your own leg?"

"One got me... on my ankle. If I didn't..."

"If you didn't, you would have turned, and that would have put your family in danger. You saved them." I checked Mark's vitals. His fever was burning him up, and the wound was infected, but not with the Z-Contagion.

Mark grimaced. "I'm a big, damn hero."

"Aint you just," I said and he smiled. I could tell he was in a lot of pain. I knew I had to keep him going. "Once we get back to my place, I'll have someone make you a kickstand."

I stepped outside and waved to Q. Cathy looked worried. She had every reason to. If we didn't get here, Mark would be gone before the next day. "We've got medics and medicine. Mark's going to be okay."

Cathy put the kids in the back of the Chopper and Q and I carried Mark on a makeshift litter.

"You guys ever ride in a chopper before?" The kids shook their heads and looked excited. I grinned and climbed into the front seat. I started the preflight checks and started the engine. It only took a moment for the engine to get back up to temperature. When I engaged the rotors, I looked over at Cathy. She sat in the co-pilot's seat and had pulled the earphones on over her head.

"I didn't know George could fly. How long has he had this helicopter?" Mark asked, Q groggily.

"We just found it." Q grinned at Mark.

Cathy looked at me with wide eyes as I pulled up on the collective, lifting the Blackhawk up off the ground. "Don't worry. Someone showed me how to drive one of these… Once."

I could see Cathy gripping her seat with white knuckles.

Once up in the air and moving again, I notified base that we had recovered our lost sheep. "But we don't have enough fuel to return. We'll need a gas station."

"Roger, Ogre. Stand by, we'll locate one for you."

"10-4, standing by." I leaned back into the seat. Q pulled up to me, putting his head close.

"We can find a truck." Q offered.

I looked back at Mark and the kids. I shook my head "Not enough time." I mouthed so no one would hear. Q nodded.

"Fort George Actual to Master Ogre."

"Go for Ogre... and don't listen to Musket about titles."

"Uh, Roger that, Ogre. We have a possible safe location to refuel for you."

"That's good news. Where am I heading?"

I got the vector and nudged the cyclic, changing my course heading. "Copy that. We're on the way."

## Izzie: Fort George.

Isabella de Castro looked at herself as she brushed out her hair, the curls coming from her mother and the color from her father. Looking in the mirror she saw the bed, just an air mattress and a couple of bunk pads, and wished he was here. From the first floor she heard gunfire then explosions. Dropping the brush she grabbed for the Glock Louie had given her. At a low ready she swung out into the hallway, catching movement at the far end. One of the RAF men from Lossiemouth coming around the corner, his L85 raising towards her. Bringing the Glock up and catching a flash sight picture, she felt her finger squeezing the trigger, one-two, one-two, one-two, following him as he fell to the floor. Spinning around she saw Paul coming from his room, his Mossberg 590 aiming down the hallway. Automatically, she reloaded, pocketing the used magazine.

"What's going on?" he asked

"I don't know. Sounds like over at the kid's rooms and the Ops center. Follow me."

Other Crimsons were coming out of their rooms, seeing Caroline she told her to search the RAF man's body and secure this floor. Taking the steps two at a time she reached the portico to the Hill's private rooms as a grenade went off, dust and pieces of plaster blowing out into the hallway.

"Mike! Izzy and Paul coming in!"

"Come In!"

She swung in, the Glock questing for targets, seeing Mike behind a heavy desk shaking his head.

"Target left!" Paul shouted, the 590 booming, the buckshot catching a civilian, one of the Father's charges, in the upper back, just as Big Mike's FAL fired, hitting her in the throat, a grenade falling from her limp hand.

"Grenade!" Izzy shouted spinning back into the hallway with Paul, opening her mouth to equalize the pressure like she'd been taught. When the explosion faded she and Paul reentered the portico seeing Mike battering a man with the butt of his rifle, a roar coming from his lips.

"Mike! Mike!" It's Izzy!" she yelled as he swung up the FAL.

"The Boys!" she pointed at the door, pantomiming. Mike spun, running to the doors. Kicking them open and stepping back as a burst of P90 fire erupted at chest level.

"Kilo, Bravo! It's Izzy, Mike, and Paul!"

"Come ahead Izzy!" Kilo shouted.

Stepping in the room she could see that the boys had overturned the bunks facing the door. Mike took them to the latrine putting them in the heavy bathtubs there admonishing them to stay put this time. Paul stood by the door, his 590 aimed towards the portico, thumbing more shells into his mag-tube.

Mike came back giving her the OK, and she saw the blood on his neck and chest from the shrapnel. She made him sit against the wall and loosened the straps of his armor, bandaging the ragged gashes there.

With the task finished, she watched the doorway for reinforcements or targets, whichever showed up first. As she did, she felt for the Star of David her parents had given her for her Bat Mitzvah.

"Please Lord, keep my man safe and send us help." she whispered in Hebrew, hearing footsteps in the hallway.

## Sarge. Fort George:

Sarge stopped by Ops and listened to George and Q's progress. They had been guided to a likely re-fuel point and were already planning the future relief mission to Urquhart Castle. Sarge was immersed in the details and not paying attention to his surroundings when he felt the concussion of rounds being fired close by his head and then the noise caught up a fraction of a second later.

He fell to the floor to get out of the line of fire barely in time. He glanced to where the gunfire came and saw a British airman was spraying the room with his L85. His partner closest to Sarge was pulling a grenade from his vest. A snarl spread across the Sarge's face. He had been running with his E&E chest pack and only had a small Ruger SP-101 .357 Mag and a big Cold Steel Rajah II folder. Too many people were crowded around the Ops center for Sarge to shoot at the airmen. He flung open the Rajah and leapt at the airman with the grenade. He had just hooked the grenade ring when Sarge clamped down on his hands and stabbed him twice in the lower back. The traitor screamed and arched his back violently and threw his elbow up into Ferguson's face. The Sarge lost his grip on the traitors hands and the grenade went flying back toward his buddy in the doorway. The Sarge grabbed the traitor again and jerked him back onto himself and then rolled away. The concussion from the grenade slammed them both into the corner and knocked the Sarge out momentarily.

When he came to, he could see the grenade thrower staggering toward the wrecked radio sets. He got to his knees and scraped around for his Rajah blade. He found it and lurched after the traitor who was scrambling to get away with a back full of shrapnel. Fresh blood wetted his back, freshening the blood stains that had dried on the back of his jump suit. The Sarge grabbed him by the collar and rammed the big folder up under his crotch. Sarge lifted him up with it then slammed him down. The traitor screamed and balled up in a fetal position, clutching his groin and Sarge tore the knife out and came down on the back of his neck and buried the blade in his spine. The traitor he went limp.

Sarge immediately turned to the doorway for the shooter and fell on his face. He couldn't hear and his balance was failing him. The lights were flickering and his vision was too dim to see how badly he was bleeding but he could feel his ears and nose were wet and sticky. He felt so thirsty and choking for air. The doorway was chipped and blasted from the explosion and the heavy oak door was lying across the hallway.

The shooter was sitting in a torn heap against the jam, his lower jaw missing. He was still alive and laughing as he choked and gurgled on his own gore. A rifle magazine was embedded in his clavicle area. Sarge struggled for strength and crawled up to the gunman and hit him as hard as he could in the side of his head, but it was a flailing, weak-as-kitten-piss punch. Sarge pulled the SP-101 and put it to the gunman's head. But the gunman was already dead so he saved the bullet. He was too tired to pull the trigger anyways. He fell forward onto the gunman's tattered legs.

Sarge felt hands lifting him up from the front and set him against the opposite jam. One of the SF communications troopers that had been on break was yelling at him, but Sarge couldn't hear. Father Mulcahy appeared before him and leaned in. He wiped the blood from Sarge's face and suddenly he could see better after that.

Mulcahy turned and looked at the dead shooter for a moment, then reached out and tore open the airman's uniform blouse. Deep in his chest was carved the demonic possession symbol. These two bastards had played it cool and infiltrated when George and his boys had brought back the food and ammo from RAF Kinloss. *Hiding in the control tower my ass! Infiltrators! How many more?* Despite Sarge's injuries, his mind was already racing with possibilities. The Hills! Despite his loss of hearing, he yelled at Father Mulcahy to secure Debbie and the kids. He smiled and gave a thumbs up.

"Don't worry. They're okay! They're okay!" At that Sarge fell back and passed out again.

He woke up in the infirmary a short time later. A tremendous ringing in his ears made him shake his head and curse. A nurse he remembered from Utah turned toward him and shined a light in each of his eyes going through the standard concussion checklist. He could hear her voice as if it were muffled by a mattress, but couldn't understand her words.

Father Mulcahy was standing in the doorway and came forward to his bedside. He had a small dry erase board in hand and wrote:

*"Hill family safe. Mike of Crimson Grd stopped 1 of my flock & stranger no one remembers before. Tried to force way to Hills w/ grenades & rifles. Mike banged up but pissing off med staff. Won't lie still. Iron Mike!"*

Mulcahy drew a smiley face at the end of that last sentence. Iron Mike, Sarge laughed and winced from the pain. He laid back and rested. *Good*, he thought. *Good.*

## Go for Ogre

It wasn't a long flight to Faslane. Nearby there was a UK Navy base, HMNB Clyde. Our fuel stop. I flew over it, getting the layout. Along the fence near the road, zombies had piled up and were pressing against it.

"How many rounds do you have, Q?"

"A full mag, Boss."

"How many zeds can you get with that?"

"Enough, if you fly straight."

As I passed over, getting ready to line up for a strafing run, one of the zeds looked up. It had red eyes. "We've got a Red Eye down there, in the center of the group, blue jacket."

"Got him."

I turned the chopper and lined up for the pass. "Plug your ears, kids." The children obediently covered their ears with their hands and Q started taking well aimed, single shots. The first round dropped the zombie in the blue jacket and other rounds started to methodically drop the rest. When Q ran out of rounds, most of the zombies were laying on the ground.

"Good shooting, Q."

He just grunted and muttered about more ammo.

I flew around one last time and picked out a place to land. I came in directly, with a nice and easy approach, and set the Blackhawk down on the grassy field as a bunch of Her Majesty's Sailors lined up at the edge of the field with rifles leveled at us. "Everyone stay put. I'm going to go talk to them."

"No your not." Q interjected. "Stay in the bird. If this doesn't go well, you can still take off and at least get part of the way back. If something happens to you, we're all done for. No one else can fly this thing."

I didn't like this, but he had a good point. "Okay."

Q stepped out of the helicopter, slowly, with his hands up. One of the soldiers motioned him forward. Q walked to the line and a lot of talking went on. Gestures, a thumb back in our direction, then the lead Sailor nodded. The rifles then pointed to the sky or the ground. Q looked back at me with a cocky grin and gave me a thumbs up.

I shut everything down and slowly stepped out and walked over.

"Do you boys have a Doctor?"

"Yes, Sir." The Sailor saluted and grabbed the large radio off his belt and called for the medic.

"Thanks for the help. We were starting to get worried.

"Well, once we took out the Red Eye the rest were..."

"Red eye?" The sailor asked.

"Yes, there was a Red Eye."

Another sailor piped up, "I told you I saw a zombie with red eyes. What are they?"

"The Red Eyes can control other zombies. One can control thousands. If you have zombies acting in any coordination at all, there's a Red Eye someplace. You kill the Red Eye, the zombies are easier to deal with." We didn't mention the black-eyed litches or their powers.

"Well, they didn't have much coordination here."

"Oh really? Go look at your fence. They were letting you chew your own fence down so they could break through it in mass instead of trying to climb it." Q pointed "Look at that main post. It's shot off at the base."

"We need fuel. I was hoping that Her Majesty might spare some."

"We have some to share, but where are you going? The dead hold Great Britain now."

"Not all of it. We have cleared Inverness and hold Fort George."

"That old relic?"

"The old defenses there work well, and her cannons have been used with great success. It's just the type of defense we need against these hordes." I said, indicating the fences and dead that lay still on the other side. "A lot better than chain link and razor wire. We've already repelled a massive attack. This place wouldn't have withstood it."

The sailors looked uncomfortable. A medical team finally arrived and I showed them to Mark. The lead medic was a trauma specialist and surgeon. He opened up the bandage on Marks leg. "That's an ugly hack job you did there, Lad."

"Sorry, Doc. I was just practicing for the other one. You know, I don't think my insurance card is up to date."

"A sense of humor, that's good." The look on the doctor's face said otherwise. He turned to the other medic. "Start an IV, we needed to push antibiotics yesterday." He looked at the kids and Mark's wife huddled in the helicopter, clinging to Mark's arm. "Let's get the kids inside, it's getting dark and they look like they could have a hot meal. Madam, if you would be so kind, please."

Cathy led the kids out of the helicopter to the buildings, following Q and a couple of the sailors. Once out of earshot, the Doc turned back to Mark. "I'm going to give you some morphine for the pain." Mark nodded. "And then I'm going to have to clean up the wound." Mark closed his eyes and nodded again.

The Doctor gave Mark a maximum dose, and then looked at me. "You are going to have to hold him down. This will be unpleasant."

The doctors worked on Mark's stump, cutting away at the necrotic meat, trimming the sharp bone shards down and made flaps that they could close over the end and sew shut. The operation took less than hour and when it was over, Mark was asleep and the Blackhawk was refueled.

"Thanks Doc. I owe you big time. Mark is my brother in law."

"I was told you have Fort George."

"That's right."

"I've never seen it. Read about it in school is all. Built to keep down a Jacobite uprising."

"And now the Jacobites use it."

The Doc threw back his head and laughed. "One must love histories ironies. Maybe we'll come up for a visit."

"Do that. You would be most welcome."

I called Q on the radio and told him we were ready to fly. Then I got on the chopper's radio. "Ogre to Fort George."

Nothing.

"Ogre to Fort George Actual, come in Base."

Nothing. I tried three more times with no luck. I started the engine and it was up to temp by the time Cathy and the kids returned. Q checked the kids, making sure they were seated in and shut the side doors. When he strapped in himself I looked at him. "We're either out of radio range, or we may have a problem."

"Probably just the radios considering the terrain and distance." Q shrugged. Moments later we were racing back to base at full speed.

## Trouble on the Homefront

Ft. George was below us as I circled. Five minutes prior we had seen two Merlin helicopters, both with the Red Thistle logos on the sides, flying south east. The radios seemed to work now, at least to the helicopter. It was good to hear some familiar voices. Paul was leading a pick up mission to Castle Urquhart.

Everything seemed fine from the air, but the lower I got, the more that impression changed. My girls were standing in the courtyard at a parade rest, rifles slung. Izzy had a look on her face that I couldn't read: anticipation and frustration. Another woman, also in armor, was with them. She wore light grey with white pauldrons. It was Debbie. Musket was there, as was Sarge, with grim looks on their faces. My boys, all armed with rifles were waiting as well. Kilo and my twins were in their armor, rifles also slung.

I set the Blackhawk down slowly and as gentile as possible. As soon as the wheels were down, Izzy and the Girls came forward. Q didn't even get unbuckled before Izzy was on him. April and Joy had seriously stern looks on their faces. "Don't do that again." April said quietly with more emotion behind it than she let out.

"I knew you would come back alright." Joy was more confident. Then again, she wasn't pregnant.

Debbie coughed as she stepped between them. She looked absolutely majestic in full armor with a chopped-down Crusader Templar hanging at her side.

"What happened?" I climbed out of the helicopter.

"Everyone is okay. Mike's recovering."

"What the hell happened?"

Next thing I knew Debbie was crying. I looked over at April and her eyes were welling up too. Joy filled me in on the infiltrator situation. Oh hell. How come I didn't see that coming? I looked up as the rotors slowed to a stop. High in the air, I saw a huge black crow, circling, and I had the distinct impression that there were otherworldly powers at play here.

"There's something else, Ogre." Sarge leaned. "Remember those cuts on that corpse we looked at in the clinic? Those symbols?"

"Yeah, how could I forget."

"This guy had those same cuts too. Not as deep, but the cuts were there."

I nodded my head. "Thank you, Sargent Ferguson. Alright, we'll deal with that in minute."

I turned to Debbie, she was looking down at the ground. "Right now..." I lifted Debbie's head. "Let me show you what I found."

As soon as I slid open the wide door, a young girl leapt out, "Aunt Dee-Dee!" The two young boys with the same curly blond hair jumped out too. I helped Cathy out and stepped back. The excited chatter woke up Mark, who groaned. I climbed into the chopper and checked him.

"How are you feeling, Mark?" His fever was already almost gone and he was no longer sweating.

"No pain. It's a nice change. Where are we?"

"Your going to be fine, Mark. You and your family are safe. You are at Fort George."

"You have your own fort?"

"It has cannons and everything."

"Figures as much."

Cathy explained what happened to Debbie as I signaled for some help. Uncle Musket helped Sarge with the litter and took Mark to our quarters.

Debbie and the kids went with them to make sure Mark was comfortable and to catch up with her sister about everything.

Sarge was struggling, I could see it. His fresh bandages had growing red spots on his forehead and neck. "We found this, George. You need to see it." In his hand was a bloodstained piece of paper.

"What is this?"

"We found it on one of the traitors."

I opened the note. It only had a few words, but with dire meaning.

"*Package at Mawgan. Once armed, will deliver to FG. ETA 4 days. See you below.*"

*Package? Armed?*

I looked up at Sarge. "Does this mean what I think it means?"

"We think so."

"When was this written?"

Sarge shook his head. "We've no idea."

"Then we have to roll fast. They had come with us to Lossi, so they had to have gotten this note when they got back."

Sarge nodded.

"So we have a little time. Find out where Mawgan is."

I looked at the Girls. Caroline, Rebecca and Izzy were standing ready. "I want a formation of all the Crimson Order and all personnel we've picked up, rescued, or have just shown up. Everyone. Man, Woman, and Child."

"Okay," Sarge said. "When?"

"Right now."

"Right." Sarge turned and limped away.

Fifteen minutes later, I had what I had ordered. The courtyard was full of people, in ranks. Even the children, including my own, were standing tall as well.

I walked in front of the ranks of the Crimson Order as I explained the necessity of exposing infiltrators. Then I ordered all the CGs to remove their shirts or armor. They did so without question or hesitation. They pulled off their clothes and let them drop to their feet and stood at attention. The Girl Squad did as well, showing me their bare backs, and more. No ritualized scarification from cuts, but I didn't know Caroline had an eagle tattooed across the shoulders. Didn't expect that.

As I examined my Crimson Order, Big Mike... Iron Mike had limped out and joined the formation. He stood by Caroline who helped him pull off the hoodie he was wearing. "Sorry I am late, Sir." There was fresh blood from wounds under bandages... shrapnel had penetrated the weak points in his armor. His back however, was clear of the cuts we were looking for. I went over to the big man and shook his hand. I looked him in the eye as I thanked him again, then took a step back.

I motioned for the CGs to recover and waited a moment for them to get their shirts and armor back on. Then I turned to the others. There was some objection. I raised one hand and made a bladed motion. As a unit, the CGs went through the ranks and checked those forcefully who didn't comply. The girls checked, much more gently, the children, even the youngest.

"We've got one!" One of the CGs called out, throwing the man he was checking to the ground. The man wrestled but the CG had him pinned with the man's shirt up off the back exposing the skin below. I ran over. I saw ritualized patterns of ink, twisting Celtic knots, and, in the center, the Celtic symbol of the Trinity. But no cuttings. "He's fine, let him up."

The man was an airman from Lossiemouth, wore wings on his chest. He was a pilot. "I'm sorry for the inconvenience, but we have to be sure, we have to check everyone."

"And who checked you?" He spat on the ground.

I took a step back from him. "April, Joy...remove my armor."

On each side of me, the girls unbuckled and removed my plate from the waist up. Once that was off, I shrugged out of my quilted padding and UnderArmor T-Shirt. I turned around and let everyone see. I had plenty of scars, but no ritualized scarification or symbols. The angel on my back was not cut, but the exit wound from the bullet I caught in Utah looked like it tore a hole in one of the angel's wings.

"Are you satisfied, Airman?" I gritted my teeth as I spoke. "I'll not have anyone question my authority here. Everyone is checked from now on before they are allowed in the fort. Medically for signs of bites or infection... and spiritually... for corruption."

"And what if we find one?"

"Purify it with fire." I growled and pulled my shirt back on, but held off putting on the armor again. I looked at everyone in the formation. "Look around you, everyone. Look at the faces. Everyone here has been checked and found clean. If you see someone that hasn't been checked... someone who has hidden from us... tell one of the Guards. Any infiltration puts everyone at risk. Think about that. Dismissed!"

As people started to wander away, "Airman." I caught the man with the Celtic tattoos. "I'm sorry we got off on the wrong foot. Please understand, I only want to keep everyone safe... I almost lost my sons, because we didn't check people. We got lax."

"I'm sorry, Sir... I... understand."

"No, please. These are tense times. I need everyone to work together. Those wings. You're a pilot."

"Yes, Sir. I fly a Tornado."

"Oh, really? And where is your aircraft?"

"Back at RAF Lossiemouth."

"Do we have any other fighter pilots here?"

"Yes Sir. there are five of us."

"Lossiemouth is a little too far away to keep your jets there. Can you boys ferry them to Inverness?"

"Yes, but the runway there will have to be cleared first. And we'll need..."

"Everything you need from Lossiemouth we'll have moved to Inverness. I'm putting you in charge... Mister..." I looked at the name tag. "Mister Hawkins. Get all the other Airmen from Lossiemouth and Kinloss. Take a couple trucks, clear Inverness and then retrieve your supporting equipment and supplies... and your aircraft. You guys are not hanging up your wings any time soon. I need an Air Force."

Hawkins beamed and snapped a sharp salute, "Yes, Sir! You'll have your Air Force before lunch tomorrow!"

"See to it then. Dismissed."

I watched Hawkins dash to the garrison. I turned around and was face to face with April and Joy. They looked at me closely.

"He smells like an old shoe." April said to Joy.

"And he needs a shave. He looks like a vagrant." Joy observed, scratching the beard that had taken over my face, hiding the magnificent goatee I used to have.

"I guess we better clean him up." April sighed. "No one else will."

The Girls had been expecting me and had hot water ready. April gave me a plate of roasted rabbit, cheese, fresh baked bread. I ate like a grizzly, while they drew a bath in the tub with water hot enough to steam my glasses. I had no idea how hungry I was. When I finished my meal, I slid into the tub, the first soak in a bath I'd had since we came to the UK. A great change from the cold showers I'd been taking.

While I was in the tub, I started to fall asleep. Voices woke me. Debbie came in. "Hey babe." I smiled.

"Thank you..." She said, sitting on the side of the tub in her armor. "I don't know how you found them... but thank you."

"I don't know either. I just had a picture of them in my mind... and it seemed familiar. I just knew where they were. I just wish I knew three days earlier. Mark would still have his leg."

I splashed hot water over my head and looked up at Debbie. "We'll get Musket to carve him out a cool peg leg or something. You like the Armor?"

Debbie nodded. "You look good in it. Where did you get the rifle?"

"We got some mail this morning. Some rifles, Gundoc sent them and some ammunition. You got a letter from the President."

"Good, good. What about the armor support I requested?"

"That's the bad news. He can't spare any. He said he was going to send some, but they went to Italy instead."

I nodded, "So Zack went back to Italy. Ammo is good. I'll take the ammo. We needed it. How much did we get?"

She laughed, "a lot."

Debbie kissed me on the forehead and left.

I closed my eyes and let the heat of the water soak in. After awhile I climbed out and wrapped a towel around my waist. I started shaving with a straight razor at a small basin of warm water, when I heard someone splash water in the tub. I looked over and saw April grinning at me as she slid her naked body into soapy water. "Can't let the hot water go to waste."

"No, that would be a shame."

## High Altitude - Low Opening

The next day I was sitting on top of some ammo crates from one of the 10 pallets that had been delivered while I was gone. I was eating mutton on the bone. April had found a case of Red Bull someplace and made me a Gator-Bull. I was feeling great again.

I was watching Sarge drilling the youths, fine tuning their rifle marksmanship, along with my boys, my three adopted girls from Japan, and some of the teenage kids we've found here in the UK. All of them were wearing armor plate and learning to shoot in it. Sarge shook his head at the British kids. They had never fired guns before and it showed. A couple of them showed promise, but the others... they were going to take a lot of work.

Sarge shouted, "Alright, we're going to break for lunch now. Be back here in one hour." He walked over and took one of the mutton legs as a flight of five RAF Tornados dropped out of the cloud cover and lined up one at a time. They did a low and slow pass over the Fort, their wings heavy with ordinance slung under them. The lead jet waggled its wings. Sarge looked up and watched the jets pass by before he looked back at me. "Those yours now too?"

I nodded. "We'll need them when we go to RAF St. Mawgan."

"When do we leave?"

"In a few hours we'll roll out."

"Why are we waiting?"

"I don't have a pry bar." I said, chomping into the roasted mutton. Sarge raised an eyebrow and then all the sudden got my meaning.

"You've got to be kidding... are they still? The man has the stamina of a Clydesdale."

I looked over his shoulder and coughed. Sarge just took a bite of meat.

"Morning, guys!" Q said with a grin on his face. "What's for breakfast?"

"It's Noon. Have some mutton for lunch." I said.

Q looked up at the grey sky, "Noon? Seriously? Well, you can't tell with the weather here."

Sarge and I busted out laughing. Q ignored the laughing and looked up at the aircraft forming up to land at the Inverness airport. "When did we get jets?" I laughed again.

We gathered in the Ops Center. We had new radios and systems scavenged from RAF Kinsloss, but the walls were still pockmarked from bullets and fragments. We had a 17-inch laptop, connected to systems in the US. We were looking at Satellite images from last night. RAF St. Mawgan was black. The only lights were from a few fires here and there. Cooking fires or burn barrels. But no electricity.

"If they have no electric lights, there is a good chance they don't have radar. They won't expect an aerial insertion."

"You mean a jump." The Sarge swallowed.

"I mean a HALO jump." I said as I zoomed in the image on the screen. Q coughed. I went on. "We can take a Nimrod from Kinloss. We can drop from here... and land... here." I pointed. "It's away from the fires, so there is likely to be fewer eyes on this area. After we land, the Tornados are going drop to ordinance. Cluster munitions here, and here. That's going to reduce the resistance to a more manageable level. Then they are going to drop bunker busters on the target." I pointed. "And as soon as those hit, we move."

"And what are we looking for?" Sarge asked.

I shook my head. "Looking for? We're not really looking for anything."

"Then what are we going to do?" Sarge asked.

"We're going to kill everything and everyone in these buildings."

"Fuckin' A." Q whispered.

"And if the bunker busters didn't destroy the package, we'll set charges and blow it ourselves." I said flatly. "We can't leave anything behind for the adversary to use. Especially anything with a half-life."

Sarge was grimacing, with his arms folded. I could tell he wasn't cool with the plan. "We have to be heavy handed here. We won't have time to be selective. We won't have time to cautious. This is a hit and run type raid. We come in when they are not expecting, we hit them suddenly, we hit them hard, and we disappear before they can react."

Q was nodding. Sarge grimaced.

"If we could do all of this with just an air-strike, that would be great. But we can't afford to miss, we have to confirm the package was destroyed. And just as important, the guys working on it. If we leave them alive, they could just get another one and get it activated as well."

Sarge was pacing back and forth. His face was flushed red. "So how do we get out? What about exposure?"

"Exposure will be minimal, but we'll use masks to keep from breathing anything in. We're not going to play with it. In and out, and then we'll get out of the area in boats. We will have two Archer class patrol boats that will pick us up here." I pointed to screen.

"They'll be waiting off shore at a distance, but still in view of land. When the bunker busters go off, they'll come in for the pick up. It's going to take them a few minutes to get in, giving us time to mop up and to get to the pick up point."

Q leaned in. "And if someone doesn't make it to the boats?"

"They'll have a long walk home." I said.

"Why not use our new helicopters?" Sarge asked. It was a valid question.

"Because I think they have some intel capability and a large helo flight might tip them off. We need as much of a chance for a surprise as we can get."

Q was making some notes, "The time-line here is real tight, Ogre."

I nodded. "I know... but this is the only way. We can't afford any mistakes. Anyone... anyone that goes, they get too badly hurt... they don't make it to the boat... they will be left behind. The boats can't wait for them. It puts everyone at risk. The whole leave-no-man-behind thing... we can't afford it, but it's necessary. Everyone moves on." I looked at April and Joy, "Even for me. After the package is confirmed destroyed, the mission is to get out. We don't know what defenses they have in place or what reaction strength they have to respond to this so speed is critical. After the boats signal their departure after pick up, the last Tornado drops napalm on the whole area."

I stood up and looked at everyone. The Tornado pilots, the CGs, Sarge, Q, the Girls. "If you can't make it to boat... just get out of the area as fast as possible, take cover."

"But..."

"Just make it to boats, Sarge. Does anyone have any questions?" The room was silent. "Everyone go take some time for yourselves. Make yourselves square with your Maker or whatever you want to do. You have 30 minutes before we head out."

Everyone was quiet as they filed out of the room.

## Getting into Position

Thirty minutes later, Ogre's Raiders assembled at the Merlin Helicopters. We rode the Merlins from Ft. George to Kinsloss where their was a Nimrod fueled and standing by. On the runways at the Inverness Airport, five Tornados were getting ready to launch. The Archer PBRs were already near their station, motoring just a few knots an hour, over the horizon from the target.

We climbed in the Sub-Hunter, and, before the door was even shut, the big goofy looking plane was rolling.

"I wish we had a Herc for this." Q muttered.

"We did... and you crashed it." I slapped Q on his back as Sarge snorted.

The Navigator came back to us, "One Minute!" He opened the door. The Nimrod was high and flying slow, but wind whipped us. I stood and checked my watch.

"On Your Feet!" I shouted and everyone stood up.

Sarge looked like he was just trying to breath. I could tell he was afraid and not happy about this, but he saddled up anyway. The definition of brave. Good man. I had gone over everything about jumping with my Girls, but anything can happen on a jump. I grabbed April and pulled her close and kissed her on her forehead. "You're going to be okay." Then I kissed Joy on her forehead. She was near panic, but she was keeping it together. I felt Joy relax, a little. "You'll be fine, Joy... You can do this." She nodded and put on a brave face. I pulled my mask down over my face and tightened the straps. We were wearing our normal kit under the jump suits. Heavy armor plate was back at Ft. George because you can't jump with it. I looked at everyone once more. Sarge, Q, the Girls and all the Crimson Guards. I got thumbs up and nods.

"Ten Seconds." The navigator shouted.

I shuffled to the door. I was going to be the first one out. I looked out and saw nothing but clouds below me and stars above me. Then I felt the slap on my back. "GO!" The Navigator yelled. I took a deep breath and threw myself out of the perfectly good aircraft. My stomach was in my throat but I was able to swallow it back down. The sound of wind and the feel of fluttering fabric was all I had. The small air-bottle was feeding dry cool air into my face mask and I tried to breath in normal regular breaths as I watched below me.

The clouds floated up to meet me, and, as I fell through them, I noticed moisture beading up on my face mask. It was going to be raining on the ground. This was good. No one looks up when it's raining at night.
I looked at the altimeter on my arm. I was right there. I counted... Three... Two... I broke through the clouds and saw the ground below me... One. I opened my chute. Looking up I checked the lines and everything looked good. That done, I looked at the ground again and searched for my landing zone. At first I couldn't find it and then I breathed a sigh of relief when I did. Steering to it I lined up and set myself for a nice glide down to the far side of the zone, a large parking lot that was behind a building from our target building and empty of cars. Trees were behind it so we had an avenue of escape if resistance was too stiff. As I glided in, I saw zombies on the other side of the building, but no one else around and none of the zombies noticed.

A couple zombies were near where I wanted to land. I brought up my rifle, one of the 6.8 ACRs topped with an EOtech with a nice AAC Suppressor. I gave the zombies a burst each and dropped them with hits into the hips and legs, then let my rifle hang on the sling as I braked and touched down running to a stop. I cut the lines to my chute and let the canopy drift away as I shrugged out of the harness and then ran over to the zeds and put a round into each head.

With the Drop Zone secured I scanned the sky. I saw April was already on the ground, canopy disconnected. Good girl. Joy was drifting down right in front of me. Her feet touched the ground running and she crashed into me. Joy's mass knocked me to the ground. She was on top of me. "THAT WAS AWESOME!" Then her chute billowed and pulled her off of me. She dragged for a few feet before she got disconnected and started jumping up and down. I peeled off the jump suit as I watched the others land. Everyone else made it down. Joy jumped on my back. "Lets do it again, I'm so excited... right now! That was better than sex!" She was breathing hard.

"Easy girl... Business first now. Get ready." I checked my watch. "Any second now." I motioned for everyone to take cover. We ran against the building and ducked low.

## Package Located - Charges Set

Cluster bombs detonated like rolling thunder shattering windows and sending shards of shrapnel whistling through the air. I poked my head up and looked through the building. The far wall was shredded and nothing moved on the far side. I ducked down again as I heard the engines of jet fighters over head. A massive explosion, followed by three others in quick succession shook the ground. The overpressure took our breath away, and chunks of debris was falling all around. Concrete, an office chair, a burning motivational poster of a kitten hanging on a clothes line.

Our turn. I was up and running on the balls of my feet, keeping my weapon up and my eyes scanning. Movement from the left. I turned to engage, but April was already jackhammering the target.

Alpha Team entered what used to be a building. The damage was extensive. The bombs had shattered the structure and left upper floors looking like broken freeway on-ramps. The facility had been a large building. We found some stunned survivors on the outside edges of the ground floor, and we shot them. One of them had Red Eyes, just before a 6.8 slug sent each one flying in different directions.

We secured the ground and Bravo Team came in and found the stairs. The first bomb had punctured through all the floors and into the basement before it detonated.

Q pulled out the Geiger Counter and it chattered like crazy. The area was hot. He hesitated, checked his airmask, and flicked on his tactical light. He lead Team Bravo down the ruined stairs and stopped half way. There had been a room full of people here at one time. The place was immolated and the Geiger Counter showed radiation levels that were very high. Q's light shown on the weapon. A warhead from an ICBM. It's housing was cracked and it was thrown into a wall, but it was still more or less intact. "There we go." Q motioned and Bravo team ran to the warhead and set the large shaped charges they carried.

"Halo 6 to Ogre. Package located and charges set."

"Roger that, Halo 6."

Once set, they pulled out and joined the rest of us outside. Everyone was accounted for. Q came up and knelt beside me. He held up the detonator's remote, winked, and pushed the button.

I felt a big concussion from below. "The package is ruined... Let's get out of here." Q shouted.

I motioned for him to move out. Q slapped Izzy on her butt and she took off first. Then the rest of his team started running before he picked himself up. Some of Alpha Team members had located a truck big enough for everyone to pile into. We would take the truck to the docks. Again, part of the plan that worked perfectly. So far, everything was going great. We drove to Watergate Bay, when the truck slid to a stop. The small road leading down to the beach was blocked.

"End of the line, people!"

We piled out and all of a sudden I knew something was wrong.

Zombies were all around us. It was as if they had been waiting for us. Everyone opened fire in every direction as we pushed our way to the beach. From on top of the cliff, I could see the makeshift pier, floating out into the water, tied with cables to the stakes. It was high tide so it was only a short run across the sand to the floating pier. We ran for it. Bravo going first, Alpha covering.

Tracers opened and one of the CGs in Bravo Team crumpled and fell. There was no saving him as the front of his head was visible through the back of his head. The team kept running. I followed where the fire had come from and brought my weapon to bare on it. I saw movement and I fired a round. A Red Eye with a rifle stumbled and fell off a deck overlooking the beach. More movement by the boathouse. I fired more rounds. As soon as the red dot in the center of the holographic sight touched a target, I fired again. Rapid fire acquisition and engagement, I fired off the trigger reset and my gun was feeling like I might as well have just put the gun on auto. Lots of targets were coming our way. At first, we had zombies and then we had more Red Eyes. One of them was packing an LMG version of an L-85. This one fired a burst in our direction. I heard Sarge yelp and looked as he went down.

"NEIL!" I shouted.

Sarge crawled back up against the broken wall he was taking cover behind. "Just a graze." He said as he pulled the weapon he had across his back. I had thought it was a shotgun. Now that I saw it clearly, I saw that it was an old M-79. He broke it open like a shotgun, shoved something fat into the breach, and snapped it shut. He looked up at me as rounds zipped over his position. "Where is that SOB?"

I was pinned pretty good now from that LMG but I popped an eye over edge and fell backwards as bullets started chewing it. "Same place." I pointed with my thumb down to the ground. He nodded.

Sarge shouldered the Thumper and got set. He popped up, fired, and dropped back in a split second. There was a loud crack sound and the firing stopped.

April and Joy provided overlapping covering fire as Sarge reloaded. I popped up and saw fire in the distance. Orange and yellow flames, coming in our direction. Damn it. A black-eyed litch. I hate those guys. I fired rounds at it but it kept coming. "Time to GO!" I shouted.

Sarge fired his M-79 for the fifth or sixth time. Then picked himself up and ran for the boat. His new girlfriend ran after him with her long hair streaming behind her. "See you on the yacht," he said as he ran past me.

"April, Go." April peeled off and sprinted towards the floating pier. "Joy, Go!" She finished spraying her magazine and took off, doing a speed reload as she ran.

I pulled a frag grenade off my vest. I was going to throw it, turn and run. The Fireman was close enough I could see his black eyes through the flames. He laughed like an evil James Earl Jones, and I could feel the cold hollow feeling of the darkness behind those eyes. I pulled the pin on the frag and threw it. The grenade flew only 20 feet before it stopped and hung in mid air like Bullet Time from *The Matrix*. It detonated with a muffled "whump." It sounded like a firecracker under a bucket.

I could feel tendrils of power wrapping around me as I ran, but it had no effect on me. I didn't let it. But I could feel it around me. I kept running.

Suddenly light and shadows shifted and I dodged to the left. A ball of fire flew past me and exploded on a parked van. The van was instantly immolated. Joy looked back at me as she ran, she was almost at the docks. A few more steps and she leapt onto the PBR. The first PBR was already pulling out at full throttle. Good. I watched as the first PBR starting firing into buildings overlooking the beach with its 20mm.

I was almost on the pier when a blast of heat and light struck my back plate as another one blasted the sand in front of me. I was thrown into the air like a ragdoll. As I flew I caught a glimpse of April screaming. I struck a large black rock and felt myself cartwheel into the water. The PBR throttled up and pulled away, from under the water I saw the cavitation and watched as the boat left. I swear I could hear April screaming as I sunk deeper into the water.

I was stunned from the impact and my left arm hurt, and didn't want to move. I knew my lungs were empty because I had the wind knocked out of me. I could panic, scramble, and still sink... instead I kept my calm and waited until I felt my feet touch the bottom. When I did, I let my legs coil under as I shrugged out of my body armor. As soon as it was off, I kicked off the bottom and pumped for the surface. My lungs were burning. I could see the surface but it was too far away. My chest heaved and I swallowed some seawater, which made me cough. Just when I thought I wasn't going to make it, I broke the surface. I coughed and sputtered, throwing up seawater. I bobbed in the water under the floating pier, hidden from any eyes on the shore, chest and eyes burning, but I was alive. Back on the bottom, my tactical vest. My radio, my M&P and spare magazines. I could hear the PBR's engines roaring as they disappeared north.

Suddenly the area was bathed in an orange glow as the napalm exploded over everything. The water was cold. I couldn't stay here much longer, but I couldn't come out either. Any adversaries still alive after the napalm strike would be looking for me or anyone else that didn't make it. I decided to swim for awhile, since I was already wet and I didn't want to catch fire. I could hear the wood of the buildings crackling as the napalm burned everything. At least the gunfire and fireballs had stopped.

## Ogre Gets Wet

I swam northwards along the coast until I was exhausted. I had just hoped that I had put enough distance. I had passed the beaches of Mawgan Porth, thinking those areas were too close and probably populated by unfriendlies. My arm was torn from barnacles on the rock I had struck, but the cold salt water helped stop bleeding. Sharks however, were a worry. Luckily I didn't find any.

Most of the shoreline was jagged rocks, cliffs, and more jagged rocks. Then I found a small beach with low cliffs and even in the rain I could make out trails leading up to the top. I pulled myself out of the water, crawling on the sand with one arm. I was so cold that it hurt. My body was numb and exhausted. I knew if I collapsed, hypothermia would take me if the crabs or a wandering zombie didn't. So I fought gravity and stood on shaky legs. I took an inventory of what I had on me. I had a Leatherman MUTT tool clipped to my belt. My Glock 23, with only one magazine. My Becker Combat Bowie and the neck knife under my shirt. That wasn't much. Everything else was with my vest. I pulled myself along a trail that wound its way from the beach to the actual ground. My feet were lead, but at the top I looked across a flat vast field. I saw a building in the distance and stumbled to it, staggering like one of the undead.

The building was a barn, with hay or straw or whatever it was, stacked neatly, and stacked high inside. I climbed up to the top and cut open the bails and pulled the straw over me. I shivered until I passed out.

Back at Ft. George, the teams landed. They climbed out of the Merlins and walked somberly to the garrison. Sarge and Q walked past Debbie, unable to say anything. They bowed their heads as they passed. It was April who went up to her.

When Debbie screamed, Sarge turned back, wanting to scream too... but he was pulled away.

"No... He's not dead. He's Not!" Debbie fell to the ground and beat her fists against it. "He's alive! I know it!" Cathy ran out to her, picking her up.

"You left him!" Debbie screamed. "You abandoned him! You stupid slut!" She pointed at April. "You whore!"

April broke down again, Joy took her arm and half carried her to her quarters.

Debbie wheeled and pointed at Q and Sarge. "You left him behind! Damn you!" Cathy pulled her back to the garrison. "He's not dead!" She screamed. "He's not dead!"

Q looked down and walked slowly away. Sarge looked up at the sky and his knees hit the ground.

It was late into the morning when I awoke. Near the farm houses I found a small car, a Ford Mondeo. There were no keys in it. I looked at the house and considered my options. I entered, drawing my Becker. There was a dried-out corpse in the kitchen, and upstairs was a zombie, a teenage girl with no hair on her head. I left her head on the floor. A photo on the wall of a young girl, the zombie I had just ended. She had been beautiful once, blond and blue eyed. In the photo was a young man, her arm proudly through his. A boyfriend, perhaps. A lover maybe. A world of possibilities before them, all cut short. I shook my head as I looked back down on the one I had dropped. I felt sorry for a moment.

I searched the house for the keys and found them. I traded my still damp shirt for a cotton shirt and a wool sweater. There was a man of the house that was someplace else, and his pants size was larger than mine, but they were dry. I tightened my belt and made do.

In the kitchen was a jar of canned fruit, the only thing these people had left. "Thank you, good folks, I hope I can repay the debt one day."

Outside I went to the little Ford and opened the door. The cabin light came on and when I put in the key, the dash lit up. "Thank heavens." It took a little cranking before the engine fired, but it did and it felt strong. I pulled out of the farm carefully, smiling.

I ate the pears and drank the juice and threw the jar out of the window of the Mondeo as I drove through Engollan and headed north. The roads were clear and I made good time. The stereo had a CD in it. *Prodigy*.

I saw a sign, just outside of Penrose, and I decided to check it out. An old RAF airfield from the great war. I stopped the car as I looked at the plane that sat there on the airfield under an old hanger. The hanger looked as ancient as it was. But the plane looked as good as new. That is for a small squat looking mini bomber. I jumped out of the car and ran over to it. A De Havilland Mosquito. I went to the undercarriage and found the crew hatch wasn't there. "This better not be a damn mock up." I followed the undercarriage to the nose. Gun ports. "Ah! The fighter variant!" On the right side of the nose was the door. I opened it and climbed in, to my disappointment, I found the battery to be dead, or removed, and the tanks drained.

Crap. I would've loved to have flown a Mosquito. It was one of my favorites.

I looked out of the cockpit and saw another plane, sitting beside it was a small cart. "Well George," I said to myself with a smile, "I guess I'll just have to take that one."

Twenty minutes later I was climbing at full speed. The plane handled much like my old trainer back in Utah, but so much more responsive and more powerful. I turned the Spitfire north and opened the throttles.

"Ha ha!!"

I flew low and fast, at full military power, then pulled up and climbed. I couldn't help but to do an aileron roll. I'd have to find a P-51 Mustang and fly that to see which was better.

As much fun as I was having, I had to get back home. I looked around the cockpit. The only navigational aid I had was compass, but it looked wrong. I tapped it. "Blast." It didn't even twitch. I pushed the rudders left and then right. "Damn." It still didn't move.

Without navigation I'd have to follow the geography, which was easy enough to do. Thinking about it, it was quite easy. I laughed and turned the aircraft towards home.

I flew north till I found Loch Ness. Something you can't miss really. I followed Ness north east and climbed to 20 thousand feet. From there, I could see the geography of the land around me. I saw Inverness, and the claw like promontory that sat Ft. George, and my home. I stayed high until I was closer, then did a shallow descent to pick up speed.

I buzzed the fort, doing a barrel roll over it and came back doing a loop. Then aileron rolls till I made myself sick. I was having too much fun to land, but the fuel gauge told me I must land soon. Pity.

I walked through the entrance of the Fort and saw Sarge. I raised my good arm and waved with a smile when I was blind sided and knocked to the ground.

"You did it on purpose!" April was sobbing. "You knew that was going to happen."

I grimaced. "Yes... I know." I tried to explain as she hit my chest with her armored fists. "And I knew what would happen if you guys didn't leave. It was the only way!"

Joy ran up and pulled April off of me. She pulled April up and then helped me up off the ground. She wrapped her arms around me and wouldn't let go. I held her head. "I knew I'd be fine... But we lost one of our own... Clark... I didn't see that happening. If you guys didn't leave they would have crushed the boats with rocks."

Sarge walked up. "You saw what?"

"Rocks. The Red Eyes had rocks on the cliffs, if the boats stayed, they would have thrown the rocks... rocks the size of Cooper Minis. And I knew if you guys left the napalm would get them and everyone would be safe."

"How did you see that?"

"Ask Oogie." I nodded towards Sarge's woman. She just looked at me with a slight nod.

Our conversation was cut short. "You knew? You saw? And you didn't tell me?" Debbie swung. Her punch caught me off guard and I was lifted off my feet, which went over my head as I hit the ground. My wife packed one hell of a punch. "You bastard!"

I was about to black out. "There's a spy... I couldn't tell anyone." I said out loud, but what I was thinking was "So good to be home again." Everything went dark.

## Mohtahe Okohke

It was getting to the point that I feared going to sleep. Nightmares haunted me, and I'd awake almost as tired as when I laid down. In my dreams there was a young, thin woman with dark skin and dark hair. She was pretty as she smiled at me. She looked Native American, like Oogie, but without the curves. She would smile and beckon me closer. As I approached her, she would look down. Then when I stood before her, she would look back up with a face that was skeletal, covered in dried skin that pulled away from her teeth. She opened her mouth and flew at my face. I'd wake up breathless. The dream was the same, until just last night. Last night's dream, I asked her name. Before she looked down, she said "*Mohtahe Okohke*".

Mohtahe Okohke. I spoke to Oogie of this and told her of the dream. She acted as if I was jesting until I said her name. When I said the name, Oogie froze. A look of horror in her eyes. "I know this name." She said and turned quickly and walked away.

"What does it mean?"

It means "Plague of Crows" she called back and hurried her steps.

Rosa was getting the hang of roasting mutton, learning from a local Scottish lass we picked up from the Urquhart Castle. Somehow Uncle Musket had found a few new Tavern Wenches that made sure that everyone had food when needed in the dining hall. Most of the food available was stews and breads, but Rosa was learning the art of roasting over fires. This made me hopeful that, at sometime in the future, we might have a good flank steak.

"Scotland has taught me a new appreciation for the simple things in life." Uncle Musket announced. "I never before would have favored cold meat, and hot beer."

I had a laugh as Musket called a couple little girls to him and whispered in their ears. They giggled and approached me cautiously. They looked to be five or six and completely adorable with girly hair and large smiles. They both made proper curtseys and lowered their heads. One of them giggled again as the other asked "Are you really our new king?"

"What?" I had to laugh. That was funny. I looked over to Musket and he threw his head back, laughing so hard he fell backwards. The little girls ran away laughing and skipping.

"Musket!" I roared. Musket had tears in his eyes from laughing so hard.

I took the mutton and walked back to the Ops Center. Snow was falling in large flakes. April took up stride besides me. "I love the fur. It suits you. Who did it?"

"I've no idea. It was on my armor this morning. And considering it wasn't out of my sight for more than 20 minutes, I'd guess it was Oogie."

"Sarge's woman?"

"I think so." The fur was from a brown bear, fashioned into a cape and over my shoulders hung the huge claws. The cape had a hood, lined with fur in and out. Around the greaves was more fur, that covered the lower legs and the tops of my boots. It was quite warm. "No one else could have done this."

"What makes you think it was her?" April asked as Sarge came around the corner on the way to the Ops Center. His armor was also covered in furs, but it was wolf, with a head over each shoulder. "Ah... I see." She said. "He looks like that guy from *Gladiator*." I nodded in agreement.

# Spirit Walking

Reports of encounters with Red Eyes or the black-eyed litches in Scotland were growing fewer. Scotland was almost cleared, but the undead still came in, marching from the south. Patrols would find them and dispatch them quickly, but the task seemed unending. I had aerial scouts use the powered gliders from Kinsloss, which flew over the countryside, watching the progression of these undead pilgrimages. After weeks of observation it was determined that these marches originated from London.

I had a feeling that would be the case; it was a hunch that I hadn't acted on before for lack of evidence. But now I had proof. The troubled dreams showed me a building that I knew was in London, but I didn't know what building it was.

I sat down with a book that was filled with photos of all the famous buildings in London. I had a mug of mulled cider and sipped at it as I turned the pages. None of them seemed to be the building I saw in my dreams.

There was a knock on my door. Caroline and Rebecca both sat up straighter in their seats, pulling up their HK UMP .45s. Both had fully loaded 25-round magazines, filled with hollow points.

"Come!" I called out.

Oogie stepped inside with her head slightly bowed. "Master Ogre, please forgive my intrusion."

I stood up, "Miss Oogie, please, come in. Have a seat."

Caroline and Rebecca relaxed and lowered their weapons. Oogie nodded and sat down. She was beautiful, tanned skin and dark eyes shaped like almonds, with long, jet black hair. She was very feminine, but she had an overwhelming sense of strength. No wonder Sarge loved her so. "What can I do for you, Miss Oogie?"

"It's me that must ask that same question. What can I do for you? I've sensed some trouble in you. What is it you are looking for in that picture book?"

"I saw a building in my dreams. Several times, the same dream, the same building. I know it's in London, but I don't know where."

"You are looking for it wrong, Sir."

"Oh? How do you suggest I do this?"

Oogie smiled at me. "Let me show you."

Oogie asked me to dismiss the girls guarding me and I hesitated at first, but then realized that it wasn't for her or my privacy, but to protect them.

She then taught me about "Spirit Walking", or as I had heard of it before, "Remote Viewing". Oogie taught me things that tickled the back of my mind, as I felt that I had known already.

"Send your spirit out to the mess hall. Look for your brother, the Musket. Think about Musket in the mess hall."

I closed my eyes and breathed and did the mental-exercises she had taught me. My breathing slowed, my heart rate slowed, and I opened my mind. I felt myself falling for just an instant and I opened my mind's eye and I was seeing in the mess hall. I could see some members of the Crimson eating and laughing. April was there, talking to Caroline. They were whispering together. April spoke of her pregnancy and she was upset that I wouldn't show her affection. I looked down at the floor, not wanting to look at her, even if she wouldn't see me. I felt like such a bastard, so I continued with the task at hand. Musket wasn't here. I heard the sound of his voice. Upstairs. I moved upwards and was suddenly in the rooms above the mess hall. There was musket. Shirtless, sweaty... and in the middle of consensual adult relations with some woman, one of his Tavern Wenches. The shock of this sight broke my will and suddenly I was back in my quarters, with Oogie laughing.

"You knew what I'd find."

She laughed an easy, good natured laugh. "I saw Musket going upstairs with his woman before I came here." Her laughter had no malice to it, just a delight in the humor of things. I laughed too.

Sudden she stopped laughing and leaned in. "*But it broke your concentration, Master Ogre!*" Her voice carried an old power and in that moment I thought I saw light behind Oogie's eyes. A bright silver light. This startled me.

When I was ready, I sent my mind's eye out and I saw the building I was looking for. And I knew who occupied it. Plague of Crows.

"I don't understand this, Oogie."

"What don't you understand, Master Ogre?"

"We're in the UK, but the entity that I'm hunting, the one that has been antagonizing me... is like yourself, Native American."

Oogie laughed. "You can say, Indian if you want."

"Why is she here in the first place?"

"Plague of Crows is very old, very powerful." She began. "The power she draws from is here. Something she is tied to."

"Before you arrived, Sarge was sent a stone. One that he didn't let anyone see. You are tied to that stone."

Oogie smiled, "You learn quickly."

"You find what she is tied to, you can destroy her."

"So where is your stone, Oogie?"

"It's near here." She smiled. "Hers will be near as well. Though probably not in the same place, but close enough."

"So how is it that Sarge won your affections?"

"I've been with Neil for a long time. It was only recently that I've shown myself to him." She smiled again. "He has great honor in his way. As do you."

I shook my head.

"Here." Oogie pulled out a small, leather bag. "This is from your home ground. I was going to give it to you when you were ready."

I took the bag and opened it. Inside was dry reddish soil. It smelled of sage, juniper and scrub-oak. It smelled like my Utah.

"Thank you, Oogie."

She smiled and stood up. "No, thank you, Master Ogre."

## She Took it!

We sat in the Ops Center, and I was listening to the ideas of how best to approach this. Q had been silent the whole time. Our RAF boys just wanted to level the place, and I had little problem with it, but we would still have to go in on the ground.

Q finally spoke up. As he did, I could see the events unfolding in my mind, and I knew it was the right way to go as I could see it clearly.

"Well what do you think?" Q asked as he sipped his coffee with a confident grin behind the mug.

I pointed to a spot on the map. "We'll have to take RAF Wyton first. We can fly straight there and that's it. We'll have to refuel there. The Nimrods can bring ammo for resupply there. We'll need much more than we can carry.

Top off for the OBJ, then come back and top off again for the flight home."

I closed my eyes and looked at the objective. Spirit Walked. Remote Viewing. Call it what you will. I saw a door... heavy, wooden.... I walked to the door and pushed it open. Inside it was dark. There was a woman there, thin with long, black hair. She was pretty, until she stepped forward, and then I could see she looked old and dead. She laughed and I was chilled to my core. Then she sneered at me and lunged, her hand as quick as a cobra, she lashed out at me with fingers like knives.

I fell back off the bench I had been sitting on. Knocked backward. My face felt raked and hot, I reached up and touched it and my hand came away bloodied. It felt like I had been stabbed through the eye with a firebrand.

"Judas!" Sarge yelped and jumped up.

April screamed.

I couldn't see out of my right eye. "What? What happened?"

Q jumped up and stuck his head out of the door, "MEDIC!"

"What happened!" I yelled. The pain was incredible. It was like my very brain was screaming.

Sarge knelt down by me, grabbing a cloth and pressing it hard against my face. "You pissed someone off, son."

Suddenly Oogie was there, looking down me. "What did you see?"

I described the woman I saw, in detail. Down to her clothes. Sarge kept pressure on my face, "What happened?"

Oogie hissed. "She tried to take his sight! She almost got all of it... instead she only took half."

Sarge looked at her. "Who is it, Oogie... no riddles... who was that?"

Oogie put her hand on my head and closed her eyes tight. "She is very old... older than me. She is the Grandmother of Death. The first daughter of Lilith. Her name is Mohtahe Okohke. She's worse than a Shape Shifter... she's a Skinwalker."

Neil looked up at Oogie. "Plague of Crows!" He shook his head. "No, she can't be. Plague of Crows was killed. Her spirit was bound. That's what all the legends say."

Oogie stood up. "The story was a lie. She was never killed... but she was bound. Someone cut her loose." Oogie then left the room by her unique way.

April knelt down where Oogie had been. She touched Sarge's hand and he pulled away the cloth, which I saw with my left eye was saturated in blood. "Can we save it?" She asked quietly.

Sarge looked up at her. "Save what? It's not there."

April choked and looked back down at me. "She took it." She whispered.

"Took what?" I didn't want to hear it but I had to.

"She took your eye."

The pain was unbearable, but I gritted my teeth and sat up. I pushed Neil off me as I climbed the bench to get to my knees. I grabbed the laptop Q had been using and ripped the battery out to kill the screen. I used the dead screen as a mirror. Four fresh claw marks across my face, bleeding, with blood pouring from where my right eye used to be in the socket. I dropped the laptop and roared with anger I couldn't control.

Q and Sarge grabbed me and put me back on the ground. The corpsman came in and looked at me. "What the hell?"

## Traitor in the Camp

The next morning I was back on my feet and in my armor again. Instead of my rifle, I had my Mossberg 930 SPX shotgun, "Cara" slung across my chest and my sword across my back. Another pilot would be flying the Blackhawk now. I was grounded since I only had an eyepatch where my right eye used to be. A large Ruby was set in the center of it. My girls were on each side of me, keeping close. Both armed with swords and Marine IARs. They were going heavy.

"You sure you're up to this?" Sarge asked, with more concern than he wanted to show. He knew I was hurting. The pain meds didn't help. "We can do this... you don't have to."

"The bitch is mine." I growled. "Saddle up." I walked to the Blackhawk and climbed in.

I couldn't help but to think there was reason that Plague of Crows tried to take my sight. She didn't care that I saw her. Evil tends to like to gloat. Show off? Make me afraid? No, it was something she didn't want me to see...here. The helo's rotors were spooling up. One of the Merlins was already starting to lift off the ground.

The Father was there with a sprinkler, throwing prayers and water at the bird for each man on board. Then he hurried over to the next one and did the same. We were used to this sight and never questioned it. Then it dawned on me. He's not blessing anybody... He's counting.

"Ogre to Q."

"Q, here." He responded quickly. I could see him in the Merlin across the field as we lifted up off the ground.

"Why is our good Father counting everyone?"

Q jumped out of his helicopter and approached the Father. There was scuffle that ended with the Father's blouse pulled over his head and Q's knife drawn. I had my doubts that Q would take such dramatic actions against the Father, but from the Blackhawk I saw Q's blur of action, and the father slumping to the ground. Good man. The Blackhawk dropped its nose and accelerated.

Then the nagging question came to my mind. When and how was the father corrupted? Was there something else that had corrupted the Father?

"Ogre to Ft. George Actual, Over."

"Go ahead, Master Ogre." It was Musket.

"Get to my brother-in-law, Mark. Put him on the radio."

"In a jiffy."

Mark had been the Bishop of his ward in London. *Was* being the key term there. But he was still very close with God. And he was a fighter. He got his family out of London and all the way to safety. An impressive feat, especially since he only had one side-by-side shotgun that was taken off the mantel and a box of shells.

"Yes, this is Mark."

"Mark, switch channels, up two."

I switched channels and waited. "Yes? Hello?"

"Mark, we've got a problem."

"What can I do?"

"The good father has just been killed."

"The Catholic?"

"That's the one."

"What happened?"

"He was somehow corrupted. Someone turned him, cut the demonic sigils into him. I don't remember him ever leaving the Fort once he came... because he wasn't marked when we checked everyone."

"How do I..."

"Follow the spirit, Mark. Feel them out. Find them."

"And when I do?"

"Kill them."

There was silence on the other end of the radio. "I... I don't know..."

"Mark, everyone at the Fort is in danger, and more so the longer this guy - or girl - is running around. Your wife and kids, Mark. My wife and kids... Everyone's. You're the only one that can do it."

"Okay."

"Good hunting, Mark."

"Same."

I sat back in the helicopter and closed my eye. April was studying my torn face. "You're still good looking." She said as if she was studying something under a microscope. "The new cuts are parallel to the older scars, so it's not much more damage than you had before."

"Oh really?"

"You would make a scary Santa Claus, but I think you still look good."

I had to turn my head a lot farther to look at her. I could see sympathy and concern in her eyes.

"Thanks."

I checked my shotgun and my shells. My slugs were hardened penetrators from Federal and Dixie Gun Works Tri-Ball. The buck was Federal Premium 00 with Flight Control Wads. Nothing really wide spread, but I had good range if I needed it.

My pistol was an HK45, which replaced the Swampy I lost in the water with my tactical vest. The HK and its mags were held in carriers attached directly to my multi-cam armor. This also gave my gloved hand more room in the trigger guard. My sword made sitting less comfortable, as it was along my back, but it was more comforting and I had a feeling I'd need it.

The four helicopters were on the way to the airfield. Once secured, the Tornadoes would come in and stage from there. They would provide air cover to help us get out.

## Dead Zeds Walking

The Airfield of RAF Wyton lay before us, and, even before we got over it, I could see there was a problem. The spy back at Ft. George had already let the adversary know we were coming. They were ready for us. Formations of the undead were lined up across the runways. Thousands of them. Large balls of fire drifted up at us, but at this range the pilots had no problem evading.

"We should have had the Tornados strafe the base."

"Too late for that now."

The helicopters were at their fuel limits which meant we had no other option but to take this field. Fifty men with small arms and blades against at least a thousand.

When we got over the airfield, the door gunners opened up with their M-134s "Spare no rounds! We take the field, we can get resupplied. Make this a full push effort! Let'm have it!"

One of the Merlins flew a little too low and was hit with a blast from a Red Eye's force impact. The Helicopter was knocked sideways in the air, but the pilot kept control and gained altitude and pulled away from reaching arms.

I ordered my pilot to make a fast pass over the Red Eye that hit the Merlin and as we went by, I unloaded my 930 SPX at it. Tri-Ball rounds had a devastating effect on most things struck, but unless a ball hit brain, it had little terminal effect on the undead. From my pass, I knocked a lot of zeds over, but many of those were able to stand back up. The Red Eye didn't. The girls started to assist the door gunners with their IARs, and the undead started dropping in rows.

"Wizard Three to all live units, we are critical low on fuel, over."

"Wizard Two, same situation."

I looked out at the field and saw that it was still thick with the undead. We moved to the far end where the undead was the thinnest and set all the choppers down.

Everyone, including the pilots got out to fight. We fired until we were almost totally out of ammunition and then it came down to hand to hand. Instead of doing a transition from my shotgun to my sword, I just detached the gun and let it fall to the ground. Before I could draw the blade, I had to punch one zombie to the ground, then I flipped another one over my shoulder as it jumped on me. Once free of the zed on my back, I was able to pull my sword free from over my shoulder. As soon as it was free, a large zombie, a huge biker in leathers came rushing at me. I gave him a overhand swing as hard as I could. The cut split him from nose to tail, then I stepped over both halves.

The girls did the same as soon as their IARs ran dry, which wasn't much longer. We worked our way forward, from the helicopters, cutting a swath through the dead. Blades flashing and parts of limbs and heads were flying.

Zombies pushed in on me, and I had no room to swing the sword. I drew my Becker bowie and used it to make quick stabs straight into the heads of the zombies as they tried to bite me. Their teeth found only my armor. Their hands though, found edges of my plate and would grab them and jerk. As quick as they would grab me, I'd chop down on their hands with the big black blade that was now red. We pushed through, and room opened up for my sword. I swung as hard as I could, a wide arch that severed the arms and torsos of the walking dead around me.

April came up behind me, she was armed with two shorter swords, one in each hand. Both blades were red and were slinging blood and gore with every stroke. She was screaming under her helmet.

Joy was fighting just as ferociously, if not more so. Somehow her helmet was knocked off, and her blond hair was flying wild behind her, blond with highlights of blood. Her teeth were gritted tight and her eyes flared.

I caught a glimpse of Sarge's team. They were a walking meat-grinder. They too had run out of ammunition and were fighting with blades and axes.

The Red Eyes were the hardest. When we found them, they would hurl other undead at us because they were no longer able to just grab us with their power... but they could throw. If you weren't careful, they could try to rip your weapon out of your hand. We quickly found that the best way to deal with them was with a fast rush and then sever their heads. It worked, but it was hard to do.

We fought for most of the morning until finally, the field was ours. We had crossed the field and made it to the hangers. Each team had made it across, and we had only taken a few casualties.

I flung the zombie that was hanging off of my armor, trying to chew through my elbow armor. It was slowing me down. The thing somehow pulled my helmet off as I threw it over my shoulder. The zombie hit the wall with a wet cracking sound. Before it could get up again I kicked it in the head hard enough to break its skull open.

I turned to Joy who was finishing off a fat zombie. She put her boot on its head, so she could yank her sword back out. As I looked, a zombie was hurtling at her like a freight train. It was another Beefeater and this one even somehow kept its silly hat. I stepped in front of her and clothes-lined the zed hard to the throat. The zombie slammed to the ground where I casually stuck the tip of my sword through its cranium.

We were all breathing hard, but it was done. I found my Great Helm and put it back on. "Ogre to Sierra Flight."

"Sierra copies." The Nimrods had been flying a holding pattern.

"The field is ours. Come on down... don't mind the mess."

"We need to clear the buildings, Sir." It was Q's voice. I looked around and I saw that he was standing not too far off. He was wiping off his blade on the shirt of one of the dead-undead.

"Let's get reloaded first, if you don't mind. What's inside can stay there for a moment. I need a break."

## Clouds in my Eyes

We were eating meat pies filled with beef, potato, onions, peas and carrots. I was told to dip it into green sauce. It was pretty good, considering the alternative that was packed for me by Debbie was a jar of pickled fish. "What are those things?" April nodded to the two strange looking aircraft sitting at the end of the runway, once ready for take off.

"Those are Victors, used to be England's strategic bombers, now they are refueling tankers."

"Can we use them?"

I shrugged, "I don't know. At least not right now."

"You know, you take a tanker like that," She chewed her meat pie and swallowed. "You could fly all the way to China."

I was about to take a bite of pie, but stopped and looked at her. China. Where it all started. I finished eating as I considered it. No, if we were going to try to crack China, we'd have to get Japan first. We had Marines there, hopefully we still did.

Joy had gathered the weapons we had dropped, my shotgun and the IARs. I looked over at the Nimrods. They were unloading the ammunition while others were getting the refueling done for the helicopters.

The other men were reloading magazines and distributing the ammo to those left that could still fight. Medics attended those who could not.

"We ready to do this again?" I looked at my Girls. They stood up and nodded.

I keyed my radio, "Ogre to all units, are we ready?"

"Bravo Team, Standing Ready." Sarge said.

"Charley Team, Standing Ready." Q answered.

"Delta Team, Standing Ready!" Musket barked.

"Alpha Team is heading to objective one, now. All teams, clear your objects."

April ran her IAR dry again, "Reloading!" As soon as the girls were back up I called that I was reloading as well. I stowed my Bastard Sword back across my back and transitioned back to my shotgun. I started feeding the tube full of Tri-Ball again as I looked around. The large room was full of now dead undead. Claw marks scarred my armor, scratching lines of white steel through the multi-cam paint. We had cleared the building and now I stood there at the window looking out across the bloody field. Bodies were everywhere and the crows were descending on them. I heard a cough behind me.

Craig was one of the men in my team. He had been with us since Arizona. A sturdy man. His armor was bloodied and dented. He knelt before me, his helmet was lost. And so was one of his armored gloves. As he knelt, I noticed a twitch in his face.

"Craig, what's the matter?"

He looked up at me. His eyes were already cloudy. "It's my time..."

I shook my head, I couldn't believe this. "When did you get bitten?"

"In the airfield, Sire. Right after I ran out of ammunition." He held up his shaking hand. The pinky finger was bitten off at the stump and most of his hand was now blackened. "But I kept fighting as much as I could... But..." His body was racked in a spasm and he grunted as he fought for self control. "I can't go any further... I'm cold... hungry... I can feel my body dying." He looked up at me, "I want to die... still human." He said through gritted teeth and shook his head violently. "Please, my... my... Lord Ogre."

I looked around, the Girls and others of the Crimson Order were standing around us, heads bowed.

I was taken back, but I had to do his final request. "You are a good man, Craig. Thank you for your honorable service. I release you from your Oaths."

Craig smiled with frothy blood coming from between his clenched teeth, as I drew my HK45 and placed the muzzle between his eyes.

"Thank you, Sire."

He was still human when he died.

I knelt beside Craig and closed his eyes as I did mine and said a prayer. April was quiet as she pulled out a small spiral notepad from a pouch at her waist. She flipped through many pages and came to one where there was space, and wrote down Craig's name. "Craig J. Huber, Battle of RAF Wyton." The other men in my team gathered around and knelt besides Craig's body as well. We were all quiet for some time.

Unsurprisingly it was Joy that broke the moment of silence.

"What's with the 'Lord' thing?"

Several of the men looked up at her with surprise at the question, glancing at me as if I might be offended.

"I don't know if it was something Uncle Musket's been up to or not, but most of the British survivors had started referring to him like that." Alan said.

"Could that be why they never come up to me to talk to me... but talk to you, April, Sarge or Q first? Requests for anything go through the Central

Ops first... but never directly to me."

"The kids do..." April offered.

I stood up and sighed heavily as I put Winchester PDX1 slugs into the side saddle of my Mossberg 930SPX. "The boys will bow slightly, and the girls will curtsy before they run off."

"I thought it was part of their game." Joy said. "a British thing."

"It's a thing..." I dismissed the subject. "Is everyone reloaded and ready?" The men stood and nodded.

We went back out to the airfield where the helicopters and everyone were there, ready and waiting, including several Tornado fighter bombers. I walked past them.

"It's not too late, you know." Commander Hawkins said.

"Too late for what?"

"We're loaded heavy. It would be easier to find your crow plague in the rubble than going in and rooting it out."

"I wish it was that easy, Mister Hawkins. If I thought that would work, I'd much rather take your suggestion. I have no problem with delegation."

"I'll try to remember that. Good luck on your hunt, Sir."

"Thank you. I'll try to leave something for you and your wing to do."

"I'd like that very much, thank you, Sir."

Q stood by the Blackhawk with some of his team. I hadn't had the time to talk to him about the Father back at Ft. George.

"I saw what happened on the ground back at the Fort," I said.

"Yeah I didn't want it to go that way, it all happened so fast I just reacted." Louis looked down at the grass. He had talked to the father a lot more than me or Sarge did. When we wanted to talk religion, we met with Mark, who had become the ecclesiastical leader for most of us from Utah.

"Well, what's done is done." I didn't know what to say, so I dodged this issue. "Time to get your game face on." I squeezed his shoulder and headed back to the Blackhawk, making the 'wind-up' gesture.

"Next stop, the Tower of London."

Along the flight, Sarge called for some music and Q played some classic rock.

"So why is this Skinwalker in the Tower of London?" Joy asked. "Why wouldn't she have taken the palace or something?"

It was a good question. "The Tower is pretty much a fortress, a great place to set up a defense. But I think more likely it's because it was a place of a great deal of suffering and misery over the centuries."

The four helicopters flew in single file, snaking along the river Thames. The city was huge and sprawling and everything seemed to look the same: lots of old buildings punctuated with hideous modern ones. I soon lost my bearings until I spied the HMS Belfast, then I knew exactly where I was.

Luckily for all of us, Wizard Lead's pilot was English and knew precisely where he was going. I looked back and saw the Merlin helicopters drop low over the water and launch the zodiacs. I looked up and could see the dart-like shapes of the Tornados, they were on station, waiting for me to call them to destroy something.

My pilot put the Blackhawk into a gut-wrenching diving turn and then suddenly flared. We were at the Tower.

I signaled for the ropes to be dropped. "Wizard Lead in position." I called on the radio.

"Wizard Two in position." I looked over and saw a Merlin on station over the west wall, ropes falling out of it.

"Wizard Three Ready." It was Sarge, over the Wakefield Tower.

"Wizard Four is go." Q signaled. He was at the south, making his way through the Traitor's Gate.

I nodded to the others and grabbed the rope. Two seconds later, I was on the roof of Saint Peter's. "

"Ogre's down!" I called on the radio. I moved out of the way quickly as the others quickly followed. Within mere moments, the helicopters were pulling away, back over the river and gaining altitude. I checked my shotgun again and searched the area. So far, the only thing moving besides us were the tower's ravens and the thousands of crows that covered the walls and buildings edges. They were so thick, we practically had to kick them out of our way. Some screamed at us in anger. Others just watched, with a calm consideration that unnerved me.

We dropped through the door and went through Saint Peters with little resistance. Regardless of our loud and obvious insertion, we used our suppressed weapons to neutralize the few zombies we found inside. We only did a cursory search of the church, because it wasn't our target; it was just our path in.

I pushed open the door and looked out. In front of us was the executioner's block and just past that, the tower green. But I couldn't take my eyes off the White Tower. There it was. She was in there. Waiting for me. I could feel it.

## Visit from the Dead

We had come up two stories of what was nothing more than a museum of Middle Age history. Glass from display cases was shattered in every direction. Then I noticed it. I squinted at it with my one eye. That was it! The door. The door that I saw before the Indian witch took my eye.

I froze, staring at the door.

"What is it?" April asked, sensing a change in me.

"She's through there."

April looked at the door. "Who?"

"Plague of Crows."

Joy spun and brought up her automatic rifle. She fired a long burst into the door, blasting it to splinters. When she was done firing, I walked up to it. My shotgun was leading the way and kept it covered as if the door itself was a threat. When I gave the door my boot, it burst open without resistance. Inside was dark, but I could see a stone stairway. The rock was chipped and pockmarked from Joy's bullets, but nothing else was there. I didn't hesitate to flick on my shotgun's tactical light and started up, keeping the shotgun aimed up. I moved as quickly as I was able while being relatively quiet. Not that it mattered considering the way we knocked.

At the top of the steps the door was ajar. I pushed it open and let the light's beam shine through. Whatever had been in the room before was gone, and the remaining furniture was shoved against the walls. All save for one tall, high-backed chair. As bright as my light was, it was not able to penetrate the shadow that fell across this chair. I stepped forward, entering the room. The girls came through on either side of me, sticking close. The others flanked as well, but spread out. We slowly walked forward. The gloom was thick, and even the air felt heavy.  The beam of the Fox Fury Hammerhead light was 320 Lumins, but it was only able to show a silhouette of a figure in the chair.

"*I've been waiting for you... for eons.*"

The figure whispered from across the room, but it sounded like she was talking right into my ear. I knew who it was.

She stood up, her long, straight black hair draped down over her shoulders falling to her waist. She was tall and thin. Her arms hung loosely at her sides, almost as if she was relaxed.

"You've been waiting to die, Mohtahe Okohke."

She hissed at the name. She raised a hand at me and pointed. At first the hand looked like that of a young woman, soft skinned and olive colored. But then it was suddenly gray and skeletal with skin that looked like dried parchment. "*Don't think you are the first to threaten me. I do not die as easily as you might hope.*" Then she said something in her native tongue that I didn't understand.

Darkness filled the room and everyone around me became still. Shadows swirled around her and us, and in those shadows I could see faces, each one a mask of hate and anger. Some looked like they were screaming. Others like they were gnashing their teeth, trying to bite those still living. Some were laughing... but silently, and I thought it looked like they would have been crying if it wasn't for the hate in their eyes. They wove in and out and around us. All the while, Plague of Crows was laughing. No one else moved.

I looked at April who had been raising her rifle. I could see her thumb on the safety switch, pressing it down, almost snapping it into the "Fire" position. I glanced over at Joy. A small spout of flame was frozen, jetting out of her rifle's muzzle brake with a projectile a few inches in front of the muzzle. I could see the pressure waves from the frozen muzzle blast distorting the scant light around it.

When I looked back at Mohtahe Okohke, I noticed her other hand holding on to something close to her chest. It was hanging from a cord around her neck. I watched as her hand flexed around it, squeezing it.

"*I have you.*"

Suddenly she was right in front of me, her hair pulled back from the sudden movement showing me her face. On one half of her face, she was young and beautiful, the other, old and skeletal and dried. She grabbed me by my throat, but I was unable to move quick enough to do anything. The hand close to her chest opened and revealed the thing around her neck. It was an eye tied with threads to the cord.

It was my eye.

She laughed and I felt a sensation that scared me. I was being pulled down. I felt my soul being ripped from my body. I felt the distant part of me... my physical body, falling to the ground as everyone else sped back up to normal speed. Automatic fire, shouting... and then screaming as if it was a hundred miles away and getting farther. I felt the other part of me, my spirit, being pulled down, like I was underwater and being dragged deeper below. I looked up and saw the light diminishing into a single point as I was rushing down.

Hands were around my ankles. I looked down and saw a skull looking up at me, grinning from the center of a corona of black hair. There was nothing in the eye sockets.

I prayed. As soon as I started, the hands released me. I could hear nothing. But I was no longer falling, no longer being pulled. I was standing beside something, it seemed like rock, but I couldn't see it. I looked around and saw that I was wearing my armor but I had no weapons. My armor was silver, like when I first found it... the steel polished bright. I called out to April, Joy, Q, Sarge, anyone. But there was no answer. I was alone.

Or I thought I was alone. Something large was coming at me, a shadow in the darkness, huge and heavy and full of menace. I turned and ran, but I didn't know if I was getting away, or if it was gaining on me. All I could do was run. It felt like it was at my heels. I looked back over my shoulder at the darkness, and all I could see was a shapeless mass of ink-like blackness. Wet, heavy thuds echoed my own footfalls.

Ahead of me in the black was a spot of light. Not so much like a spark, but a distant brightness in the gloom of fog. I ran for it putting everything I had into speed.

I could hear laughter behind me. The slow and low rumbling laugh of something big and less human and more Lovecraftian. I neared the glow of light, and, as I got closer, I saw that it coalesced into a figure of white. White clothes and white hair. I ran to the figure. I saw that it was reaching out to me, beckoning me, but I couldn't see any detail, because it was too bright. The closer I got to the figure, the further away the darkness.

Soon I was surrounded by light and I could see that the figure was that of a woman, shapely and familiar. She spoke and I knew it was Jen. She held a sword that was as bright as hot fire and the thing that had been chasing me was driven away.

"Jen." I didn't know what to say.

She looked at me and smiled. "You've fallen a long way. You were almost lost."

"Where am I?"

"You are at the brink... and you almost went over the edge."

"This is limbo?"

Jen giggled and took my hand. She had that gleam in her eye.

"Some call it that. Come. We shouldn't be here." Her hand was soft and warm, like it was the last time I held it before she died.

"Am I dead?"

Jen didn't say anything as she walked beside me, leading me.

"I thought when you died, it was family that came... ancestors..."

Jen glanced sideways at me. "I'm part of your family now. My old family, well, they are not in the same place."

"Plague of Crows..."

"She tried to pull you down, but failed."

"How?"

"You had faith. You showed it. She won't be able to do it again." Jen squeezed my hand. "I wont let her touch you again."

"How can I stop her? She's undead, but she's not like the others."

"No, she's not. She still has a human heart."

As we walked we came to another figure. A tall, slim man wearing a 50's style jacket and slacks, with his hand casually tucked into his pockets. He wore a fedora with a jaunty tilt to one side.

Jen gave me a kiss on the cheek and a hug and was suddenly gone.

"Boy, you can get into some trouble when you put your mind to it."

"Grandfather!" I looked at him and could tell he was my Mother's Father, but he looked younger and healthier than I had ever seen him. He looked like he was about thirty. He jerked his head in a "Follow me" motion.

As we walked he lectured me about history. He spoke of a knife. A small flint blade that was found by early American explorers and it ended up in the British Museum.

"Her name was Wings of Crows when she was a girl. Because of her hair. It was long and black and always flying behind her. That was before her tribe's enemies came."

Grandfather stopped walking, and I looked around and found that I was in an ancient native American village.

Wings of Crow was only eight years old when the other tribes attacked.

That was five days ago. Her tribe lay dead, scattered, bloating in the sun. Only she remained alive of the hundred and forty four. The attack had come suddenly while Wings of Crows was swimming in the shallow creek. They were Navajo and Ute warriors, large, fierce, and covered in war-paint. She hid in the reeds, scared and shaking and holding her hands over her mouth so she wouldn't cry out. She knew if she was found, she would be killed. She could hear war-cries and screams coming from her village in the canyons. Her home was built into the side of a cliff, like most of the others. She was Anasazi, and her tribe was the last of her people. From the creek where she was hiding, she could see her home. She watched as a large Ute warrior pulled her mother from the door by her hair. Suddenly the big Ute pulled a knife across her mother's neck, opening it like a big smile. Then he threw her mother off the cliff. Wings of Crow screamed inside, but made no sound. Not until she knew the warriors had gone.

"She didn't know why they attacked. The Navajo called her people "Ancient Enemy" but she never did anything to the Navajo. Now her namesake birds flew in great numbers, so many it would shade her from the sun. At night, the coyotes would sneak in and drag the smaller bodies away... but the crows, they didn't care. They would perch on the faces of the still bodies and peck at the meat. Some would feast till they couldn't fly anymore and would hop away when she threw rocks. The only body the birds didn't peck at was the bloating corpse of her mother. She guarded her mother and would throw rocks and swing her stick if a bird came too near. She was waiting for her father to come back. He would know what to do. In the mean time, she wept and threw rocks and retched at the stink.

"She had water and food in jars, roots, and grains... but she was alone. After a time, not even the crows would come near. Her father never came back.

"As time passed, she would try to lure the birds closer, but they didn't want roots, they wanted meat. Having pecked at all the rest of the bodies, and after the coyotes, the only body that was left was her mother. They could smell it, and they were still hungry. She would use her small knife to slice off a bit and toss it half way to a crow and the crow would look at it, then at her, then hop over. Pretty soon she had dozens of birds coming near, all wanting another bite of mother. When one came within reach her hands sprang out and caught the bird by surprise. She quickly pulled it in and bit hard into the back of its neck. That was when the rest of the birds jumped on her and her mother."

Suddenly the birds were gone and my Grandfather was there again. We walked towards a door that was filled with light. "Find the knife, my boy. You know where it is."

As soon as I went through the door I suddenly had the sensation that I was laying on my back. I opened my eye and saw the overcast London sky and snow falling from it. I was moving, with my feet leading the way. It was like

I was floating. Then I realized I was being carried. I looked around. I saw a Nimrod and could hear the sound of jet turbines running. They were carrying me on their shoulders to the plane.

"Carefully let me down please."

The men who carried me were too startled and I was dropped unceremoniously on the ground.

"Oh! Sorry about that!" Sarge apologized. The girls shoved the men away and grabbed at me. "You were dead!" I could see streaks of eyeliner, making the girls look like they were wearing raccoon masks and I felt sorry for their pain.

I rubbed my head, "Mostly dead... that's still slightly alive." I grabbed my girls and held them. They were shaking and crying. I could see they were not the only one's relieved. I felt cold and thirsty. I had been gone for sometime. "I could kill for a Gator-Bull."

April laughed, "We're all out. I have water." I nodded and accepted the Camelback. I drank deeply from the reservoir and emptied it. April looked at me, holding my face. "Where were you?"

"You don't want to know... seriously... you don't want to know."

April gave me a funny look, like she knew I was hiding something and that she would get it out of me later. I changed the subject. "Where are we?"

"RAF Wyton. We were going to put your body back on the plane to Inverness."

"How long was I... gone?" I looked around.

Sarge knelt down close by. "Four hours."

"Sitrep."

"The Tower of London has been cleared and cleansed. We found a Plague of Crows medicine bag." Sarge held up a brown leather pouch. "Well, Oogie found it. Behind the chair in the room where you fell. It's a key to her powers. Now that we have it, she's going to be playing defense now. And I bet she's going to want it back."

"What's in it?"

"Ash, bones, a few teeth, and..."

"And?"

"Your eye."

Huh? No. That can't be. I saw it on her... around her neck. "Let me see it." Sarge held out the little sack and I looked in it. There was an eye in it, but it wasn't mine. And it was more dried out than mine would have been. "Not my eye. Someone else's. Someone's taken before mine."

"Who's could it be?"

"I don't know. But I suspect we'll find out. Should we destroy the pouch?"

"No. At least not yet."

"I take it Oogie will let us know." Sarge nodded. "Casualties?"

"Six... Five now that you've returned."

"Where's Q?"

"I don't know. After you fell, he took Izzy and a couple other guys and they disappeared. He said he had something to take care of and we've not heard from them since."

I stood up. My weapons were gone, but I was still in my armor. "Where's my war-gear?"

Joy ran back to the Blackhawk and brought back an armload of weapons. My ammo pouches, my shotgun, my suppressed HK, and sword. The girls attached the pouch to my armor again when April stopped. "Oh, I thought this was your sword."

She was looking over my shoulder. "What?" I reached back and my fingers found the hilt of a sword, but Joy was holding mine. I wanted to draw the sword and look at it, but I had the feeling to leave it. "I... I found a new one." I took my old sword and loosened the strap on the scabbard and put it over a shoulder, so the sword hung at my side.

"I've got something to do. I'm going back to London."

## Ugly Little Hybrid

Walking through the British Museum, I could hear the sound of our armored footsteps and the tinkling of falling glass from shattered display cases. I had the small flint knife tucked into an empty magazine pouch on my chest plate. I carried my shotgun with one hand and had my Becker BK9 in the other.

There were a few zombies in the museum, lurching around, stupid and uncoordinated, until they saw us, then they came straight in, unable to wait to be butchered.  No, zombies were not the problem. The Red Eyes were the problem. They had learned quickly that throwing things with their telekinetic powers was a good trick. Instead, it made me think of the end fight between Luke and Vader in Empire. I'd face one Red and something would slam into me. I'd turn, and something else would slam into me from another direction. I had a trick of my own. The Reds soon found that Shotgun Slugs penetrate damn near everything they could hide behind.

The knife was in the Native American display section in a glass case. I felt bad smashing the case and taking it, but they had it labeled wrong anyways. I knew it was the right knife, because I had seen it before. I also knew it wasn't from the Fremont Indian tribe. When I first saw the knife, I could have sworn that it glowed. It was a simple little knife, napped stone blade that looked like quartz affixed to a simple bone handle with a sinew lashing. As simple as the knife was, it's effectiveness couldn't be questioned.

"That's it?" April asked. "It's a rock tied to a bone."

I turned to the mannequin dressed in buckskin clothes and drew the blade across the leather. It split open like a well done haggis. "This is it." I said.

We marched out of the museum and climbed into the Blackhawk. Without breaking pace, I went through the Blackhawk and out the other side. A bright yellow Prius was parked quietly across the street. I immediately pulled out one of my thermite grenades. The car was locked up tight, but a quick blast from my shotgun opened a window. I let the spoon slip from my thumb and with a "sproing" it flipped up into the air. I tossed the heavy cylinder into the front seat of the ugly little hybrid and turned back to the helicopter. The Prius was burning nicely when I climbed back into the chopper.

"Had to do it didn't you." The pilot observed while handing April a twenty-dollar bill. Not that money had any use anymore, paper currency was still used in casual betting. April took the bill and tucked it into her vest with a smile.

"JJ, you have to take the time to enjoy the little things in life."

"Where too now, Boss?" The pilot asked, shaking his head.

I thought about it. She wouldn't still be at the Tower. She left there when she pulled me down. I could have said that she pulled my soul down, but that wasn't right. I don't have a soul. I am a soul. What I have is a body. She pulled me down, and I left my body. So when she left, she went someplace else, because she still has a human heart, she still has a body too. I thought about her, and suddenly I knew where she was. I found it easier to spirit walk now that Oogie had given me the Medicine Bag and with a little practice. I looked into the palace and saw her. She was chanting and drawing a pattern within a circle as she sat on her heels within it. She looked up at me and hissed and threw a powder up in the air and suddenly I couldn't see her anymore. I had seen enough anyway. I opened my eyes and I was sitting in my Blackhawk again.

"Buckingham Palace." I said as I started reloading Cara and filling my shell pouch again.

Joy pulled off her helmet. "Damned Reds give me a headache." She said while looking at the dents.

April was thumbing cartridges into her 60-round magazines. Every fourth round was a tracer. "If you shoot them, they can't throw stuff at you." She grinned.

As we approached the palace, we were a mile out when we saw one of the Wizards circling the place. "Looks like we found Q."

The Merlin Helicopter darted down, and we watched a brief battle as the men on the ground were extracted. Two armored figures were injured. I didn't recognize the first one, wearing standard mail and plate. The other, I did. He was being half dragged, half carried in his Roman style armor. The small armored warrior helping him was without helm and her long curly dark hair told me it was Isabella. Within seconds the Merlin was lifting off and climbing into the air.

"What do you want to do Boss?"

"She's still in there." I could feel her presence. An almost tangible thickness in the air just like at the Tower. "Drop us down right where Wizard Three left."

There were dead zombies all around the area, and several were still moving, watching us. When the gunners opened up the world was filled with screaming fire of electric Gatling guns. The zombies were mowed down, clearing our landing. The Blackhawk flared and touched down. Before the wheels were on the ground, I leaped out. As I jumped, I pulled my new sword and started to swing. One of the last zeds reached out as the sword sliced it through like it was a rolled rice mat. I carried the swing around and hacked the other one in half.

I wanted to tell April and Joy to stay in the chopper, but it would have done no good. The girls were already out with their weapons up and ready. I signaled the pilot to take off again and he didn't hesitate to pull up.

I watched the Blackhawk take to the sky and the Merlin circle once. Izzy called on the radio, "Q's seriously hurt, Sir."

"Roger that, Izz... RTB. Once you get your injured to medical, get another team ready and stand by."

"Uh, but... Sir..." I could hear the conflict in her voice.

"Mission first, Isabella. You know Louis would tell you that." I hated saying it. I knew how she felt.

"Yes, Sir." I could hear her gritting teeth and saw the Merlin bank away and head north west.

The girls were kneeling, covering the area with their IARs. The Blackhawk's gunners ripped off occasional long bursts of suppressive fire into areas I couldn't see. I didn't have to say "Let's move." As soon as I stepped out the girls were on their feet and flanking me.

We entered the royal palace.

Long halls echoed the smallest sounds. We followed the trail of blood and gore and soon I was stepping into the throne room. I could smell the acrid scents of cordite and blood. Damage from weapons fire and shrapnel was everywhere. Sections of wall with ancient paintings were scorched, and some were still burning, others were covered in splattered blood.

"What the hell happened here?" April muttered.

"That's exactly what happened here." Joy answered.

"Shhh." I whispered. On the floor was a decorated circle. Ancient symbols were written in and around the circle, along with intricate patterns. This is where I had seen her. I could hear voices. All around, voices were whispering and black vapors were coming up out of the floor. Then I made out the distinctive laughter that caused a chill up my spine.

"Mohtahe Okohke... Plague of Crows... Show yourself, Skinwalker. I'm tired of your games."

Suddenly the black mists came together in a swirling vortex that took the form of a woman. Her long hair continued to swirl. She gave me a skeletal grin as her form solidified.

"*Skinwalker? Someone has been talking to you.*" She hissed. The ghostly dark forms surrounded me.

"That's not going to work this time."

Plague of Cross said something in her ancient language and looked at Joy. I have no explanation as to why, but I suddenly reached out to my left with my armored hand. Mohtahe had lunged faster than I could have followed, but I caught her by her throat. Her hands were outstretched, bloodied fingertips just a fraction of an inch from Joy's face.

Joy shrieked and flinched backwards.

I tightened my grip as I pressed her back, away from Joy. Through the mailed glove I felt a coldness that was numbing my hand. It stung, and out of reflex I wanted to let go. Instead I put my shoulder behind my hand and threw the Skinwalker as hard as I could, at the same time I pulled up my shotgun with my right hand and fired. Tri-ball shot impacted her, blasting large holes through her body and she was sent sprawling. Before she could hit the ground, she gestured with one hand. Suddenly a zombie corpse was hurled at me, spinning me like a saw-blade. It hit me and knocked me down.

Mohtahe laughed as she picked herself up. The holes from the shotgun blast disappearing as fibers reached across the gaps and wove new flesh where before their had been none. She reached down and picked up a corpse by the head like it was made of silk cloth. She lifted it and let it go, but the body hung there like it was nailed in mid air.

"*You tire of games... maybe we should play a new game.*" She spoke as she grabbed the body and pulled here and there and the flesh and bone stretched like clay. She pulled the face, extending the jaws like a muzzle of a wolf. She pulled the arms, stretching them, then the fingers. Before I could get back onto my feet, she touched the back of its head with her open palm and the creature blinked at me with dead fish eyes. It crouched low and snarled like some sort of wild animal.

April started to fire, but another thrown corpse smashed into her, knocking the IAR from her hands and sending her to the ground.

At first I thought my 930SPX had jammed but I glanced at it and realized that it had somehow run empty. Its bolt was locked back.

The gollum creature moved towards me, prowling like, hunched and cautious. It moved wrong, spider-like, as the Skinwalker had given it joints where their shouldn't be. It opened its mouth, and I saw its teeth were like a mountain lion's.

Joy's weapon ran dry with almost no effect on the monster. She then raised the weapon up and charged the creature, bringing the hot barrel down on its head with a scream. There was a bone-crunching sound as the barrel impacted what used to be a human skull. Joy raised the gun again, but the creature swung. A long, heavy arm caught Joy in the midsection, and she was thrown across the room like a toy action figure.

I reached back over my shoulder and grabbed the hilt of my sword. It felt hot to the touch as I pulled it out. As I raised it over my head, I sensed the room suddenly grow brighter. The creature facing me flinched away from it at first, then looked at me with a sneer. It howled as it sprang forward, galloping like a strange horse before leaping. I stepped to the side as I swung. With a flash the sword came down and passed through the head, just above the neck. I blinked away the residual image of the sword's swing. Blue flames followed the blade that Jen had given me.

"*NO*!" The Skinwalker shrieked with rage as she flung herself on me. I swung and an arm was severed. She screamed and swung again. Another arm flew across the room. As soon as I cut one, another arm was in its place swinging at me again with new claws. I don't understand how she's doing this, all I know is that I have to cut this bitch down. Down... good idea! I ducked and swung low, taking her legs out from under her. She fell and rolled backwards and sprang up as if she wasn't touched. She can't be killed... she can't even be hurt... not by guns, not by swords. But I knew how to kill her.

She lifted more corpses and they were animated as soon as she let go. But they were weak and I cut through them like they were smoke. She was getting weaker. We fought across the room as I slowly pushed her back. When we got to the throne I backed her into it and she sat down hard. I drove the sword through her stomach all the way to the hilt, pinning her to the chair. She screamed and lashed out, but I blocked her hands and reached inside her defense and grabbed her by the throat. Then I saw something in her black, hollowed eyes. Something I hadn't seen before in her. I saw fear.

"You are finished, Skinwalker."

She laughed in my face, but it was filled with nervousness. I let go of the sword and reached up with my right hand and found the little quartz knife. Suddenly she stopped laughing. As I pulled the knife, the blade glowed like it was neon.

As I pushed the knife into her chest, between her breasts and through the sternum, Plague of Crows screamed in silence. She opened her mouth, but no sound came out. The knife cut like the flesh was melting away from it. As I cut, she seemed to shrink and soften. I pulled the heart from the chest, connective tissues stretching and breaking. She convulsed, then shivered, then was still. I looked at the heart. It was withered and blackened but still pulsed in my hand. Soon it stopped.

When I looked back at Plague of Crows I was so shocked I almost fell backwards. Sitting on the throne, pinned to the chair with a sword and a huge gaping hole in her chest... was a pretty young girl with long dark hair. Wings of Crow.

## Long Live the King

As I pulled the sword, the girl fell out of the chair and crumpled to the floor. I looked down at her and saw her for what she was. Plague of Crows was gone and what remained was the tragic end of a young girl. The only curious thing about the body was the lack of blood.

I looked at my hand, the heart that I held, crumpled to dust. Any blood she had was long dried. The sword in my hand looked like just another sword. It no longer glowed or possessed any other worldly attributes. I sheathed it again and suddenly felt tired. It felt like the passing of a storm. Either that or Gravity just increased. I turned to look at April and Joy, who were picking themselves up off the ground. Crimson Guard poured into the room with their mix of weapons, M-4, Steyr Augs, and SA-80 rifles. With them were former members of the British Royal Marines and RAF security forces.

"Sir, the Palace is secure. Units are pushing zombies down the streets and away from the Palace."

"It was strange, Sir. I was fighting a bloody Red when suddenly it's eyes turned white and it was just a normal zombie again. The other zombies lost all the coordination they had... they were just all zombies."

"Who was that?" One of them asked.

"That was the Skinwalker." I said with a quiet voice. "I released her."

"So she died and lost contact with the zombies, no more control, no influence."

I nodded and just that small effort made me dizzy. I stepped back, into the throne and sat down heavily and unintentionally. I looked down at my hands. This was good news, but possibly too much of a good thing. "Let's not overstretch ourselves. Set up a perimeter and do a house-by-house, room-to-room clearing to make sure we've established a safe zone within London. Bring in reinforcements to relieve fatigued squads and resupply. Tomorrow, we'll push the perimeter further out... and the next day after that. We'll not stop until we've retaken all of London."

I looked up and around the room. Everyone was kneeling, including my CGs, Izzy and Caroline, and my personal body guards.

"What's this?"

No one answered at first. The shout started in the back of the room, with the Royal Marines. "Lord Protector of the Realm, our King!"

"LONG LIVE THE KING!"

"LONG LIVE THE KING!"

"LONG LIVE THE KING!"

I stood up. They were cheering. "What? April..." I held out my hand to her... wanting her to stop. She looked up at me, "My Lord."

"Joy?"

"Your Majesty."

"Where's my shotgun?" The 930 was passed up front within moments. I took the weapon and attached it back to the single point sling, and then I noticed that the front of the magazine tube was severed off at an angle. Crap. I'll have to get a new one now. I don't think we have a lot of Mossberg parts on hand here in the UK. Oh well. "Girls."

They stood and turned, stepping beside me on either side. Izzy and Caroline stood with me as well. The cheering filled the room. I didn't like this, but I played along. I held fist in the air. The cheering was energetic and primal.

"Time to go." I turned and walked out of the throne room. The girls lead the way, clearing our path. As I left I heard the shout of a British Officer. "Right! You heard His Majesty." He started barking more specific orders and assignments as we headed outside.

The sky had been gray and snowing when we went in, but now the clouds had gone. The sky was blue, and I felt the warmth of the sun on my face. We climbed into the helicopter and lifted off. "Now what's this king bullshit?"

April just smiled. "Don't try to fight it. You're the King of England now."

"How?"

She just shrugged. "You're the authority... the boss. You've been so for some time, and now you just took the throne. I guess that's how it works here."

"I think it's sexy..." Joy smiled at first then looked surprised. "Wait. What would that make us?" She was asking April who then looked at me.

"I have no idea. I'm not a king. Let's not be silly."

"They say you are. With that, they are saying that they are your subjects."

I didn't know what to say about it. Instead, I leaned back and closed my eye for the rest of the flight.

As soon as I fell asleep I found myself back at Fort George. But there was nothing there. No people. No vehicles. Not even any buildings. Just the walls. I looked around and could hear only the wind. I walked out into the center of the fort. I felt empty and alone. Then I heard a chuckling. I turned and there was a huge demon standing there. Tall and its skin was red and its horns and teeth were black.

"You killed my little sister."

"She was a bitch."

"I was quite fond of her."

"That's your problem. She asked for it."

"She didn't ask for you to come to England."

"I didn't ask for her to rip out my eye, either."

The demon's grin spread across his face like a canyon. "I'm sure she had a reason."

"And I had my reasons for killing her."

The demon started walking to me. Each stride shook the ground. "And I suppose you are going to think that you'll want to kill me next."

"I don't even know you." I said as I reached over my shoulder for my sword, but it wasn't there.

"We don't need to fight little lordling." He reached out a hand the size of a large frying pan. "We can still be friends. How about I let you keep England and you stay out of Europe?"

"Go to hell."

The demon's grin turned into a sneer. "That's what I thought you would say. Unfortunate." The demon's hand balled up into a fist and before I could do anything, he punched me. It was like a truck hit me and I was flying through the air across the fort and over the wall... Flying...

April gently shook me awake. "RAF Wyton... My Lord."

I sat up and looked out. We were descending, the Merlins landing first and then we sat down in the center. I saw Izzy dash off at full tilt to the medical camp, looking for Q.

I grabbed a radio, "Ogre to Wyton Control."

"Wyton Control, go ahead your Majesty."

I looked over at April who winked at me. I shook my head. "Everyone's gone mental now?" I keyed the radio, "Where's Q and what's his status?"

"Ah, he was in the brig interrogating the prisoner, then he went to find Izzy. I think they are in her quarters."

Wait, what? "I thought he was injured."

"My Lord, I believe the last thing he said to us was 'I ain't got time to bleed.'"

"Wait, prisoner? What? Where's the prisoner?"

By this time, one of the CGs approached. I didn't recognize him, but he was one of the new CGs that swore in after we got to the UK. He had a Scottish accent and sported a ruby in his eyebrow piercing. "This way, my Lord." The man bowed as he spoke. We headed to the brig and bumped into Louis on the way.

"So, King Of England huh?" Q said.

"That's what they tell me." I shrugged.

"Eh, You'll still be the Ogre to me." Q said, holding on to Izzy. "By the way, Merry Christmas." Q said, tossing me a small leather thong she had worn around her neck. Tied to it was something that had belonged to me. My eye! I had looked for it after I had killed her. I wanted to burn it. Now I can.

"How did you get it?"

"I grabbed it when I got close. I couldn't kill her though."

"Thanks." I said.

"I guess it is Christmas... even though it's a week or so away, I should give you something." I acted like I was looking around for something. "I guess... uh... I guess I'll just give you Edinburgh."

"What?"

"Edinburgh. You know the big city in Scotland."

"Yeah, yeah... I know the city."

"Good... that's good. It's a bit of a fixer-upper right now, needs cleaning up. But if you want it, that makes you the Duke and that makes me your King. All feudal contracts apply, that's how it works. I give you land and titles and you recognize my sovereignty. Evidently it's a game the Brits have been playing for centuries. Like Monopoly, they call it Monarchy. So, you want to play, yes or no?"

"Will a big 'hell yeah' do?"

"I'll take that as a yes. Walk with me. I want to talk to you about something real quick." We walked outside and headed out to the airfields where the Tornadoes were landing. "Now, I had an idea that I tried to use with Inverness, but it didn't work because of the Red Eyes keeping the zombies away. But they are gone now so I think we can make use of them now. Here's one."

We came to where one of the RAF mechanics had been working on a nightmarish machine. "What is that?" Q asked.

"That was a Land Rover engine. Now, it's a Zombie Processor. I got the idea from Half Life Two. Musket has been working on them." I gave a nod and the mechanic pressed a Remote Key Fob that started the engine. Once started, the tall blades unfolded and started to spin. Fast. The man pressed the button again, and the engine stopped and the blades folded back up into a tall mast. "Place a few of these in an intersection, you have to bolt them down with concrete nail guns, put some bait in the middle of the intersection, get to a safe spot and turn it on. Zombies swarm the way they used to... they get processed."

"Bloody hell..." Q whispered.

"Yes. That's the idea. Whenever you're ready... just a new tool in our arsenal. Sarge has already taken eight of them."

"Where do you want me to set them up?"

"I'm going to leave that to the Duke." I said as I started to walk away.

"Who's the Duke?"

"That would be you. Remember? The big city in Scotland. It's yours now." I said over my shoulder. I noticed that he wasn't so much holding on to Izzy, as she was holding him up. He was hurt more than he wanted to admit. I slowed down and let him catch up. "Come on, I want to see your prisoner. Tell me about him."

On the way to the brig, Q filled me in on what happened. When he was done, he looked at me with genuine concern. "What am I going to do with this guy?"

I just shook my head. "Well Q, he's your find." I motioned to the door. "Let me see him."

Q stepped inside, Izzy helping to hold him up. The Doc was dictating some notes to a nurse when he looked up and saw Q.

"You're still on your feet? Must have the constitution of a horse." he said.

"Clydesdale actually." I said entering the room.

"Goat." Q shot back, smiling.

"Clydesdale." Izzy whispered to me with a grin. Louis coughed and held his hand out to a strange looking guy shackled to the bunk in the corner. "This is Will. Or at least he says he's Will. He won't give us a last name, and he doesn't have any ID on him."

I looked at the young man and said, "Hello, Will."

## The Sugar Plum Fairy

"Who are you?" Will said.

"Well, they tell me that I'm George Hill and that I'm now the King of England." I watched as he digested that information.

"Nice to meet you. I'm the Sugar Plum Fairy." Will said as he wrapped his arms around his knees, feeling smug about himself.

"Oh crap." Q breathed.

"That's funny. You're a funny guy. I like that. Now, let's get down to the brass tacks. You helped save my man, Q. For that I thank you. But I don't know you. So let me tell you what's important to me. Trust. I have to be able to trust you. If you stay with us, you do what I say, when I say it. I'm not going to micromanage you, but I have to trust that you get your job done. Do you understand me?"

Sugar Plums nodded his head. "Yeah, whatever you say."

"Whatever I say? I don't think we are quite clear." I looked over at Q. "Q, this man saved your life."

"Yeah, he did, Boss."

"But if I asked you to kill him, would you?"

"Without hesitation." Q said, his hand moving to his pistol.

"Why would you do that?"

"Because you are the guy in charge and you've kept everyone... most everyone alive... and you have a habit of being right."

"Izzy."

"Yessir."

"This man helped you save the man you love."

"Yessir... without hesitation... Same as Louis, and also because I've given you my Oath."

"So you would, you'd shoot him in the head."

Izzy looked from me to Will and unsnapped her handgun and started to draw it.

"No, no, no. That's good, Izzy, that's good. I don't want him dead just yet." I turned to Will again, "So, Sugar Plums... Can I trust you?"

Will looked around the room. "Yes. Yes you can."

"Good. That's good. You're a sneaky bastard. I need a guy like that. Q here, he's a bigger hammer kind of guy. I need a sneaky bastard kind of guy for a job. As soon as you're up to it. You interested?"

"Yeah, I guess... Sure. I'm up for it... uh... what is it?"

"I've sent four men into Northern Ireland. They have not come back. I want them found. Also, I need to know the status of the people there. I suspect the IRA has it locked down. They have guns. And I suspect they have control. I just want to know what's going on there. Can you get me some information?"

"Uh..."

"Oh, and one more thing. I need you to stop by an island and check up on someone... the Isle of Mull. Duart Castle. His name is MacLean. If he's okay, he may be able to help you. If he's in trouble... Call in the Cavalry. Before you leave, I'll have a letter for you to take to MacLean. "

I turned and started to walk out. "Let him out, but don't let him leave the grounds of the Fort without checking with me. And for the love of all that is holy, get that man a hot shower, food, and something to wear with less holes in it."

I marched myself back to my quarters … my new quarters that is. Debbie wasn't keen on letting me into "our" room and she still wouldn't talk to me. I can understand her wanting some space now, and that was fine. When I got into my room, I found that a bath had been drawn and was waiting for me.

I closed my eye and let the hot water soak into my bones. The hot bath felt like heaven, and I almost fell asleep. After I took my bath and put on some warm sweat-pants and a sweat-shirt, I laid down on the bed and put my hands behind my head.

Once again, April didn't let the hot water go to waste. She stripped naked and slipped into it. I didn't mean to look, but I noticed that she was a starting to "show". It was going to be obvious soon to everyone that she was pregnant and keeping her condition secret was going to become impossible. "So what are you going to do with this whole 'King' thing?" April asked as she stretched a soapy leg up into the air.

"I'm going to split Scotland and Ireland off, make them their own countries again. Scotland has lost its national identity. It's sad. That and the British Government's Health and Safety Ministry is why there is only about 2,000 people left alive on this whole island. Their Nanny State bullshit killed them. And if we don't make Ireland independent... they would eventually go to war for it. I'll just give it to them. I'm part Irish too, so I've always been sympathetic."

"So why send Sugar Plum to the IRA?"

"Because the IRA has kept Northern Ireland mostly intact. Took them a lot of time, but they now have a safe zone like what we had in Utah. After they got rid of the Zeds and the Reds. Or so I've been told. I don't know for sure, so I'm sending Will. I don't know if I can trust him yet, so he's expendable at this point, and he still doesn't know enough to be a problem if he's captured and interrogated. " I could tell that she didn't like the answer.

"Why are you sending scouts into Ireland anyways?"

"I have to know how to approach them. I want them to be willing to play ball."

"For what?"

"For when we invade France."

April laughed. "You can't be serious."

I opened my eye and looked at her. "You are serious!"

"Of course I am. There is something we have to kill in Paris, and then we'll establish a new Parliament and set up democratic elections."

April stood up and stepped out of the tub. "You said *something* when you should have said *someone*."

April towel off and pulled on her Raiders football jersey and climbed into her bed. She had the bottom bunk.

Joy slipped into the tub with a grin. "I've always wanted to go to Paris."

"Well, that's down the road a ways, but we'll be there in the spring." I started to fall asleep.

Joy leaned back in the water, "I can't wait."

## A Good Afternoon

It looked like a small Bull Elk, but was the size of a deer. A Red Stag. It grazed unaware of my presence. When I stalked close enough I pulled my rifle up to my left shoulder and sighted carefully across the sights of the .375 H&H CZ 550 Safari. The Stag took a step and raised its head. It sniffed the air and looked in my direction as I pulled the trigger. The rifle boomed and recoil raised the muzzle. I lost sight of the Stag for a moment as I cycled the bolt with my left hand, reaching over the scope. Shooting a rifle left-handed was usually no problem, but this big, heavy gun made it more awkward. The Stag was stumbling around like it was drunk.

"A fine shot, my one-eyed King." Lucas whispered. He was grinning and so was I. We were far north in Scotland, in what used to be a military reservation. The British Army used to train here. When the Stag finally fell over, I stood up. The .375 was a lot of gun for the Stag, but I liked the heft of the rifle, the lines, and the brush busting capability. It felt good to shoot it, even if I had to do it left-handed.

Joy and April were already driving up in the Raptor when I stood over the Stag. It was kicking weakly and I could see frothy blood coming from the mouth and the wound. I knelt on the neck and pressed the Stag's head into the ground. Using my big Becker, I slit the throat. Blood was still pumping, staining the fresh snow red. Soon the pumping blood started slowing and it wasn't long before it stopped.

Lucas handed me the cup and I filled it with the fresh blood. I drank the blood and passed the cup to Lucas. Lucas looked squeamish but took a sip. April then took the cup and drank deeply. When she smiled, it was a completely ghoulish grin that made me laugh. Kilo looked like he was going to be sick.

I stood up and wiped the blood from my blade before I sheathed the knife again. "This is a good one." I glanced at Kilo, "As soon as we get this one sorted, we'll find one for you." Kilo just nodded.

Lucas started quartering the Stag as I caped it out with my smaller Becker. Once the Stag was in the back of the truck we started a new stalk. We went another two miles before we found another Stag. This one was even bigger than the one I took. "Look at that." I whispered. Kilo slunk up from behind and came to sit beside me. "It's big."

We were two hundred yards away. "Let's work our way over to the left, go around that hill and we'll be in forty yards."

"Or I could just take it right here." Kilo sighted his rifle and held right over the kill zone. It was a quartering away shot, but the Hornady loads would have no problem with this. I put my hand on top of the barrel and pushed the rifle down.

"I know you can, Son. But killing isn't the point of the hunt." We made the stalk and crawled up the hill through the snow. Kilo pointed his rifle and we waited. After about ten minutes we saw antlers crest the hill. Soon the Stag was in full view, at only 30 yards. I heard Kilo take a deep breath, then, as I looked back at the Stag, Kilo's rifle boomed. He was shooting his chosen hunting rifle, a long-barreled 1895CB in .45-70. The Stag was struck in the center of the chest and immediately fell over.

"Alright!" I shouted as I jumped up. Kilo levered the action and carefully lowered the hammer before he stood. He had his trademarked half grin on his face. "So, go finish him."

"Okay." He slung the long rifle over his shoulder and pulled his Ka-Bar knife out as he approached the Stag. Doing what I did on mine, he pinned the animal down while it was still kicking and slit the throat. Soon the animal stopped moving. He stood there looking at the stag, and then into the cup of fresh blood.

"Tradition." I said.

Kilo tilted his head back and drank the cup empty.

"YES!" I cheered him and gave him a high five.

"It could use a little pepper."

Lucas approached the kill. "Looks like a trophy worthy of the Lodge!"

I beamed. We took photos. This was a good afternoon.

Joy and Rebecca drove the Raptor up, soon followed by the other vehicles: a couple Humvees and an LAV. CG troops helped take care of the stag, and it wasn't long before it too was quartered up and in the back of the Raptor. Up overhead a Merlin was circling, and, I knew above that, a couple Jets were flying CAP. I shook my head. As much as it spoiled the whole idea of hunting, it was still good to get away. As much as this was.

"Your Majesty," Alan approached with an iPad. This was a man that had been with me since Utah.

"You used to call me Ogre... what happened to that?"

"You became King." He said.

I took the iPad and looked at the screen. The team had made it to just outside of Belfast. They had picked up the trail of the other scouts. They had been out of contact for the better part of a day now and missed their check in time. Being in Indian country, schedules can become a problem. But I didn't feel like I needed to worry.

Will, aka, Sugar Plum, was expendable at this point. An unknown element. That could change depending on the outcome of this mission. I kicked myself for my harsher disposition, but since we've had people taking the demonic marks and turning on their fellows, I've been less trusting.

"Keep monitoring. We'll give them another twelve hours to check in before we take action."

"Yes my Lord. If I may ask... what action would that be?"

"A bigger hammer." I said as I handed the iPad back and climbed into the Raptor. From in the cab, I could see the coast. Out in the ocean I saw a patrol boat. The red thistle on the side of the bow marked it as one of mine. *Oh come on.* This King business was even more annoying than being the President.

The more I thought about Will and the scouts I had sent, the more I became uncomfortable with their situation. I closed my eye and tried to see into Ireland. I could see the Island and tried to move to it, but there was a wall. Something blocked me and I couldn't get close. Old magics. Old spells. It was no use. I called out and heard only an echo of my mind's voice. When I looked down, I saw a face, but it was unfamiliar. A sly smile and blue eyes under dark hair. Then I was pulled back. I opened my eye and saw northern Scotland again, and April's hand on my arm.

"You okay?" She asked.

"How's your Irish accent?" I asked April. My eyes glanced down at her body. She was as beautiful as ever, but now her breasts were swollen and she was showing. In her armor that she normally wore, it was better hidden. In more regular clothes, she looked like a pregnant woman. It was time to find a place for her where Debbie wouldn't gut her. And me. The initial thought was to take her to Ireland with me. But suddenly I didn't want her at risk. Her or the baby.

"I don't have any. How's yours?"

"Mine is fairly good," I said wearing the accent. "I could pass as Irish if the conversation was brief. But let's hope I don't have to try. I would rather concentrate on my own mission."

No, she wouldn't be coming, and she wouldn't be staying near Inverness. I had an idea.

## Home of Clan Cameron

The road to Achnacarry Castle was small, twisting and forced me for the first time to put the Raptor into four-wheel drive because of the snow. Following the Raptor was a pair of Humvees pulling a trailer and the M-ATV. We came to a stone and iron gate that had been shut, chained, and locked with a gigantic old padlock.

Achnacarry Castle, the ancestral home of Clan Cameron. I was finally here. I've been itching to come here since we first landed, but The Bigger Picture kept me from my journey. We could have flown, but I wanted to drive. Back in the day Achnacarry Castle was the training grounds of the British Commandos. Snow and ice crusted the chain and gates, and it didn't look like anyone had passed through in some time. There were no tracks in the snow on either side of the gate. I grabbed the lock. It wasn't just large, but it was also heavy.

I motioned for some cutters.

Two of the CG jumped out of the second Humvee and brought out a small cutting torch. Well, that would work better than some simple bolt cutters for sure. I stood back and let them work. In about two minutes the lock was open, chains pulled through the bars, and the gates were pushed wide open. I climbed back into the Raptor and started rolling, slower than before.

As we rolled slowly through the estate, I had a feeling that we were not alone. Tracks in the snow, too wide for deer. "Guns up! We might have company, so ID any target carefully." I said, over the radio. The canvas cover for the turret ring was pulled in and Joy climbed up. The cold air wasn't much of a challenge for the Raptor's heater, but the sudden rush of cold air made both Joy and April shiver. I heard Joy pull the charging handle, locking the bolt back and getting the big gun ready to fire.

With a glance in the side mirror as we came through a curve, I saw the other vehicle's gunners up and ready covering their sectors. We drove out of the trees and saw the Cameron Museum. The building was a small cottage. We passed the Museum and continued up the road to the Castle.

"That's a castle?" April asked.

"I love it!" Joy exclaimed.

I pulled to a stop. Achnacarry Castle wasn't so much of a castle as it was a large estate house built from stone. The original castle was destroyed and this one was built in 1802 to replace it. I knew the history, written in dozens of books. But that was nothing like seeing it with my own eyes... eye... it was so beautiful that it took my breath away. Especially with the snow on the roof, glowing light from some of the windows, and the wisp of smoke from one of the chimneys.

"Looks like someone is home." I said.

We pulled up in front of the castle and even before I opened my door, I saw movement inside. There were tracks all around the grounds here. I stepped out of the truck and approached the door, which opened before me.

"I wasn't expecting deliveries." The old man said. He had long, gray hair coming out from under his beret. His old jacket was well worn, and of old military issue. He had a slight hunch, but his eyes were bright and clear... and mischievous. "Well don't just stand there... you're letting the heat out and I've only got so much wood cut."

Joy was suddenly at my side, one hand casually behind the curve of her well shaped hip. In that hand was a loaded M&P pistol. April was still in the Raptor, and CG had the truck surrounded. Their new Oaths were to protect April at all costs. These guards were now hers.

"Thank you, Sir. I appreciate the hospitality."

Joy and I stepped in and the old man shut the door. "Now who in the bloody hell are you and what do you want?"

"My name is George and I'm of Cameron. I came home for a visit. Didn't expect to find anyone here. Alive."

The old man's eyes went wide. "I knew it! You're the new master of Fort George, the one they are calling the new King of England! I've heard the talk on the radio."

"That's me, and that's what they are telling me. I'd have preferred to have just remained myself, the Ogre."

"My humble apologies, my Lord. Had I known you were coming..." The man bowed his head.

I held up my hands, "No, please... Don't do that... Ah... Mister.."

"Ah... Where are my manors? I am Duncan Clarkson." The old man was hesitant, but held out his hand then pulled it back a bit afraid he may have done something wrong. I reached out and took his hand.

"I'm pleased to meet you, Duncan." I smiled and Duncan seemed to relax. "It's a pleasure to meet family. We're of the same Sept."

To this Duncan's eyes gleamed. "Well then! Come in, come in... We have much to talk about. Have you been to the Achnacarry before, Son... Ah... Your Majesty."

Joy snickered quietly behind her hand at the old man's discomfort. I shot her a glare. She nodded towards her pistol and I shook my head. She pulled the gun up to her waistline and tucked it in.

"Duncan, my friends call me Ogre, my family calls me George. Please, call me either you feel comfortable with." I indicated to Joy. "This viscous beauty is Joy Ansfrida. Joy is one of my body guards. And if you listen to too much gossip, one of my mistresses. But that much isn't true. Even if I have thought about it." I turned to her and winked. She just smirked. "She's fought with me almost since the beginning."

"Ah, pleased to meet you..." Duncan tipped his head, "My Lady Ansfrida."

"You can just call me Joy." She smiled.

"Welcome to Castle Achnacarry, Joy." He took her hand, "Its about time we've had some joy in this old castle."

"Duncan, you said 'we'. How many are there here?"

"Ah, well... You understand of course that we didn't know who you were or what your intentions were."

Duncan opened the door and blew an old silver whistle. Around the grounds several of the shrubberies stood up. Some of the bushes were holding Bazookas, others Bren Guns, and the rest a collection of Sterlings and SA-80's. All the men and the few women were wearing face paint in white, gray and greens.

"And if I was hostile?"

From next to the vase on the table, a large book obscured a short barreled Sten Gun. "I would have been forced to defend myself as everyone else took care of your friends in the trucks."

I threw my head back and laughed. "One must never forget this is the home of the Commandos as well as the Clan!"

Duncan's eyes gleamed, "God's truth, my King."

I keyed my radio to all units, "Stand down everyone... we are among friends and family here."

With that, the bushes stepped forward as the gunners in the trucks safed their weapons. The doors to the Raptor opened and April climbed out. The other trucks unloaded their occupants save for the M-ATV which were going to continue to run security.

"Duncan, I require your utmost discretion in the handling of my biggest indiscretion of my life. This is April Peterson, my other bodyguard. And she is my mistress."

"My Lord surrounds himself with beauty." Duncan approached April, and kissed her hand with a slight bow. "My Lady. As beautiful as the blossoms your name recalls. I am at your humble service." April blushed as Duncan bowed low.

April was surprised. "Ah, nice to meet you too, Sir."

"You are all Americans?" Duncan asked.

"No, not all of us. Several here," I nodded back outside. "We picked them up in Scotland. RAF, Royal Marines." Introductions went around.

"Duncan, my friend..." I said, patting him on the back. "I've never been here before. Is there a tour?"

We let Duncan Clarkson show us around the normal tourist things and indicated to Joy and April rooms they could use. "Ah, if you wish you can use either room, your Grace." Duncan didn't quite know how to approach it. As the girls went into their rooms, I pulled Duncan aside.

"April is carrying something very precious. She's with child."

Duncan nodded.

"With my child."

His eyes went wide for just a blink. "Ah... I understand."

"That's good. Because my wife wouldn't. She knows about April and I. But she doesn't know about this."

Duncan started tsking with his tongue in his mouth. I was beginning to think that this was a bad idea. Then I realized that was just him thinking. "So you need a place that is safe and secure to sequester the lady and child when it comes."

So he does understand. "Exactly."

"So you brought her to your Uncle Duncan." The man clasped me on my shoulder with genuine warmth. "You do us, and Achnacarry a great honor, Sire. This old house will not soon be forgotten and I won't be just a tour guide." I could see a glitter of new moisture in his eyes. "You've given us new purpose."

A large smile spread across his face. "This is an auspicious occasion. I think this calls for a feast. Such as we have."

"Duncan, let's keep this part of it as low profile as possible. But to eat with everyone, that would be my honor. If you don't mind, we brought some food. Some meat and cheese. And we have bottles of Orange Juice, but that's for April. I'm told OJ is good for pregnancies. Helps the baby as I understand."

Duncan nodded as we went downstairs again. "To help with security and for the chores of the house, I'm leaving a detachment here with April."

I saw Duncan's back stiffen. "They will be under her command of course, but they will also be under your direction. You've run Achnacarry and I would like you to continue to do so. Now you have some more responsibility, but more hands for the daily work now. Maybe my Uncle Duncan can take some rest now and then. I imagine there is good fishing around here in the nicer months."

We ate with the men and women of Achnacarry that night, and dined on venison, cheese, and canned olives both black and green.

## Ogre Goes Secret Solo

The next morning, I had left Achnacarry, left my bodyguards, my team, everything behind. My girls and the CG members protested, because finding a new home for April was only part of the reason I came here. No one would be missing me for a few days. Officially I was resting and recovering at my clan's home. Otherwise, no one would have let me go. If anyone called for me, I was out hunting. A stretch of the truth, but not a lie.

April kissed me, on the cheek. She came in for my lips but I turned my head. "I'm sorry, but this is for the best." I kissed her on the forehead and tried not to see the hurt look in her eyes. Joy gave me a hug and told me to be careful. I made my promise to try to be as careful as possible. I swore the rest of the CGs to secrecy and then I turned back to Duncan. The old Commando said that he wished he could come with me. He, probably more than anyone else here knew what I was getting into, even more than me. One of the last things I did was to take the Blue Force Tracker out of the Raptor and had it installed in Duncan's old Land Rover Defender.

I took my Raptor to Naval Station and caught a ride to almost within sight of Ireland's shores aboard one of the Patrol Boats. From there, I took a Zodiac to shore. The Zodiac had enough fuel to get in, and get back to the Navy Station... and enough speed to get away if something gave chase. I hid the Zodiac under a small pier with fishing nets providing some camouflage. It was still very dark, very early in the morning. There was no one around this little town that consisted of only a few small houses, a couple sheds, and this little pier. There was a small fishing boat tethered to the pier, but it was floating away, pulling at the rope. A good storm would send the boat adrift. In one of the houses I found badly decomposed bodies, left since the undead plague first started.

The home was typical, rural Irish fishing village. I found some clothes to change into: rough army trousers with cargo pockets and an oversized wool sweater. I changed into the clothes, pulling the sweater over my black T-shirt, body armor and shoulder holster. Over the sweater I pulled on an old oiled canvas jacket. I found a cap that looked just like what the singer from AC-DC used to wear. The treasure find was the old messenger bag. I threw my spare mags, radio, grenades, and the L34 suppressed Sterling Duncan gave me into the bag. Last thing I did was to pull off my ruby and black eye patch and replaced it with an old brown leather one.

I looked in the mirror and saw what could pass for any run-of-the-mill, old, beat-to-shit Irishman. I had let my facial hair grow out for the last few weeks, and I really looked rough. Groovy.

Making my way from Orlock, I went cross country to Bangor. I wanted to avoid people as much as possible. As I crossed the last field, into Bangor I noticed people walking around, going about their business. As I neared the buildings the stench of rotting corpses hit me. It was so rank, it made my eye water. I found an open pit where bodies were simply thrown in. The sun had come up and there was enough light to see that not all the bodies were zombies. Some were young men that looked like they died human, but died stitched with gunfire. *What the hell was this?* We were told that Northern Ireland had been under control. The zombie plague had been contained and controlled. To my left, there was an outbreak of gunfire. Loud and stark against the otherwise quite stillness.

I heard a moaning erupt, and a couple more shots. All was quiet again. I walked past the corpse pit and into the streets where some people were walking around. Women in coats carrying bags from a shop. No vehicles that I saw. I stood there a moment trying to get my bearings. The sky was cold and overcast, and I had a hard time finding my direction all the sudden.

"I've not seen you around here. Where are you from?"

I turned around and found a police officer standing there. He was wearing a flak vest with patches that said PSNI and the word POLICE across the front. "I came in from Groomsport, looking for a decent breakfast."

"Ah, Groomsport you say? I heard its a ghost town there now."

"There are a few of us left. To think we had a bad time during the troubles... all I can tell ya is that I'm sick of fish and would love some eggs for a change... a proper breakfast. And a pint if there is any to be had. I've not been here since the world went to hell."

"Well, the best one is still open. The Ava. But it's a ways into town. There's a bus that should be coming by, it's going to go right past it."

"The Ava? Still in operation, that's the best news I've heard in months. Thank you, Constable, Sir."

The officer tipped his hat and walked by. I looked for the bus stop signs and saw them. I remembered which side of the road the traffic was heading to go into the deeper portion of the city and crossed the street. I noticed as I stood by the bus stop that the police officer had walked some ways away, but stopped. I acted casual as he was doing, but I noticed he was watching me. A couple other people came to the bus stop, they said curt "Good Mornings" but everyone seemed to mind their own business, hands in their pockets, heads down. Nothing to see here. Just old houses painted in peeling white. I put my hands in my pockets as well, acting as if I was cold like they were. Given all the layers I was wearing, I was more than warm enough. These people seemed to be chilled to the bone.

The bus came within minutes and everyone climbed on. I was half expecting a London style double decker, instead the bus was a modern metro style like most anywhere, save for the paint job, a crazy bright blue that looked out of place here as it would anywhere else on the planet. I had coins, and, as I followed the others on board, I watched how they paid and how much. I did the same and had no problem. The bus driver didn't even look at me. I took my seat in the back and carefully glanced out the window where I saw the officer talking into the handset of his radio as the bus pulled away.

As we drove, I noticed a couple small cars go past, and a truck full of what looked like some sort of soldiers, but they were all wearing face masks. I had the feeling that riding all the way to Ava was poor idea, so I got off at the next stop. I was almost in the center of Bangor when I saw something interesting. I had walked down a couple side roads, and found a small pub called McDonald's. The smell of good food was coming out, so I went in.

The people inside were talking quietly and eating well. Large plates of food. Eggs, black sausages, toast, and pints of Guinness. "Can I help you?" The girl was a young twenty something, with long red curly hair and striking blue eyes. She reminded me of Rebecca, but with a rounder face and curvier hips.

"I'm starving to death and need a good breakfast, if that's not too much of a bother."

"Have a seat and I'll see to it." She gestured to a small table.

A few people glanced at me but didn't seem to pay much attention. I sat my bag down beside me on the bench seat. I was up against the wall and had a good view of everything. In a matter of moments, I was served a tall glass of dark liquid with a cream-colored head.

"What happened to your face? If you don't mind me asking." The red-haired girl set the glass down and made the motion of wiping off the table.

"Got into a wrestling match with a girl as pretty as you... but she was undead and not such a good conversationalist."

She laughed. "She tried to kiss you, eh?"

"I tried to tell her no as politely as possible."

"I'm sure you hurt her feelings."

"Well, I get that a lot, you know."

The girl chuckled as she went to the other tables, checking on the patrons. After awhile, I had a full plate of food in front of me. The Guinness was good, and went with the traditional breakfast very well. The sausage was particularly good. I listened carefully to the conversations in the pub. I could make out bits about the IRA, and other groups that were fighting for control of the region. Belfast was a war zone now. Seems like the people here didn't much care either way as long as some sort of control was established and things normalized.

After I finished eating and listening, after the other patrons wandered out. I waved the girl over and paid for my meal. "So what are ya really here for?" The girl asked, with her piercing blue eyes looking into mine. She had leaned in close and her long hair fell off of her shoulders, framing her face like lion's mane. As I looked in her eyes I could see she was drastically sharp, and that I was in trouble.

"To be truthful, it was the eggs. But I enjoyed the sausage almost as much."

The corners of her lips curled up slightly. "That's why you came inside, I can believe that. But what are you here for? You're no local. Your accent is good, but it's not quite right. You sound like someone who's trying to blend in."

She nailed me. I dropped the accent when I whispered. "Your right. I'm not from here. I'm looking for some people, some friends. I'm on my way into Belfast, where we lost contact with them."

"I knew it." She smiled. "I remember faces, and I've never seen yours before around here. But you do look familiar." Her eye narrowed as she looked at me.

I put my accent back on. "Well you caught me. A man looking for his friends... You should be a member of MI-6."

The girl sat down. "Belfast, you said. Well that's a tough bit of travel. How are you going to get past the check point?"

"I didn't know there was a check point."

"Just outside of town on all the main roads." She flipped her hair then blinked her eyes at me like she was waiting for me to say something.

"Well, then I'll probably best stay off the main roads then. I'm sorry. What's your name?"

"It's Deirdre." She held out her hand.

"George."

"I'm pleased to meet you George."

"Pleased to meet you too, Deirdre. Thank you for the food, and the chat. I should be going now." I stood up.

"I have an easier way to get Belfast." Deirdre grinned and held up a key ring. "I have a Polo parked in the back."

I stopped and looked at her, holding up the VW key. "Why would you want to help a stranger you've never met before?"

She walked over to the bar and picked up the small newspaper. My picture was on the front page. I was wearing my multi-cam armor and held my shotgun. I was walking away from a helicopter. It was taken at Fort George. "Ah damn it." I grumbled. "Why does anyone need spies when we have reporters?"

Deirdre's eyes flashed wide with her grin. "I knew it!"

Suddenly my suppressed HK came out from under my sweater and was pressed up under her chin. "You know nothing, girl. You didn't see me. You just saw a tired old fisherman. Am I clear?"

"I saw the new King of England and served him breakfast... and instead of leaving me a tip he pulls a gun on me. Typical English. But we better get moving if you want to make it to Belfast."

"You still want to help me?"

"I'm from Edinburgh." Her accent changed all the sudden. "I came here on holiday before this great plague that doesn't let people die. I just want to get home again. I don't know if I have any family left or not."

I sensed that she was telling the truth. That part at least. I slipped the gun back into the carrier pouch. "You help me find my friends, and I'll help you get home. I know the Duke." I looked out the window as a police car pulled up out front. *Crap. So much for just sneaking out.* "Come on, let's go." We went out the back.

We ran out the back door and quietly shut it before the cops came in the front. Deirdre's car was a small, yellow VW Polo. We jumped in and I let her drive. Deirdre pulled off and we were half way out of the alley when the cops came out of the back door and saw us. I glanced back and saw one of them running down the alley after us as the other ducked back into the cafe. The cop running started to draw his pistol when we turned the corner.

To avoid the police we took a zig zag path that made our way to the highway. We soon were on the main highway heading to Belfast, and we came up to a checkpoint. The three armed guards at the checkpoint were taking up positions already as we approached.

"Just play it cool, girl." I said as I slipped my right hand into my messenger bag and took a grip on the Sterling.

"This is no problem." Deirdre said as she pulled up to the stop. I didn't like this one bit. Something felt wrong. She rolled down her window. "Hello there boys!" She smiled.

"What's going on Deirdre? Who's this?"

One of the other guys shouted "Did you bring us some Eats?"

Deirdre looked at me and I saw her smile disappear. "I've got something better. George, the new King of England."

"You lied." I said.

"More of a fib, I'd say."

The man to the left of the car, just outside my door started to unsling the Sten Gun he had over his shoulder. I pulled the trigger on the Sterling, firing through the bag. The 147 grain slugs punched through the car door and into the man's chest. I hit him five times in the upper chest. Dierdre screamed and grabbed at me. I gave her a quick elbow to the face as I dove out the door. I hit the ground as a shotgun blast tore through the windshield and into the seat I had just been in. I glanced up and saw one of the guys moving past Deirdre towards the rear of the car. I pulled the Sterling out of the bag and fired through the car as I moved to the back, away from the guy with the shotgun at the front. At the rear of the car, I found the guy hitting the ground face first. Another shotgun blast sent more glass flying and Deirdre screamed again. The man with the shotgun broke open the action of his double barrel. He was empty. I stood up and covered the guy with my SMG.

"Stop that." I said. The man looked up at me as he shoved a shell into the breach. The Sterling rattled in my hand and I could hear the impacts of my bullets crashing into the man's face. He was dead before he hit the ground. I turned my gun on Deirdre who was still sitting in the driver's seat. Broken glass and some pellets had peppered the side of her face.

"I'm very sorry you did this. That was a very stupid thing to do, girl." Without moving her head, she turned her eyes to me and blinked. "This isn't what I wanted for you." I put the muzzle of the Sterling against her ear and pulled the trigger. She slumped over into the passenger seat twitching.

"Shit."

I pulled a fresh magazine from the bag and changed it as I went to the vehicles that formed the barrier across the road. One of them, at the end, was a white Mitsubishi SUV. No keys. A quick search of the bodies yielded a couple things. One was the Mitsu keys, and the other was a Walther PPK .32, which I checked quickly before putting in my pocket. Sitting on the saw horse was a handheld radio and a cell phone. I took both, tossing them onto the passenger seat of the Mitsu as I climbed in.

In the Mitsu was an SA80 rifle with a couple magazines. Good, that might be handy.

The old SUV fired right up and soon I was rolling in the right direction. As I was driving into Belfast I turned on the handheld radio. I could hear chatter. Someone was organizing an attack on the "outsiders". I hit the gas.

The drive wasn't all that long, and the radio chatter was all about looking for a little yellow VW, and then about how it was found. There was nothing about a white SUV. This was a good thing. This meant that they were not looking for me in a vehicle, and probably not heading into Belfast. I imagined that they were thinking I might be on foot, possibly wounded and not able to go very far. I continued on the highway, praying that I'd find some signs of my scouts, and Will, the sneaky Sugar Plumb.

It wasn't long before I was out of range of the Motorola hand held and it went quiet.

As I got near Belfast, I saw up ahead another check point and quickly pulled off the road. Now where to? I checked the glove box for maps or notes or anything that could help me. There was a lighter and a pack of cigarets that looked like they were several years old. There was a nut and bolt, probably to something under the hood, or from the Mitsubishi's ride, a part of the suspension. A critical part. So, no maps, no outlined detour to get around the checkpoints. I looked around and saw that the small, dirt road I had turned off onto was through a farm. I followed it, through some tree lines and across some fields and then saw another road going into the city. Following this road, I was tempted to stop and try to find where that nut and bolt was supposed to have gone. However, considering the engine's temperature, I was not sure I wanted to stop and risk it not starting again. The engine liked to run hot, and by hot, that meant into the red line. The oil and check engine lights were both on. Come on you piece of crap... don't fail on me.

The road turned out to head into Belfast on a street less traveled. There were a few cars on the sides, but nothing else moving. I drove around more open areas, not going deep in the city, where I could see were more vehicles, more soldier-looking types with sour faces and rifles. I found one location where the scouts had planned on coming, but there was no sign they were here at all. I kept going. There was a police car of some type, but the word Police had been painted over with spray paint. The cop within was in the back seat. Driving was a man in a mask and old military coat. I watched as another masked man dragged an old geriatric man from his house. A woman came out screaming as the masked gunman shot the man. The woman fell to her knees holding the old man and the gunman shot her too. I saw too much for any one man to have to see in his lifetime. I turned my attention to another task and went back the way I had come.

There were some stores here, mostly supply shops, light industrial stuff. It was starting to get dark, so I pulled in behind some old buildings that looked like they hadn't been used in years. I parked the Mitsu behind one of them, making sure it wasn't visible from the road.

I checked out the building and then went to the next one, farther away from the vehicle. If it was located, the commotion might give me time to escape or hide.

This was as good of a place to hunker down as any place. As the sun set, I looked out the upstairs window and noticed something about Ireland that I liked. No crows so far. That was a plus. Traffic on the road was nonexistent. No vehicles. No people. I kept away from the window but continued to look out at the street below, staying in shadows. Off in the distance I could hear occasional gunfire.

When I heard the sound of a truck approaching, I held my breath. It sounded like it was slowing down. I crouched low and got closer to the window. It was moving slow as it had just come around a corner and the driver was trying to find gears. I could hear the transmission being tortured to give up the location of the next gear. "*We have ways of making you shift.*" I was amused at first, then looked down at it and saw something that I didn't understand. It was a cattle truck of some sort. Inside the open-topped trailer, I could see the dirty, bloody heads of people, packed in the trailer like sardines. One of them was looking up and I saw it's dead, milky white eyes looking up into the sky. Zombies. The truck was carrying a load of zombies, still alive, still ambulatory. The truck driver had found the gear he was grinding for and the truck lurched forward. What the hell was that about?

I watched the truck go up the street till it was almost out of view, but then it stopped. The driver and the passengers in the cab got out. They held AK's. I had to get a closer look at what was going on. In my pack I found a compact pair of Swarovski binos. With the glass I could make out what the men were doing. One had a radio and was directing the others. They were setting up steel lines to form a fence, a funnel. Once done, they climbed up to the sides of the trailer and opened the gate. The zombies poured out and started running in the direction the fence lead them. I could feel the weight of the moans as they emptied from the truck, and worse were the screams that came to my ears moments later.

Weapons, I thought. They were using the zombies as weapons. Smart, and horrid at the same time. I'd not have thought of doing that. I couldn't help but to shudder when I imagined the person that could and did think of doing that. I listened to my hand held, scanning through the different channels and listening for what chatter I could understand. The picture I was painting in my head was one of an island in utter chaos and the warring factions were using the chaos as a tool to try to get advantage over the others.

I pulled out a can of Kippers and a bag of walnuts and a bottle of water to wash it down. This was my dinner.

No, Northern Ireland wasn't ready for me, and I wasn't ready for them. The reports from the scouts in the southern part of Ireland was pessimistic. Massive depopulation. Survivors holding on by mainly fishing. We would hit them with some supplies to help them get through winter. But there was nothing useful for us there. Northern Ireland however, could be very helpful one day. Maybe after things settled down, after someone claimed victory, maybe then we could come to an agreement. I turned my attention back to locating my men, and getting out. I went back into the room I'd call my sleeping quarters. I laid down, using my bag as a pillow, as comfortable as it was filled with magazines and grenades. I closed my eye and thought of women who loved me. It was the only comfort I had here.

My first night's sleep in Ireland was upstairs in a shop that sold bathroom tile, and my bed was table top.

The next morning I heard more radio chatter. This time it was about unknown men, trespassers, Englishmen, and invaders. My scouts! I listened carefully trying to follow the game play by play. They were not captured. Good! They were killing and eluding their way out of ambushes and the Irish didn't know where they were going next. When the Motorola radio died, I threw it across the room. I ran out to my Mitsubishi and jumped it.

Suddenly, the Blackberry in my pocket vibrated to tell me that I just received a message. I pulled it out and checked the screen. Two words and numbers. "RAPID TRANSIT 2-20." The two words which meant the scouts needed a fast extraction... by helicopter. The numbers meant location. The second location, and the time to get there. Twenty minutes was the fastest the chopper could prep, launch, and get to the location. This meant that the scouts were in trouble.

Not all bad news, I reasoned. At least this told me a couple important things. First, that one or more of the men were still alive. Second, right where they were heading. Especially since I helped select the locations. The second extraction point wasn't far from here. Even though I had no direct way to communicate with any of them, I decided to be as helpful as possible. I pulled off the road at the Irish equivalent of an IFA store. Farming supplies, tools, feed, and fertilizer. Lots of fertilizer. The store was gutted of most of the stuff, but they still had what I was looking for. There were a couple people there, looters. Just like me. They made no objection to me rolling out my cart stacked high with some cleaning supplies, 50 pound bags of fertilizer and granulated chlorine for pool treatment. Not that I planned on swimming. I threw them in the back of the Mitsu and jumped in. I had a little time, but none to spare. I headed to the extraction point where I examined the terrain. If they were coming, they would be moving fast.

I found a good choke point along the only half-decent route to the extraction point. What also made it a good choice was a parked Toyota Prius on the side of the road. I had a some explosives for just this purpose, but not big enough for what I wanted to do. I didn't have many options on just how to construct my IED, so I just used the Mitsu, draining the oil from the oil pan to mix with the ammonium nitrate. The oil was hot, thick, and black. Almost sludge. But it would work just fine. The back of the SUV contained one charge, the Prius had the other. Large fertilizer-oil charges would do the trick, effectively creating a large "Muff-Charge". To set these off, I set both command detonating mines to blow at the same time.

As soon as I had finished getting everything ready I scrambled behind some cover about 75 yards away. I could see the mines through the windows, clear line of sight. Nothing to get in the way of the signal. Also, nothing to get in the way of any shrap. I had to be careful.

The plan was simple. Good guys would drive past to the extraction zone. Bad guys would approach and the SUV would go up, taking them out or at least causing some distraction. All I had to do was wait, but it wouldn't be for long. I could hear engines, so I tucked into the rifle tight and got ready.

A red Land Rover Discovery came barreling around the curve into view. As it approached, I saw that it was full of men that I recognized. The Disco flashed past, one of the men riding Trunk Monkey was firing. I looked back down the road and saw a black van in chase. The side door was open and a man with a black ski mask was firing out of it. Neither the masked man nor the Trunk Monkey were doing a lot of hitting. Just as well, this situation was

about to get resolved.
The Disco made it safely past, and I watched with anticipation as the black van closed in on the Mitsu on the side of the road only a hundred yards away. Timing was everything.

I picked up the remote. A harmless little thing, it weighed almost nothing. I flipped the switch on it, arming the system. I lifted the cover to the little red button. A small LED made the button glow red, like an invitation to push it. I didn't even touch it yet, but I let my thumb hover over it, ready to mash it down and send the signal. The black van was almost at the Mitsubishi. Just before it reached it, I pressed the button. There was as flash of light and then a massive concussion that felt like it took the air out of my lungs. I ducked quickly behind the tree I was using for cover. The blast was far bigger than I had intended. I could hear the buzzing of high velocity fragments. Bigger vehicle parts started falling down around the whole area.

I peeked around the tree and looked. The Mitsu and the Prius were gone. Where they had been were nothing but wide craters. The black van was also gone, but there were parts. Most of the van had been blown out and away, along with its occupants. Some parts remained. An axle and a wheel, but no tire remained. Part of the engine was sitting in the middle of the road like it had just been dropped there. Nothing remained attached to it save for some exhaust pipe. I stood there for a moment, taking in the scale of the destruction I had unleashed. Part of me laughed and I said to my self. "I think I just rolled a Twenty." The other part said that I had a helicopter to catch if I wanted to get a ride home. More IRA would be coming here pretty soon. An explosion of this size was going to attract some unwanted attention. This wouldn't be a good place to be in a little while. Besides that, a good-sized brushfire was already going. Time to jet-moto. I tossed the old SA-80 rifle into the Mitsu's crater. I had thought that I might keep it, but I noticed a jagged piece of metal sticking out of the receiver. Looks like it caught a bit of shrapnel. Oh well, I'll get another. Jogging to the extraction point, I kept my Sterling in hand, keeping just inside the treeline. I knew this wasn't the fastest way, but I made good time regardless.

I saw the Merlins coming in overhead and picked up the pace. I found my rhythm and was making good time. I crossed the distance and came out into the open where one of the Helicopters was just touching down. Men in camo instantly brought up arms and covered me. I held my Sterling up over my head as I slowed to a walk. I understood that they would have a hard time recognizing me. When I got closer, I called out. "Anyone going," I huffed, the run was harder than I had thought, "...back to Scotland?" The weapons dropped.

I recognized MacLean as one of the Scouts that I had sent. He was dirty, sweaty, covered in mud, blood, and camo paint, and he wore a huge grin on his face. "Ogre?"

"The King?" One of the men questioned. "It is him!"

I glanced at Will whose strange eyes were blinking in surprise. I looked back at MacLean. "Couldn't let you amateurs have all the fun. What was that van doing following you?"

"Well, the natives were a little frisky." He shrugged.

"Anyone have a drink here?"

One of the scouts pulled out a canteen. "That was you?"

"Should have known you would drop a nuke on Ireland." Maclean laughed as I unscrewed the lid to the canteen.

"Had to cover your tracks, didn't I? It wasn't a Nuke. It was just a fertilizer bomb." I tossed back the canteen and took a long pull.

Whiskey. Hadn't expected that, was expecting water. It burned going down. But now that I knew what to expect, I took another snort and handed the flask back. The man chuckled. "You'd give your King cheap whiskey like that? Isn't there some sort of rule about that?"

I turned to the pilot of the helicopter and leaned in, yelling a little over the sound of his engines. "If I could get a lift to the Naval Station across the way there." I pointed. "I left my truck over there." The pilot nodded and motioned with a thumb to hop in.

I climbed into Merlin Five and set my messenger bag down. The pilot looked back at me and I gestured with my finger. "Let's ride."

I looked down at MacLean as the Merlin lifted off the ground. "I'm going to want a full debriefing at our appointment in a week. Make sure you bring Will!" I tossed him the keys to Mitsu. "See if they validate parking!"

The Merlin turned then dipped its nose and accelerated eastwards. The ride was low and fast, skimming the water. Soon I was back on the ground in Scotland and in my Raptor, racing my way back to Achnacarry.

# SEVEN

## Meanwhile, Back at the Castle

At the Castle there were a few more vehicles than I remembered when I had left. I pulled up beside the M-ATV and climbed out. It was late and I was tired as hell. I was caught of guard by my bodyguards who both tackled me.

So did I miss anything while I was gone?" Duncan came out and I handed him back the Sterling. "A fine weapon, thank you, Duncan. I put it to good use and it served admirably."

"It would be my honor if you kept it."

"Thank you, Duncan. I would love to."

April whispered in my ear. It was the old Good News and Bad News routine. I listened to her good news, which was about the baby kicking her. Then the bad news.

"Q was here?"

"The Duke came hunting for you and was pretty upset. He knew something was up."

"How?"

April held up the Blue Force Tracker that was ripped out of the Land Rover. "He said to put it back in the Raptor when you got back." I took the BFT and tossed it to the same man that had installed it into the Defender, then pointed to the Raptor. "Fine, I'll send Q the message that I've finished my hunt."

I had no idea what to make of that. If he was down here, and not back in... Something was going down. Delegate and Trust, I said to myself. I shook my head. Delegate a task, trust they will accomplish it, and then take it from there.

"At first light, we're going back to Fort George."

"What? You just got back! Stay awhile... I've missed you guys!"

"I know... I know. But I really got to be back."

"Why? What's up?" Joy asked, as April turned and walked off, obviously upset. Joy looked at her and then back at me. She wasn't happy either.

"We've got some serious plans to make." I said as Joy went off to find April.

I pulled a bore snake through the barrel of the Sterling. I had the weapon disassembled for cleaning. The Sterling was a simple weapon, simple to the point of being crude. It made an AK look sophisticated. I dabbed some Slip-stream grease around the firing pin and the bolt before I reassembled it. As different as the Sterling was, I had become very fond of it. Especially how quiet it was. With the suppressor attached, it was one of the quietest guns I'd ever fired. The accuracy was pretty good too. Duncan had more than a few of these. He was no mere grounds keeper. After I got the Sterling back together and function checked it, I went to look for him.

He was at the wood pile, splitting logs with a maul. I watched the old man swing. He hit with authority. Without looking at me or turning, he knew I was there. "So you had a bit of a holiday on the emerald island?"

"Yeah, it's a great place to visit. Hopefully one day I'll go back."

"If you do, you should use a radio detonator. More reliable."

"I don't want to know how you know that, do I?"

The old man's eyes twinkled.

"You were never just a caretaker, were you, Duncan?"

The old man swung the maul one more time, sticking it into the stump he was using at a chopping block. "No."

"What did you do, Uncle?"

He jerked his head and motioned for me to follow him as he walked to the castle. I followed him into his room where he pulled down a photo album from the top shelf of a book case. It was thick and heavy, full of old photos. He started thumbing through the pages, slowly, letting me see them but not saying anything. He didn't have to. The photos told the story. He was a Commando and after the war he came back here as an instructor. He trained a lot of new commandos over the years. Class photos of his trainees filled most of the book. Many of his trainees became SAS. This was the most impressive resume I'd ever seen. I looked at old Uncle Duncan and knew that this was a man that knew where all the bodies were buried.

"Can you still teach, Uncle?"

"If you send me good students, I can teach them."

"I think you will meet my Sons soon. And some of their friends."

Duncan just nodded with his eyes closed. "It would be my honor."

I stood, "No, Sir. It's mine."

I shook his hand and looked Major Duncan Clarkson in the eye.

"Anything you need. Any time. You let me know. We're going to re-open your school."

Duncan grinned like a wolf.

# Return to Fort George

We left the next morning. As the helicopter lifted up off the ground, I looked out and saw April standing there. She looked like she was pouting. She was officially retired from the Crimson Guard, even if she would always be a sworn member. She wasn't happy about it at all but knew I retired her for a reason. She had someone more important to nurse-maid than myself. Looking at her, motherhood suited her. She looked almost majestic standing in front of Achnacarry, her hair had grown out like a lion's mane, and her breasts had swollen to go along with the more pronounced curves of her hips. She wore jeans and a sweat-shirt and kept an ACR slung across her back. She was distracting me. She had changed, but no more than I had changed. I had been letting my hair grow out long as well, and I had the beard growing out full. It helped keep the cold off. I scratched it as the Blackhawk flew me back to Fort George.

It was March now. The grey sky felt heavy, and I could smell the rain that was about to drop. When I glanced at the Blue Force Tracker, I didn't see any threats marked, and everything seemed fine. Yet I felt apprehensive. Maybe it was those crows circling overhead. I looked up and watched them. They didn't seem to be excited or agitated. They were just there. As always. I opened the door and stepped down out of the Raptor. It was as quiet as a graveyard save for the small clinking of my armor. The crows didn't seem to mind me; it didn't feel as if they were watching any more. They were just being crows. Unfortunately, I had learned to really not like those birds.

It was getting to be time to return to Achnacarry, April was going to have the baby soon. The doctors were planning on inducing labor tomorrow. Reports from Achnacarry said she and her baby were doing fine, and that April was going on a little shopping trip to gather up baby stuff. My plan was to head down there and surprise her. I had thought about calling and telling her I was coming and that I'd come with her "shopping", but popping in might be fun. I hadn't seen her or spoken directly to her these last couple months. I didn't like this. It bothered me a lot. Because regardless of relationship trauma, she had become a dear friend, and I cared for her a lot. Love? Well, in a way. Not like my love for my wife (who was still not speaking to me). Even if I dishonored myself and her, April was still... special to me. Joy was looking forward to seeing April as well, and was probably even more excited than I was. Joy gathered the packages and loaded them up into the Blackhawk.

A hunting trip and a visit to the Commando School was the official reason for the trip. Kilo was down there now, learning more about field craft and tactics. During the next training cycle, my twins would be going too.

"We're ready to go, Sire." Joy never missed a chance to rub in the royal thing. I wouldn't rise to the bait.

"Yes, of course. Saddle up, Lady Ansfrida." I motioned for the chopper to spool up with my finger in the air and tossed my backpack into the back as Joy stuck out her tongue at me.

## The Warrior Woman

April's convoy pulled up in front of a little shopping center in Fort William, a town south of Achnacarry, but the closest place with any decent shopping. Or in her case, sanctioned looting. The store was similar to a JC Penny's, featuring clothes and other nice things without being too full of themselves. Most importantly, it had infant clothes and supplies. April held her belly as she climbed out of the Excursion. The baby gave a strong kick to protest the unwanted movement. She seemed to like riding in the vehicle, with the soothing vibrations and sounds. April rubbed her belly. "It's alright, sweetheart. We're here now. Going to do a little shopping for you, get you some nice, cute little outfits and some cozy blankets to keep you snug. You'll like them, I promise!" April coo'ed to her belly and then shouldered her ACR.

She turned to her security team and nodded. "Clear it." Mother to be or not, April remained a warrior woman.

"Yes, My Lady." The soldier was curt and motioned for the team to enter. Four men with rifles up and ready quickly breached the door with a heavy knocker held between two others. The door burst open and the four men entered, going in opposite directions and flicking on their weapons lights.

After a few minutes they came back. "Clear."

The curt soldier had been one of the Royal Marines before the world went to hell. He stepped into the building and looked around then back at April. "It's safe."

April couldn't keep her ACR in front of her anymore thanks to little Kyra, so the rifle was muzzle down under her right arm. Under her left, in a shoulder holster was her M&P 9mm. The nurse assigned to attend April always insisted she leave the guns in the truck or let one of the big, hairy men carry them. April looked her and roller her eyes. "It would be mad to go around unarmed. How can I ask people to help protect me and my baby if I'm not willing to protect myself?"

The nurse was always flustered at that.

Once inside, April's warrior instincts were pushed aside, and the mothering instincts kicked into overdrive. "Oh look at these... they are so cute and tiny! And pink!"

The Marines all sighed collectively, and gave the lady space and to avoid looking directly at small pink things.

GEORGE HILL

# *Once Bitten*

Jeffry was only five when the zombies came. He tried hiding in the racks of long clothes after he watched them bite his older sister. "Stephanie, please, stop." He begged, but she didn't. She bit Jeffry's hands and arms, biting off fingers and pulled a chunk of meat out of his bicep. He screamed until he couldn't scream anymore. That was a long time ago. Stephanie had wandered off, out the back door after someone else. Jeffry just hid in the long clothes again. Dresses with bright colors. Then the long clothes weren't so bright anymore. Everything went grey. He waited. And waited. He was hungry. He wandered the store, and found all the doors were shut, and he didn't know how to open them. He moaned, but no one came. No food came. All he knew to do was to hide in the long clothes. Jeffry slept. And waited. Hiding.

April was filling her arms with baby blankets and fleece onesies. She'd filled a whole shopping cart full of things pink, yellow, and green. She found a little dress with white frills and flowers. "Oh look these little flowers! Adorable!" April turned and saw a long flowing sundress on the rack on the other side of the isle. It was the same color. "We'll match!"

She went over and pulled the dress out and held it up. "George couldn't say no to me in this."

The soft, long thing Jeffry was hiding behind was suddenly pulled up and away. Jeffry turned his head and looked. Food. Meat. Blood. Food. Eat!

April was looking around the store to see if there was a hat that might match when she felt a tug on her arm. "Huh" She glanced down and saw a little boy just as it sunk its teeth into her hand and crunched down with his sharp, little teeth. She felt the pain just as blood spurted up onto the dress she was holding. She screamed and pulled away, jerking her hand back and some of the zombie's teeth with it.

April dropped the dress, still screaming and pulled the rifle across and smashed the zed on the head before shooting it to pieces. The Marines reacted instantly to the scream. Guns up, they came running. The nurse, who had been pushing a cart full of diapers, dropped everything and stood in shock not knowing what to do. April grabbed her bloody hand and squeezed it, trying to stop the blood. She was still screaming. "No! NO! Oh No!"

The Marines surrounded her, one of them kicking Jeffry's ruined corpse in the head, knocking him away from April. Not that it mattered, the zombie had no face left and nothing inside the remains of his skull.

April was rushed out the door, into the waiting Excursion, and the convoy headed back to Achnacarry as fast as the vehicles would go. Soon the big black SUV pulled away from the slower military vehicles and roared through the Scottish countryside like a meteor.

"Hold on, we'll get you home. Your going to be alright." The Marines were telling her. They got on the radio calling Achnacarry to reach the doctors there.

"Can you start an IV?"

"Yes, we can do that."

"Good, push saline to get it started. What time was she bitten?"

"Ah, about two minutes ago."

"Drive fast." The Doctor said into the radio, looking at the hypodermic full of the Anti-zombie serum. If they could get here in time, maybe there was a chance to save April. Maybe.

## She Loves You

"Are you guys sure about the name? Kyra?" Joy asked, for the umpteenth time.

"April picked it. She said she always liked that name. That's good enough for me."

"Kinda goes with the other Celtic names of your kids."

"Not that it matters, but it does. It's a cute name."

"Any meaning to it?"

I shrugged. "I don't know. We'll have to ask April when we get there."

"She really loves you. You know that."

I looked down at my boots. "Yeah, I know."

"She has since she first saw you."

"Yeah, I know."

"Do you? Really?"

"I know.

"It's okay to show her some in return."

"I..."

"What? It's okay to fuck her, but not to love her, even a little in return? What the hell?"

"Joy..."

"What? When was the last time you even smiled at her? Called her?"

"You're not making this easy for me."

"It's not easy for her either, and she's going to have your baby. As if you needed another one, you have what, nine of them... this will make ten."

I looked at her, sitting there. She had a point. There was no reason to bring up the fact that the three girls were adopted. Instead I paid close attention to my boot laces.

"Just show her you care." Joy looked out of the helicopter at the ground below. "That's all I'm saying. I know you do. Just show her."

The drive was too long, and too much time had passed. The doc knew it even as he pushed the serum directly into April's heart. April's fever was 105 and climbing, and the bite on her hand was looking more like a third degree burn. It was blackened, with dark streaks reaching up her arm.

"My baby."

As the Blackhawk started descending, I saw people run out to meet us. The nurse, some of the Guards, and a Doctor. Something was happening, and it wasn't good. "What the hell is going on?"

"Shit." Joy growled.

Even before the Blackhawk touched down, I jumped out. "What's going on?"

"Come with us, your Majesty, please!"

I followed, the doctor was almost running. Joy was at my heels. "What's happened?"

"Lady April was bitten."

"What? SHIT!"

I burst into the room of what had been a library and was now an ER. "NO!" I yelled, but my shout didn't change reality. I ripped off my heavy gauntlets and ran to the side of the bed and grabbed April's hand. It was like it was on fire. She was tied down, arms and legs strapped to the bed-rails with heavy leather belts. It looked like some dark-age torture as April writhed. "No! No! No!" I couldn't even think straight.

She opened her eyes, "George?" April was weak and her voice was a forced grunt through clenched teeth. I could feel that she was in agonizing pain as the zombie plague was burning her out of her own body.

I rubbed her head, pushing the hair away from her face. She was pale and covered in sweat. "I'm right here." I squeezed her hand and looked at the doctors. "The serum. Did you inject her? Is it working?"

The doctor shook his head, we gave her all we had, but it was too late. I'm sorry."

"You're fucking sorry? Sorry?" I didn't know if I should shoot him or punch him.

"We're trying to save the baby now." The doctor's ever so calm voice was pissing me off and I wanted to hit him. A lot. But I knew he was doing his job. "We're going to do an emergency caesarian, it's all we can do now."

"Is the baby alright?"

"We don't know. We don't have the equipment to monitor the baby, it was supposed to get here tonight."

Helplessness wasn't a feeling I was used to. I hate being helpless. But there was nothing anyone could do to help April. She was done for. I looked at the heart rate monitor attached to April's arm. It was showing more beats than a drum solo. April's hand squeezed my own, "George..."

I looked down at her and I saw the fear in her eyes. She was almost in a panic, but holding on. As I looked in her eyes, I could see clouding over as the infection permeated her whole body. "Yes, I'm here, April. I'm here."

"I... I love you so much..."

Oh God... Why are you doing this? This is too much. I could feel tears run down my cheeks.. "I love you too, April."

"Do you?"

"Yeah. I do." At that moment, of course I did. I didn't want her to die. I didn't want her to feel this pain... this isn't the way I'd want anyone to die. From the corner of my eye I saw sudden movement and glanced up. Joy had turned and rushed out of the room, almost running with a hand over her mouth. I didn't even know she was there. I looked at the doctors and the nurse who was pulling a cart full of polished silver tools. Several of them scalpels of difference sizes, forceps, and things I didn't even want to know what they were for.

"I want to just see her..." April choked. "Let me see her first... then..." April convulsed.

"Then what?"

"Kill me."

I squeezed her hand and watched as the doctors ran a pair of shears over her clothes and pulled them open. Pants, shirt, everything.

I saw the doctor pick up the scalpel and I turned away, looking instead into April's face. I don't think she felt the pain of the cutting, she was in enough already. I held her hand as I watched her face and listened to the doctors cut.

"Looking good, color, oxygenating." Then the question I wanted answered, but couldn't bring myself to look. I didn't want to see. "Is she infected?" One doctor asked.

There was a pause and I thought time stopped along with my heart. "No, seems clean."

I heard a shrill cry as the baby started wailing.

"Let me see..." April pleaded.

The nurse brought the baby up to where April could see it. Red and wet and screaming. One of April's eyes was completely white but she still recognized the infant. "Kyra... Beautiful..." Through the pain and madness, April smiled. Then she looked at me. "Please.." She was struggling to form the words. "Take... my... life..."

I waited a moment longer for the nurse to take Kyra into the other room.

"Goodbye, April." I kept hold of her hand as I drew my pistol and pressed it against her forehead. April closed her eyes and there was a small smile that curled the corners of her lips. "Love" she said, the instant before I shot her between the eyes. I held her hand until her body stopped twitching.

That was it. She was gone.

"Love", the last words exhaled from her lips.

I holstered my sidearm and went into the other room, not looking at April's body and what we... what I had done to it. "The baby." I said.

The doctors were scared stiff as it looked to them that I was about ready to shoot every one of them. Maybe I was. The nurse had Kyra wrapped in a soft blanket, and held her close. I took a step forward, and she held the baby out to me. I took the girl in my arms and held her. She weighed nothing. Smaller than all my boys ever were. Little Kyra, now a motherless bastard. I dropped to my knees and wept holding the baby.

Everyone slipped out of the room, quietly. I didn't care. One person though, came in. She was sobbing as well. Joy put her arms around me and little Kyra and cried with me.

The nurse was able to make arrangements. She had found a young mother who would serve as Kyra's Wet-Nurse and foster-mother. Her name was Angelica Mayweather, and was rather horsefaced, but amply qualified to naturally feed an infant. She had a little infant of her own who was born at Fort George a few weeks ago. When she agreed to help, we had Madame Mayweather flown to Achnacarry immediately. Kyra was nursing even before her mother was put into the ground, into the hole I dug myself with a pick and entrenching tool. I didn't want anyone else to help.

Kilo had taken a break from his training, to come tell me that he was sorry. But I don't think he meant it. Only a few people from Fort George and Edinburgh came down. April was seen as a trouble-maker, but it wasn't her fault. It was mine. All this was my fault. If I hadn't slept with her, if I hadn't gotten Jen killed, if I hadn't... if... if... if I hadn't done... everything.

"I know you're hurting, son." Duncan said to me, quietly with a hand on my shoulder. I was sitting in the library alone with a tall glass of the best single malt stuff Duncan had. The ad-hoc ER equipment was removed, but the .45 diameter hole in the floor remained. I sat in the chair staring at the hole, wishing it was in my own forehead.

"The best thing to do is to live how your loved ones would have wanted. That's how you honor them."

I didn't say anything but swirled the amber liquid in the glass and drank down another mouthful as I looked at the old man, then back down at that little black hole in the floor. I don't know how long I was there, or when Duncan had left. But I was vaguely aware of the dark outside the windows, then the light, and then it was dark again. I didn't eat. Couldn't even think about sleeping. I sat in the chair, only getting up to piss the whiskey back out, or to open a new bottle.

When I finally left the room, it was dark out, late at night. I took a cold shower, shaved, and changed my clothes. I physically felt better, outwardly human again. But any motivation in me was gone. I laid back on the bed and finally fell asleep.

When I woke, Joy was sitting on the edge of my bed. "She has green eyes."

"What?"

"Kyra. Her eyes are bright green. They are amazing. Like perfect emeralds."

I thought about the little baby for a moment. I hadn't seen her since she was born. "How's she doing?"

"She's doing okay. As well as any baby. I suppose."

"Where is she?"

"Downstairs... she's nursing regularly now."

"Now?"

"She was having a hard time getting going, but she's doing fine now. At least that's what I'm told. I don't know. I don't know much about babies."

"I should go see her. How do I look?" I stood up.

"You look like shit."

"Great." I went into the bathroom and splashed water in my face and looked in the mirror. Yeah, I looked like crap. My face was grey, gaunt and sick looking where it wasn't racked with scars and my damned empty eye socket. I found my patch with the ruby in it and put it on. It didn't help much.

Downstairs, I was offered breakfast. "No, I want to see my baby."

"You need food."

"I need to see my daughter."

"Maybe after..."

"Where is my Kyra? Say one more damn thing other than where she is, and I'll kill you where you stand."

The nurse pointed to a door. I looked at the short lady again, up and down, then without speaking another word I turned and walked through the door.

Madame Mayweather was sitting in a rocking chair with a bare breast hanging out and a little baby up over her shoulder, patting her back. "Is that Kyra?"

"Yes, your Grace." She turned the baby and held her out to me.

Joy was right. Kyra had the most amazing bright green eyes I had ever seen, and dark hair, tinged with auburn. Just like April's. For the first time in days, I smiled.

I held the baby for a long while. I didn't know how long. When I handed the baby back, I told Mayweather to contact me should any need come up, and as soon as the baby is weaned from breast milk, which should be as soon as feasible.

Outside I found a formation. Royal Marines and Crimson Guard stood shoulder to shoulder at attention. Their faces were grim and their weapons were held at their sides. One of the men stepped forward. His name tag read Corbett and he snapped a salute. “Sire, Lady Peterson’s security detail.”

I nodded and returned the salute. Corbett stepped back into the line. I walked back and forth examining the small platoon.

“You men had a very simple task and you failed it. The Lady who was under your protection is dead.”

I walked over and stood in front of Corbett. “The first thing I wanted to do was to have you all executed.” I saw some of the men bristle or shudder. “But we can’t afford to lose men who have learned a valuable lesson. You all now know the price of failure. The cost of a slip of vigilance. But you didn’t pay for your mistakes. I did. And April did. And a little baby girl will continue to pay it for the rest of her life... never knowing her mother. But she will know each of you, and your failure. That’s the price you will pay. Each of you will be reassigned. Report to Sargent Ferguson at Fort George within four days time for your new orders. Failure to do so will result in a more dire consequence. Dismissed.”

When I left Achnacarry an hour later, it was only because I had to wait twenty minutes for the pilot to return from the firing range, which was several miles away via snow-covered dirt roads. We lifted off in a swirl of powdered snow from the rotor wash. I sat back in the seat and didn’t look down until we went over April’s tombstone. It was small and alone on the crest of a small, bald hill. From the air, it looked even smaller, and more lonely.

## Chilly Homecoming

We landed at Fort George and as soon as we touched down, Joy jumped out with her pack and weapon and started walking to her quarters. I wanted to say something, but had no idea what to say or where to start, so I let her go. We'd talk later. Above my head the Blackhawk's rotors slowly turned to stopping. The pilot went through his post flight, and I left him to it. Grabbing my pack and my rifle I turned and stood face to face with Debbie. She had a crocodile's grin on her face.

"I'm so sorry to hear another one of your whores died. That's too bad." Debbie's voice was laced with poison. I turned, ready to lash out at her and unleash my anger and frustration on her. Then I saw her eyes. She was daring me to. She wanted me to. Because that would make everything easier. And then I understood how she felt. The small death inside me that I was feeling, was what she had been feeling for a while. I wanted to be anywhere but here right now. "At least you finally have a daughter now. That should make you happy. I hope she doesn't turn out to be as much of a slut as her mom and dad was."

I walked away.

"Hey, I'm talking to you!"

I kept walking. Debbie yelled more hurtful things, but I knew I deserved them so I didn't fight... I just walked away.

In the mess hall, I sat alone with a pan of scrambled eggs, cheese on top, and blood sausage. I ate because I needed the food. I stabbed a piece of the sausage with my fork and chuckled as the juice poured out. April would have squealed at that. She hated blood sausage. Damn it April.

I put my fork down and held my head in my hands. It wasn't just April. We had lost so many good people. Those of us that had come from the US, our numbers shrank continuously.

"You have grim thoughts, brother." Musket said.

"I do."

Musket nodded and set down a pint of Guinness in front of me. "I'm sorry I didn't make it down for the burial, had I known, I'd have come. I know the Lass was important to you. She was a good girl... Is... Is a good girl. I was out hunting when the word came in. When I got back, it was already done."

"It's alright."

"No. It's not. Someone should have stood beside you."

"There was nothing you could have done, or said."

"I didn't say I would have done or said anything. Sometimes just being there is the important thing."

"Yeah."

Musket sat there, sipping his Guinness and not saying anything else. He was right.

I saw Joy come into the mess hall. She looked as bad as I felt. At the counter she took a tray and the Tavern Wenches gave her scoops of food as she went down the line. Eggs, some toast, grits, and a glass of fresh milk from the dairy cows we had gathered.

She saw me and looked down, taking a seat at another table. It was my turn to comfort someone else.

"Thanks, Musket." I said and clinked my glass against his. He nodded, sagely and took another drink.

Before I made over to Joy's table, Musket was already calling for the company of something soft and curvy. "Wench! My lap is getting cold!"

I had to chuckle as I sat down. Musket had a way of making you feel better. Joy was smiling as well.

"You don't mind if I sit here, do you?" I asked.

"No." She was quiet as she forked eggs into her mouth.

"I remember when I first met you. April and Jen. You guys scared the crap out of me."

Joy looked up for a moment before turning her eyes back to her food.

"I had talked to April about that day. But I've never talked to you about it. April had said that she was about to shoot herself until I pulled up in front of that store. I don't even remember what store it was... some book store."

"Barnes and Nobles." Joy muttered.

"Yeah, that was it." I nodded. "Jen was waiting for those guys that had run off to the mall... and you. You were just waiting for Jen."

Joy drank down some milk, almost emptying the glass. Her lip was covered in white film which she wiped off with the sleeve of her shirt. "I remember that day." She set her glass down. "I remember watching April. She had that rifle. She'd put the muzzle in her mouth and then yank it out. She did it several times. She had even taken off her shoes to see if she could reach the trigger with her toe."

"She was serious? I thought she was exaggerating."

"No. She was going to do it. It might have taken her another hour to get up the nerve."

"Did you say anything?"

"What could I say? I might have used the rifle next. We had no hope. It was obvious those idiots weren't going to come back. When you pulled up, you scared us. But then you gave us something we didn't have before. Hope."

"And now?"

"A cause."

## Sword and Mace

I stood on the battlements of Fort George and listened to something that we had not heard for so long that it seemed like foreve r. Birds singing. Gulls and other seabirds swooped down and pecked for small fish and crabs along the shore below the wall. In front of the fort, the snow had melted off, grass was growing, and spring was really here. Our Spinners had made short work of the walking dead who were out in the open. After that it was a simple matter of room clearing. Block by block, house by house, room by room, teams went through towns and cities. The cold made the zombies slow and weak and this let us save on ammo. We made good use of blades, hammers and maces. After losing April, something inside of me changed. Solace was found in my sword and mace and violence.

It seemed fitting that things changed on the first day of April. The letter from Northern Ireland set old plans in motion again. According to the letter, Ireland was under control. The IRA factions controlling Northern Ireland had fought each other to a final end, and there was now a victor. I sent a letter back, agreeing to official recognition of his rule of Northern Ireland, and to give control of the rest of Ireland to him, under the stipulation that Ireland remains loyal to me, and we work in cooperation. Basically a modern version of the feudal contract. But letters were only words on paper and that just wasn't good enough for me.

"I can't believe your going... this is crazy." Joy was against this, but I knew she would be.

"Have to. It's the only way to be sure."

"But remember the last time you went? It was a disaster."

"I wouldn't call it a disaster. Everyone got out, but no, it didn't go like I had planned."

"That's because it was a disaster."

I looked at Joy as she stood there, hands on her hips, giving me that look that she and Debbie are so very good at giving.

"This time I know where to go and who to talk to." I held up the letter. She didn't seem impressed. "We have been getting communications from Northern Ireland for some time now. And agents have reported a stabilized situation there. It's a good time to meet. The plan is that I go in, low profile, meet and greet and see if everything goes the way I like it... I recognize the new leadership of Ireland, their independence, and in turn they support us as an allied nation. With that support, I could have an additional army of about two thousand soldiers. This would be a substantial increase in man power and get us ready for the French operation."

"Yeah, I can understand it. But I still don't have to like it." Joy was fuming. Especially since she wasn't going.

"It's the only way to validate all this. I have to see for myself."

"And I'm not going, but Caroline is."

"This mission is about subtlety, stealth, and keeping a low profile. Besides, Caroline graduated the Commando School at Achnacarry, and I want to see if that training as done any good."

"I'm not going to like this, even after you do come back. You will come back."

"Of course I will."

Joy then did something I would never have expected. She threw her arms around me and gave me a hug. "You better." It was a quick hug and she turned away quickly and walked away. I watched her walk for a moment and shook my head. Joy, always the tough one, scared of the dark though, and now worried about me. Huh. I laughed to myself as I walked down to the boat.

Caroline was already on the boat waiting for me. Her bag was in the wheel house and she was sitting on the small seat looking out across the water with some binoculars. She was dressed like I was, woolen trousers, oversized wool knit sweater, stocking cap, work boots. Under the sweater was a tactical vest, armor, and her weapon hanging from single point sling, anchored with some Velcro around the barrel, keeping it tight against her body. She looked cute and altogether nonthreatening.

She was packing a H.E.R.A. Arms mod, a neat, little kit that turned her full auto Glock from a pistol into a compact sub-machine gun. It was light and compact and the same mags fed her compact pistol she kept behind her back. It wasn't a lot of firepower, but it should be more than enough.

I was packing the same weapon I went to Northern Ireland with last time. The suppressed Sterling. Backing up the Sterling was an old Commander 1911 .45 with a suppressor to match. I don't know what happened to my HK, and I didn't feel like sending out for a new one. Of course, I also had my knives. Blades which had saved me more times than I could count.

Unlike last time, I also brought a number of grenades, modified modern grenades made into "Tiger Tails" so they could be thrown farther. The best weapon I had was a good Sat-Phone with a flight of gunships on speed-dial. The phone was not one that the IRA would be able to track or locate as it didn't touch the cellular network. We had found out the hard way that it was the cell phones that allowed the scouts to track and close in on us. I wasn't going to be caught flat-footed again. I looked the part like I did last time, with the simple brown leather patch over my empty eye socket, and longer hair and beard than ever before. I didn't look like the king of anything. But then again, that was the whole point.

When I climbed aboard, Caroline untied the lines and got the boat ready to get underway.

## Back to Ireland

I flipped the switched for power, fuel pump, and ignition. Soon the boat's engine burbled to life and sat there chugging to itself. Everything looked good on the boat. I glanced back to the dock and I thought that I saw someone standing there, watching. For an instant I thought it was April. When I blinked, the dock was empty. I knew April was gone, but only from this world. Like Jen, like so many others. Like me one day. "Ghosts... too many ghosts." I pushed the throttles forward to the stops.

Who was watching, and I didn't see, was Debbie. Standing high above on the battlements. She just stood there for a moment longer and turned back to the Fort, walking slowly with her arms folded around herself.

Caroline didn't say anything, she pretended to busy herself with the boat as if we were really going fishing. We cruised for about a half hour before I looked back at her from the cabin. She was pretending not to be looking at me.

I checked the GPS, and set the course before I turned back to her and saw her glancing away again. "What?"

"I didn't say anything." She had a slight smile as she coiled a rope.

"You were thinking something."

"Well, maybe I was..."

I crossed my arms. "Out with it."

"Joy's been with you longer than I've been. She's a good fighter. You should have taken her instead of me."

"I couldn't. Dragging her along on every mission, I can't do that anymore to... people I..."

"People you what?"

I turned back to the cabin and checked the heading. I didn't want this conversation. Caroline came into the cabin. "People you love. That's what you were going to say."

"Yes."

"I know you were close to April. The way you've been acting proved that... I'd say you were closer to her than you were with Jen. And at the Commando School, I saw the grave. All of us would go by it, every day. As a reminder to not slack off. They said you dug the grave yourself. Was that true?"

"Yes. I dug it alone."

"You must have loved her a lot."

"Of course I did. She was with me since Salt Lake."

"And she was a lover."

"No, not really. We had sex once. Only once, and I don't even really remember it." I fiddled with the throttle, upping the RPMs slightly.

"Jen and April are gone, and now you fear losing Joy too. Is that why you've banished her to Ft. George."

"I didn't banish her."

"Maybe not, but it might as well be."

"She's earned some down time. April was close to her as well. Inverness is the safest place in the UK... on this side of the planet. She's protected."

"She wanted to come."

"She would have been going into harm's way for no good reason."

"I'm going into harm's way."

"You swore an oath."

Caroline held up her ruby ring and looked at it. "So did Joy."

"That's different."

"You love her, and you don't love me. So I'm expendable."

"It's not that. Not at all. You've graduated the Commando School, so I thought I'd put your training to use."

"So did a lot of other people, including Kilo."

"Again, you swore an oath. And that makes you..."

"Your mistress?"

"That makes you only one that was approved. Look, I never wanted anything like that to happen. I'm married, I have my sons. I didn't want to..."

"You never wanted to, but you took lovers. Gorgeous girls."

I turned away from Caroline. "We fought through some tough situations together, but they weren't lovers."

"I fought through some tough situations with you too. I swore my oath too."

"Swearing that oath didn't mean you were going to be..."

She cut me off, "I thought it did."

"Caroline."

"I'm not as pretty as them. I know that."

I turned back to her. "Stop this! I didn't take anyone as a lover. How come no one understands that? The CGs were not my harem."

Caroline laughed, "That was kind of obvious after you started admitting men."

"Is that what you really thought?"

"That's what we all thought."

"So why did you join?"

"I wanted to fight, I wanted be in the thick of it... doing something important." She looked down at her feet, "Being with someone important."

I looked at Caroline as she leaned in the doorway, rocking with the boat. She was pretty, in a girl-next-door sort of way. Then I realized that I really didn't know anything about her, about her life before the uprising. I remembered when I first saw her, when she was wanting to join the newly formed Crimson Guard. I remembered how she was quiet and shy, and how she'd look at me with huge eyes and then quickly turn away.

"So tell me..."

She looked up at me.

"What did you do before the zombies came?"

"Huh?" Caroline was surprised at the question.

"We've got some time before we get to Ireland. This isn't a fast boat. Why don't you tell me about you, before the world went wrong?"

She sat on an upturned bucket and looked out the window as she spoke. I had never heard her talk so much in all the time I had known her. I would never have guessed what she was before.

We could see the coast ahead of us in the moonlight. Ireland. Again. The water glimmered as we approached. We had a meeting scheduled at a location not too far away, but I wanted to get there first. So I figured two days early. Get there, recon the area, make a plan. I figured two days, because if I was them, I'd get there early to do the same. I wanted to get there earlier, to watch them do it. At least that was my plan.

## It's a Canary

It was dark as the boat motor chugged at an idle, momentum carrying the small vessel to the pier. I let the boat drift in while Caroline jumped over and started working the ropes. When the boat was secured, I looked around. This was exactly where I had landed before. Under the pier was a Zodiac, still there waiting where I had left it. The fishing nets covered it. I checked it using a red-filtered LED light while Caroline stood watch with her suppressed Glock SMG.

The Zodiac was in good shape, so we didn't need to waste time prepping it. We had other things to do. The meeting was going to be held in a small house, rather out in the open between two large fields. I had picked the spot and the time just before we left. It was a house I had passed the first time I came through, so I had an idea of what I was getting in to.

But that wasn't where I was heading now. Overlooking that house, across the field, was a taller house. If I was going to set up a sniper overwatch, that's the obvious place to put it. I counted on the Irish not to have too much imagination.

As we approached the overwatching house, we heard the soft moaning of an undead person. It was walking across the field, out in the open. As it shuffled it would moan a little at the back of its throat and then look up into the night sky as if it was expecting something.

I motioned for Caroline to get down. She crouched down and slunked up behind me in total silence. "Take it down." She breathed.

I pulled my pistol out and took aim. Something tickled the back of my mind and I stopped.

"The first time I came through here there were no zombies. Now, since we have a meeting that's going to happen here, there's a zombie." I put myself into the Irishmen's shoes. Yes, they do have an imagination. Clever.

"Just shoot it."

"Can't shoot it."

"Why not?"

"It's a canary."

"A what?"

"A canary. You know, a little yellow bird." I glanced at Caroline. Her face told me that she didn't get it. "It's sort of an early warning system. Coal Miners used to keep canaries in cages, they'd take them down into the mines with them. If there was any dangerous gas, it would effect the birds before them and then they could get out. This zombie is a canary."

"How do you figure?"

"Given our history in dealing with the undead, they think we would just take down the zombie as soon as we saw it."

"Yeah, so?"

"So... if we did, then they would know we came through the area. They are keeping an eye on it."

As we watched the zombie, I noticed something. There was a cable around one of the zombie's legs. It was tethered to a stake sunk into the ground. "Look at that. See the line from its leg? This guy was placed here on purpose."

"So what do we do?"

"Do? Nothing. We go around it."

Caroline kept an eye on the lone zombie as we went wide and made our way to the house. The door was unlocked, and inside it was very dark. Using red filters on our lights, we quickly cleared the house and found it to still be abandoned. There was an access to the attic by pulling a cord which pulled down a ladder. I climbed up.

The attic was dusty and cluttered, but large. It had been used for storage.

Boxes and trunks were everywhere. I made my way to a small window and looked out. The view was directly across the field to the meeting house. This was a perfect spot for a sniper.

Caroline came up after a few minutes. “What are we doing here?”

“I’m putting an insurance policy in place.” I finished setting the small charge and getting the radio ready. “Any food down there?”

“There was a bag of rice, but some mice got into it.”

“Might as well leave it to them then.”

“That’s what I thought too.”

“We’re done here. Let’s go.”

Caroline went back down and I packed up my gear and picked up the scraps of wire. I started down the stairs when Caroline came back.

“There’s people coming!”

“Where, how many?”

“Three guys, with rifles. Coming from the west.”

I looked out the window and saw the men. “Come on.”

We ducked out the door and headed back east. We made it past the zombie and into the treeline. From there, we watched.

The men used bright, white lights to search the house. Their progress was obvious. Beams of light scanned through the windows and panned across the fields.

On the radio, I heard their voices. “Looks like Old Patrick is still stumbling about out there.” One voice said.

“No ones been around here then. Especially not the English, or those Mericans. They shoot everything without a pulse.”

“Good Old Patrick, finally of some use.” Another voice said.

We listened for a while, tuning out when they started talking about shagging female zombies they had chained down.

“Disgusting bastards.” Caroline grumbled.

We had made our way to a small house on the coast to the north before the sun came up and spent the day listening to the men at the Overwatch House. When we heard anything interesting, we took notes. Names and places. Everything was being recorded, but the notes were helpful as to the what and when.

Towards the end of the day we had some good information. The guy we were going to meet was named Manus. He was in charge of the IRA, and had pretty much taken control over the region. He was coming, along with another man, named Jacob. He was Manus’s second in command, and he was against working with the English in any way at all. It was Jacob that had sent these three men to set up a sniper hide over-watching the meeting. If we made too many demands, conditions, or twitched wrong, or if Jacob said the code word, they were to kill me, then kill Manus. This would put Jacob in charge. He was going to use us as an opportunity for insurrection and proof to the Irish that they can’t trust us.

This meeting was for only Manus and I, with only one assistant each. We would approach the meeting place at the appointed time, on foot. Simple enough.

Jacob was going to be a problem. Caroline agreed to be ready for him. In the mean time, Caroline demonstrated some remarkable skill in cooking. Before the zombie uprising, Caroline had been the Chef in a top restaurant in Park City, Utah. Cooking had been her main love, cooking, and her RX-8 sports car. She'd race up the canyon to work, and back down to home in Sugar House. We had talked about Sugar House, the stores there, the farmer's market and the book stores. That common ground was important, even though Salt Lake and Park City were very far away. She had a boyfriend, who was also a Chef, but he proved to be less interested in her than just having a fling with another Chef from another restaurant.

Caroline had brazed chunks of fresh rabbit meat and was letting them simmer in a sauce that she made from tomatoes she had found growing unattended in a small garden. Some herbs were growing there as well, so she put them to use with the tomatoes. There was a bottle of wine that she used to cook with, even though she and I didn't drink. I don't consider Guinness to be "drinking", the stuff is practically milk, but even I don't drink it very often.

I watched Caroline work in the kitchen. She had speed and efficiency and a delicate touch with the knives. Her baggy sweater and armor were off, but near by. It was the first time I had seen her out of multiple layers of protection. She was small, almost frail, but her muscles were lean and defined. She was stronger than she looked. Her hair was brown, long, and falling to the bottom of her shoulder blades now that she had let it down. She wasn't bad looking at all, and her butt was a cute little thing. Caroline looked over and caught me watching her. She smiled and kept working.

I heard my name on the radio and was snapped back to taking notes. I wrote a brief outline of the conversation I was hearing. Manus, seemed to be in a tough position. Which is probably why he agreed to the meeting so easily. The chances of Manus walking out of the meeting alive was very slim. The chances of Caroline walking out, were even slimmer. We would have to change this.

Soon Caroline set a small, metal plate in front of me and handed me a fork made of pure silver. "They were kind enough to leave the good silver."

The food smelled wonderful. The spices and the wine-sauce were a stark contrast to the normal fare we had all been eating. When I tasted the rabbit, I had to sit back and just savor what was in my mouth. "Oh man... this... this is amazing."

Caroline smiled, "I'm glad you like it." She took a small bite and chewed it, with the smile still there with closed lips.

"If I had known you could cook like this..."

"That's why I didn't tell you before. If I cook, it's just for me... or for you. I'm not cooking for an army. Your Rosa can do that."

After dinner, I washed the plates while Caroline manned the radio, but the conversation had pretty much ended. I left the plates in the sink, clean, but in the sink. There were no dish racks to set the plates to dry in, and I didn't have a dish towel. It was well passed dark when I decided that we should call it a night.

"You want first watch or should I take it?" Caroline asked.

"You rest. I'll wake you when it's your turn."

She didn't need to be told twice. From her small pack she pulled out a poncho liner and wrapped it around her shoulders. Next thing I knew she was curled up on the couch, facing the back. She didn't take up much room on the couch that way, and within minutes she was in a deep sleep. I let her sleep until after five in the morning before I woke her. The night had been peaceful and completely uneventful. When she got up and noted the time, she gave me a grimace which almost made me laugh as I manned the couch next.

The day before the meeting, we observed Manus's men scouting the area. They placed a few zombies at different locations which looked like they would be in our line of approach. It was a three-man job.

Using my binos, I saw that the zombies were held with long poles and metal loops, like what an Animal Control officer would use to take control of a dangerous dog or something. Two men on the poles, the other man would anchor the zombies by a foot to the ground with a cable. This wouldn't hold a zombie forever, as it would soon enough pull it's foot off with repeated tugging.

A small van trundled along the gravel road, every house they came to, one or two men with AK-47's would jump out and check the house, and then they would continue.

"We're going to have company."

I looked around. We could hide, but what was going to be the give away was the clean dishes, sink, and stove. Also, the smell of cooked food still lingered. I threw open the door and a couple windows. Hopefully the breeze from the sea would take the smell away and replace it with the salt and sea-weed smell that permeated everything. Caroline caught the gist and opened some other windows and grabbed the clean dinnerware and threw them in the cabinet under the sink. We grabbed our stuff and went out the back. We ran behind an overturned row boat and crawled under it. The space was cramped under the boat, but we had enough room to unlimber our guns.

The small, white and yellow van pulled up to the house and a couple guys jumped out. One was tall and skinny and kept a cigarette hanging on his lip. He was wearing an oiled canvas jacket and dirty cargo pants. The shorter, red-headed guy had a face full of curly facial hair. He wore a military jacket and blue jeans and what looked like brand new bright red Air Jordans. They walked to the house, and the shorter man entered. The tall, smoking guy sauntered around to the side of the house and pulled out his junk and started watering the wall.

"Crudeness..." Caroline hissed. I felt her breath on my neck. From the corner of my eye I saw her hand reach up and flick the power on the EoTech holo sight on her weapon.

Short-Red came out the back door and called for the other guy. They both went back inside. A minute later, four more guys jumped out of the van. Some had more AK-47s others had Steyr AUGs. The men ran inside and we could hear a ruckus going on. Banging and crashing.

"They found something." I whispered.

"Oh crap."

"What?" I asked.

"Leftovers."

"There were leftovers?" Crap, I'd have totally eaten it.

"I left them in the fridge."

"Seriously?" I gritted my teeth. "Guys always look in the fridge."

"Always?"

"Always. Its what we do. It's like looking at women's breasts and rear end. It's instinct. We have an ingrained curiosity and hope that there might be a bacon double cheeseburger and a Coke in there. It's a psychological thing."

"Men are stupid."

"Uh huh. I'm not the one that left food in a fridge that doesn't even have power." I looked over at her and she was grinning and rolling her eyes.

The men in the house came out. Some of them walked around the house, looking around. I lifted the muzzle of my SMG and flicked the safety off. Caroline pulled her weapon into her shoulder. If we had a fight, it was going to be very short and lively. But we were not going to go easily.

A couple men took some steps toward our hiding place, but they were not looking at it. They were looking around, off into the distance. Still, I tightened my finger on the trigger as I placed my front sight in the face of one of them. I was ready to kill. *One more step.* I was thinking. *Just one more step, and it's on.* I could take three of them in one long blast before they even knew where the shots were coming from.

The tall guy came out the back door a moment later, with the container from the fridge. He had a spoon and was eating the food. We didn't hear what he said, we were too far away. But the men went back to the van and everyone piled in. As the van drove off, I moved my finger off the trigger and up onto the frame. I didn't realize it, but I had been holding my breath.

So had Caroline. She let her breath out with a sigh. "That was close."

"We couldn't have picked a more obvious hiding place." I growled.

"It was all we could get to."

"We were lucky... Damn lucky." I shook my head. "Too close." I crawled backwards out from under the boat and stood up, looking up into the grey sky.

"What are you looking for?"

"Some reason to make this meeting tomorrow."

"You wont find it up there."

"I probably wont find it all

"So we're going to go back?"

I shook my head. "No, we'll make the meeting. Come on. We need to find a new place to crash tonight. They're going to watch this place." With that, we slung our weapons and packs over our shoulders and started walking.

We headed along the rocky coast until we found another house, one that had already been searched. This was a little house, not much bigger than some good-sized tool sheds. But it was clean, and relatively warm inside. Better yet, it had a large sofa. It was all that we needed. The body that had rotted on the bed made that an unsavory option, but the sofa was only dusty. I pulled a stool over and put my feet up on it. Moments later I was falling asleep and Caroline was leaning up against me, snuggled in and pretending to sleep too. I didn't mind her pretending.

Some time later, I awoke with a start. It was dark outside and Caroline was gone. I bolted up and grabbed my Sterling. My stuff was untouched, and Caroline's stuff was still here. Her weapons, pack, armored vest, and her boots. What was missing was her. "What the hell..." I muttered.

"It's okay... I'm in here!" I heard her voice from the closet. She must have heard me.

"What are you doing in there?"

"Boiling some water. I'm using a flame and didn't want to break light discipline."

"Oh. Okay then."

"You want some tea?"

"Er... sure."

"Just a minute or two longer..."

I stretched out, trying to relax. It was a rude way to wake up, but I was definitely awake now. I peeled off my armor and took off my boots. The shirt I was wearing under the vest was matted. I peeled out of it and shoved it into the bottom compartment in the pack. I pulled out a clean AC/DC shirt and pulled it on. It felt much better. At the small sink, I splashed water onto my face. As I was washing up, Caroline came out, with a small pot of steaming water and a couple blue pouches. "Mountain House". Dehydrated food packs. They were actually pretty good. Both pouches were the "Sweet and Sour Pork". That she had food wasn't surprising. What was surprising was that she was wearing silk and lace. Pink. It was short and obviously wasn't made in her size as it was hanging off of her. She set the pouches down and poured the hot water into the cups she had ready on the table.

"Caroline.... you... look..." I stammered.

She looked up at me with just her eyes and smiled. “Tomorrow might go very badly, so I want to be comfortable while I can.”

“Ah, don’t...”

“This is what I normally wear under my fatigues. It feels good, reminds me of who I am. And the silk reduces chaffing.”

“Ah. Okay then.” I took the pack and the fork. “I love this stuff, for camp food, it’s pretty good. Not as good as what you can cook, but I’ll take it.”

“Joy had said you liked the Sweet and Sour Pork and Green Tea.”

I didn’t know what to say.

“Honey?”

“What?”

“In the tea.”

“Oh... yes...”

“You should sit down... you look like your about to fall over.”

I sat.

“The pouches are supposed to be sealed shut for 8 to 9 minutes after you pour in the water and mix. So we have a little time.” Caroline purred.

“Time for what?” I was suspicious and nervous.

I was relieved when she pulled out an old paperback. *The Grimnoir Chronicles*. I had to laugh.

“Have you read this?”

“Yeah, I’ve read everything Larry’s written.”

“Really? I love this guy.”

“Yeah, he’s a great guy.”

“I heard you knew him.”

“Knew? I know him. He’s still alive.”

“Really?”

“Oh yeah, he’s running MHI teams all across the West back in the States. He might come over to this side of the ocean. I sent him an invite to take over Portugal. Spain too.”

Caroline read *Grimnoir* while I paced impatiently for the minutes to tick by. I was hungry. I was also more than ready to get this meeting underway and be done with it.

The next morning we got ready to move out just as the sun started to peek over the horizon.

## Meeting Manus

As we approached the meeting house, I had the distinct impression that there were cross hairs on my back. Caroline clicked her tongue on her teeth as we walked. The sound of the tongue clicking and the sensation of being aimed at put me on edge. Unknowingly, one hand rested on the hilt of a knife, and in the other, my thumb rubbed the safety lever of my Sterling.

The other party approached, right on time. Two men. One was tall and broad shouldered with long hair and beard that matched my own. He wore similar clothes but had on a flat cap that was pulled low. The other man, just as tall, but slighter built must have been Jacob.

We came from both directions and we arrived at the porch at the same time. We stood there looking at each other for a moment. The tension was electric and the crosshairs on my back made me itch. I finally held out my hand, raising it slowly. "I'm pleased to finally meet you, Manus."

Manus looked at my hand for a moment, his eyes squinting like he was trying to find the trap. When his eyes came back to mine, he softened a bit and raised his own. "I'm surprised you wanted a meeting at all. Your normal routine has always been to shoot first."

"Normally, where we've gone, there hasn't been any organization or stability of any sort." I took my hand back and nodded. "But you've created both. Last time I came to Ireland the whole place was in civil unrest, but reports have it that there is now a semblance of normality."

"We've had our struggles, that is to be sure." Manus walked the side of the house and set down his MP5 against it. On the other side of the front door, I leaned my Sterling. Our seconds did the same. Jacob had a short pump action shotgun, a Winchester Defender that he set down with great reluctance. Caroline's Glock SMG leaned against my weapon.

"There," Manus said. "Let's go inside and have a conversation." He tilted his head towards the door. "King's first."

"After you, this is your Country, sir." I said.

Manus walked inside and I followed. Caroline was close behind me. I noticed out of the corner of my eye that Jacob looked back at something before he stepped in.

Manus sat at the oaken table, taking a seat on one side. I sat opposite. "Before we begin any further discussion, Manus, I'd like you to read something. For your eyes only."

I pushed a folded piece of paper across the table and Manus took it. As he read, I pulled out the small radio transmitter from my pocket and pulled the antenna up. Before Manus looked up, I pressed the button.

The sound of a dull thump reached us, some windows rattled.

"What was that?" He asked.

"That was the playing field being made even. Please, read that."

Manus went back to the note and kept reading. "Are you sure of this?" He said, looking up with anger flaring in his eyes.

"Absolutely. I transcribed everything as I heard it."

"What's this?" Jacob was starting to get flustered. "What just happened?"

"I just set off a small charge right above your sniper team. Nothing too big. Just enough to do the job."

Jacob looked out the window and across the field. The house 600 yards away had a wisp of smoke slowly uncurling from the blown-out attic window.

"Sniper team?" Manus asked. "I didn't have a sniper team. I honored the agreement."

"I did too." I said, "but Jacob here didn't."

"This is a trick. There was no sniper team, he just set off an explosive. This is a lie."

"Manus, how did I know the name of your companion here and write it down before the meeting?"

Manus looked at the note again and handed it to Jacob, "How can you explain this, Jacob."

Jacob took the note and started reading. "These are all lies!" When Jacob looked up, Manus was standing and had a Glock 36 pointed at him.

"I expected a trick today. But I expected it from the English." Manus fired a shot. The slug crashed through the bridge of Jacob's nose, expanded perfectly, then busted through the back of his skull, pulling bone and brain matter with it, decorating the wall with gore.

Caroline's own Glock pistol came out and up and pointed at Manus. I remained still, watching. Manus didn't even look at Caroline as he put his 36 on the table, well within my reach. He sat back down, heavily.

"I suspected Jacob for some time now. You only confirmed my suspicions. Call me John." He said.

"John." I nodded. "You can call me George. Now, we can start over on a better footing for both of us."

"I suppose I owe you a favor then... Your boat."

"What boat?"

"Your little rubber boat you hid under a doc. Before you start it, you will want to pull the leads off the detonator."

"You found my Zodiac."

"We did. The bomb is inside the engine housing, you'll see it."

"Thanks for the warning."

"The least I could do." John nodded and looked back over at Jacob's body. "That was my brother in law. I don't know how the hell I'm going to explain this to my wife."

"My sympathies." I reached over and put a hand over Caroline's gun, lowering it.

"I'm not sure if what you said was the truth or not... my normal reaction would be to consider it a lie."

"But you couldn't afford the risk that I might have told you truth."

"No. You put me at compromised position."

"By letting you know what Jacob was up to, I took you out of a compromised position. I put you in a stronger position."

John Manus sat there, leaning back in his chair looking at me.

"I need you in a strong position, John."

"You need?"

"Yes. I need. Ireland is yours, John. Not just Northern Ireland... all of Ireland. There is no one left to oppose you now and Southern Ireland almost completely depopulated. It's all yours. And I officially recognize you as Lord of the Irish."

"On what condition?"

"None." I leaned back in my own chair. "Other than official recognition in return, no conditions. It's done."

"What do you want, King George... the Ogre King?"

I smiled at the nickname. With that little casual statement, John just told me that he was just as well informed about me as I was of him.

There's lots of things I want. But from you, I only want friendship."

"You don't want Ireland?" John was cautious.

"I'm part Irish, part Scottish... But no, I have no desire to rule Ireland. And I don't want England to rule Ireland again. In fact, my headquarters is in Scotland. England is, you could say, under Scottish rule now."

John chuckled. "If only my grandfather could have heard you say that."

"Since we're friends now... I could use some help."

"Oh?" John raised an eyebrow and stood.

I stood as well, I wasn't going to have him above me. "More of an invitation really. I'm planning on throwing a party. In France, and I think it would be great if you could come over and play with us."

John laughed and held his hand out for me to shake. I took it and pulled him into a back pat. "That sounds like a good time. I'll have to check my date-book." John's laugh was a wide, open, head back laugh.

"I think the future looks brighter now." I said.

"I've got some things for you. A couple gifts." John said with a smile.

"That's completely unnecessary." I objected.

"No. Please, it's my honor. A celebration of our accord. Their coming now."

From the distance, I could hear an engine. A small Nissan truck approached. I could see two people in.

"If it's a hot meal... that would fantastic."

"This is better than a hot meal... for your brother, 'Musket'. I don't think you will personally like it."

The Nissan pulled up and in the back was four large kegs. The Guinness logo was stamped on them. The guys in the truck stepped out, and it was hard to notice that one of them wasn't a guy. She was short with long, black hair. Once the kegs were off loaded from the truck, the girl came over. She stood in front of me and glanced over to John.

"This one is for you. I understand you only trust female body guards... attractive ones. Much like the late Colonel ."

"?"

John laughed again. "Just joking... but it's true, no?"

"It just worked out that way."

"I can imagine. This is Sinead. She's well trained, and loyal." John turned to the girl. "Sinead, this is George, the King of England, former President of the United States, current invader of France, and a friend of Ireland and myself. You are now his, to serve as he sees fit."

"Yes, Sir." She said to John then looked back to me.

"John said you were trained. How so?"

"I spent 3 years with the Óglaigh na hÉireann and then the zombie outbreak happened."

"The Óglaigh na hÉireann... Ireland's Army? What did you do while you were a soldier?"

"EOD then Intel."

"Really? EOD? I've a friend that's EOD, that's a tough field."

John leaned in and whispered. "She's the one that rigged your little rubber dingy."

"Most of the time you take the direct approach. Finding the boat was easy." Sinead said with a grin.

"I like her." I said to John.

Sinead looked me up and down. "I like you too... but the full beard doesn't suit you. With your patch it makes you like borderline insane."

"That's just what I thought too." Caroline interjected. "Oh, and pick up is on the way."

"No one likes the beard?" I said to myself out loud.

"Don't ask me, I'm a biased jury." John said scratching the sides of his thick beard.

"John, I have a helicopter…"

"Three." Caroline corrected me.

"...Helicopters coming to pick me up. You don't mind if they enter Irish air space, do you?"

"Are they armed?"

I nodded.

Caroline said "Heavily."

"I supposed that's fine... you wouldn't hurt your new friend after he just gave you such wonderful treasures."

"No, of course not."

Caroline turned away and tapped some keys on her little PDA device. She turned back and said "Three minutes."

John walked back over to the house and picked up his rifle and the shotgun and took them to the truck.

"You really don't like the beard?" I asked Caroline.

"No, not so much. The goatee looks good on you though."

"I think so too." Sinead said.

"So other than being a cute, bomb-making blunt person... what else can you do?" I looked at the dark-haired Irish girl. She was late twenties, early thirties, serious looking, and had an AUG slung tight across her back.

"I can sing."

"That's not what I meant."

"I've killed over twelve hundred of the undead."

"How many not undead?"

She looked down. "Too many."

I looked at Sinead, up and down, taking everything in and gauging every word she had said and how she said it. "You're an assassin."

She suddenly looked back up to me, into my eye, and I knew I'd nailed it. I looked over at John who was getting into the Nissan. "John, why did you give me an Assassin?"

He called out with a grin, "Because I don't trust her. She's dangerous. She's your problem now." He shut the door and the little pick up pulled out, heading west, the way it came.

I could hear the choppers coming. "Is that true? You're dangerous?"

"Not to you, uh, Sir." She had a pain in her eyes. "I follow orders. Your orders now."

"There something you need to tell me?"

Sinead glanced over at Caroline. She was hesitant. "Sinead, this is Caroline. She's one of my Crimson Guard. The rubies she wears, the nose piercing, the eyebrow piercing, earrings and the ring on her finger... The rubies mark her has my most trusted of soldiers. The ring on her finger marks her as one that is personally sworn to me. I trust her with my life, as others in the CGs are trusted with the lives of my loved ones. Since she is in this inner circle... anything you can say to me, you can say in front of her. She will of course brief the others in that inner circle of the Crimson Guard, if it's important."

Sinead took a step back. "It's not something I wanted to talk about."

"What happened?" I said in a tone that meant I would have answers, now.

She clinched her jaw, and I saw a proud defiance in her eyes. "Some of Manus's lieutenants tried to rape me."

"Go on."

"I killed them."

"How many was some?"

"Four."

"Was it necessary?"

"I thought so, yes. Considering that they were trying to rape me without my consent."

"Then what's the problem?"

"Manus was the one with the problem, it was his friends that I killed."

"Ah, I see." I turned around as the first helicopter flared and landed perfectly. The other two, Apache gunships, flew circles around the area. They reminded me of huge wasps, sleek and hanging with weapons. England had purchased a great many Apaches from the US and even had a facility that built them locally.

Crewmen jumped out of the chopper and I pointed to the kegs. "Get those loaded."

"Yes, your Majesty!" The men dutifully and eagerly went to load the kegs as soon as they saw what they were.

But before we climbed into the Super Puma, we had one thing to do. "Sinead, I have your first order."

"Yes, Sir?"

"First off, I am now your King. So, please refer to me in such manner."

She bowed her head. "Sire."

"Good. Now..." I cleared my throat. "I need you to take off your shirt."

"If your Majesty wants to see my tits..."

"Your back. We need to see your back."

She looked at Caroline. "It's okay, I'll explain why on the helicopter once we get going."

Sinead pulled her AUG off and handed it to me before opening her vest and then pulling all her clothes off above her waist. She stood there with her small breasts pointed at me. She was proud and didn't blush. I twirled my finger to indicated that she turn around and she did, pulling up her hair.

On her back were markings, but not what we were looking for. A large Celtic cross was tattooed up her spine.

"Very nice." Caroline said. "I like the ink work."

"Thanks, I got it in Tralee." She said, pulling her shirt back on and taking her rifle back. As she was climbing into the Super Puma she looked at Caroline. "You have any ink?"

"Yeah I'll have to show you sometime."

"So, what was this about?" Sinead asked with a smirk, "If you wanted to see my tits you could have just bought me a drink."

I shook my head and climbed into the helicopter as I nodded to Caroline and then to Sinead. Caroline rolled her eyes and started to explain the cuttings and marks to our new team member.

The flight back to Inverness was direct as the helicopter was fitted with external tanks. The escort birds however had to peel off as they were getting low. They headed to their own airfields while other helicopters took up positions. Long, sleek-looking choppers that looked like Air Wolf, but slung with as much firepower as an Apache.

When we landed at Inverness, there were people waiting. Joy stood out from the rest, as she was the only one not in armor or a uniform. She was wearing a tactical thigh rig, with plenty of magazines on her belt. *That's my girl.* I thought.

The doors of the Super Puma slid open and crewmen jumped out. There were hand-trucks ready to take the kegs. "Make sure Uncle Musket gets one of those for his own personal use... where is he?"

"Last report he was seen heading deeper into Germany with some big dude that looked like the Techno Viking."

"Fine, well, put it in his quarters as a welcome back gift for whenever he checks back in."

I turned to Caroline, "Find Sinead a room, show her around and... I'll see you guys later."

"Sure thing, my Lord." Caroline smiled and winked at me as she jumped out. Sinead followed, giving me a look and then running after Caroline. I grabbed my weapon and pack and stepped out of the chopper. Debbie was standing there. Her eyes were filled with fire.

"I saw that."

"Saw what?"

"You know what I saw."

"What you mean, Sinead? The Irish insisted I take her with me."

"The little Irish girl isn't what I was talking about. She's short, flat chested, and needs a sandwich... she's not your type."

Debbie turned and stormed away.

"Hey, not even a welcome home?" I called after her. Debbie flipped me off without looking.

"Welcome home, your Majesty." One of the crewmen said.

"Shut the fuck up!"

"Yes, my Liege."

I shot him a glare and he grinned as he hooked up a fuel line. I started walking back to my quarters, Sterling in hand and pack over my shoulder. This wasn't going to end well.

As I walked to my quarters, Joy fell in beside me. "You came back."

"Told you I would. Anything happen while I was gone?"

"We received another letter, my Lord." Joy handed me the letter. It was heavy parchment, sealed with a thick, wax seal.

"When did this arrive?"

"Just this morning."

I tucked it into my vest and continued on to my room. I threw my gear down on the bunk and pulled the letter out and set it on the small table under the window. Once I got cleaned up and changed into some fresh clothes, I pulled out a knife and slid it under the wax carefully opening it. What I read, made me sit down in my high-backed wooden chair. I pulled the table closer to me, as it was far easier than moving the chair. Under the seat of the chair was a large stone. I didn't really care for the chair all that much, but I liked the rock.

*"To: His Highness King George, Master of the Realms.*

*From: His Highness, Sir Yancy Gunn. Master of the Gunn Clans and last Heir of Her Majesty Mary "Queen" of Scotland.*

*Subject: Freedom.*

*Your Highness, may you live for ever.*

*It has come to my attention that you are in desperate need of warm bodies, equipment, and support information concerning France and other locales. I offer to you our full-fledged loyalty and support as we did for Sir Winston Churchill back in the day. You will find in these files the latest tactical and strategic information, along with radio frequencies and codes for digital communication setups with our databases.*

*I also offer to you the use of one thousand fully trained and battle hardened troops of my Highland Guard of The Claymores, one hundred Diviners of Wisdom, twenty hand-picked Black Ops Specialists, and my very close friend and Adviser Sir Sean. I do not give his last name due to secrecy you understand. But he has been partial to the nickname 'Gunn-guy'. He will contact you directly once the data connections and codes are made secure.*

*Signed,*

*His Highness, Sir Yancy Gunn. Master of the Gunn Clans and last Heir of Her Majesty Mary "Queen" of Scotland."*

I read the letter three more times. This was it. This promise of fealty was a huge boost. I called for my cadre and had Sarge read the letter out loud. When he finished, there was stunned silence for a few moments, then cheering. This was indeed a big boost. Not just to our strength, but to everyone's morale. Spirits were up.

"This is good news, but maybe I can put a cherry on top." Sarge said with a sly grin as he hit his fist against his Roman style armor.

"What do you have up your sleeves?"

"We had some new arrivals from the states."

"Oh? Anyone we know?"

"You remember a Lt Jackson?"

"Jackson? Police, Air Force or Guard?"

"Cadet."

I shrugged. "No, not so much."

"You should. You saved her life. Or so she says."

"Jackson you said? Ah! She was an ROTC Cadet, got shot. Yes, I remember her. How is she?"

"She got better. She's now CG. She's going to be going down to Achnacarry soon."

"Good, good."

"And there is some radio talk show host that came out. Walters... Mark. Said you knew him. You remember him?"

"Mark? Awesome. Where is he?"

"We have him and his family at Castle Stewert, the one on the way to Inverness."

"Good, good."

"He wants to be addressed as Lord Walters."

"Absolutely. That's fine. He can have the Castle Stewert and the surrounding grounds."

"That's very generous."

"Well, he's a friend. Make sure he's armed. Oh, let's have that keg of Guinness from Musket's room sent over as a welcoming gift."

"What about Musket?"

"We'll get him some more when he gets back. Now. We have some serious business to do."

"Uh, Musket is back. He's already tapped that keg. He's been in his quarters ever since."

"Fine. We'll get Mark a keg sent over as soon as we can."

"Right on. Okay, what's this important business?"

"Plan out how best to invade France."

Sarge grinned.

## Attack Plans

Before we could tackle France, we had to have some support structure, and our supply logistics needed to be revamped. This was assigned to Musket. The task might have seemed strange, but the reality was that Musket was able to get things done, make things happen to get what he wanted where he wanted it and when he wanted it. Even down to the girls he had serving it.

In three weeks we had food and fuel and all manner of supplies laid out and ready to go in organized supply trains. I wouldn't have believed it if I hadn't seen it several times before. Once again, Musket proved his metal.

We had six medical personnel at Fort George and three in Edinburgh. If we rolled out to France with all of nine medics, this would be a disaster with all our people, a thousand Gunn Clan and two thousand Irish. We needed more medics on board. This meant we had to go recruit some people out of their comfort zone.

I left my quarters and walked out across the fort's grounds. There was a hospital we were sending scavenged supplies and food to outside of Coventry down in the West Midlands. I think it was time I paid them a visit. As I walked, Joy fell in lock step. With her was Caroline and Sinead.

"Where are we going, my Lord?" Joy asked as if she already had gear and supplies ready.

"Coventry." I said.

Joy repeated it into her radio. "Coventry."

I heard two clicks in the radio and up ahead I saw the large Kestral helicopter and the pilot start up the chopper. It had large fuel tanks hanging under stubby wings to give the bird more range. It was fueled and waiting. When I got to the chopper, I looked in. Door guns were loaded and the Crew Chief was smiling at me. Under the seat was my battle pack. I looked at Joy who just winked. Turns out she did have everything ready.

"Am I that predictable?"

"No, not at all." Caroline said. "We didn't know the destination."

"We're going to visit the hospital there."

"I didn't expect that." Sinead muttered.

"Anyone we know a patient there?" Joy asked me then called into the radio. "We'll need four more riflemen to the King's Helicopter."

"I hope not. This is a recruiting trip." I said as I looked around the fort and saw men running our way with rifles and packs in hand.

"We're almost there, Sire." The pilot said.

"Have you been there before?" I asked him.

"Absolutely. I dropped off a load of Squadies two weeks ago. The place is a wreck, but Miss Pix is putting it back together."

I watched the ground roll past below us. Up ahead I saw the city, but we skirted to the left and headed to a large building complex. University Hospital Coventry. I only knew it by the stream of requests that came through Fort George, and that some of the medics at Achnacarry were from here. It actually had a working MRI and Radiology department. How it was working, had my curiosity. We didn't have electricity working to this area yet, so they made their own.

We slowed down and circled the area. Door gunners were gripping their weapons, scanning for threats. I saw the big hospital landing pad. Right where the "H" was, there was the tail boom from a Life Flight bird sticking up out of it, like some sick piece of modern art. The area around it looked scorched. No need to ask what happened here. I noticed several trucks with trailers lined up. The trucks were full of cut wood.

There were burned out cars around the parking lots, and some of those cars were pushed up to form a wall, like how you push snow out of the way to clear a lot in the winter. In the middle of the parking lot were several large tents.

"What are the tents for?"

"Most of the hospital is burned out." The pilot said as he slid the helicopter over the building to set it down in the almost completely empty employee parking lot.

The CG Riflemen we had in the helicopter bounded out and checked the area as soon as the wheels hit the ground. Once it was safe, the men nodded back to the helicopter, and the pilot shut the engine down. I dismounted and started walking to the building. Black streaks rose from the upper floor windows of half the building. A stream of smoke rose from the far end.

A man in a white lab coat ran out. He wore thick, rubber gloves and boots with heavy goggles on top of his head. He looked like some sort of mad scientist or Doctor Horrible. He had an old Enfield .303 in one hand. The CGs with me snapped up their own rifles. "Drop your weapon, Sir. Nice and slow."

The man in the white coat stopped and held up his empty hand. "Yes, yes." He lowered the rifle and set it down. "Don't shoot me!"

I stopped in front of the man. "I'm George. Here looking for some volunteers."

"George?" The man looked at me, then at Joy and Caroline. Sinead grinned at him."

"Your the new K, k, king?"

I nodded. "That's right." Joy said for me. "And you are?"

"Knowles, Roger Knowles, your... Lordship?"

The man was scared for some reason. "I don't imagine that you are the one in charge here." I said.

"No, not me. I'm just hired help." Knowles looked increasingly nervous.

"What do you do here, Roger?" I asked him.

"I'm a doctor." He said as he tried to hold his chin higher and his chest out.

"That's like saying you're a scientist. Doesn't tell me anything. What kind of doctor are you?"

"Pediatrician."

"That was before the world went to hell. What kind are you now?"

"Uh, I guess every sort, if you put it that way."

I nodded. "I can imagine. So who is running the operation here, Roger?"

"That would be Miss Pix, your, your Holiness."

"No, I'm not Clergy, Mister Knowles... Miss Pix, eh? I've heard the name before. Is she around here?"

"She's inside."

"Take me to her."

We followed Roger Knowles inside. Joy and Caroline on either side of me, Sinead behind, and three of the CGs following. The fourth stayed with the chopper and crew.

"Where's Pix?" Roger would ask people he passed, they all said the same thing. "She's at the reactor."

*Reactor?* I thought. *Is that how the hospital is running?*

As we continued down the hallways, Roger pulled his goggles down over his eyes and soon we found why. The hallways down here were covered in soot. Smoke hung in the air, and the rooms were all abandoned. Soon we could hear voices. A man's voice and a woman's voice.

"Then you are just going to have to solder the pips again, don't you think?" The woman's voice carried out of a blackened room. We stopped as a short figure in a bright red jump suit stepped out of the room. She wore boots and gloves like Roger, and also wore goggles over her eyes. She had chocolate skin with long raven hair, and a crooked grin crossed her face. She walked right up in front of me and looked up into my face with one fist against her hip. She had no fear of me or anyone with me.

"Roger, someone left this rotten, old King in my hallway. Be careful not to get any on you."

"You must be Pix." I said, looking down at her.

"You can call me Nivi." She said.

"Having trouble with your reactor?"

She cocked her head and just looked me. "Yeah. Take a look."

We went in the room, and the smoke was stinging my eye. Inside was a gigantic boiler built from the trailer of a tanker truck. Under it was constructed a gigantic fire box with a man that would stoop to pick up a new log, kick a lever with his knee, then throw the log into the fire just before the door slammed shut again. Up above, hundreds of lines of copper pipes ran in and out and around the boiler.

From one junction, a finger of steam was shooting out and giving off a whistle like a tea kettle.

"This is our reactor." Nivi Pix said. "We use the reactor as some have chosen to call it, to heat water... we get hot water of course, which is nice... and we use steam to turn the turbines, those are in the other room over there, to generate electricity.

I looked around. "So the hospital is steam powered."

"Most of the time." she said.

Nivi gave us the tour of the place. "So what did you do before the uprising?" I asked her.

"Oh, I was a nurse."

This took me by surprise. "You were just a nurse?"

"Just? Just a nurse?" She gave me a "Huh" and started walking a bit faster.

"I didn't mean it like that, Nivi. That came out wrong."

"Well, I wasn't a nurse here. I used to work at Primary Children's Hospital in Salt Lake City."

"Salt Lake? Really?"

"For reals." She stopped and turned. "Are you the same George Hill that nuked Salt Lake?"

I shook my head. "It wasn't a nuke."

"Well, I'd like to go back home one day so I hope you didn't tear it up too much." She started walking again. "Some friends of mine came out here for a little Vay-Kay and well, all the flights home got canceled all the sudden. I've been stuck here ever since."

"What about your friends?"

She looked down. "They didn't make it."

"So how did you end up running this hospital?"

"My friend Ashley got hurt pretty bad and I brought her here. No one was doing anything but going crazy. Someone had to grab the reigns, so I did."

The more I talked to Nivi Pix, the more I was impressed and the more I liked her. Especially when she ran out of pleasantries and turned to me. "Okay now, Mister Governor of Utah, President of the Confederated Western States, President of the United States of American, King of England." Her eyes flashed as she spoke, "What do you want with me?"

I smiled down at her. "Just you of course, oh, and as many as can be spared of your people who are good at handling trauma."

"What?"

"I need medics."

"As many as can be spared, you said."

"Yes."

"I can handle letting go..." Her wheels were spinning in the wrong direction.

I held up my finger, "We need you and the very best people you have. Medicine and Surgeons, experienced ER people, those that can handle stress and trauma... we need all of them."

She looked at me with one eye squinting. "What are you up to?"

"Oh, nothing much... just a trip to France."

She squealed and did a little dance, and I knew she was in.

# NINE

## D-Day

It was only two weeks later when I was once again standing on the battlements of Fort George, looking out over the water, and watching the seabirds. I turned my eyes from nature, to a more serious business.

The Merlins and the Blackhawk where getting prepped. Apache attack helicopters were already gassed up and loaded, and in a few moments they were going to head out. Ground vehicles were still being loaded onto the landing craft.

I looked for Joy and found her checking on the weapons of the Ford Raptor, my personal truck and assault vehicle. She was about to have it loaded up on the landing craft.

"Are you sure you want to do this?" Sarge was always the voice of reason.

"No, Neal... I don't want to do it... not a bit." I shook my head.

"Then why are you?"

"Has to be done."

Sarge nodded. "If you wait till summer, I'll have 20 more recruits ready to go."

"If we wait, we'll be stronger... but so will the Adversary. At least now, we have a slight advantage."

Neal coughed. "And what advantage is that?"

"They think we're waiting till the summer." I looked back over my shoulder at the gallows Uncle Musket had built. Swinging from the rope was the body of the spy that had been informing on us. She was just 16 years old. The scarification was hidden under her long hair. Her name was Victoria, one of the first rescues. She had been playing us from the beginning, recruiting the others that we had found due to their overt actions.  Her's were the quiet whispers from the shadows that haunted us.

Neal saw me look back at the body of Victoria, and his shoulders sagged. He looked down and closed his eyes. Neal had found her himself. Trained her with others, including my own sons. And he never picked up on it. How could he? Who would have guessed? She was just a girl.

"She was turned before you found her, Sarge. She was planted."

"She could have..." Sarge shook his head. "We could have brought her back."

"There's a lot of Could Haves and What If's... but what happened, happened of her own choice. At least we used her to our benefit one last time."

"A small comfort." Sarge looked down at his feet.

"I'm just glad you're coming on this one. I need all the help I can get."

"I always wanted to see Paris."

"Really?" I said. "I Never pictured you as the romantic type."

"I'm not. I just want to take a piss on the Eiffel Tower."

I threw my head back and laughed. "Then let's get going!"

Sarge and his woman climbed into his assigned Merlin. He gave me a thumbs up and smiled. My team and I climbed into the MH-60M Blackhawk, which was fitted with the external tanks and rocket pods. I looked at the pilot, JJ, who was already strapped in and had the bird preflight checked and ready. He looked back at me, "You sure you don't want to fly this one?"

"I'd love to, JJ but kings get driven everywhere they go." I said while tapping the black leather patch with the ruby set in the center.

"I'm sure you could talk to someone about flight regulations."

"It would be unwise to break the rules on this one. Maybe if I was just flying solo. Besides, I trust you to fly us smooth and safe."

"Will do just that, Ogre King." JJ pulled up on the collective, lifting the powerful helicopter up into the air. Within minutes the airspace around Fort George was filled with helicopters. Some gunships, the rest filled with troops. Below us, the ships were steaming at full power, leaving long wakes behind them. Patrol boats, landing craft, and former British Navy cruisers, Destroyers, and the HMS Bulwark.

The invasion of France was now underway.

## Taking the Beachhead

I looked over the pilot's shoulder as we approached France. The coastline spread out before us, while the small fleet of miscellaneous ships crashed through the waves below us. Landing craft headed straight for the beach, while support ships took up their positions. Brownwater vessels peeled off, heading to the inlets to drop off special teams.

"Feet dry in one minute, Sir." The JJ spoke in cool tones, but I saw the small tremor in the hand holding the cyclic. I could feel the tension in him through the helicopter.

I placed my hand on his shoulder, trying to be reassuring. “Excellent! The sooner we get on the ground, the sooner...” My pep talk was cut short. We were close enough to the shore now to see it clearly. The beach crawled. Thousands of zombies lined the beaches, waiting for us.

“Ogre to all units. Weapons free. Clear a path, boys.”

As soon as I said this, the support ships opened fired with guns and rockets. Our cruiser had turned broadside, and its five-inch guns swiveled around to take aim. I could almost feel the concussions from the air. The radio freqs filled with chatter.

I looked out the side of the Blackhawk at Wizard Three and gave it a thumbs up. Sarge signaled back as his helicopter peeled off, heading to their objective. Between the Blackhawk and the Merlins, Apache gunships dove in on attack runs, each one sending out lances of smoke from their rocket pods.

From the shoreline rose great fireballs. Some were explosions that sent undead bodies flying in every direction, some whole, some in pieces. Other fireballs flew out across the water, hitting boats and immolating everything on board with demonic fire. I saw one of the Apaches stop in mid-air like it had run into an invisible wall, its cockpit crushed. The gunship fell gracelessly to the waves below, just missing a landing craft.

Over the radio, some of the chatter turned to screams as the LCs hit the sand and undead started to board almost instantly. Zombies had been laying in wait under the sand.

As we crossed the sand, I saw one LC drop its ramp as the LAV surged forward. Zombies were crushed below its wheels as the turret swung side to side firing at everything. A Red Eye in front of it started to raise its hands. Salt spray and blood splatter started to lift off the LAV. The gunner in the fighting vehicle had no time for the Red Eye’s magic and hit it with a single 25mm round to its chest. Chunks of undead flew everywhere, and the LAV rolled over and past the litch as if it had never existed.

Armored men took the beach with sword and gun. I saw one of my friends, Mark Walters, weapon in each hand, cutting a swath through the zombies with his sword and blasting others out of reach with a Krinkov. You can’t expect him to stay out of the action.

The port of Calais was in front of us now. Before we could take the city, we had to take the port. We needed to land more men and equipment and that required bigger ships than what could land on the beach. The zombies were thinner here at the port, but there was still plenty of targets for us.

Next to me, Joy opened up with her IAR, supporting the door gunners who were firing the miniguns almost constantly. I felt the Blackhawk flair as it neared the ground. It seemed as if the nose went almost vertical before it leveled and touched down. Joy was out first, and I was right on her heels. Four more birds landed at the same time and everyone spread out. The undead were thinner here now, but that could change quickly. I directed snipers to points of advantage. Paul, who went by “FMJ” and his spotter, were my personal snipers and I wanted them up high. If I called a shot, I wanted that .338 Lapua to be able to hit it. I pointed. "Position yourself up there."

Paul hefted his Accuracy International and gave me a nod before he turned and ran for the large crane that would give him complete coverage of the whole area. Across the port was the ferry terminal, and I could see one of the ferries was still docked.

"Get that boat off my dock! I want it out of there. I need that dock cleared." I pointed at the offending vessel and one of the Crimson Guard turned around to get a better look before calling orders on his radio.

A moment later he turned back to me, "Sir, the Gunn Clan is moving on it right now."

"CONTACT!" One of the CGs yelled and instantly shots rang out. I brought up my old Remington 870 Police shotgun and started picking my shots. Normally, I'd not have bothered at this range, and, with the shear number of zombies that came running between shipping containers, but the fancy HE shells we had found needed to be put to use. One shell could take out half a dozen zeds, and I had eight in the gun, on tap. It would do just fine for now. If the undead got too close, I had my blades, as always. Overhead I heard a distinctive noise.

Over the normal gunfire, I heard the high-speed shriek of an electric-powered Gatling. Then came the long, bright finger of fire. It reached down and touched the mass of undead, carving gashes in their ranks, shredding zombies everywhere that orange glowing finger touched. To help the gunfire, I fired my grenades in rapid succession, and while they were no where near as potent as a 40mm, it made quite a mess.

Some of the undead moved with a coordinated purpose, so I knew there was a thinking mind behind it. I grabbed my Swarovski CTC 30, extended it, and pulled it up to my eye. The spotting scope gave me a vivid picture of the zombie horde. There, wearing a green footballer's jacket, a Red Eye. I clicked my mic, "Paul, Red Eye, wearing a green jacket, near the orange shipping container!" I said, dropping the fancy spyglass back into its pouch and shoving more HE shells into the shotgun.

"Roger that, target in sight... on target... sending."

I looked in time to see the Red Eye's head explode. Even from this distance, it was apparent: .338 Lapua is not a gentile round.

"Good shot." I said, into the radio.

The radio clicked twice, signaling Paul's acknowledgment.

"Reloading!" Joy called out as she executed a speed reload with the IAR and 100-round Surefire magazines faster than most guys could run a plain M-4. While she slapped her bolt release I pulled the trigger a few more times, exploding the undead who were clustering in groups. Stupid zombies just don't pay attention to intervals.

Soon the surge of flesh eaters had abated. As I was reloading again, I noticed the ferry was pulling away from the dock. A few minutes later, other ships were coming in, these filled with military vehicles. I watched as they unloaded. Some trucks, APCs, armored cars, and some others that I was particularly glad to see. They were wide, squat, tracked, and completely menacing: Challenger Main Battle Tanks. Calais was ours already. The undead just didn't know it yet.

Units that had taken the beach moved through the city as units from the port put the undead into a vice grip. Thanks to the heavy armor, we swept the city, and, within hours, Calais was mostly under control. We didn't do a door-to-door sweep, but the streets were cleared in our containment zone.

The roar of airpower overhead almost broke my concentration on the line of vehicles coming off the beach in the distance.

"Status reports on Task Force Bravo and Charlie."

"Task Force Bravo is moving in on Laon-Couvron. Sir, they have made contact with remnants of the Chasseurs Alpins. They've now joined with Bravo."

"Ah, the Alpine Hunters... this is good news... how many of them are left?"

"About 140 of the 7th Battalion."

I nodded. Less than a company, but enough to make two over-strength platoons. This was good news indeed. Especially since they didn't resist our trespassing.

"Sir?" One of my CGs turned and looked at me.

"Yeah, what's on your mind?"

"Laon-Couvron used to be a US Air Force Base, but it was closed. Why are we taking it and not another base?"

"Remember how I used to be the President of the United States?"

"Yes, Sir."

"Well, one of the strategic plans in place was to maintain that base. Which includes stockpiles of equipment and supplies: food, fuel, and ammo. We've also directed military units that couldn't make it to Ramstein, to rally there."

"Who do we have there?"

"I don't know. That's why I sent Q there straight off." I lowered my scope and looked at the CG. "Now, what about Task Force Charlie?"

"MacLean and the 'Master Sargent' should be another 20 minutes before they reach Paris-Orly."

"Good. Things are going according to plan better than I could have hoped."

"Vehicles approaching, Sir."

I turned and looked to the west and saw familiar vehicles racing towards us. A Ford Raptor, an M-ATV, and a battered Humvee. Running with the Trio was a pack of Mastiffs and Ridgebacks.

"Very good."

When the Raptor pulled up to me, the door opened and Kilo climbed out grinning. "Need a lift, Old Man?"

Joy looked at me with her crooked grin, "You gunna let Prince Kilo talk to you like that?"

I sighed. "I can tolerate a lot of insubordination from those I love."

"Did she just call me a Prince?" Kilo looked struck.

"She sure did," I said while I climbed into the driver's seat. "And you sure are, so get used to it."

"That was below the belt, Joy." Kilo said.

Joy smiled as she climbed into the Rapor and took shotgun. Kilo took the turret position and readied the .50 caliber. The rest of my CGs piled into the other vehicles.

"Can I call you old man?"

"If you do, I'll have to spank you."

"Promise?"

As we pulled out, a flight of Westland Apaches moved forward overhead, scouting out and clearing the way with chainguns and the occasional rocket.

## Roadblock Ambush

The A26 was in a state of ruin with abandoned cars. Many of them were left with the doors open as if the occupants just bailed out of them and ran. A lot of collisions and cars that had been driven into the shoulders. Overtuned cars scattered across the highway like punctuation marks.

A closer look revealed that many of the cars were riddled with bullet holes. A few of the cars that looked harder hit, were still occupied with corpses. Some were fully decomposed, others half dragged from vehicles and were victims of post mortem animal feeding. Bones, stains, shredded fabric. Any survivors in the area never came back here.

"Boss, you seeing this?" Caroline said from the turret seat.

"Someone lit them up." I replied as I wove the Raptor through the gaps. "I would like to know why."

After a few hundred yards, we found the reason. A road block across both lanes. Military vehicles were parked bumper to bumper behind a hasty built barricade. Some of the bodies here were wearing uniforms. FAMAS rifles were scattered amongst the corpses.

I pulled to a stop and waited. The other vehicles in our convoy pulled up, and the gunners in the roof mounts swiveled in all directions looking for movement.

"Looks clear, Dad." Kilo said.

I keyed the radio, "Alright, lets get some dismounts to open a door for us."

"Roger that."

In the rear-view mirror I saw soldiers spilling out of the trucks, forming a perimeter, and expanding that perimeter to secure the area. Others soldiers moved forward to the barricade in staggered lines on either side of the Raptor. They moved with their weapons up and at the ready. Everyone knew we were in "Indian Country" and no one was taking chances.

Most of the soldiers were wearing their new K-Plate armor, which was lighter and quieter than the steel plate we had abandoned during the deep winter. K-Plate was made of layered Kydex over heavy leather. It was far more comfortable and still offered great protection in case a soldier got caught in an undead dog-pile. Testing consisted of putting Uncle Musket in a K-Plate suite and dropping him in a pit with a dozen hungry zeds. After five minutes, the zombies were dead and Uncle Musket was in a seething, panting rage but otherwise unphased. He was angry we put him in the pit, even after we reminded him that not only was it his idea, but that he had volunteered to do it.

Another advantage of the K-Plate was that it was easier to make it fit the individual. Joy's K-Plate fit so well that it was almost erotic in the form-fitting details that the artisans put into it. The Multicam pattern helped break up the form, but admittedly it was still a turn on for the men who admired it.

We also found that we were using the swords, maces, and axes more and more in conjunction with our modern firepower. They don't run out of ammo, and a zombie has a hard time biting when they don't have heads. That's the one thing that always works well against the undead, a good blade.

I got out of the Raptor after the soldiers passed. Joy was instantly at my side with her IAR.

"This is where they always jump out." Joy grumbled, tucking the stock of her weapon into her shoulder.

"You make it sound like there is a conspiracy about obstacles in roads."

Joy looked at me, "No... but this is where they always jump out."

I knew she was right, but the edginess in her tone is what made me tense. A took a couple more steps before I cycled a shell into the chamber of my shotgun. Joy didn't say anything, but the corners of her lips curled up ever so slightly.

"My Lord! Take a look at this!" One of the soldiers waved me over. The cab of the truck was riddled with weapons fire. Mostly small caliber stuff, but there were larger hits. The corpse in the truck was not much more than a rag-wrapped skeleton, but for the small hole in one side of the skull and the much larger hole on the other side seemed to suggest a hit from a rifle.

The bodies of soldiers, Gendarmerie and regular Army, both scattered around and in the trucks. All fallen from gunfire.

"Something's wrong here." I said as I looked around. "None of these men..."

"This one was a woman."

"None of them were killed by zombies. They were in a gunfight."

Joy was counting something with her finger in the air ticking each item. I raised an eyebrow. “We have thirty three bodies of soldiers, there are twenty rifles and a few handguns. So the attackers took some weapons, but only a few of them. I find that strange.”

I nodded my head.

One of the CGs asked, “Okay, what’s so strange about it?”

“They didn’t take any spare magazines. They don’t need more ammo or they don’t need this ammo.” I said. “Send a SITREP to the other task forces, let them know that we have possible hostile forces in country, and they are probably well armed.”

Before the RTO could send anything, we heard a low guttural moaning in the distance.

“Contact Left!”

Joy’s IAR snapped up as she scanned the area searching for targets, along with most of the other soldiers. When the target appeared, no one fired.

A loan zombie stumbled out from the trees. It was wearing shreds of clothes and was missing its lower jaw and its tongue hung down to its chest. Around its neck and shoulder was slung a FAMAS rifle. What made everyone pause though was that the zombie didn’t just let the rifle hang loose like we had seen in the past. It was holding it in a low ready position. The zombie jerked around in our direction and moaned as it started to raise the weapon.

“FIRE!” I shouted.

The zombie opened fire first. Ineffective fire that mostly went over our heads, but a couple rounds tinged off of one of the trucks.

About a dozen weapons engaged the target at the same time, shredding the zombie into undead confetti. The soldiers at the barricade started working in earnest, picking up sandbags, and boards and throwing them to the side of the road. Others disengaged parking brakes and put the rigs into neutral before starting to push them out of the way.

“Send that report! The zeds are using weapons!” I shouted at the RTO, who responded with a nod and was instantly on the horn.

“Anyone hit?”

Everyone checked themselves, and all were okay. I looked back and up at Kilo who was behind the M2 with a smoking barrel. His eyes were wide. I looked at him funny. He had been in the heat before.

“What’s wrong!?”

Kilo simply pointed to his shoulder. There was a large furrow through his left shoulder’s K-Plate. The father instinct in me overcame every other and I ran to the Raptor, leaping up to the top over the hood. The gash through the plate was only a graze on the outer layer.

“Any other hits?” I patted him down, looking for anything else. “Any other hits?”

Kilo looked down at himself and patted himself. “No... I’m fine. I’m fine. I’m okay.”

I took his head in my hands. "My boy..."

"Hey." He said.

I looked at him.

"I just got shot." He grinned and let out a small chuckle. He raised his goggles up to the top of his head. "I never got shot before."

"Don't do it again." I grabbed him and held him close. "Never again. Okay?"

"Okay."

Kilo seemed to have taken it in stride, but I was shaking. I jumped off the Raptor and started walking to where the zombie was. The clothes were not any sort of uniform, not military, not law enforcement, just business casual. The Famas rifle the zed had been holding was struck several times with rifle rounds. The gun was trashed, but I kicked it away regardless.

Joy and Caroline came up beside me, while Sinead stayed with the Raptor. "You okay, Boss?" Joe said, softly.

I looked down at my hand. There was a tremor. The undead didn't scare me, demon-possessed Skinwalkers didn't scare me. The thought of one of my boys getting hurt though, that scared me. I kept my face down to the dead zombie. "I'm fine."

A minute or so later the call came over my radio. "Roadblock is cleared."

I turned back to the Raptor. "Let's roll."

Three minutes later we were going again. More cautious than before. We headed for Paris.

## Ogre Calls Orkin

The sky was getting dark when we approached the outskirts of Paris. Huge city, lots of roads going in and out. It would take years to clear this city alone. Which is why I had another trick up my sleeve that I hadn't told anyone. This was better than a MOAB, horse sacrifice, or cats strapped to motorcycles. But first we had to make sure all the main routes out of Paris were closed off. Units spread out around the city, pushing up physical barricades and manning machine gun nests to cover the main avenues. By morning, we had Paris completely encircled. We were spread thin, but it would have to do. Paris was now under siege.

"Sir Sean is getting ready to assault the city." Joy said, looking up from the report.

"You're kidding. Please tell me your kidding."

"In his ready orders to his men, he passed on the phrase, 'Zerg Rush'. He thinks you meant for him to be the Zerg."

"Send him the message... 'Stand by and be ready to withstand a Zerg Rush'. Tell him to prepare and bolster the defenses on his assigned sector. We must hold everything in Paris, in Paris."

Joy shook her head as she typed into the Blue Force Tracker and sent the instant message. "He is enthusiastic."

"He is... he's been bored. The winter was too quiet." *For him,* I thought. "And so far France has been too easy to walk over. It's soft, even their zombies. No wonder everyone with an army has taken their turn on them. France is white bread."

"White bread?"

"Food, soft and fluffy, easy to eat." I could hear the aircraft coming. "But, that's going to change soon."

Joy raised an eyebrow then heard the aircraft as well. She looked up into the sky and saw the tankers approaching. "What's going on?"

"Three days from now, he's going to find he is far from bored."

"What do you mean?"

I gave Joy the run down.

The tankers were filled with Agent X. Just developed in the USA, this was a biological agent using a retro virus that would attack and kill one of the three strands of bacteria that help comprise what is known as the zombie plague. Specifically it kills the bacterium that gives a zombie extra energy. Without that bacterial assistance, a zombie essentially starves to death. Unfortunately, the zombie feels that its getting hungrier. So much so that it becomes frantic, panicked even in its need to feed on something. Sometimes this panic would turn one zombie against another. Other times it would cause the zombie to do things that zombies wouldn't have otherwise had the strength to do. Such as ripping open cars and trucks, smashing through otherwise solid walls. This usually occurred on the third day. While the zombies burned energy at such high rates, they depleted their energy at the cellular level, down to the Mitochondria, essentially burning it out. This causes cellular death, and eventually the whole zombie falls down, completely spent and completely dead. That usually happened on the fourth day. Agent X worked very well in the US, even to the point of clearing out the streets of Milwaukee without so much as even firing a shot. The down side is that it only effects the undead that come into contact with the spray. If a zombie is in a closed building with no air coming in, it won't be effected. So, normal clearing operations are still required, but it makes the job so much easier.

"I love it." Joy smiled. "Zombie Spray."

"Precisely. The only problem is that on day three, they are really agitated. It's like kicking a hornet's nest. You kick it, they swarm out, all pissed off, and then the next day they are all on the ground dead as door nails."

"So all we have to do is keep the zombie boxed in and wait for them to fall over dead."

"That's the plan."

"Should I warn the others?"

"Absolutely."

The tankers, heavy with Agent X, descended to a lower altitude as they passed overhead. As soon as they hit Paris proper, they started spraying. A red mist followed the planes, curling in the vortices and falling slowly over the crowded streets. The undead didn't seem to mind much. Some looked up and moaned at the aircraft. Others moaned in answer, but didn't know why. The rest just continued to wander, looking for fresh meat, flesh still plump with blood.

One zombie watched the planes with her red eyes. The planes crisscrossed skies, dropping red juice that wasn't blood. They mocked her. Her lips curled with hunger and hatred. The red juice landed on the back of her hands and she felt it on her face. At first she just looked at the drops on her skin, wondering what this was. Then the droplets started to blacken her skin. She hissed and pulled back into shadow.

"You wouldn't have thought Sir Sean was so bored, with his Harem of four girls." Joy smirked as she sent the message with the BFT. "It's a wonder he has any energy left."

I put down my spyglass and looked over at Joy, "Perhaps his girls are not as good as mine."

Joy chuckled. "Yeah, but you only had one of us."

I looked down, thinking about April and the betrayal. I couldn't dwell on it, let it ruin me. I had things to take care of here and now, so I might as well make peace with it. Stiff upper lip as some of the Brits might say. "Divide and conquer. I read my Sun Tzu. I wasn't foolish enough to take on all of you at once." I tried to joke, but it didn't feel funny.

"You are a smart man. You wouldn't have survived."

"I try to pick my battles." I said, lifting the spyglass back up to my eye, looking at the tankers. Flying with the tankers were a couple C-27 Spartans. These looked like small C-130 Hercs with only one engine on each wing. Smaller but very efficient. These Spartans didn't carry any Agent X, instead they carried 7.62mm and .50 caliber Gatling guns and 40mm grenade launchers. Flying above those was fighter support. Some units had called in reports of fighter aircraft, so we pulled in our own. No sense in being unprepared. If the Adversary had operational aircraft, it would be nice to swat them down.

"He picked a bad one to fight." Kilo grumbled from up in the turret, where he was eating a sandwich.

*Yeah*, I thought. *I know*. I climbed out and went to the back of the Raptor and broke open the Yeti cooler. I pulled out a Red Bull and an Orange Gatorade. Caroline was in the back with her rifle across her knees. She was wearing her K-Plate with her helmet off and her hair was let down. Over her hair was her radio headset, and around her neck was the throat mic. She had a small pair of binos that she used to scan the area.

"So how come you never let anyone else make you a Gatorbull except April?"

"It's not like that, Caroline. April just knew ahead of time when I wanted one. Even before I did."

"I wish she was here... she'd have loved seeing Paris." Caroline sighed.

"I'm glad she's not."

Caroline looked at me with a tilted head.

"This isn't the way to see a place that you've always wanted to see. It would have been nice for her to have seen it before everything... or maybe after we've cleared it out. But not now. This is an ugly time. I don't even want to see it."

Joy came around the back of the truck and climbed up. From the Yeti she found a can of Sunkist. "And what about the Queen? She was asking to come."

"Knowing that she's safe is the only way I can do what has to be done."

Joy sat on the side of the truck bed and popped open the can. "But what about me? You don't worry about my safety?"

"Of course I do. Which is why I keep you close by."

"I thought I was supposed to be *your* Body Guard... when did that change?"

"I think it was at Cheyenne Mountain."

Joy looked at the orange soda. "I was so scared. I've never been so scared."

"And I knew I had to protect you."

"Those were good days." Joy lifted the can and tilted her head back. She closed her eyes as she drank. Then she said "I miss April and Jen."

"I know. I do too."

"Do you really believe that I'll see them again?" Joy looked me right in the eye as she asked.

I drank some Gator-Bull before I answered. "Yes, I do."

"You don't think I'll be in hell for loving Jen?"

I shook my head "Joy, I think we're in hell now."

Joy looked around, "I thought hell would be hotter."

That night, Joy's comment became true. Paris was burning. Agent X had a greater effect than all the testing had shown previously. Within just hours of the spray, the zombies were absolutely enraged. They tore into each other, they tore into parked cars, and they tore into the defenses that were keeping them contained. Small arms fire, had little effect at all if the targets were not hit in the head.

Most sectors were reporting engagements, especially those along the eastern side of the city, where we were. We had small groups of zombies, enraged and crazy fast coming at us. Paul with his .338 Lapua AI was able to drop most of the individual zeds, but then they started coming in bigger groups.

One large group of running zombies came into view, the biggest group we had seen yet.

"Mark Nineteens, engage that intersection," I pointed with two fingers. "Lay down some frags and put some along that street there, and there."

The Captain saluted and turned to relay the orders to the gunners. I raised my spyglass in time to watch a pair of zombies spring over the barricades like bounding xenomorphs from the movie *Aliens*. The shrieking was almost similar, enough to give me chills. What the hell? More jumped over, then others. Soon it looked like a river overflowing its levy. The LAVs opened up with their 25mm cannons and everyone with a rifle was firing. Screams and shrieks and gunfire was so loud, you couldn't hear yourself think. The zombies even looked like xenomorphs as their skin was blackened and burnt with bones visible through their tightening skin. Agent X for some reason worked too fast here. There were too many zombies, and they were coming. I opened up with my grenade rounds from my shotgun, but it felt like I was throwing rocks into an incoming tide.

"We're losing containment here." Joy said as she speed reloaded a new magazine into her IAR.

"Losing nothing..." I emptied my shotgun and started reloading. "We're holding this."

Another LAV pulled up behind our position and starting firing over our heads. The gunner was firing continuously. Other vehicles pulled up besides the LAV, and my Raptor. I looked up at Kilo, who was in the turret, heating up the M2. I moved over to Caroline who was firing over the fender of the Raptor. "If it gets too bad, take the Raptor and Kilo and head back to Calais. Your job now is to protect Kilo. Above everything else."

She looked at me strangely, but saw that this wasn't a matter for discussion. "Yes, Sire." She nodded.

I turned back to the swarming zeds. They moved too fast. This wasn't any effect of Agent X. This was something else.

The overwhelming firepower was holding the surge of undead. Some of the zombies had rifles and would open fire in our direction. Large caliber rounds answered, splattering the gunslinging zombies and those behind them. But the zombies kept coming. What they lacked in coordination or tactics they made up in volume of bodies and ferocity.

My shotgun ran dry so I let it fall as I drew my sword. My pistol would be useless right now. "I'm out."

Joy emptied her last magazine and dumped her weapon. She drew out her sword with one hand and lowered her visor with the other.

"I'm empty too."

All around us the guns stopped firing with the noise being replaced with the ring of steel being drawn from scabbards. I lowered my visor and nodded to Joy. "Ready?"

"No." She said, as the first zed came into reach. Then the fighting really started.

The first zombie to approach me was cleaved cleanly in two from armpit to armpit. The next one slammed into me, almost making me lose balance. Fingerbones like claws raked at the K-Plate and tore at the equipment on my belt, and I could feel fingers reaching under the seams in the armor. I looked into the dead white eyes of the zombie that was clawing at me. Its grinning skull made a lie of the boney smile, and I could feel its hatred of the living. I could hear it in its shrieking. I heard another scream, off to my left, cut short and from a quick glance I saw an armored head fly over the sea of undead. One of the CGs had fallen. I shoved the zombie in front of me away, and smashed its skull in with the pommel of my sword. I looked over at Caroline and saw that she was separated from the Raptor, trying to fight her way back to it. Kilo was standing on top of it with a large two-handed mace, each swing, crushing a swath of zombies, keeping them off the truck. I wanted him out of here, now. I needed Caroline to get to the truck. I tried to make my way to her, but the zombies were all over us, hands were pulling at me. I swung the sword, cutting down several zombies, only to have the blade wrenched from my grip. The zombie that pulled it held it up and screamed. The only thing I could do was to ball up my fist and punch. The zombie was knocked backwards, but it had dropped the sword and it disappeared from my sight. "Crap!" I pulled out my Becket combat bowie with one hand, and filled the other with my mace. Hands and arms got the knife, anything that came in to grab at me. The mace found their skulls and dropped them where they stood.

I heard another scream as one of our French soldiers that had joined us was pulled down. He screamed and I caught a glimpse of him. There was a zombie trying to twist his head off as others bit down into his unarmored shoulders and arms.

Joy was spinning and slashing with her sword, she was a blur of sharp-edged steel, and any zombie that came too close lost pieces of its self.

I made it over to my own sword, but standing over it was a Red Eyed zombie. She looked like she could have been pretty if it wasn't for the black spots that covered her naked skin. She hissed like a cat.

"Your soul will burn, Ogre King!" Saliva poured from her mouth and her swollen, blackened tongue licked her lips. It looked like a rotten slug and left a ring of slime around the creature's mouth.

I could feel her try to lift me with her powers but it didn't work. She screamed in rage and crouched, her hands held out wide. Doing something I had never done before, I threw my mace. Before the Red Eye could spring, my mace flew straight and true and struck her square in the mouth with a spray of blood and teeth. Over the din of the battle, I heard the bones in her jaw and face break. The Red Eye was knocked down, but I knew it wasn't out. Undead hands grabbed my arms but I shrugged them off as the Red Eye started to rise again. It's pretty face was a ruined mass of pulp and shards of bone and shattered teeth. The eyes though, were just fine and they looked at me. I swung the big bowie knife as hard as I could, but the blade passed short, missing the Red Eye completely. I was about to swing again when Red Eye fell. Part of it falling one way, the top half of its head falling the other. I looked around, the mace was within reach. I bent to pick it up and a zombie grabbed me from behind. I reached over my shoulder, took a handfull of undead flesh, and flipped it over my shoulder as I continued to reach for the mace. As my fingers wrapped around the grip, I was knocked sideways by another zombie. My bowie found its ribs, all the way to the hilt. This didn't do anything to zombie, but it gave me a handle to use for leverage as I rolled the zombie away from me.

An armored hand grabbed my wrist and I looked up to see Joy. She helped me to my feet before spinning on another zombie and splitting it head to tail. Around us, the zombies were pressing in. I heard the engine of the Raptor fire up and I glanced over. Caroline had made it inside and shut the door. Kilo was back in the turret with a pistol in both hands. Any zombie that jumped onto the Raptor got a shot to the skull as a reward.

Suddenly helicopters were overhead. Miniguns opened up and bright orange fingers of death that reached out and touched the zombies. The stream of fire played across the swarm of undead, back and forth like it was watering a garden.

There was a cheer from the men with me. Even I cheered. I killed another zombie before I found my sword, and once I had that back in my hands, I was able to start taking heads again.

The tide of battle had turned in our favor as we started pushing back. Soon I had men around me and not zombies. We formed lines and killed our way back to the barricade, putting Paris back into containment as the helicopter started working its guns over the streets on the other side of the barricade.

As the chopper flew low and slow overhead, we caught a glimpse of who was inside. In the door of the Merlin I saw an armored figure of a woman, large breasted with long, red hair pouring out from her helmet and across the bright white shoulder plates. In her hand was a long barreled automatic rifle finished in a gloss white that matched the armor. She looked magnificent and frightening.

One of the French soldiers shouted "Jeanne d'Arc!"

"No, that's my wife!" I shouted back.

"The Queen!" The men started cheering.

"Mom?" Kilo stammered.

A space was cleared out and the chopper landed. As soon as the passengers got off, the bird lifted back up and started shooting again. The Queen's personal guard were all in shining silver plate armor. They fanned out as she approached me. They were all women, tall, strong, but as beautiful as her. "Your Majesty." Debbie said.

I bowed slightly, "My Queen... You know how to make an entrance."

Debbie lifted her visor. She had dark makeup around her eyes and her lips were blood red. "I learned from watching you. I thought you could use a hand. My Valkyries and I were bored." She quipped as she swung her rifle over her shoulder. I noticed on the mag well a familiar logo. The rifle was

Crusader Templar. Gundoc had been busy. Hanging off Debbie's belt on one side was a short sword with a wide blade, and an HK MP7 on the other side.

"I thought you were at Fort George." I said as I slammed my sword tip first into the ground and sheathed the Becker. "But I am very glad to see you." I said, lifting my visor. The air felt cool on my sweaty face. I walked over to her and took her armored hands into mine. I leaned in and gave her a gentile kiss. As I pulled back, I saw that Debbie's eyes were closed and only a moment after did she reopen them. "Why did you come, my Queen? It's not safe yet."

"We wanted to see Paris. And you."

"What do you think?"

"Overrated."

"Paris?"

"Both." She said with a grin.

A couple helicopters overhead made passes with miniguns, rockets, and chainguns. They were finishing off some of the remaining swarms of zombies that were heading to the barricades, taking away the mass of their surge and cutting their numbers down to manageable sizes. I looked around. The men were picking up discarded weapons, reloading magazines or getting a drink. The battle was a victory, but I wouldn't say we had won. We had lost more men. As long as the Adversary whittled away at our numbers, they would eventually win. There were only a relative handful of us, but they had hundreds of thousands, millions even. We had to be more careful. Here, the zombies numbered beyond thousands, but we held them in check. The other units reported the same. We still had containment.

"How many did we lose here?" I asked.

"Five, Sire." The CG had given me their names and Joy was recording them in the book.

"Five? Are you sure, I thought it was only four."

"Smyth was bitten."

"Where is he?"

"He's in the back of the LAV over there Sire." He pointed.

I walked over to the LAV and there was Smyth, laying there. His friends around him. When he looked up and saw me, he smiled. "My Lord, to what do I owe the honor?" He said, trying to smile, but I could see that he was in a lot of pain. Undead teeth had found bare skin at his neck. It was a small bite, but that was all it took with the Z-Plague. Tendrils of infection had already reached out from the wound, like twisted spider legs that crossed his neck to his face. As I looked, I could see them spreading.

"The honor is mine, sir." I knelt. Those around me bowed their heads.

"Please, Sire." Smyth said. His teeth were clenched, but there was no anger or remorse. "It was my honor to fight with my brethren. Vengeance for my family, and my friends."

"Where are you from, if you don't mind me asking."

"Cumbria, near the river Leven. You could throw a stone into it from my front door." Smyth smiled as he remembered it. I watched as a dark tendril of the plague reached across his face and touched the right eye. The eye started to cloud over like milk poured into a bowl. The left eye remained blue and bright.

The men around him picked him up and carried him out of the LAV and set him gently on the grass. Smyth was composed as much as he could be, but I could see tremors in his hands. It wasn't fear, it was pain. "How would you like it, son?"

Smyth looked at me, "Sire, I'd like Willas to have the honor. I was married to his sister, God rest her soul."

Willas had been kneeling at his side. He had tears on his cheeks. "I, I can't do that, Chucky."

"You can, Willas. Please. I want you to do it."

Everyone took a step back and Willas pulled out his pistol, an old battered Browning High Power. "Ask someone else, Chucky."

"Send me to see Laura before I can't recognize her."

Willas took Smyth's hand and squeezed it. With his left hand he put the barrel of the Browning to Smyth's temple with the barrel angled down so the bullet would pass through the deeper part of the brain and exit into the ground.

"Laura." Willas said. Then the shot. Then everything was quiet.

I walked back to my Raptor. I sat down heavily on the Raptor's tailgate. One of the CGs handed me my old Remington. It was covered in blood that had only partially been wiped off. I shook my head as I cleaned my weapon and topped it off again. I refilled my pouches from the boxes of ammo in the back of the truck. My HE shells were getting low so I used more buckshot. A rifle would be better, but with one eye, I felt like this was a more effective path.

I watched as the Queen went from person to person, talking to each of them, lifting their spirits. Morale was improved as she went around. It was good to have her here. She had talked to Willas as Smyth's and the other bodies were loaded into a truck. I couldn't hear what was said, but their was a moment when Willas actually smiled. He'd be okay. We've all had losses before.

I noticed also who Debbie didn't talk to. Joy, Caroline, and Sinead. The girls kept their respectful distance from Debbie, and Debbie returned that.

I looked at Sinead, who had stripped out of her armor and was in just her UnderArmor shorts and a tank top. She was rinsing off her armor, which had been completely covered in blood, head to toe. I don't know how she fought, but she had bathed in blood. It was disconcerting.

"You're staring." Joy said as she stood next to me.

"Did she roll around in puddles?"

Joy looked over to Sinead who was now rinsing out her hair. "You didn't see her fight?"

"No, did you?" I asked.

Joy nodded. "Yeah."

"How did she do?"

"I almost felt sorry for the zombies." I saw a shiver in her as she talked. "There's something about that girl. The way she fights. It's wrong."

"What's wrong about it."

"She loves it too much." Joy said quietly.

I looked back and Sinead who looked up at me as she flicked her hair back . She winked at me, closing her right eye slowly and grinning at me. Joy was right. There was something wrong with her. I picked up my sword and ran a cloth down the blade before I sheathed it again. Maybe there was something wrong with all of us.

## Pebbles

Hours later, the swarming throughout the city had stopped as the zombies were out of energy and they became lethargic. No more rushes on the barricade, no reports of surges anywhere. The zombies were running out of steam.

I scanned the streets on the other side of the barricade and the zombies far beyond it that shambled slowly. One of them stood out to me. It was different. "Someone hand me a scoped rifle." I said.

An ACR topped with an ACOG was handed to me. I took aim and fired a shot. The zombie with the white, painted face crumpled to the ground. "Mimes... fucking hate mimes. Worse than clowns." I muttered.

I turned to my staff, "Anyone see a mime, shoot it on sight... zombie or not."

That night I was sitting in the C2's tent. We had set up camp and security. The threat from the city was dissipating fast as we had already observed some of the zombies starting to drop dead from the Agent X. It had worked, but not as it had worked in the USA. What should have taken days only took a matter of hours. This was wrong. There had to be a reason. Biologically, the Z-Plague was the same here as it was in the USA, and the biology of Europeans, even the French, were the same as Americans, so there was no logical reason for the Agent X effects to have been different. I wanted to know why.

"You've been studying the screen for some time now, Sire." One of the CGs observed.

I didn't look up, but kept gazing at the screen, pulling the time frame back and letting it advance.

"Two hours now." Joy said. "C2's been over all of this."

I grumbled, "Then C2's missed it."

Joy leaned over. "Missed what?"

"Pebbles."

At this the C2 bristled, "Pebbles? Your Majesty..."

I sent the images to the big screen with a click. "Pebbles..." I used the Viridian laser pointer I took off my shotgun. "In the water."

The green dot showed the motion I wanted everyone to see. "It starts here... 'plink' and the movement spreads outward, like ripples in a pond." The scores of zombies started to move from that center point... subtle, like a push. But the push was there. The moaning couldn't be heard from the overhead Sats, but one could almost feel it. Panning the image to the outskirts of the city, that subtle push turned into a tidal-like surge.

"They were reacting to the spray and then to our presence... the moan communication." The C2 stated.

"You think? Or you just assumed? Look at the time." I said. "The pebble was before the Agent X spray started... in fact, the pebble happened just about the same time the aircraft took off."

The C2 looked at his PDA the up at the screen with eyes wide. "That's..."

"Like what we were dealing with in London." Joy said quietly.

I nodded. "Which is why the Queen needs to be not in France. She needs to be back in Scotland, at Fort George."

Debbie stood up. "My place is here, with my husband. I am not going anywhere."

"Everything on this side of the Channel just got a lot more dangerous." I said. "We've seen the zeds use weapons, move in coordination, use ambush tactics... and... I can't believe the reports, but there are reports of undead operating tactical aircraft."

"Then come back to the Fort with me, but I'm not leaving your side."

I shook my head, "Debbie, I love you, but I don't want you here. I want you to be safe."

Debbie's face got red and her eyes narrowed. "I want you to be safe too. I saved your ass today."

I stood up and took her hands. "Please, I can't go forward unless I know you're safe... I can't worry about you and worry about everything else."

"I am..."

"Distracting, my love, my Queen. Please. I can't have you in harm's way."

After some more time, she finally consented, and, in the morning, she would be on a Gulf Stream jetting back to Fort George. We arranged for a pair of escort fighters to fly in formation with her jet the whole way back to Scotland.

In the mean time, Debbie sat beside me at a large table in the mess tent. I was eating some sort of grilled fish that Caroline had prepared and talking with some of the Cadre.

One of the CGs came forward, stood briefly at attention, then took a knee, bowing deeply. She wore steel plate armor and had her weapon slung tightly across her back. Her blonde hair was pulled back into pony tail behind her head, but she had long bangs which framed her face. Her features were sharp. At first I didn't recognize her, but then it came to me. "Yes, Rebecca Hallbrook, please stand."

"Your Majesty," she coughed. "I request to join your personal protection unit."

"I thought you were with Louis Q's detail."

"Felt like a third wheel, Sir. Besides, the Duke has a whole new squad, his Dragoons. I was redundant and I don't like feeling redundant."

"What about Izzy?"

"She's occupied. Q has her busy, then she keeps him busy. I told them I was coming here, and the Duke signed off on it."

"Well, I'm glad you're here. I can use the help. First off... your steel plate armor... we've upgraded. You need to get fitted in the new stuff."

"My Lord, if it doesn't bother you too much, I'd rather keep the steel plate."

"Are you sure? Why?"

"I feel safer in it."

"By all means, if you prefer it."

Rebecca smiled and bowed. "Thank you my Liege."

I laughed, "Stop that, Rebecca... come here."

She approached with her head down. I threw an arm around her. "Welcome back to the team." I gave her a hug and smiled at her. "It's good to see you again."

Debbie looked at me funny. "How do you know her?"

"I found young Officer Hallbrook of Phoenix Metro out in the Arizona desert."

"What was she doing out there?"

"About to be fed to a zombie by some Mexican Cartel."

"And of course you always save the pretty girls."

"Of course." I laughed.

"The King never hugged me." One of the big CGs muttered, loud enough so he was overheard by everyone.

"Two reasons for that, Iron Mike." I responded. "First off, I don't want your sweat all over my armor. And second... I fear the return squeeze would break my spine!" I said laughing. We all had a chuckle.

I returned to the seat at the table and spent some quiet moments with Debbie.

## Demon Dreams

After dinner was finished, Debbie and I retired to our own tent. Debbie was reluctant to get close to me again like we had been before, and I didn't blame her. I was happy enough to just be able to go to sleep with an arm around her and no armor between us.

As I slept, I dreamed of standing on a beach of fine sand with scattered shells. Small crabs and gulls were my only companions on the beach. The beach seemed to be a small island that reminded me of the movie *Pirates of the Caribbean* where the drunk Captain was marooned. I walked around the island and came to my original footprints and decided to follow them. I had nothing better to do. The sand felt good and hot under my feet. As I walked, I noticed another set of footprints in the sand, they were right along the water line, one foot in, one food out of the waves. I stopped and looked at the foot prints. They were larger than my own. As I looked at them, I saw how the water started to fill them in. These prints were very new as the action of the small waves quickly erased them. These prints were very new. I looked around the beach but saw nothing until I suddenly turned around. Right behind me was a large being, red skinned, tall, with black horns and black teeth. The demon laughed.

"I was beginning to think you were ignoring me." The demon said with a rumbling low voice.

"I was trying to."

The demon laughed. "Don't try to raise my ire. You won't like me when I'm angry."

"Why? Do you turn from red to green and get bigger and stronger?"

The smile fell from the demon's toothy face, and he suddenly balled up a fist and punched me. I flew across the beach and landed in the surf. I stood up, spitting salt water.

"I told you not to cross me. That was just a love tap."

"I was hoping that it wasn't the best you had, because my wife hits harder than that."

The demon laughed and cracked its knuckles, "Oh how I would so love to show you... a great many things." When the demon's knuckles popped, each one sounded like gunshots.

"I came here to talk with you, little Ogre King. One more time. One last time."

"One of these days, very soon, I'm going to find you."

The demon took just a few quick steps and crossed the distance to me within a blink of an eye. He swung a backhand fist that caught me in the side of the head. I was instantly knocked out, but I woke as soon as I hit the water again. I stood up, expecting to be dizzy and unfocused. But I wasn't. I saw everything with stark clarity. Including the demon as it stomped across the island, coming to me. I was knee deep in the water so I walked forward. "Hit me again and I'll kill you."

The demon laughed and swung a big red fist at me. Everything seemed to slow down and I ducked under the fist, this was fairly easy as I didn't have that far to duck, the demon was much taller than I was, by at least two feet. I came up hard with an upper cut. I put everything I had into it. It felt like I punched granite, but the demon's open mouth clapped shut, and the huge red beast was lifted off its feet. Time seemed to come back to normal as the demon landed flat on its back. If I hadn't been dreaming, I'd have sworn I had broken my hand.

The demon laughed as it rolled backwards and came up onto its feet. "Frisky little Ogre, aren't you? I like it when they are playful... but come now. Please. I have much to offer you."

"What can you offer me?"

"Everything!" The demon's eyes went wide as it smiled at me. It had a big, wide toothy smile that looked like the grill of a truck more than any friendly expression. "I can give you this whole world! It's yours to rule! All you have to do is one simple thing."

"What would that be?"

"Worship me."

"I already have a god."

"One who hates you, Ogre! He said it himself! A natural man is an enemy to God!"

I took a step back. I didn't expect that. It hit me harder than his fist did, and the demon knew it. "He calls the love you had with April a sin! Whoredoms, and adultery, an abomination before God. Your baby girl, such a sweet little thing, born outside of his grace, so he took her mother. From her and from you... and she loved you so much. All she wanted was for you to love her back, but you couldn't do that... tied to your beliefs that just doing that was wrong! You were wrong, Ogre! YOU WERE WRONG!" The demon said through clenched teeth, its long, finger with black nails pointed at me in accusation.

"But you can make it right! You can see her again, I can give you another chance. You can be with her again... forever."

I took another step back. I knew these were all lies, but they still cut me. Lies from the Father of Lies.

"Bend your knee, Ogre King, and I will give you back the one that loved you the most. I can give you power! I can give you the power to command the dead! Think of it! With a sweep of your hand, all the dead will return to dust! No more fighting, no more killing!"

I shook my head.

"I can give you gold and silver! You can buy armies and navies! You can rule the whole world! You can buy women, the most beautiful in the world. Just bow to me!"

I started to get very angry now. "I already have armies." I took a step forward.

"I already have navies." I took another step forward and the demon took a step backwards.

"I already have the most beautiful woman in the world as my bride!" I took another step forward.

"I already rule!" I screamed and leaped at the demon. I swung my fist and hit him in the eye. I hit him again and again. The demon fell backwards into the sand. I grabbed one of its horns and stomped down hard until I had crushed its head under my heel. When I looked around I realized that I was no longer on the beach, but back in my tent. I was sweating. I tasted salt water in my mouth, but it could have been sweat. I didn't know. I looked around the tent. Debbie was awake, on the far side of the tent, her blanket pulled up under her chin with wide eyes. "What's the matter?"

"You scared me. You were yelling."

"I'm sorry."

Debbie quickly got up and pulled on her clothes. She picked up her armor and called for one of her Valkyries to help get her into it. When she glanced at me, it was as if she was looking at a stranger. As fast as she could, she got her armor on and left the tent, her Valkyrie on her heels. When they left, Joy ducked under the flap and came in. "Are you okay, my Lord?"

"I... I... Yes, I think so. I just had a nightmare is all."

"Some nightmare." Joy shook her head. "Can I get you a drink?"

"I could kill for a Gator-Bull right now."

"Can I make it for you?"

"Sure, if you would like."

"I would." Joy left the tent as I changed clothes. She came back with an Orange Gator-Bull and a hot roll, stuffed with cheese and sausage.

"Thank you, Joy." I said, and took a long pull at the drink. I sat down on the small stool and picked up my greaves. Joy knelt down and started buckling them. "Thank you."

She looked up at me and smiled. "It's nothing." She was quiet as she buckled the other one on my other leg. The armor was deeply scratched, but it did the job and was still serviceable. The bite marks on the arms were the worst of them.

"What do you dream of, Joy?"

She stopped what she was doing and looked at me. "What do you mean?"

"When you dream, what do you dream of?"

She sat back down on her feet and he hands fell into her lap. "I dream of a place far away from here... Jen is there. April is too, now."

"Where is this place?"

"I don't know, but it's beautiful."

"Do they talk to you?"

"Yes, they do."

"What do they talk about?"

Joy stood up quickly, "I don't want to talk about this." She turned to leave but I grabbed her arm.

"Please, Joy. Please, tell me."

She looked at me. "They tell me to be very careful or you'll be killed."

I could tell there was more, and she wasn't telling me. "What else do they say?"

Joy looked down. "That they will see me soon, and to not be afraid."

I let go of her arm. "What?"

"That's what they said." She shook her head. "But it's just a dream." Joy helped me with the rest of the armor. "Dreams don't mean anything."

"Some don't." I said. But some mean a whole hell of a lot, I thought, keeping it to myself. I was very uncomfortable right now with all this dream stuff. Joy turned to leave again.

"Does April say anything else?"

Joy opened her mouth to say something, then shook her head and ducked out of the tent.

I sat in silence on the stool and ate the roll and finished the Gator-Bull. It was still dark outside. Debbie was by the jet, talking to someone. As I approached, I saw that it was Kilo. She gave her son a hug and Kilo hugged her back. He looked back at me and walked away, heading quickly to the mess tent.

"He's grown up quite a bit lately."

"He has. He's one of the best men I have."

"Don't let him get hurt."

"I won't. Just before you showed up, Caroline was about to extract him... they were both in the Raptor about ready to take off for Calais." I shrugged, "But then you showed up, so they stayed."

"Maybe I should have been a little late."

"You arrived precisely at the right time." I hugged Debbie, not wanting to see her leave. "How's the boys?"

"Oh, you remember you have more sons now, do you?"

"Well, Kilo is the first borne and heir to my empire."

Debbie ignored that, "The twins are at Achnacarry going through your school there, and the others are doing just fine at Fort George. Grandma is taking good care of them."

"Grandma? Which one?"

"My mother of course. All my family as at Fort George now."

"All of them?"

"Yes, even Basil."

"Basil? That's great, and his family?"

"Yes, they all made it." She smiled.

"That's fantastic! They had been out of touch for so long. Where were they?"

"They had made it to the cabin in Idaho and held up there until things settled down."

The Gulfstream's pilot approached us. "It's about time to go, yes?"

I nodded, "It is."

Debbie looked at the jet, then back to her personal guard of her "Valkyries." They boarded after I gave Debbie a kiss on the forehead.

"Be safe." was all she said as she ducked into the aircraft.

"Your majesty." The Valkyries said as they boarded.

I stood aside and watched as the jet throttled up and moved down the runway. Soon it was climbing into the air, disappearing into the clouds.

I sighed and turned back to the camp. The walk was quiet as Joy, Caroline, and Rebecca followed at a distance. This was a good thing as talking wasn't something that felt right at the moment.

# TEN

## Ogre Does the Opera

I headed back to the C2's tent and sat down, looking up at the big screen. The C2 had pulled up detailed views of "The Pebble", the location where everything in Paris had started.

"What am I looking at here? I don't recognize that place." I eyed the building. It was large, ornate and monolithic. Gold statues stood on the corners of the roof.

"I don't know, either, Sire." The C2 shrugged. "But that's where everything started from."

"Your Majesty." A French accent sounded over my shoulder as I looked at the screen. "I think I know that place."

I turned around, it was a French soldier with a huge, floppy beret. I looked him up and down. "Yes?"

"It's the Palais Garnier, my Lord... The Paris National Opera."

I looked back at the screen. "Great. A Demon with a sense of drama."

"What can you tell me about it?"

The French trooper just shrugged his shoulders. "I have never been, your majesty. I have only driven past it on rare occasion."

From what I knew about this demon, from our little chats, I ascertained this is where he would be. His efforts to buy me off meant something. Why bother if he was really as powerful as he made himself out to be. Which meant that he wasn't. Or at least he was afraid of how powerful I might be. Either way, he was afraid of me for a reason.

We needed to get near the Opera House, what the French called "Palais Garnier". Q wanted to get as close as possible and do a little recce. I gave him the green light, and he said something about the sewers before he took his team and headed out. I didn't know what he had in mind, but he was welcome to that route. Of course, it was probably the safest route, seeing as no one in their right mind would want to take it. It was probably the least watched.

We sent drones in of all sorts. Some flew at high altitude getting big picture views, while others ran like pod racers through the streets getting us the low-level images. We had a couple robotic helicopters that were used to search and examine anything that brought up more question marks. Unfortunately both went black after transmitting a final image of a bright flash. The source of the bright flash was not known, but I didn't think it was any electronic malfunction. I had a feeling they were burned out by a something that didn't want to be seen.

The streets of Paris were mostly cleared of the walking dead, thanks to the Agent X spraying. Corpses littered the streets, but at least they were not moving. The ones that were moving, seemed to have somehow survived the spray, but not without effects. The Agent X had caused large areas of flesh to slough off, leaving bare bone. How these zombies were still ambulatory was unknown. When you have no tissues connecting the upper arm to the lower arm, one would think the hands wouldn't still be able to grasp. But they did. This was something beyond Nature and seemed more magic. That was an uncomfortable feeling. But we had seen the Adversaries use magic before. Telekinesis, Pyrokinesis, and such. But this goes from some sort of spiritual or demonic possession into pure necromancy. This wasn't a good thing.

A video feed from a Predator showed one desiccated zombie ripping the doors off of what looked like a hotel, freeing the zombies that were inside... zombies that had not been exposed to Agent X. This behavior suggested a controlling force was still in effect.

I was tired of looking at screens. "I'm going to have to get in there."

"Sire, please."

I held up my hand to silence the protest. "Get ready to roll out."

Joy picked up her new weapon, an L86-LSW. The barrel of her IAR had been shot out and it had no rifling left. No replacement was available, so she took the best she could find. She topped it with an EOtech and she seemed to like it. They were able to make the Surefire mags work with it, so it had just as much firepower as the IAR had.

Well, I'll be able to put this beast to the test sooner than I thought."

I held the heavier armor in reserve, and we used the swifter and quieter vehicles instead. The Raptor, the M-ATV, and the up-armored Humvees, only four vehicles for our incursion.

Most of the weapons we carried were suppressed. We wanted a lower profile mission, if it was possible. I had a can attached to my HK pistol, but not to my Shotgun. During my fight with Plague of Crows, my Mossberg 930 SPX was ruined, and its replacement, my 870 Police Tactical was a great shotgun, perfect for zombie defense. But for offense against zombies, it left something to be desired. Debbie had left it in the Raptor for me before she took off.

The note said "*From Debbie, Please be safe. Oh, and Gundoc says hi.*"

It was one of Crusader Weaponry earliest guns, and one that I had always been enthusiastic about. Joe must have come across a CNC Mill that no one was using. The Crusader Warhammer was essentially an SR-25 type gun, rebuilt to chamber 2 3/4" 12 gauge shells. Along with the weapon was a pack of magazines and several 20 round drum magazines. The Warhammer was a comfortable addition to my arsenal, as it could be reloaded as fast as a carbine. The Warhammer's controls were ambi, so running it left handed was not a problem. Joy, insisted on playing with the cool new toy and said that while it was reliable, she didn't like the recoil. I didn't mind it a bit. I zeroed the sight for slugs at 100 yards.

I also had a Crusader Broadsword in .375 Ogre. This was topped with an ACOG. The ammo supply was limited, but Joe said more was on the way. I kept it in the rack with my Savage 10BA, "Lilith", if I needed it. The Warhammer would be my main go-to weapon for the time being.

"Joy?"

"Yeah, sir?"

"Send a message to Gundoc, he's in Colorado..." I held up the Warhammer and inserted a full drum magazine, but didn't chamber a shell. Cruiser Ready was the safest way to carry a shotgun of any type. "Tell him that we need him here as soon as he can make it. Tell him to get to any Air Force Base in operation and I'll send a plane as soon as he notifies us that he's made it."

"I'll get the word out."

I put the weapon on safe and shoved it into the rack. Everyone ready to go?

I looked in the back of the Raptor. I had Caroline and Rebecca in the back seat, Kilo up in the turret, and Joy in the front passenger seat. In the bed, the Yeti was chilling with some fresh ice and cans of Red Bull and bottles of Gatorade, and lots of Sunkist for the girls. We were ready to go.

As we rolled through the barricades and entered Paris, one of the drone operators caught a glimpse of something on the screen. He leaned in and looked carefully at the grainy image. Something had started to crawl out of a dark alley. It moved strangely, almost as if it was crawling along the wall of the building instead of on the ground. The creature darted back into the shadow before any detail was discernible. The drone operator shook his head and leaned back... just another damn zombie.

We drove fast through the streets of Paris, following the path the BFT had mapped out. In the back seat, Rebecca's attention went to the boom box in the back seat. She turned it on and pressed play. "Boom Boom Pow" started playing. Joy looked at me and I looked into the back seat. "Black Eye Peas?

Really?"

Rebecca smiled, "Hey I just pressed play, this is your music box."

Joy looked back, "That was Jen's boom box."

"Jen? She was the short girl with the big hooters? What happened to her?"

Joy stopped smiling and turned around.

"What?" Rebecca asked, "What did I say?"

"Jen died." Caroline said, then leaned in close and whispered into Rebecca's ear, "Jen and Joy were a thing."

Rebecca sat back in her seat. "I'm so sorry, Joy."

Joy shrugged, "It's okay."

The Black Eyed Peas continued to sing about their modern techno greatness. "Wasn't this the theme song to that stupid GI Joe movie?" I asked, trying to lighten things back up.

"I don't... yeah, yeah it was." Kilo said.

"I hated that movie." I said and laughed. I glanced over at Joy who smiled and turned to look out the window.

We wove through overturned vehicles and crunched over fallen dead. There were old bones and new bones scattered around, and blast marks from our helicopter's rockets and the scorching from the fires started by riots and undead masses didn't hide the simple fact that Paris was a filthy city. It smelled of rot and sewage and corruption. I didn't like this place at all and would have chosen to have just gone completely around the place, if it wasn't for one thing. That big ugly red bastard that wouldn't let me sleep at night. I was going to sleep well soon enough. "*Soon enough, you jackhole.*" I thought to myself.

Kilo was up top in the Raptor with a hushed ACR 6.8 and the big Fifty. Every once in a while I'd hear a quiet pop as Kilo cleaned off anything lurching about as we drove past.

The song on the music box changed to Prodigy's "Breath". This was a little more to my liking. Suddenly from behind us one of the Humvees opened up with a .50, its report blasted over the sound of the loud music. I looked over and saw tracers zip down a side street, but didn't see the target.

"Ogre to Tango Three, what are you firing at? Over."

"Unknown, Ogre. I saw something big, but it moved too fast."

"What was it?"

"I really don't know Sir." The Tango Three's gunner said.

Over the radio Sinead in the passenger seat of the M-ATV came on. "Sir, I saw it too. I don't know what it was, but it was big. Really big."

"Well what did it look like?"

Sinead didn't answer. "What did it look like?"

"Ah... "

I looked over at Joy. "What the hell is wrong with my crew all of a sudden?" Into the radio I said, "Well?"

“Sir... it... it looked like a Big Foot.” Sinead finally said.

“Tango Three, is that what you saw?”

“Roger. That’s what it looked like.”

Joy held up her finger, “That location marks the same location of one of the downed Rotor Drones, or near enough to it.”

“Alright then.” I turned on blinkers and opened the radio channel again. “Let’s take another look. Gunners, get ready.”

I looked back and saw Kilo go from his ACR to the fifty and I heard him charge it. I flipped a U-Turn and the short column of vehicles went back the way it was, then turned left onto the side street we had passed. About a half a block I saw some marks that indicate bullet strikes. “This is it, Sir.” Joy said, looking up from the BFT and looking around.

“Is this where you saw the thing, Tango Three?”

“Affirmative, Sire.”

We sat there for a moment and looked around and listened. Nothing moved, not even a breeze. Everything was perfectly still. “Dismounts, on me.” I called into the radio.

“Why do you have to do that?” Caroline asked.

“Do what?”

“You have to Captain Kirk everything.”

“Do I look like Shatner?”

“No, but you act like Kirk.”

I had my hand on the door latch but let go and sat back. “There are green chicks around here.”

“No, you keep beaming yourself down when you could let a team do it.”

I looked back at Caroline. “First, no one here is wearing a red shirt more than me. Second, I’m not about to ask anyone to do anything that I wouldn’t do myself. Third, I lead from the front because the view is better, and if you don’t you are not leading, but you’re being a backseat driving REMF.” I opened the door and jumped out, Crusader Warhammer in hand.

“What’s a REMF?” Rebecca asked.

“A REMF is a Rear Echelon Mother Fucker.” Kilo said as he climbed up out of the turret, “Caroline, take the Fifty.”

“Sir.” She said as she climbed up and took Kilo’s place.

I looked back into the Raptor. Joy was already out and by my side, while Caroline was up in the turret. Kilo jumped off the back of the truck and slung his ACR on the single point sling and looked around slowly taking in everything like he had learned in his training. Windows, doors, shadows, under vehicles. The stock of his rifle was in the shoulder pocket but the muzzle was down. The finger was along side the frame of the weapon, and his thumb was up on the safety lever. Good lad.

I looked in the Raptor and Rebecca was still in the truck, messing around with gear.

“Officer Hallbrook, would you care to join us or would you rather wait in the car and listen to MP3s?" I said into the radio. No one laughed outright, but there was a lot of smirking. Rebecca practically fell out of the truck as her rifle caught in the seat belt.

"When we are coming up on a stop where we could get into action, you take one hand, unlatch the seat belt, and move the belt up and away from your gear so when we do stop you can get out quickly. I'd have thought they would have taught you that in the police academy."

Rebecca stiffened, "Yes, Sir."

"Sire." Joy hissed.

"Sire." Rebecca looked down.

I looked over at Sinead who was biting her lower lip. "Sinead, you are now in with us. Rebecca, you are now in Tango Two. Everyone, search the area."

I started looking around, not knowing exactly what it was I was looking for. Trash and debris was everywhere.

"What are we looking for?" Kilo asked.

"Crashed ROV that looks like a small helicopter." Joy said.

"Bigfoot" Sinead said.

"Whatever might be out of place." I said.

On one side of the street I looked up at the bullet holes in the wall. Tango Three's .50 cal had torn out chunks of old brick from the side of a building. I could smell the residue from the HESH rounds he had fired. I could also smell a heavy, musky scent, like the cross between skunk and wet dog. It was thick and made my upper lip and nose curl into a sneer.

"What's that smell?" Kilo said, covering his nose as he looked around.

"Tango Three's unknown target."

"Do you think it was a Bigfoot?" Kilo asked me.

"Son, to me, BigFoot is a Monster Truck that runs around dirt-filled arenas with other monster trucks. I don't know what Tango Three saw."

"That's too bad." He said.

"Why is that?"

"I'd like to hang Bigfoot's head up on the wall back at Fort George."

*That's my lad*, I thought as I patted him on the shoulder. As I did that, I noticed something on the ground. I went over to it and knelt down. Circuit board fragments.

"I think we found part of our missing Rotor Drone."

The circuit board parts lead us to other parts, and a section of rotor blade. The section was scorched and shattered.

"It's like an RPG hit it." Iron Mike said. I looked up at the big CG and nodded.

"Yeah, it does. But that would have been a hell of a good shot." I said.

There was no other parts to recover. Whatever had shot it down had taken off with the wreckage.

"If they took the little chopper, they probably took the other one too." Joy said.

I nodded in agreement. "Yeah, I think you're right." I circled my finger up in the air "Saddle up!" I said, and everyone went back to their vehicles.

Once we started rolling again, I looked into the back seat. Sinead was grinning at me in the rear view mirror. I looked back at the road and then back into the mirror. She was still grinning. "You are one creepy chick, Irish."

"You replaced one of your own yanks with a little Irish girl such as myself."

"You are still creepy."

"Yeah," she said, sitting back. "I get that a lot."

## Opera Stake-out

Our objective rally point was a hotel within view of the Palais Garnier. We approached the building from the east, taking care to not allow ourselves to be seen by anything from within the Palais. The teams in the Humvees bailed out and instantly went about securing the building. They moved with speed and efficiency, clearing out a couple dozen of the undead that were locked behind unlocked doors.

Within minutes, we were in an upstairs room, looking out the window at the Palais directly.

Zombies were milling about, some going in, some coming out. At first it seemed like there was no order, but then we realized that the zombies that went in, seemed to come out with a purpose. They would mill about a little while, but would eventually take off in different directions. Some time later, they would come back, mill about, and then return inside. Something was going on.

I heard a small vibration and glanced over at Joy. She plucked a small Nokia cell phone from a vest pocket and flipped it open.

"Maclean is demanding to talk to you, Lord. Evidently he is at a hospital. Doctors are demanding you talk to him. It seems he makes a very poor patient." Joy was trying not to laugh. "Men can be such babies... it's not like the doctor is going to shove a speculum up inside him."

FMJ was setting up his sniping position on top of a table he'd pushed near the window. "Get him on the line. Paul, make sure you put your sunshade on. We don't want some reflection to give away our position." FMJ nodded as he pulled the legs down on his bi-pod.

Joy walked over to the huge, soft bed and fell back into it as she started tapping little buttons.

I turned back to the Palais and lifted Paul's Leica GeoVids to my eye. To me, it was just a bino. If I still had my right eye, I'd have seen the range to target reading. I watched the traffic for a moment before handing the Geovids back to Paul. "Let me know if anything changes, FMJ."

"Right on..." Paul nodded. "You don't mind if I light up do you?"

"Naw, go ahead, but when the sun starts to go down, put it out."

"Roger that, Boss." Paul's grin stretched out into a wide smile as he pulled out a thick cigar. "Say, you think if I find a Ferrari that I could keep it?"

"I don't know, Paul. Are you sure you really want one?"

"Yeah, I am. I know it's not the most practical of cars these days, but it's been a thing with me."

"Go ahead, if it makes you happy."

Paul nodded slowly as he lit his cigar.

Joy started talking, "Hey Maclean... what are you doing in a Hospital? You hurt? Really? Good, you probably deserved it for some past sin. What's going on?" Serious? And how's Will? Sugar Plum is okay? Yeah, we're going to need you guys up and ready. Me? I'm laying on the softest bed I've ever felt in this awesome old hotel here in Paris... Yeah, in Paris. No, he's still in his full battle-rattle. Work before pleasure you know. He's doing fine, still trying to use binos with both eyes... but he's fine."

I walked over and kicked her foot. "Don't be a smart ass."

Joy giggled. "He wants to talk to you." She held up the Nokia.

I plucked the phone from the her hand. "How come you're in a Hospital? No... No... I don't want to hear that shit. Get your convalescing ass up and atom. I need you and your team over here Riki Tiki. Something is going on. Something big. Where's Will? How's he doing? I need him. I need that spooky, sneaky shit he does. I need some eyes inside the target before we go in. Uh huh. Yeah... Put the Doctor on."

I walked back towards the window. "Is this Doctor Jessup? This is George... That's right, that George. Stop, shut up. Here's what I need you to do... Fill Maclean full of painkillers, stimulants, and a full spectrum of anti-everything... and send him on the way. He has a job to do. He can rest later." The doctor went into a full monologue before I could cut him short. "Listen up Doc, if I have to come get him myself, I'm going to fillet you open and staple you to the fucking wall like a scene out of *Hellraiser* or some crazy shit like that, make you look like a Jackson Pollock painting... so get him up and ready to go before I start getting rude. Good. That's what I want to hear. Thank you Doctor."

I tossed the phone back to Joy. "Damn Sawbones. Wants Maclean and Sugar Plum to rest for a week."

"I'd like to rest for a week." Joy said.

"You are resting." I said.

Paul was chuckling as he peered through his rifle scope. "You have a way with words, Boss. Ordering a Doctor around like he was your bitch." He shook his head.

"It's good to be the King."

## Zed Couriers

We watched the zombies for hours, trying to find the patterns that I knew were there. We picked up on a couple of notes. The zombies coming back had bags. Messenger bags, backpacks, or purses over their shoulders. That was easy enough to see, but then we noticed that when the zombies came back, the bags seemed heavier and when the zombies came back out, the bags were empty.

"What do you think they have in those bags?" Paul asked.

I had an idea, but I only said "It doesn't matter. I don't care if they are fetching groceries."

"Brrraaaaiiiinnnnssssss...." Joy growled.

"Please don't ever do that again."

"Scared?"

"No, but I did almost shoot you."

Joy rolled over onto her stomach and stretched. "You'd miss me."

"I know I would." Paul said.

I shook my head and keyed my radio, "Ogre to all Tango units, radio check. Over."

Kilo, Caroline and Sinead were all waiting in the vehicles, keeping low profiles and quietly watching the occasional shambler that made its way past. CGs were holding the ground floor secure. Everything was fine, but I started getting that itch. Something wasn't right.

"You guys stay here, keep observing." I said and picked up my gun and headed out the door. Standing at the stairwell, was Iron Mike, large and armed with an M-240. He was leaning casually up against the wall, watching the stairwell.

"Sire." Mike stood up straighter.

I held out my hand, "no, take it easy."

He looked at me with an eye that said he wasn't looking at me, but into me. Mike's VIP Protection background gave him years of experience and insight into people. This is why he had been my first pick in keeping my family safe. It also allowed him to see that I had become worried. "What's the situation boss?"

I looked at Mike and I knew I couldn't brush him off. "I don't know, big guy. How are you feeling?"

"I feel fine, Boss. Nothing wrong here."

"Keep alert, Mike."

"You expecting something?"

"I don't know." I walked downstairs, all six floors.

Down in the lobby on the ground floor, the men had pushed up furniture and created barricades. Above these barricades, were some heavy weapons. M-249s.

"How are you boys doing here?"

Everyone jumped up. "No, no, no... you guys take it easy. Everyone okay? Anyone pick up on any problems?"

"No, Sir. We're all green lights. We were just enjoying some quiet time."

I noticed that Rebecca looked down when I approached her. "You okay, Becca?"

"Fine, I guess... Sire. I'm sorry."

I cut her off. "It wasn't you, Rebecca. I decided that I needed to keep a closer eye on our adopted Irish girl." There were things I wanted to say about that situation, but I didn't know how to put them into words, so I just moved on. I checked everyone out, and nothing seemed out of order.

When I headed to the door, Kilo was sitting very low in the turret of the Raptor. He saw me pull the door open and peeked up just enough so I could see him and he put his finger to his lips. The universal "Shush" sign. Before stepping outside, I slowly looked around the doorway, down the street. Several zombies were lurching their way across the intersection. When they had passed, I looked up and down the street in both directions. When it felt clear, I darted out to the Raptor and climbed in, quietly shutting the door. "Hey guys."

Kilo slipped down from the turret, "Hey Pops".

Caroline was laying down in the back seat with an iPod with one ear bud in and her nose in a Marcus Wynne novel. Sinead was in the driver's seat, with the seat leaned back so she could stay low. She was sharpening a long thin blade.

Everything seemed fine, and I didn't know what was wrong, but something was wrong here. I looked out the windshield and didn't see anything amiss. When I looked out the back window, I saw the hulking form of the M-ATV sitting there, its M2 machine gun pointing upwards.

"Guys, I know this truck is more comfortable... but I need you guys to change over to the Mat-Vee."

"What? Why?"

"I don't know. Just do it for me. I want you guys behind more armor."

"Maybe we should come upstairs?" Caroline asked, sitting up.

I shook my head, "No, that doesn't feel right. I just want you guys in the Mat-Vee."

"Okay, Dad. We'll switch."

"Good. Move as soon as you can."

As I went back inside, Kilo and the girls were already moving to the M-ATV.

"Tango One is now in the Mat-Vee. Tango Two, you guys get the Raptor."

"Hey, Sweet!" One of the guys said. "I'm driving!"

# On the Alert

I headed back upstairs, passing Mike with a pat on the shoulder and went back into the suite. Joy had stripped out of her armor and was stretched out on the bed diagonally. "Joy, get back into your wargear ASAP."

She woke up and rolled off the bed to her gear. "Ten four, Chief."

Some time later everything still seemed fine, but I was growing uncomfortable. The zombies outside were moving in their same patterns. Nothing there had changed.

I was looking out the window when I noticed the sun high in the sky. It was directly over the Opera House. It would be getting dark in a couple hours. Then I noticed the Red Eye that was looking up at the window.

"Paul..."

"Yeah, Boss?"

"Did you put the sunshade on your scope like I told you?" I said as I turned and looked in his rifle case.

"Uh..."

I held up the sunshade. "Paul..."

"Oh..."

"Damn it, man!"

"I..."

When I turned back and looked out, I saw the Red Eye running inside the Opera House. "Oh shit. Guys... we've got to get rolling... Now."

I picked up my Warhammer and pulled Joy up off the bed where she had been napping. As I got her to her feet, we felt a sudden reverberation that shook everything. Like the beat of a huge bass drum, that we felt but didn't hear. "The pebble." I said. I realized that the concussive wave wasn't a physical wave, but a blast of psychic energy... and it didn't shake everything, just my perception. I instantly started getting a headache and became sick to my stomach.

Paul was opening the straps in his rifle case. I glanced out of the window again and saw the undead that had been milling around the opera house, all moving towards our building. "Leave the case! There's no time!"

I pushed Joy to the door.

Mike appeared outside the door, "Sire! We've got movement outside, lots of it!"

"We've got to get to the trucks." We were six stories up in a building with no elevator.

I keyed the radio. "Ogre to Kilo... Kilo, are you in the Mat-Vee?"

"Just like you said, Dad."

"Get the guns ready. Expect contact very soon."

"Roger that."

"We're on the way down."

Joy followed Mike out into the hall with her weapon ready. I was on her heels when I heard Paul's voice. I turned back and I saw Paul standing in the doorway with his rifle. "I'll hold them off from here!" As he spoke the room behind him started glowing with an orange yellow light that was rapidly getting brighter.

"Get Down!" I shouted.

Paul had just started to turn to look when the blast hit. The demonic fireball exploded at the window in the room, and the concussive blast slammed Paul into the wall across the hall. He hit the wall half way up to the ceiling with the sickening sound of things crunching that shouldn't be crunched. He fell to the floor like a discarded doll, broken and unmoving, leaving an FMJ shaped indention in the wall, save where a heavy wood beam intersected the outline. The room he was thrown out of, was already fully engulfed in flame.

"Paul!"

I ran back to him, but I could see it was already far too late. Compound fractures in the clavicle jutted out through the armor. The upper arm and his right shoulder were twisted like his arm was coming out of his back. The side of his face was crushed, and an eye was evulsed. He was gone. "Paul..."

I could hear the fire in the room crackling and smoke was pouring out into the hallway. I looked into the room and saw that most of the outer wall was blasted open. Over the sound of the fire, I could hear the moaning of the undead outside.

I ran to the stairs and started down. Small arms fire erupted. First it was a few guns, then it was a lot of guns. More guns than we brought. I didn't know who was firing, but it sounded like everyone. The radio chatter was frantic. Kilo was screaming orders to the CG outside at the onset of the engagement from the safety of the M-ATV as ordered. Some of the CGs had jumped into the Raptor, which was the closest to the hotel's door. The zombies swarmed the Humvees and the Raptor. Kilo watched from the Driver's seat of the M-ATV, as Zombies tore into the Ford truck, climbed up to the open turret and crawled inside.

Kilo watched in horror as the Ford Raptor rocked on its suspension. He saw a hand streaking blood against the window as a zombie stood on the hood, grinning as it fired a FAMAS full auto into the windshield.

"Dad, it's fucked up out here."

I could hear Caroline's voice over the radio, "There's too many!" Then Kilo yelled at her, "Get back up on that gun!" I could also hear the gunshots and bullets pinging and ricocheting off the M-ATV's armor.

"Kilo! Get out of there! Go! Now!"

"Father!"

"GO!"

Through the radio I could hear the M-ATV's engine fire up and rev hard. I could hear the tires shrieking over the din and the M-ATV's .50 open up. In seconds, the sound of the .50 disappeared in the distance.

"I'll send air support, Dad! And the tanks! Hold on!"

"I'll be fine. You get back to the lines!"

I made it down to the landing just above the first floor and saw Joy coming back up. She had panic in her face. "They're shooting! They have guns!" She had blood splatter on her, blood that was not her own.

"Where's Mike?" I asked.

"Where's Paul?" She asked.

We both knew the answers to the questions. There was another explosion above us. A fireball had hit the hotel again. More gunfire opened up downstairs, and we heard crashing sounds of breaking wood and glass and the continual moaning of a tireless force.

"They were overrun." Joy breathed hard. "All of them."

"Come on, back up." I pulled a frag off my belt and flicked off the safety clip. Joy ran up ahead of me as I started up, pulling the pin as I ran. Bullets tore through the banister of the old staircase, sending splinters flying everywhere. Joy shrieked and threw herself to the wall to get away from the incoming fire.

I looked at the grenade in my hand as I let the spoon slip off my finger tips. It rang as it went flying, and the world seemed to be in slow motion. I started the count as I continued up the stairs.

One, one thousand...

The hypersonic crack as bullets zipped passed seemed to have slowed down to the lower tone buzz of bumble bees in flight. Wooden shrapnel from the railing tumbled past my face, and I saw the altering of raw wood and two hundred years of varnish and polish.

Two, one thousand...

Joy was scrambling on all fours, with her weapon flying in the air behind her, tight against the sling. More buzzing. Chunks of plaster above us were exploding outwards as bullets tore into walls. The grenade rolled out of my hand and over the edge of the stairs, just between the narrow rails.

A moment after the grenade fell out of sight, I felt an impact against my armor. Little black bits of plastic and circuit flew through the air, and parts of my radio turned instantly into confetti. The hit had come from behind. I turned and I could see the face of a zombie. Half its face was blacked with rot and the other was bare bone, yet both white eyes stared at me. It lurched up the stairs after us, holding a pistol out in front of it.

Suddenly, time was back to normal, and I raised my Warhammer. The Viridian laser put a bright green dot on the undead and it quickly found its way to the zombie's head. I pulled the trigger. The Warhammer bucked like a jackhammer. Holding the weapon, it was easy to forget this was a shotgun. Once you fired it, you remembered real quick. Especially if you had flicked the safety lever all the way around to full auto. The recoil was heavy. Chunka chunka chunka chunka! Four fast shots before I could let off the trigger. The results were instant and dramatic on the zombie. The mass of the zombie's head now decorated the ruined walls of the hotel.

The detonation of the grenade was almost a dull thud below us, but the volume of fire coming up the stairwell was instantly cut off.

"Where are we going?" Joy screamed.

"To the roof!"

We ran up the stairs, and at the top of the 7th floor was a door marked "hotel staff only". Or I imagined it did... It was in French and I don't read a lot of it if its not on a menu. The door was locked, but the Warhammer opened it with one knock. This stairway was short and narrow and led up to another door; this one wasn't locked and it opened outward onto the flat roof.

The roof was mostly bare save for a card table, a couple small wooden chairs, and some antenna. I grabbed a chair and shoved it against the door, under the handle. It was the best I could do. Joy was panting, leaning over, catching her breath.

I ran to the edge of the roof and looked at the nearest building. The alley was narrow, and the other building slightly higher, but just below us on the building was a fire escape made of wrought iron. We could jump it.

"I think we can make this... it's not too far to jump." I was pretty sure I could make the jump, but Joy would have no problem.

I looked back at her. She was on her knees and her panting was faster.

"Joy?"

She didn't look up. Her arms hung from her shoulders, completely slack. She was leaning back, sitting on her heels, but her head was down. The weight of her weapon on the sling behind her was what was keeping her from falling forward.

"JOY!"

I ran to her and could see the neat little holes seeping red in the side of her K-Plate armor. Two bullets had entered her side. "No, Joy! NO!"

I flicked out my Emerson knife and cut away the armor as fast as I could. Joy looked up at me weakly. "I die in Paris... this isn't so bad. I could have died in a bookstore in Orem." She tried to smile through her pain. Her breath was coming in short, quick gasps. As I pulled her armor off, blood that had been pooling up, poured out like an upended mug. "Oh no! NO!"

I looked in her eyes as her gasps slowed. She looked back into mine as she smiled. "...is... okay... my... love... Jen's... here... and April." Her last breath escaped her lips as she looked at me, still smiling. A moment later, the light in her eyes went out.

She was gone.

"JOY!"I screamed into the sky as the thudding started on the doorway. A zombie pounded, but the small, wooden chair held fast, and they couldn't get through as the stair was too narrow for more than one undead to come up at a time. I ignored the zombies at the door and eased Joy's body down, and closed her eyes.

From the direction of the Opera, I could hear laughter. A deep belly laugh that reverberated the air. I couldn't help but clench my teeth as I stood. The door was failing under the weight of the zombies pushing and banging on it. Finally, it cracked and buckled. When the zombies spilled out over the roof, they found only the still body of a blond-haired girl.

Later when a helicopter came, it slid low over the building's roof, coming to a hover. Smoke curled around the rotorwash. Well-aimed shots from the suppressed Sterling cleared the roof quickly of the remaining zombies that had been milling about. It was a Scotsman that rappelled down to the roof and went to Joy's body.

"It's the King's Mistress at Arms, Lady Ansfrida."

"Where is the King?"

"There's no sign of him."

"Damn it."

"What about the body?"

"We'll bring her back. That's what his Majesty would want. Be quick about it, it's getting hot up here!"

## Ogre on the Run

It was dark and I was still running. I knew running from the hotel was a bad idea, but the choice was not my own. I had about two hundred zombies after me, some of them Red Eyes. Somehow they knew I had jumped to the other building and were waiting for me. I was down to my last magazine and the zombies were still behind me. All I could do was run.

I spun and let the zombies get closer as I took aim. *Make the shots count.* I unloaded and dropped the dozen zombies that had been on my tail. The weapon was now empty and useless, only serving as dead weight. I hit the sling's quick disconnect and let the Crusader Warhammer drop as I turned to run again.

When I came around a corner, I crashed head long into a Red Eye. We were both sent sprawling. I tumbled and instantly got back to my feet. The Red Eye had been taken by surprise, but it too rose from the ground and seemed indignant at my rudeness. The creature turned to me. It had been a woman in life. She was thin, but well dressed for the Undead. Her clothes looked fairly new and clean. Her red eyes locked on to me and she snarled. She uttered something in French that I didn't understand.

I pulled out my Becker Combat Bowie and waited for her move. She reached out one hand and I felt a force around my neck, but it didn't effect me. "Wrong move." I lunged and slashed and the Red Eye's head went flying. For the moment, I couldn't see any more zombies, but off in the distance, I could hear the all too familiar moaning.

I turned and ran again. I didn't know where I was going, but I knew I couldn't keep going much longer. I had to find a place to hold up, put up a signal. When I looked around, I didn't see anything promising, only one building, tall, narrow. It looked like an apartment building. I went to the door and found it unlocked. When I went inside, it was dark.

I pulled my HK and took a step inside, trying to control my breathing. I let the door shut behind me, quietly. Something didn't feel right... I didn't smell death or rot... I could smell gingerbread.

The blow came from behind. It was heavy. It hit me in the head and drove me to the ground. I heard voices speaking in French as I lost consciousness.

I wasn't out very long. I could feel hands pulling gear off of me. Then I could hear arguing. Not that I understood what they were saying, but the tone. They couldn't decide what to do with me.

"Nous devons le tuer. Nous ne savons pas qui il est."

"Jetons lui à l'extérieur ... laissez les marcheurs prendre soin de lui."

I cracked open my eye just enough. No one was looking in my direction. My handgun was gone. My magazines were gone. My Becker Bowie and Companion knives were gone. Luckily I was not bound and I was still in my K-Plate.

One of the voices was a woman, she was arguing with a male, a younger man... there were other voices as well. I couldn't tell how many. I moved quickly. I pushed up, kicked my feet under me, and lunged. I grabbed the woman from behind and pulled her into a choke hold. She screamed. The man she was arguing with spun and raised my gun. The safety was off and his finger was on the trigger, but it barely reached and the man's grip was awkward. He was no shooter, and I decided no serious threat either.

I reached up under my K-Plate, the Necker was still there. I always wore my neck knife as it had saved my hide several times now. I pulled the blade out and put it to up to her throat. "Drop the gun."

The man said something and tightened the grip on the gun. The muzzle quivered.

"DROP THE GUN!"

He didn't, but the look of his resolve was weakening. I looked over the man's shoulder at nothing, but the sudden look caught the French guy off guard... he looked for what I had looked at. As soon as his eyes were off me, I spun the girl away and threw myself at the guy. I flew across the small space and landed a solid punch on the man's head. The man was knocked against the wall and he slid down.

With the HK back in my hand, I was able to take control of the situation again.

"English mother-fuckers... Do you speak it?"

"I say little English, yes."

"I want my blades back, please."

"Your knives, yes?"

"Yes, I want them back, now. Put them on the floor."

There were six survivors, two of them came forward, slowly and put my knives on the ground. "Good. Now my other stuff, pistol magazines, the mace, flashlights, everything you took off of me. I want it all back, please." Once all my possessions were presented and put in the pile, I needed them to give me some room. "Now back up, please."

I put my knives back in the sheaths, clipped the light mace to my belt, and put the spare mags for my HK back into their carriers. Only then did I slip the Necker back into its place as well. "Now we can have a conversation." I kept the HK in my hand. I didn't trust these people at all.

"Conversation?"

"How long have you been here?"

"Three. Three weeks." The girl was pretty, but had an arrogant look of disdain about her.

"Who are you guys?"

"Perhaps, it is you who should tell us who you are? You now have us as... prisoners."

"No, no... I was just... Hey, you hit me first."

"You had gun. You could have been evil as you look."

"Do you think I am?"

The girl looked at me like she thought I was kidding. "Knife to my throat.. you hit Jeac... You look like terrorist. You sound American. Yes, I say you are evil man."

"He pointed my gun at me."

"He should have pointed more harder." She actually sneered at me.

"Nice... alright." This wasn't working out very well. I was tired. I had a raging headache. And I knew I couldn't trust anyone here. If I fell asleep, I didn't think I'd wake up again.

Outside was deep black.

I went to the door and looked out. The street, from what I could see of it, was clear of the undead.

"Look, just outside of Paris, is a picket line of soldiers. Safety. Food. Medical care. You get to them, you'll be alright."

"We don't need help from you... whoever you are."

"I'm the Ogre."

"Fitting title."

"You are just all sorts of pleasant aren't you?"

"Just as pleasant as you are, Monsieur."

"You're the one that hit me."

"I would call it a small pleasure." The woman smiled sweetly.

With that, I went back outside.

## The Getaway Car

I started running back to the hotel where the ambush happened. As I crossed an intersection, I caught a glimpse of a Chinook helicopter. Its running lights cast strange shadows over the darkened streets. I could hear the sounds of small engines racing up another street, but I didn't know where it was coming from or where they were going. I pressed on, with the HK in my hand.

The sound of an explosion was a surprise. I could hear the big helicopter going down. The sound of the crash echoed through the streets and I wasn't the only one that heard it. Zombies started shuffling and moaning. Some were already running.

I looked behind me, and through the gloom of half hidden moonlight, I saw a mob of zeds coming my way, heading to the crash. I ducked behind a row of cars and crawled into an unlocked Peugeot 406 Coupe. It was a small car, but only one of the few decent ones the French had ever built. The driver was a desiccated corpse, long dead and dried out. I ducked down in the back seat and waited till the mob passed. A few moments later, I peeked up, very carefully. There were a few rotten zeds shambling by, but no real threats. I noticed that a ring of keys were hanging out of the ignition. When I turned the key, I was happily shocked that the lights on the dash came to life and the gauges indicated good news. I wasn't going to question this blessing. This car had been parked here for a long time, and without any outside aide, was ready to run. This was a good thing, because I was tired of running.

When the street was clear enough of zombies, I pushed the long-dead driver out the door and jumped into the driver's seat. A 406 is not a big car, but it's quick. The engine fired up and I gave it a few revs. The car sounded eager and ready to get moving again. I put it into gear and started rolling. When I turned on the headlights, I saw that the street was more infested than I had thought. Thousands of zombies were coming my way.

I spun the 406 and hit the gas. Thankfully the car was really quick.

I raced in the direction of the crash... zombies bouncing off the hood, one cracked the windshield. I rounded a corner in a power slide, suddenly slammed on the brakes.... someone in my headlights that wasn't dead.

The high beams lit up the man who had been running. He skidded to a stop, as did I. He looked familiar. I opened the door and stood up out of car. We both looked at each other with a "WTF" expression.

"Sugar Plums? That you?"

I took a step toward him when I saw his eyes go wide. I heard the sound of bare feet slapping the ground, and all of a sudden an impact. A zombie crashed into me, almost sending me to the ground. I grabbed it over my shoulder and threw it off of me. I finished it with a single shot of .45 ACP to the noggin. I could hear more running. When I turned to look, a glowing orange and yellow finger of death reached out from above and shredded everything it touched. Parked cars, zombies alike. The tracers made a solid line from the zombies up to the roof top of some sort of fashion store for Lady Gaga wannabees. Hanging its ass end over the edge, I saw the tail of the big chopper and men with guns leaning over the edge as well. Will got on a radio and started talking to someone. He made a gesture back to me. "Come on."

Leaving the little, French car where it was, I followed him, .45 still in hand. The zombies behind us were being chewed to bits on an industrial scale, but some still lingered in shadows and under cars. Some decided to rush us, but they fell. What I didn't shoot, someone else did with suppressed rifle fire from up above. Will walked with a casual swagger as if he'd taken this stroll a thousand times before.

"Enjoy your little holiday, my Lord?"

I ignored the jab and pulled out a pen. I never go into the field without my trusty pen and note pad. I quickly drew a map and put an X on the building I had left not long ago. "We have survivors here, about a half dozen surly French... there may be more. They are paranoid and potentially dangerous... but they might like you."

Will took the paper and looked at the map. "Not too far away... alright."

"What happened to the Chinook?"

"Took a hit from a rocket. Warning alarms. We set down real hard."

"Casualties?"

He held up his arm and pointed at his elbow. "Bruise here, and I bit my tongue, but I'll be able to eat ice cream again in no time."

"Good. We lost a lot of good people, I'm glad we didn't lose anymore. Alright, I'm going up to the chopper." I looked up at the roof, then back to Will, who was already gone. I looked around for him, and there was no sign. The street was empty.

"How does he do that?" I asked no one. One more look around for any sign of where Will had vanished to and I ran upstairs to the chopper.

When I reached the roof top, there was a small cheering section to welcome me. The pilot explained that they were frantic in looking for me. When the hotel we had used had been over run, everyone came looking for me. The hotel was cleared out and they searched room to room in case I'd found a hiding place, then they started searching adjacent buildings.

I nodded, "That's great, and I knew you would... but the zombies were all over me, I had no choice but to beat feet. But I'm here now, so the search can be called off." Then I asked the questions I didn't know if I wanted answered. "Did Kilo make it back to the lines safely?"

"Yes, my Lord. He took command and organized the search for you."

"Were our people recovered at the hotel? Their bodies?"

"Yes, your Majesty. All of them."

"The body on the roof?"

"Lady Ansfrida was recovered as well."

I nodded. There was nothing I could do about that now. That time had passed. I mentally shook my mind back to the present. "We need to get back on task."

"Yes, my Lord." The Chinook pilot pulled the craft gently up into the air and turned it around. It gave a shudder through the airframe, but then stabilized. Warning lights were all over the cockpit... as was a monotonous tone.

"Can we get back to the Grand Hotel near the Opera House?"

The pilot checked his gauges twice before answering. "We'll make it, Sir... and then back to the FOB for some quick repairs and she'll be fine."

I sat down and looked around the bird. It was the first time I could take a deep breath... Joy's death, along with the others... Mike, Rebecca, my team... my running for what felt like forever... getting knocked out... I closed my eye.

## Bomb the Opera

I heard the Co-Pilot chattering on the radio. Next thing I knew the Crew Chief was shaking me. "Your Majesty... the Opera House. We're here."

I opened my eye and saw that the Chinook wasn't set down on the roof of the hotel, but hovering with the ramp down over the edge. It was time to get back into the game.

I stood up and walked off the chopper back onto the roof I had jumped from. In the gloom of the night, I could see the dark stain of Joy's blood. I turned to the Crew Chief and asked "Where is her body?"

"My Lord, Prince Kilo ordered her body to be taken to Achnacarry. He said she should be buried next to Lady April."

"Good... that's good." I'd have ordered the same thing. Smart kid.
The troops were fully assembled, I noted as I looked over the edge of the hotel. I looked at the Armor on the street. Challengers and LeClerics with Strykers and LAVs behind them.

When I looked back at the Opera House I felt it again... the pebble. Psychic energy pulsed out from the building. This time, it was sharp and painful... my head felt like it was struck with a hammer. I was staggered. The Chinook dipped down and I heard the engines surge as the chopper pulled up into the sky for safety. Below us, soldiers had been knocked down. The dead took advantage of the opportunity and surged out of the old building.

I grabbed a radio from the man next to me. "Weapons free! RAZE THE OPERA HOUSE!"

The tanks opened fire with HEAT and HESH rounds. Shells exploded along the sides of the building. A Tow streaked out from a launcher and opened a large hole. Chunks of concrete flew out all directions. All the soldiers were cheering while the tanks kept firing.

Over the sound of the tanks blasting the building and the small arms fire shooting at the zombies, we heard the helicopters coming and I looked up into the dark sky. As dark as it was, from the staccato light from all the muzzle flashes, I was able to make out the helicopters. Three Chinooks were flying in single file. Slung below each one was a small car. "What's this? What is going on?" I asked.

"Thought you would like this. This was Prince Kilo's idea." He handed me his pair of Binos and I looked up at the suspended cars and suddenly I started laughing.

"That is awesome."

"It gets better, my Lord. Each one is filled with high explosives."

As the helicopter's flew over the Opera House, the Toyota Priuses dropped, one at a time. As each car crashed through the roof, it detonated, blowing large sections of the old opera house apart. Between the explosive hybrids and the tank fire, little of the building remained that wasn't opened up to the sky. The Opera House was in ruins and it looked like about all the free roaming zombies were done as well. "I'm going down."

I looked down the side of the smoldering building. "Get me a rope." The CGs in attendance set up a rappel in a matter of moments. I tied a quick harness and hooked on. I descended with one bound and braked at the last moment, touching down to the ground without a jolt. The CGs followed me down and fanned out around me.

"My Lord! One of soldiers I recognized from Ft. George came running up, weapon in hand. "My Lord, your weapon, Sire!"

The man held out the Crusader Warhammer shotgun that I had dropped earlier. "Thank you."

We walked around the corner of the building. The remains of my Ford Raptor and the Humvees were still there. The bodies had been removed, but the blood and bits of torn flesh in the truck was still there, and still fresh. In the heat of the day, it would start to stink. Looking in the Raptor, I found my sword was still locked in place above the driver's door. I took it and slung the carrier over my back. In the back of the Raptor, still intact in the storage locker, was a pack full of loaded magazines for the Warhammer. I took the mags and refilled my vest pockets, then for good measure, slung the bag over my shoulder as well. I've never gone into a fight wishing I had less ammo. I topped off my pistol magazines, then having taken everything from the Raptor that I wanted, turned my back on it.

"My Lord, do you want us to recover it for repair?" A French soldier asked. I didn't even look at him.

"Recover the GPS, Coms and the Blue Force Tracker out of it, then torch it. Recover and repair the Humvees."

"As you wish, Sire."

I walked back to the tanks. They had stopped firing and all were quiet. There was a smear of red and chunks of gore from the tanks to the Opera House where surges of Zombies had poured out and rushed the armor. I looked around and saw that people were looking at me, waiting for the next order.

"Do we have Snipers on overwatch?"

"Of course, Your Majesty."

I turned to the Infantry and looked at them, in their eyes. "Now that the tin cans have had their fun... FOLLOW ME!"

As we moved to the ruins of the Opera House, I chambered my Warhammer shotgun and took it off Safety. After a few more steps, I hit the power on the EoTech sight and checked that it was on and on a lower power setting. I had a feeling that things would be dark soon even if the morning sun was climbing upwards.

As the sun's rays reached the torn doorway, it seemed that shadows bolted from their hiding spots to retreat deeper into the ruined building. The closer we got, the colder we all felt. I heard a shudder over my right shoulder. To my left, I heard the sound of a safety lever being flicked to the fire position, then again to Auto. "Good... Good man." I thought. He was afraid. I could feel it. It's good to be afraid. That means he's cautious, and he's going forward anyways. That means he's brave. I didn't look back to see who he was, but I was glad for his courage. I walked over long-dead corpses that had only just fallen still this night. Twisted faces of bare bone and rotten meat with expressions of hatred. I had a feeling that the look on the dead zombie's faces mirrored the attitude of France itself. If the old saying about beauty being only skin deep was true, and if Paris being the most beautiful at night as I used to hear, then I was looking at the true face of Paris France. I think I'd rather hang out on the Las Vegas Strip.

The shattered remains of one of the gold statues that used to be up on top of the roof of the Opera House was laying on the ground; it had fallen and crushed several zombies. One of which was reaching for the live flesh that was walking towards it. The man behind me to my left fired a single shot that went right through the zombie's head and out the other side, taking much of the skull's contents with it... most of which were black chunks, unrecognizable as brain tissue. I glanced at the dead zombie as I walked past. It used to be a police officer.

As we entered the building, I had the sensation that there was movement all around me. Whisperings and murmurings, just out of ear shot so we couldn't hear what was said... just that something was being said. Shadows moved across light where shadows couldn't be.

"This place is evil." Someone said behind me. I had to agree. I held up my hand and everyone behind me stopped. Two hundred men, some inside with me, others still outside. Everyone could feel the tangible malice in the air. Bits of plaster, crown molding, and decorative debris were still falling, and, other than the sounds they made, all we heard were the whisperings. I saw the burned and twisted steering wheel of a Toyota Prius and it cheered me up.

"For those that have a Faith," I turned around and looked at the men that were following me. "Now is a good time to pray."

I closed my eye and bowed my head for a moment. My prayer was simple, humble, but to the point. *"Thank you for keeping me alive so far... Help me send more evil back to hell before I'm done with this life."* I didn't know what else to say to a God that was letting all this happen to a world he'd created. Maybe he was just done with it, like a kid that grew bored of a toy. He just didn't care anymore.

I turned back around and walked further. A door had been blasted off the hinges, hanging from only a couple screws. Past the door was a darkness so deep, it seemed to pull light into it. I could hear things through the doorway, but couldn't see anything. I nodded in the direction of the door and men ran to it, queuing up on both sides, ready as if to breach the already broken door.

"See what's inside." I said, and nodded again.

The men flicked on weapon lights and I saw them count to three. Then they went in, alternating their entry so no one bunched up as they went through the fatal funnel. I motioned other men to secure the rest of the building. Some ran up a partially destroyed stair case, others fanned out through the ruins.

One of the men that breached the door came back, "Sire, there is a stairway going down. We don't know where it goes. It's very dark."

"I know." I said, pulling the Warhammer's stock into my shoulder pocket and adjusted the sling for a little looser fit. Then I took a deep breath, and went in.

The room was small, but the stairs going down looked long. The whisperings were louder, and, as we descended the stairs, we could make out words. Threats, taunts, warnings... the whisperings were in different voices, different languages, some understood, some not, but it felt like they were just on the cusp of understanding. It all felt evil and too familiar. Some of the muttering sounded and felt like they were spoken directly in my ears as if the speaker's lips were almost touching. Those whispers were worst... hate and anger... telling me I was going to be killed, that my soul was going to be ripped from my chest and devoured.

I kept going.

At the bottom of the stairs there was a hallway. The walls were black and greasy looking. The only light was from our weapon lights, and they all seemed dim. At the end of the hallway was a reddish gloom. As I walked forward, I could tell that the floor was made of stones... bricks or blocks of some sort, but the walls were different.

They looked like they were covered in congealed blood.

Here the voices were no longer whispers. We could hear crying and screaming that sounded like it was coming from the walls themselves. As I walked forward, the walls seemed to bubble outwards... faces... thousands of faces... some smiling, some screaming, others gnashing their teeth in hatred. The faces were like bubbles in boiling water. A mouth or eye would open and a short moment later, another face would push up out of it... each face different... each face unique, each one a different soul. The worst ones were the faces of children crying. Each face visible and unique for just a split second.

"Madness..." Some behind me spoke out. But I couldn't tell if it was one of my men, or one of these lost souls. I kept walking, shotgun at a low ready. I didn't dare take my eyes off the end of the hallway any more and I tried to ignore the faces on either side of me.

Up ahead, I heard laughter. Like the jovial laughter of a big brother, glad to welcome me. I stepped into a large room, ornate with gold and red and strung with bodies tied to the walls like garland. Around the room were piles of treasure. Gold, silver, and jewels of all sorts, piled high around the room.

## Angel of the Pit

A voice boomed out from the throne at the far wall and a figure slowly rose from the great chair... the figure was at least eight feet tall.

"Ah... the Ogre King is here at last, in person. How delightful!"

He was built of raw muscle and sinew and he wore no skin.

"I have been expecting you're minions... Louis, the Chosen One. Maclean, and his friend William the Sneak." His pronunciation was a little off as his lips had to move across exaggeratedly long canine teeth and tusks. "I didn't think that you would actually come personally. This is a treat." The way he said treat made a chill run up my spine. His voice was low and ageless and full of malice.

"You have me at a loss, Sir. You know me... but then again, everyone does these days. But I don't know who the hell you are."

"Who the hell? Indeed... good choice of words." He threw back his head and laughed. As he did, a name popped into my head.

*Abaddon.*

I knew this name, and I knew this was who I was talking to, who I had seen in my dreams. One of the Arch Demons, and one of the few mentioned by name in the Bible. "The Destroyer... The Angel of the Pit." I said.

The demon stopped laughing and looked at me. His smile was that of a crocodile. I heard quick footsteps behind me so I quickly glanced back over my shoulder... of all the men who had followed me... only two remained.

"To what do I owe this great honor? A visit from the great King? You are only one of three left now, you know... Kings."

"I'm sorry, I don't keep up with the tabloids."

"There is you... Ku, in China, and Hyrum in America. For now... Soon Hyrum will fall." Abaddon spoke offhandedly as he walked down the steps from his throne. "After you... unless..." His voice trailed off.

"Unless what?"

"Does the Ogre King have such a poor memory? You never gave me an answer to my very generous offer." The way the demon said "generous" sounded like a snake saying he was going to hug a bird... he even hissed the "s". "All of this." Abaddon's left hand was outstretched, palm up, innocently offering me the treasure. "All the wealth of Paris is here. I had my... subjects... gather it for you."

I looked around. The gold and the rest, piled along the walls, half way to the ceiling in thick mountains of fortune. A staggering amount of wealth. "This takes the phrase 'blood money' to a whole new level."

The demon took a step forward. "This is just a down payment, my little friend! This is just one city!" The monster's eyes flared with inner fire. "You can have it all... and all the rest of the wealth of the whole world! All you have to do is one very simple thing, for me. After all, I made you the King of England. I made you the President of the United States! I can make you so much more! I just want a little... gratitude."

"You want me to worship you."

"I am not asking too much... where much is given, much is expected. But I only ask you to bend your knee. I won't even ask you for a tithing." The demon chuckled at his own sense of humor.

"Where is the profit in that, Demon? What do I profit if I gain the world, but lose my soul?"

"Tisk, tisk, tisk, little one... what of your soul? It's already ours. You lost it when you broke your covenant with your wife, and killed how many people?" The monster shook his finger at me. "Thou shalt not kill. But you are so very good at that, aren't you?"

"The commandment is thou shalt not murder. There is a difference."

The demon shrugged, "Is there? I don't know. So many in the pit for killing and all have their own justifications and rationalizations, it's hard to tell. But don't worry, you have a special place of honor in our order. You are one of the Sons of the Morning! You were born for greatness! In this world and the next! In fact, in the next world, my place will be to bow to you!" The huge demon pantomimed making a deep bow. "But that time is not yet and you are still in this world."

The demon stood up straight again and his voice took on an edge. "Decide now, Ogre King. Do you fall, here and now, bathed in your own blood and the blood of your men. Or do you kneel before me and accept me as your Master?"

"I will never worship you, Filth. You disgust me." I snarled, "I'm sick of your lies, and I'm disappointed that you forgot something too."

The demon's eyebrow cocked, "oh?"

"You forgot that the last time we talked, I kicked your ass."

Abaddon snarled and made a quick gesture. He suddenly raised both hands held claws upwards. The men behind me were suddenly slammed against the wall and lifted screaming up to the ceiling.

Upstairs, only one of the men who had run away made it through the hallway and up the stairs. He was almost catatonic after he threw himself through the door into the light. He was covered in blood and gore, some of it his own.

"Where's the King!?" One of the CGs yelled.

"The demon... the demon!"

"What demon?"

"Huge... red... demon!"

"Where is the King?"

"Down there..." The man pointed back to the doorway he had just come through. The door was no longer there, just a blank wall.

## The Fight of my Life

My men were pinned to the ceiling, being pressed against it by unseen hands. They were screaming. One of them, pushed out with his ACR, one handed and fired on full auto. The 5.56mm rounds sprayed down on Abaddon, who seemed to have felt some pain from this. He ducked his head and shielded himself with one arm. With the other, he reached up and made another gesture. He squeezed his hand into a fist and as he did so, I watched my man crumble like a paper doll, into a ball. I heard bones crack and organs rupture. Blood gushed down from the ceiling like it was from a bucket suddenly upturned. The ACR fell to the ground with a clatter.

The other man grunted in pain as he was slowly being crushed against the ceiling.

"Let him go!" I yelled.

Abaddon continued to press and my Warhammer snapped up to my shoulder. The drum-mag in the gun was loaded was Federal Tactical, 00 Buck. Not the best anti-demon load, but what the hell... it was in the gun already. I ran forward and closed the distance between us. From only a few feet away I let him have it. Full auto, upwards into Abaddon's stomach and chest, twenty rounds. They rocked the demon backwards. Great wounds opened up in the raw red flesh and I felt hot splatter on my face. The bolt locked back and I instantly dropped the magazine and slammed a new one in. This one was loaded with Dixie Tri-Ball.

"If it bleeds, we can kill it!" I yelled, as I pulled the trigger again. Another twenty shells ripped into the demon, each oversized ball over-penetrated and chewed into the wall behind him. Bone and tissue were splintered and shredded.

Abaddon roared and swung. His massive arm caught me and I spun to the ground. The Crusader Warhammer shotgun was knocked away. Abaddon ran up on me and kicked me. The impact was absorbed by my armor, but the force was still there. All the air in my lungs was expelled, and I was thrown across the room, landing on my shoulder against a pile of gold and jewels. The armor took most of that impact as well. I gulped air, trying to breath again. When I looked up, my vision was filled with red.

Instinctively, I pulled my handgun out. I saw a hand reaching for me... I threw myself backwards, landing hard on the ground again, out of the grasp and brought the gun up. I fired until the slide locked back. Abaddon screamed again. "You maggot!" The voice seemed to shake the whole room.

I scrambled to my feet and bolted, but not fast enough to avoid the next blow completely. A massive clawed hand swung out and caught me in my shoulder and arm. The claws ripped through the armor like it was made of paper. Sharp pain exploded across my whole body, white hot and exquisite. I was spun again, but this time I retained my footing. I regained my balance and found that I was facing the huge monster.

I looked up in time to see another blow coming. This time, a fist. It slammed into my guts like a wrecking ball, then the wall behind me slammed me again. I fell to the ground. I coughed blood and puked hot bile.

Abaddon laughed. "I didn't know Kings made such fun playthings. I wish I had known before! I've wasted my time being so generous with you."

I spit out the taste of acidic copper from my mouth and tried to refill my lungs with air. As the demon laughed, I breathed deep and stood.

"I'm done playing." I growled. I reached up and pulled my sword from its scabbard over my right shoulder. The blade was white, radiating energy, crackling and giving off a hum. As I held the sword, the blood on my hand was suddenly burned off and fell to the ground like dust. I looked at the demon and saw fear in its eyes.

Abaddon hissed, "A Seraphim Blade! Where did you get that?!"

This was the same sword Jen had given me in London. "An angel gave it to me. I used it to strike down Plague of Crows. Now I'm going to use it again to send you back to your pit."

Abaddon roared as he ran straight at me. His huge legs pumped like great pistons, shaking the ground. I screamed as I ducked my shoulder and charged, sword held high. Just before we collided, I swung the sword as hard as I could.

The whole world exploded in light and pain.

I heard voices. Some familiar. Some distant. Voices calling my name. Some calling me their king. Some called me George. Some simply, "son". I could close my eye and I'd see faces I have not seen in some time. I'd open it, and I'd see men in tactical gear and armor. I didn't know if I should close my eye or keep it open.

"My Prince, he needs to be taken back to England... we don't have the facilities here in France. We've got a helo standing by. He's stabilized. He's safe to move."

"Fine, transport him immediately." Kilo said.

I felt myself being moved... I was being wheeled out of where ever I was... I couldn't see and I couldn't move.

"Where is the Duke? And Master Neil? Maclean? Where are the Generals?"

"We don't know, your Highness... they went out of contact an hour ago."

"That's just fantastic. Okay, let's pull all units back and as soon as they are clear drop the GBU-43. I want that place gone!"

"It will be so."

I recognized the voices. My Son, and the head of the CGs, Commander Roger Bisley. You could tell by his New York accent. Probably the only guy in France with a New York Accent, and one of the few people left in the world with it too.

Just then, a radio crackled. The signal was poor and full of static and noise. I couldn't make anything out save for one word. "Reavers."
The thought that came with that word sparked some energy back into me... but I couldn't move. I didn't have the strength. I opened my mouth to speak... the salty copper taste filled it and I croaked. Whoever was wheeling me stopped.

"Dad?"

Kilo came closer.

I licked my lips but my tongue was dry and thick. "Send in the Ninth Attack Wing... Let the Apaches work on the Reavers. Move the Armor in to support the ground..." That was all I could say. Speaking was exhausting. I could feel myself blacking out. Every time I did, the angels were with me. I could see them. Angels.

## Talking to Angels

The man talking to me looked familiar, but I couldn't place his name. He had an irritating way of flicking his wings when he made his points. Michael... I think. His name is Michael.

"But I ran my sword through his chest. To the hilt." I argued.

"And he ripped out your side with his claws."

"So... I'm still alive and he's dead."

"See, there's the problem."

I raised my eyebrow. "That I'm alive?"

"That's he's not dead."

"I saw him fall."

"You only killed the vessel... the body of the Acolyte that Abaddon took over. You killed the body, but the demon was only sent back to the Pit. He'll be back eventually. Once he recovers and finds a new vessel to take over."

"How long?"

"We can't know that. Lucifer is angry with him... he failed... he might not come out for some time. Might already be coming back. We don't know."

I looked down at my side. Fresh, pink flesh, newly grown where there were open wounds before. "He really got a chunk out of me, didn't he?"

Michael nodded. "Like the bite of a Great White shark."

"How am I even still alive?"

"You're not done yet."

"Where's my sword?"

Michael held his hand out and there was a brief flash of light. I blinked and the sword was there in his hand. Blade down, Michael held it out to me by the hilt. "Try not to lose this one, will you?"

"I didn't lose the one I had. It shattered." I looked up at the Archangel and he just smiled.

"They do that sometimes."

I took the sword and felt the weight of it. It felt just like the other one, but this one looked slightly different. "I like this one." Michael smiled at that.

"Thanks, I made it myself. Maybe one day I'll be allowed to teach you how to make your own."

"That would be very cool." I said, looking up at the Arch Angel.

"You know, you look just like..."

Michael cut me off. "If you say that Scientologist's name, I'll burn you to ashes."

"No, I was going to say Danzig."

"Pity."

"What?"

"I don't care for his music."

"Well, you do."

"I know... I just wished for something more Led Zepplin'ish.

"Like..."

"Like Robert Plant?"

"Yeah."

"But he looks just like Gabriel."

Michael flicked his wing in irritation.

"You like Led Zepplin?"

"Of course. We all do... classic." He moved his hand like he was dismissing me. "You should get back now."

My dream was getting strange and I could hear the beeping of the monitoring equipment. I turned around and I could see an IV stand, where before there was nothing. I looked back at Michael and he was gone.

I hate this part.

I closed my eye and when I reopened it, I was back in my room. I was covered in bandages and tubes and had wires running out from me like I was a network router. The one thing that was different was that there wasn't the sudden rush of pain. The sharp pain was merely a dull ache. I felt stronger. I could fill my lungs again and there was no gurgling and choking.

I looked to either side and saw that I was alone in the room. Simple plaster-coated walls painted white. No ornamentation, not even a clock. There was a window, but it was too high for me to look out. The light coming through was orange, vivid like a sunset or a sunrise. I had no idea which.

I sat up and almost pulled the IV stand down doing so. This was enough. I starting pulling things off me. As soon as one of the monitoring wires came away, an alarm went off. I glanced up at the machine and it indicated that I no longer had a pulse. By the time I stood up and had myself disconnected. I could hear pounding footsteps coming up the hallway. First one through the door was Caroline, followed by Geoff, a CG from Utah and after him was a pack of medical staff.

I didn't look at them. Instead I looked at the sun going down over the water. It was a sunset, and I was in Inverness again.

Caroline was on the radio, "He's awake. And standing!"

The nurses were pawing at me and I brushed them off. "Please, Sire, you must rest!" One of them was insistent.

I was slowly unwrapping the bandages from around my middle. They had been soaked in blood after a few layers. Evidently I had been a mess. When I pulled off the last bandage, one of the nurses gasped. The other one covered her mouth.

Geoff looked at my bed and went over to it. Laying on the mattress next to where I had been, was a long, thick, silver blade. He picked it up, clumsily hitting the blade on the bed rail which was severed through. "Who let this in here?" He looked at the Doctor who was standing in the doorway, wide eyed.

"I'll need my clothes, please." I said, looking at Caroline. I was very naked in a room full of people staring at me.

"My Lord..." Caroline bowed her head slightly as she grinned and walked out of the room.

I looked back at the spectators. "What's the matter?"

Geoff brought over a robe and put it over my shoulders. "They are in awe, sire. By rights, you should be dead, not standing here looking out the window at sunsets."

I nodded. "How long have I been... incapacitated?"

"A week, my Lord." Geoff took a step back, still holding the sword.

"Bring his Lordship something to eat and drink."

I held up a finger. "And status reports on everything."

Debbie ran into the room with my younger boys on her heels. When she looked at me, I saw waves of emotion roll through her. Without saying a word, she came to me and threw her arms around me and didn't let me go. My boys hugged me around their Mom.

I thought you were..." Debbie started crying. "I thought you were dead."

"I think I was. But I got better." I tried to smile.

"Don't do that again."

"I'll try my best not to die again."

"Promise?"

"Promise."

"How... how can you be standing?" Debbie opened my robe a little and looked at my side, she was stunned into silence. When she saw the wounds were healed, she ran her hand along my side. "How?"

I shrugged. "Wasn't my time... that's all I can say."

My boys were reluctant to let go of me. "Come on guys."

I sat back down on the bed and my youngest boys were excited and stayed with me for hours, talking about everything. It was after midnight when the Doctor on duty insisted that they let me rest. Debbie however, refused to leave and pulled up a chair next to my bed.

## The Queen Commands

Ft. George was quiet that night. A porter had brought me a platter of meats, cheeses, and a crusty bread, baked here at the fort. As I went through the status updates and reports on the iPad, and snacking on the food, the door opened. Someone came in, but I didn't hear footsteps. I knew who it was. "Hey, Miko."

I looked up at my adopted daughter. "Father..." She bowed, respectively. Her English was greatly improved, but her Japanese upbringing was still a foundation of her character.

"Please, don't be so formal." I opened my arms and Miko came and hugged me. "What's on your mind? And why are you wearing your swords?"

Miko was the oldest of my Japanese daughters, and most elegant and the prettiest. Her hair was long and straight and pure black. Like Wings of Crows was, but longer, finer. She carried herself with elegance and dignity beyond her years. She pulled her hair back behind her ears and I noticed her earrings. They were rubies, large ones, set in gold. I stood up and hugged her again, then held her shoulders at arm's length. "You joined the Crimson Guard... that's wonderful, Miko! When did you do that?"

"After I returned from the Commando School in Achnacarry and while you were recovering from... from whatever hurt you in France."

"I'm very proud of you."

Miko blushed and lowered her eyes. "Thank you, Father."

"I'm getting the feeling that there is something else on your mind."

"Yes... The Commander has assigned me to your protection detail."

"The Commander?"

"The Queen and Commander of the King's Guard."

"Ah... Did she give you a specific reason for your assignment."

"She said because you would not..." Miko paused and took a breath. "Be with me in bed."

I busted out laughing. "She's right about that, but I don't think that's what she said."

"No, she used other words I don't wish to say."

"I'm sure." I said as I sat back down.

"Miko, I've been following your training and education. You are – an amazing girl. You are the best in the class and you graduated training with the highest scores in everything. Your instructors tell me that you were the most determined. That's an important trait. I would be proud to have you on my detail..."

"But you do not accept me." Her shoulders dropped.

"Miko... I do accept you... but please, understand... everyone that works on my detail gets killed."

"But Miss Caroline survives. Kilo survives."

"They almost didn't. Three Utah State Troopers died. Iron Mike died. Jen died. Joy died. April died. Rebecca died, I almost didn't make it myself."

Miko didn't move. She  seemed to be holding her breath.

"I just worry... a lot... because..." I didn't know what to say... I knew what I wanted to say, but I'd never said it before to her. "Because I love you, Miko."

I pulled her to me in another hug and held her. "I want you to be safe, so I don't have to worry as much. I don't want to see you or any of my children get hurt. I couldn't stand that."

Miko was rigid, arms locked to her sides, head down. After a moment, I felt her go slack as she let out a shuddering sob. Then she threw her arms around my neck and squeezed. I felt her tears on my cheek. "Do you mean that? Truly?"

"Very much so. You and your sisters... even if they are too scared of me to talk to me."

"Yes, you were very scary."

"But you were not afraid of me." I said, and Miko laughed with a sniff.

"Yes I was. I was terrified."

"So you were scared of me, but you talked to me anyways... that's the very meaning of bravery, Miko. It's only a fool who is never afraid. It's okay to be scared, but to be brave means you are scared but you saddle up anyways. That's another reason you are an exceptional young woman."

"I love you too, Father."

My eye got watery and I looked down.

There was a knock on the door and Miko stood back up. I wiped my eye. "Yes, who is it?"

"Caroline." The familiar voice called out.

"Come in!"

Caroline entered the room and I glanced up at her.  Instantly I noticed the red mark on her cheek that wasn't there last time I saw her.

"What happened?" "Nothing, my Lord. Nothing at all. I'm just here to take Miko and our other new CG to the Master of Arms for equipment fitting."

I stood up and went over to Caroline and looked closer at her face. Her cheek had some swelling. "So the hand print on your face is nothing?"

"Like I said, it's nothing. There was a disagreement, but it's settled now. Everything is fine."

"Was this the Queen?"

"Yes."

"Was this about me?"

"Yes."

I was angry. "So how is everything fine?"

Just then the door opened again, and in walked Debbie. She smiled sweetly at both Caroline and me. "I was just making sure you had something to eat... and someone to guard you for the night."

Debbie's eyes were just about as red and swollen as Caroline's cheek. She had been crying. I pursed my lips and bit my tongue, forcing me to conceal the anger and laughter that wanted to burst out.

"Miko, sweetheart... You best go get your new gear, comms, weapons, and level three armor. I'll see you in the morning after breakfast. Okay?"

Miko looked at the other women in the room and bowed slightly before she skipped out the door.

"Okay, you two. What the hell is going on?"

"Going on?" Debbie shrugged her shoulders. "Nothing's going on... we're taking off though."

"I thought you said I had guard?"

"You do. Stacy."

At the name, Stacy Roth walked in, uniformed and armed. Stacy was the daughter of a fighter pilot that had sunk a Chinese aircraft carrier by running his plane into it. Stacy was young, but stood proud. She wore Rubies in her ears and her hair was pulled back tightly under her western style "Tactical Taco" hat. I noticed on her hips were a large bowie, and her sidearms were a pair of Peacemakers. She had a Winchester 92 slung on a single point sling. She was still the cowgirl.

I smiled and tried not to laugh. So my new bodyguards were a Cowgirl and a Samurai.

"Miss Roth, you look well."

"Thank you, Sire."

"You don't have to give me the royal treatment, Stacy."

"Yes, Sir."

I leaned back into my pillows. "Do you play chess?"

"Uh, Sir, you just almost died... it's not a good idea to get a thrashing again so soon."

# The King's Wisdom

The next morning I found myself with a sudden headache. "So explain this to me... seriously. Why the hell did you two jackholes think it was a good idea to Dog Fight with Predator Drones?" The pain started behind my eye and I rubbed the bridge of my nose. I looked over at the wreckage of the one that had crashed.

The two standing before me made some lame excuses. The drones were expensive, and the loss of one was going to be a problem, but the truth was that the recovered parts could be used to put two previously sidelined Predators back up into the air.

"You are both removed from your positions and assigned to Gathering Operations."

The two men snapped salutes, "Yes, your majesty!"

"Now get out of my sight before I have someone build a couple Crow Cages." The two men turned and marched themselves out.

I turned to Debbie, "Follow up on them and make sure they report to Masters." Debbie nodded.

The Gathering Operations were teams of folks who hunted for both food and fuel. Canned goods, dry goods that were still usable. With farming and refineries coming back on line, these operations were still important to us. Not that I would ever want to try a Canned Haggis again, but it was food. Masters was the man in charge of Gathering. His operations center was next to the Central Ops, and they coordinated efforts. It was a logistical nightmare, but they managed to get the job done. Bellies as well as fuel tanks both remained well fed.

The best news I had today had been the start up of an ammunition factory. But my delight in that was squelched when the truck pulled into the Fort with the remains of a Predator.

"I didn't even know you could dog fight them." I shook my head.

Debbie pulled out the clipboard again and looked at it for a moment. "Okay, now we have Geoffry Tellinger."

A guard opened the door and called out the name. A moment later a squat, balding man walked in. His clothes were clean, but threadbare. He walked in still straightening his jacket. He walked in front of me and bowed. The man had his dignity, I had to give him credit.

"So who are you and what can I do for you, Mister Tellinger?"

The man's pride cracked slightly, and I sensed a great deal of nervousness. "Uh..." was all he managed to say.

"Don't be shy, Geoffry."

"I've never talked to a Royal before... Sorry... I'm here because I was robbed... uh... Your holiness... er... High."

I held up my hand. "Tell me about the robbery."

"It happened last month. In Kent. I own a filling station and convenience store there. Trucks came and pumped my petrol... they bore your sigil on them. The men also ransacked my store, taking everything I had."

"You said it was in Kent?"

"Yes, Sir.... Is 'Sir' okay?"

"Sire is fine." I turned to Debbie, "Did we have gathering teams in Kent last month?"

April made a radio call to Gathering Operations. A few minutes later she nodded, "They made stops at Tellinger's shop. Once to check out what was there, the second time to collect it."

I looked at the bald man. I could see him sweating now. "Well, Geoffry, it looks like we took your property. Thank you for the gasoline. I can't give it back, but we can pay for it. Our teams don't take things that look like they still have owners with heart beats. They post notices before they collect what's usable. You didn't see the notice?"

"Yes, Sir... I saw the notice."

"Then all you had to do was indicate your continued ownership."

"I was afraid... Your men are well armed."

"So you were scared of them and hid when they came." My statement wasn't a question.

"Yes."

"And now you want payment?"

He nodded.

"I tell you what I can do for you. When we get fuel production back up and going, I'll have your tanks refilled." Debbie handed me notes of what was taken. "Looks like you only had a quarter capacity, and I'm going to fill them for you... so you are coming off like a bandit on that account."

This seemed to please the man. "Do you have any family left?"

"Just my wife, your Majesty. But we've taken in several children who lost parents."

I nodded "And what about food?"

"My wife has a garden, we are getting by."

"Geoffry, we're going to make sure you and your sweetheart and the children have plenty of food. Did we get power turned back on in Kent?"

"Yes."

"Then send some meat to the Tellinger's residence, and some dry packs." I said to Debbie, who made notes. "Veggies alone make for some boring meals."

Geoffry's eyes filled with tears, "Thank you!" He bowed.

## The Third Strain

When he had left, it was with a bounce in his step. I looked to Debbie. "Next?"

"We've got a scientist or doctor of some sort, he arrived this morning very anxious to see you."

"Alright then, let's see him." I sighed. Within seconds, a man in a lab coat burst into the tent.

"We've got some interesting news, my Lord!" The man in the white lab coat said.

I looked up from the iPad, showing me status reports from our men in the field near Switzerland. They had encountered armed border guards who wouldn't let them pass at first, and had then talked to their equivalent of an Ambassador. "What is so interesting that you'd come up all the way from London, still wearing your lab coat, when you could have sent a text message?"

I looked back at the iPad. Our men were set up in a camp in the foot hills of some mountains in Germany that I didn't know the name of. The Swiss seemed eager to play ball with us. The Swiss represented the only nation to survive almost completely intact from the uprising. Their borders had been closed since everything started, and neutrality had been enforced by armed barricades. Two days ago we received the message that they wanted to trade.

This wasn't surprising. Switzerland is not completely self sustaining. They have resources and agriculture... but they don't have enough agriculture for themselves, and they don't have the mineral resources. These things, they have to import and imports have been rather thin since the world went to hell.

We on the other hand, have a lot of agriculture and mining resources, but we lack something critical ourselves. Manpower. Most of Europe was dead, undead, or fighting to not become either of the other two.

The man in the white coat was tall and bearded. I remember his face, but not his name. Dr. Pratt, I believe. I had given him all the research we had taken from Cheyenne Mountain about the zombies. "I found it," he said.

"You found what, exactly?"

"The third strain." He said, as if I was reading from the same page and knew exactly what he was talking about.

"Yes, we know there is a third strain... three bacterial and one viral... the Zombie Plague."

"Right, but we didn't know what the third strain did." The doctor wound himself up into lecture mode to tell me what I had broken into Cheyenne Mountain to get. I didn't stop him. "The first Strain converts proteins into sugars. Feeding tissues vital energy... when the zombie is stressed, the production goes into overdrive, giving the zombie that corpse-like appearance even if the heart never stopped beating. The second strain of bacteria produces oxygen as a bi product, which is why zombies can't drown. They don't need to breath. The virus causes the brain damage that basically wipes a subject's mind of human behavior."

I was now impatient. “Yes, yes, we knew all of this... cut to the chase.”

“Well, in all the studies, we could never find what the third strain did”

“And.”

“Well the reason was because we never observed the strain under the right conditions.” The doctor said with a voice that sounded as if that response would answer all the questions. I tapped the edge of the iPad with a .50 BMG round I had been holding, and raised an eyebrow.

“Well, we had taken a tissue sample and somehow it was put in the freezer.”

“So?”

“That’s what activated the third strain!”

“Doctor... please.... for the love of all that is holy... I’m about to shoot you in the knees.”

“Cold was the right condition!”

Debbie was shaking her head. I pulled out my 1911 10mm, “Tell me, right now... or I’m going to shoot you... What does the third strain do?”

“When they get cold, they produce Threitol and Sorbitol.”

I put my gun down and sat back. “Ah... so when they get cold they produce alcohols... which act as an anti-freeze.”

“Precisely,” the doctor said, looking surprised that I knew that.

“This protects cellular walls in freezing temperatures.”

I nodded, grasping this information. “Which is why zombies can freeze in the winter, and thaw out and revive in the spring... just like that beetle does.”

The doctor looked puzzled. “Beetle?”

It was now my turn to lecture the doctor. “In Alaska there is a beetle that can freeze solid, but every spring when it warms up they revive and go about their little lives.”

“Remarkable. I didn’t know that.”

I looked at him. “You didn’t know that? I thought everyone did. Hmm.”

“Well, the zombie plague has the same effect on the human body.” He paused. “If this research could be put to use... we could prevent injuries from frostbite with an inoculation.”

“That is the exact type of thinking that created the zombie plague in the first place. Doctor, listen to be carefully. What I want from you is a way to kill the zombies... Agent X works after awhile but in the mean time it makes the zombies a hundred times more dangerous until they finally die. Agent 11 and 12 works too slowly. We need something that works fast, without turning them into even worse monsters. That is the only research I want you to be doing. If you can’t do that, you can help someplace else, like in one of the refineries, power plants, or fishing. You’re choice. Now get out of my sight before I become irritated.”

The doctor looked shocked and turned and walked out of the tent.

“A little harsh, don’t you think?” Debbie said quietly as she pulled a boresnake through her ACR.

"Maybe." I stood up and walked to the tent flap and held it open. The doctor was stomping across the field, hands in fists. I picked up the mic from my lapel. "Caroline, do you see the man in the white lab coat walking west?"

After a second, "Yes, my Ogre, I see him."

"Tell him I said thank you and give him some food rations... make sure he has everything he needs."

"Roger that." Caroline said.

I looked over at Debbie, "How many more cases do we have to deal with?"

"Another twenty six people are waiting."

"And you've been handling stuff like all this?"

"We hold court like this almost every day, save for Saturdays and Sundays."

"Basically a full work week?"

"Basically. This is your job, being King of England after all."

"Wasn't there a Magna Carta thing?"

"Yes, but there is no Parliament, dear."

"How come no one else has handled all this?"

"Because you've not put anyone in charge of civil affairs."

"Where's the Chief? Where's..."

"They are all fighting your campaign in France."

"I need to hire someone. What happened to Phil..."

"He was killed last week."

"Any news of Musket?"

"Your brother is still in Germany. He's taken over a brewery and the Porsche factory."

I shook my head. "I wanted the Porsche factory... pity."

"There's still the Mercedes factory."

"He'll probably be there by the time we get to it."

Just then Rosa came in. She had a platter of tacos, tamales, and cans of a beverage called "Cock and Bull".

"Rosa, how long have you been cooking for us?"

"It's been about three years."

"Time for a promotion."

"Que?"

"Rosa, you are now the Royal Arbitrator."

"Is this some joke?"

"Nope." I took the platter of food and went to the table. "Take that clipboard from Debbie and let's see how you do."

I sat down and started to eat while Rosa just stood there for a moment, looking over the docket. "Okay... Leslie James and Roger Ashcroft."

While I ate, I continued pouring over reports. One from France was troubling. "High-level Red Eye activity. Location of Nuclear Weapon Stockpiles." This required immediate attention and action.

I got on the radio and called for choppers and soldiers to be readied immediately. We were going right now. I got confirmations via radio and sent messages to the units in the field of what the battle plan was. Simple plan, go in, smash evil, defend good, be big damn heroes. Priority was securing the nukes so they couldn't be used against us. That done, I finished my tacos, chewing my food and thinking about getting back into the action. I knew Debbie would love for me to stay and hang out doing this King Shit... but I had no stomach for it. I'd rather be killing zombies and demons.

Rosa had tackled four cases before I pushed away from the table.

"Rosa," I patted her on the back. "You are doing great. Keep it up... the job is yours. But I still want some of your cooking once a week."

Rosa smiled and called the next case.

Debbie and I ran out while we could. We headed to the field when Caroline and Sinead came up. Miko was following them, looking like she was drowning in her new tactical gear. "The Irish have just landed in southern France."

"How many?"

"About eight thousand." Sinead said.

"I asked for two."

"You got eight." Sinead shrugged.

"I guess we best get ready to go."

"We're already set." Caroline chirped.

We took a few steps before I looked back at Debbie. She was standing there, looking deflated, knowing she wasn't going.

I hated to see the sadness in her eyes, but I wasn't going to risk her.

I smiled at her and turned back to the field. Helicopter turbines were already spooling up. Stacy Roth was already in the helicopter, leaning back, and had her hat pulled low over her eyes, her boots resting on my gear back. I shook my head and climbed in.

Soon the chopper was loaded and we were flying as fast as possible. The Kestral wasn't the fastest, but when you were skimming the trees, it felt like you were going Mach two.

Sinead and Miko had not done a lot of nap of the earth flying. Both had ridden in helicopters, but going full tilt boogie at treetop level, with the sudden climbing and diving was completely new to the poor girls. Miko was white as a sheet and gripping her seat with both hands while she watched the ground outside flash past with eyes as wide as saucers. Sinead was a distinct shade of green and had her eyes shut tight.

"I wouldn't think you would be scared of flying, Irish."

"I'm not scared, bloody King Yank." She said through clenched teeth. "I'm trying not to throw sick all over your bloody helicopter!"

Suddenly the floor dropped out of the chopper as the pilot followed a dip in the terrain. "Jesus, Mary and Joseph!" Caroline handed her an airsick bag and a pack of mints. Sinead shot her a hard glare, then a moment later made use of both. Stacy Roth just shook her head and muttered "Greenhorns."

The Crimson Guardsmen with us had a good laugh. I chuckled and looked out the window. I enjoyed the flight. The VH-71 Kestral was a fast and well equipped chopper. Similar to the Merlins but upgraded with comm gear and increased range. The Kestrals came over from the States, ferried in on C-5 Galaxies along with ammunition for the 25mm and 120mm weapons systems.

The trees below us gave way to open ground and roads. Soon enough we flashed across columns of vehicles, some with the red thistle, some with markings of the Gunn Clan, and others marking them as our new Irish allies.

We were converging on the Istres-Le Tubé Air Base. Home of France's stockpile of nukes. Our forces had been sent to secure it and found stiff resistance in the form of armed undead. Speculation was that they were being directly controlled by another demon.

I keyed the mike to my LASH radio set. "This is the Ogre to all units... Godspeed and take no prisoners."

I checked my 1911s and then my Warhammer. Everything was ready, just as it was fifteen minutes ago. The Warhammer was a new one. The old one I had with me when I faced Abaddon was ruined. It had been crushed. The HK was never found. Of course, it was hard to search when most of the ceiling had caved in on the large underground room. The 1911s were simple Springfield GIs that looked like they were completely stock, when in fact they had been slicked up by Gundoc and converted to 10mm. After the fight with the demon, a more potent round was wanted. Instead of one pistol, I now carried two of them like I used to carry my Glocks. I tried a 10mm Glock, but found the gun too bulky. Both 1911s had threaded barrels for suppressors, which was a nice touch, but I doubted I'd use a can on either one of them. For quiet work, a blade or mace worked just fine.

I closed my eye. I could hear everyone else doing their final weapons checks as well. In my mind I could see the airbase, the resistance, the minor demon in charge, and I knew this operation would go clean and easy. But I felt uneasy regardless. Suddenly, the image of a huge church filled my vision, and I was filled with dread. It was Notre Dame, and it was dark. Around the old church, shadows swirled. Deep laughter came to me, and under that, I could hear familiar voices shouting and others weeping. Something bad was going to happen. Notre Dame was a trap. I saw my friends go into the trap, but I couldn't do anything about it. When I opened my eyes I saw the fence of the air base pass below us. Tracers reached up at us as the helicopter dropped under them and then flared hard to land.

As soon as it set down, we were out and ready. I was about to yell out "Didn't we just do this?" But I looked at my team and saw that they were in no mood for any dark humor or otherwise. I looked at each one as the adversary started to take note of our presence. "Let's get going."

# John Manus' Daughter

As the Kestral took to the air, I heard the distinct hollow popping sounds of rounds impacting the chopper. None of them critical and the bird flew low over the tree line and out of sight. I looked back and saw zombies about three hundred yards away, slack jawed and limp armed, staggering towards us. There were thousands. Some of them were armed with FAMAS rifles, occasionally firing from the hip. Most wore the shredded remains of uniforms. Steve, the CG to my left, pulled up his ACR and started firing controlled, well aimed shots. Hot 6.8 brass bounced off my shoulder, but I didn't care. I was engaging my own targets. The 12 gauge grenades were airbursting just above the zombies. The small blasts were smashing four or five zombies at a time. Miko, to my right, armed with her ACR, was very selective. She was aiming specifically for the zombies who were holding guns. The heavy 6.8mm slugs would tear into the zombies through the head, exit, and strike the one behind it, dropping them or blowing chunks of flesh off their heads. Caroline's shooting was without discretion, spraying rounds into the oncoming mass at hip level, dropping zombies who were no longer able to stand or walk. Sinead's rifle was barking with the rest of them, and she was pulling her weight.

As many as we were killing with the small arms, we were not even making a dent in the numbers coming at us. The situation looked dire until two pairs of Tiger attack helicopters came in on their attack runs. One at a time they swooped in with ripple-fired rockets, then strafed with guns. One single rocket made my grenades look like 4th of July fireworks.

The gunships circled and came in again, putting rockets into the thickest clusters of undead, blowing them into chunky zombie salsa, and sending up gouts of earth. Small chunks of dirt, rock, and what was once runway rained down on us.

I glanced back over my shoulder and looked at Sinead. She had a maniac's grin that made me feel unsettled. Then suddenly that grin looked familiar to me.

"Sinead..."

She looked me in the eye.

"What's your full name?"

"Sinead Bannon Manus, my King. Why?"

"Manus?"

"Manus."

"You are John Manus' daughter."

She nodded. "I thought that was clear. He didn't tell you?"

The Tiger helicopters peeled off to the west, RTB for rearming. Coming in from the west to replace their firepower were the APCs, which led the charge by crashing through the fence line in a wedge formation and announcing their arrival with full auto fire from their 25mm chainguns.

I looked back at Sinead. "No. He sort of completely left that little detail out. That's why he didn't kill you when he found out you killed his men."

She just looked at me. "You are probably right."

"Probably isn't good enough. Am I right or not?"

"Mostly right."

"This is why we got more people than I asked for, isn't it?"

"My father would like to see me kept safe."

I nodded, of course he would. Something about Sinead didn't feel right, but I couldn't put my finger on it.

The zombies had closed in enough to recognize fresh meat and let out moans as they broke out into a run. The APCs swept through most of the zombies, and we had no problem picking off the stragglers. Soon the trucks of soldiers came in through the fence breach the APCs had made and went about the business of securing the area and clearing off all the remaining shamblers as we made our way across the field, our weapons carried at low ready.

A man with a green uniform jogged up casually carrying his AUG rifle in one hand with the sling dangling. His manner was that of an untrained man, even his clothes were Irish Military. He must have been IRA. His accent was thick. "Your Majesty, the airfield is secure. We're beginning the building clearing operation."

"Very good... Mister..." I left the question hanging.

"Cain, Sire."

"Thank you, Mister Cain." I nodded a dismissal. Cain lingered, looking at Sinead with eyes that tightened into slits when he recognized her.

Sinead looked down as she adjusted her grip on her weapon. Cain spun and jogged back in the direction he had come from. When I looked at Sinead, she seemed very interested in the caps of her ACOG's adjustment turrets. I decided that this was a topic of discussion for a later date. "Let's head for the Administration buildings, Caroline, take point. Everyone, watch your intervals."

## He Wore Biker Leathers

The business of controlling an air base is generally one of tedious work. Collecting fuel stocks, weapons, vehicles, and most importantly ammunition. It was distracting. We found several Jackal patrol vehicles, all of them filled with dried blood. Great rig for desert patrols, but total crap for protection against zombies. The markings on them indicated they were Legion. I stood up in one of them and looked in, thinking we could use them for something. Shell casings all over, dried blood all over, meat chunks... bad juju in these rides. I jumped back down.

"Take the guns and the ammo, drain the tanks... but leave the rigs."

"What about those?" Drew Osbourn, a former Captain in the British Army, we picked him up outside of London. He had lead a small platoon of soldiers and cops and had miraculously saved almost a hundred people... keeping them safe, fed, and unbitten. "Parked along the tarmac." He said, jerking his head back to the line of heavy metal... AMX-10RC. Recon vehicles that look like tanks. Eight of them.

I wasn't familiar with the AMX rigs. "Can we use them? Are they compatible?"

"They are. And we have an abundance of HE rounds for those guns."

Sounding better. "What about people to operate them?"

"We have enough men to crew them, and drivers who can run them, but gunners will need some practice."

"Alright, get the men on it. Where are we at with the nukes?"

Drew was straight forward. The warheads are getting ready to load for transport back to Kinsloss.

"Did anyone find the demon?"

"You're new to working with Irish. They found it. Cut it to pieces." Drew shook his head.

"Don't look surprised, Ogre King," Sinead said with a grin. "That's what we do."

I turned to Sinead. "I know that, little doll. That's why I only asked for two thousand."

All of a sudden the bud in my ear squawked. "Duart actual to Ogre actual." There was a lot of fatigue in the voice. I instantly turned to Caroline, looked her in the eyes and gave the sign to round up.

"This is Ogre actual. Go ahead, Duart actual."

"Friendlies coming in from the west. Hope you don't mind us crashing the party."

"Roger that, Duart. Come on it. See you shortly." I flipped the radio channel. "Ogre to all units, Friendlies approaching, so hold your fire."

Caroline started calling the CGs to rally and we started to relax a little. Maclean and Q both reported in and it was good to see them again. We talked about the wild adventures we'd all had, and it seemed that each one was a foot taller, or maybe it was just the way we stood, prouder, stronger, less afraid of what we had been through and what we'd faced. We'd come a long way, and seen and done things that we'd never be able to explain to those who were not with us. Like always, those who were there knew, and those who weren't never would.

Soon it was time for them to go tend to their teams and turn in for the night. We all needed rest. I watched my friends leave to return to their teams. I looked at the cape, Q wore; it looked like wings. Odd fashion choice, but it went well with his Roman styled armor

Then there was Maclean's new girlfriend. She was introduced to me as "Abby". But I knew that wasn't her real name, and much like Sarge's girl friend, she wasn't your normal every day girl next door. She was insanely sexy. She made Kim Kardashian look like a mud fence. Just then, in mid stride, Abby turned and looked at me. She smiled at me, with a shy look in her eyes. I smiled back.

For a brief second, I was afraid she could read thoughts. Abby winked at me then she hurried to catch up with the others on her team. I knew I had nothing to worry about with her, but I was curious about her. She was devoted, I could see that, and that's all that mattered, but I was still curious.

Miko came up to me. She was holding on to an old CAR-15.

"Is this a good weapon, Father?"

I took the weapon from her hands and looked it over. "My first issued weapon was just like this one." It felt a lot lighter than what everyone else was packing. Lighter than I remembered it. It would fit the young woman well. "It will be, after it's cleaned and oiled properly."

"I think I'll use it."

"There should be a cleaning kit around here. Caroline, get Miko sorted out. After it's cleaned up, bring it back to me for an inspection."

Sinead was sitting on the ground, rifle between her legs. "You guys never stop, do you?"

"What do you mean?"

"We've been all over France, never taking a day to rest unless you get torn up too bad and have to stay in a hospital for awhile. Always fighting or looking for the next fight. Never enjoying what you have."

"What are you talking about?"

"You are the King... and I've not seen you enjoy yourself. Relax."

I looked at the Irish woman. She seemed tired, but not overly fatigued. "You think I should order minstrels and a leg of mutton?"

"Isn't that what kings do?"

"Do I look like a king?"

"One from a couple hundred thousand years ago."

"You saying I look old?"

She laughed.

"I think you need to find some food. Get some for yourself, and bring me something too. Just not mutton."

Sinead nodded and pulled herself up. "Yes, your majesty."

I shook my head as she wandered off, muttering to herself. I started scrolling through the situation reports on an iPad. Looking at fuel levels, ammunition supplies, casualties.

"You are very tolerant for a king." A voice said with a thick Nordic accent.

I looked around. Up on top of an LAV a large man was sitting casually, dangling his legs. He wore biker leathers with his jacket open and he was bare chested under it. He was pale of skin and hair, but his muscles were well defined. He looked just like the Techno Viking, even having the same facial hair style.

I was cautious, casually putting a hand on the butt of one of my 10mm 1911's. "What can I do for you?"

Instantly Stacy Roth was at my side, her lever action held level and unwavering, aimed at the man's heart.

"I've been spending some time with your brothers. First, Zach. Met him in Germany and went to Italy and back with him." The man casually slipped off the armored vehicle and stood before me. Stacy's gun never wavered from the target. The man was massive, heavily built. "Then I ran into your other brother, Musket. We went all around, bashing skulls and bedding wenches... good times. Now, here I am."

"Here you are. What do want?"

"I don't want to be bored too much, I don't want to grow old... and if at all possible, I'd like to find Musket again."

"Find Musket?" Alarms were going on in my head.

"Didn't anyone tell you?"

"Tell me what?"

"Musket was captured."

"What? Where? When did this happen?"

The Techno Viking pulled out a map of Germany and spread it out on the ground, looked around, then oriented the map.

"Here. Two nights ago."

Stacy lowered the rifle, and I knelt and looked at the map. "That's Ramstine Air Force Base."

"Yes it is. Musket had just opened a tavern," He pointed to just outside of the base. "There. They came. Killed, destroyed, but Musket, they were looking for specifically. They took him. Kicking and screaming. Probably killed about three hundred zombies, but they finally got him."

"You said they took him.. where did they take him to? And where were you?"

"I was there, yes, fighting for my own life. But where they took him, I don't know. I only knew I had to find you, so we could go get him back."

"No, I don't know you. We'll go, but you will stay here."

"I want to go with you. I'll swear allegiance, take your Oath, and I'll help you track down Musket."

I looked at the man, up and down. He was proud, defiant, but I could tell that he was sincere and honest. "Fine, I'll take you at your word." I had started to turn away, when I stopped and looked back at the man. "What's your name?"

"Stig."

# *Looking for Musket*

The next day we were approaching the famous US Air Base in Germany.

"My Lord, come take a look." It was the Flight Navigator and he seemed to be under some stress. I rose immediately and followed him to the cockpit. The pilot dropped the nose and made a shallow decent. It was more than enough to see.

"I thought Ramstein was secure." I said almost in a whisper.

"It was... as of last week... We were here, we refueled, took supplies." The pilot said.

Ramstein AFB was key to the European survivors. The entire base was razed. Runways cratered, buildings burned, everything destroyed. The destruction was total. I felt my blood chill in my veins as I gritted my teeth.

"Can we land?" I asked, but already knew the answer.

"No, Sire... not here."

"Find a place to set down... we'll go in on the ground."

"Sire."

We found an airstrip some miles away. It was small, but a C-130 can do small. One Herc would land and off load, then the next would touch down. It wasn't long before all four were unloaded and headed back to France where they could land and refuel.

I looked at my old M-ATV and patted the fender. Ten vehicles were ready to roll. We were divided into two platoons. The M-ATV was the heaviest of them. Most of them were regular hard top, fast back Humvees... Not armored, but they'd stand against the normal undead. My Praetorians were standing ready.

I gave the signal, "Let's roll." We pulled out. Caroline driving the M-ATV, leading the convoy.

"Ogre Actual to Delta Two."

The voice that answered was low and cold. "Delta Two copies. Go ahead, my King."

"What happened at Ramstein, Delta Two?"

Stig took a moment to respond. His voice sounded... amused. "You saw it, your Majesty. I was sitting in a Humvee eating a biscuit before we landed."

The big Nordic was in Delta Platoon's second vehicle. I looked back at it and glared.

"Oh, don't be mad at me, my Lord. You know what happened, you don't need me to tell you."

"Speak plain, Stig."

"Those who have your brother." Stig said. "They destroyed the base, the whole base."

I wanted to ball up my fist and hit something. But I knew that would do little good.

## Pop Goes the Zombie

The destruction of Ramstein from the air was nothing like it was on the ground. We rolled through where the main gate used to be and drove through the ruins of the Air Base. Everyone was quiet and sober. The place looked like the set of a horror movie. What was still standing was burning, and what was knocked down, was scattered and bloodied. Pools of blood were puddled around and some of it was still red and wet. Dismembered body parts were sprinkled around like confetti.

Sinade spoke first. "Where are the bodies?"

The question prompted a physical shock response as if I had been slapped. I looked around and found that her question was valid. Parts were all over... some large, others, small. There had been children here. But there were no bodies. No heads. No torsos. Just... other things.

Sinade crossed herself, something I had never seen her do before.

The chatter started up on the radio between vehicles and I squelched it. "Second Platoon, sweep the outside perimeter and look for signs of aggressors, where they came in and where they may have left.

"Roger that, Sire."

Second Platoon vehicles sped up, passed First, then fanned out heading across the big base.

"First Platoon," I called into the Radio. "Search the Airfield first, then the remaining structures. Look for aggressors or survivors."

First Platoon vehicles acknowledged and fanned out.

"Where do you want me to head?" Caroline asked quietly. I pointed to a C-5 Galaxy that was half burned, but the cockpit section looked mostly intact.

"How did this happen?" I muttered as I looked out the window down to the ground and instantly wished I hadn't. There was the arm of a child, still clutched in its hand was a small, half-melted toy that I couldn't tell what it had been. "Hell... this is hell on Earth."

I was looking up at the cockpit of the C-5 when Bravo Two called to Bravo One. "We have Contact, North West, at the perimeter."

"Bravo Two, this is Ogre Actual."

"Go ahead, Ogre."

"What are you seeing?"

"Undead Walkers, Ogre."

Smart ass. "What are they doing, Bravo?"

"Milling about, aimlessly, my Lord."

"Copy, Bravo Two. Observe, hold and avoid contact."

"Bravo Two acknowledges, Out."

The front end of the Galaxy transport plane looked mostly intact, which was a stark contrast to the rest of the plane, and airfield. Two Praetorians stood by waiting, on my nod, they went into the large aircraft to search the cockpit.

It didn't take long. I soon heard "Two coming out!"

"Come on out!" I responded.

The Praetorians came out, one holding an object that I'd seen a few times now. The Black Box. The cockpit voice recorder. That's brilliant. I hadn't thought of that. "What did you find?"

"Bloodbath, Sire. Only chunks. Looks like a bomb went off inside."

I nodded, to the black box. "Get that to Technical, have them see if there is anything on there."

The Praetorian holding the strong box took it back to the trailing vehicle. The first one looked hesitant. "Sire?"

I looked at him and recognized his face as one that was more used to smiling casually. There was no such expression now. "What's bothering you."

"Fragmentation."

"What about it."

"Shrapnel... in the cockpit. An explosive went off in the cockpit. Like a grenade, but bigger. A lot bigger. Everything in the cockpit is shattered and scorched."

"So, maybe it was a couple grenades or a pipe-bomb."

"I've seen what pipe-bombs do, and this is different."

"What do you think it was?"

"In Iraq I saw something like this. An AP that was set off inside an M113. Looked just like this."

"A mine?" That didn't sound really all that possible... but it would explain the shattered windows, I thought as I looked back up at the plane's nose.

"Ogre Actual, this is Bravo Two." The voice was urgent.

"Go for Ogre."

"They spotted us, Sire."

From across the base, I could hear brief gunfire and explosions.

"Pull back to the airfield."

Through the radio I could hear the engine of a Humvee racing, more shooting and muffled thumps of explosions. "We're coming. So are they... uh... and they explode when you shoot them."

*What?* "Say again, Over."

"They pop when you shoot them, your Majesty."

"All units, regroup on my position, Riki Tiki. We have incoming Zeds."

We rallied all the vehicles like a ring of covered wagons from the old west. Guns out, everyone ready. We didn't have long to wait. The undead swarmed, but luckily for us there just wasn't that many of them.

We observed them coming from a distance; they were moving as fast as they could, but were just not that fast. Some of them looked like they carried large packs. Others, big coffee cans in their hands.

Sinead was in the turret and was looking through binos. "They have mines!"

"Clarify that."

"I'm seeing Soviet made mines. All types. Bounding AP mines and big... really big ones. They look like AT mines."

I pulled up my Binos and looked closer. I could see one Zed running straight for the M-ATV, huge maniacal grin, half smile, half skull holding out a bounding mine in each hand. I had no doubt they were live.

Over the open channel. "Fire."

It took about a second and a half before the shooting started in earnest. I watched as rounds impacted undead bodies, punching through. Some rounds impacted mines and did nothing. Others detonated, clearing the zombies around it. But they had enough zombies to make up the difference.

"This is how they knocked the airbase to the ground." I said to no one in particular.

I saw one zombie take a round in the hip and fall down. The heavy AT mine on its back shifted forward, crushing its head before detonating with an enormous blast that sent a geyser of dirt into the air.

Before the zombies got within a hundred yards, we had cleared most of them. One zombie with a pair of Bouncers got close enough. He clapped the fuses together and the mines erupted in a combined double blast with secondary blasts that sent fragments pinging off the M-ATV's armor.

"Shit!" Sinead cursed as she pulled herself down out of the turret. She had blood on her face. Miko, sitting next to her pulled her weapon back and turned her attention to the wounded comrade.

"Leave me alone, I'm alright!" The Irish girl snarled.

"You cry like a little bitch. Be silent." Miko said with crisp effectiveness and Sinead stopped protesting. Miko tended to the wound and bandaged it. "Just a graze, but you have a new piercing in your ear."

"Shit." Sinead growled.

Miko handed me a small bearing. "This was in her collar." The ball bearing was the size of buckshot, but made of hardened steel.

Someone was behind this. This was orchestrated. These zombies were just the leftovers after the attack. There was not a single person left alive. As was the plan. There was a small trail heading east out of the base through a break in the fence. So we knew they had come from the east. That didn't tell us much but at least we had a trail to follow. That was something. Not much, but it was something.

"Ogre to Bravo Two."

"Go for Bravo Two."

"Report to me."

The Stig bounded around the trucks and came to a stop in front of me. "So where was Uncle Musket's Tavern?"

The Swede pointed with a thick, pale finger. He pointed directly at the fence break. We jumped into the M-ATV and rolled to where the Tavern had been. Half the building had been blown to splinters, and there was nothing left inside that wasn't burned to hell. I could see in the middle of the floor where there had been a fire-pit. The bar was completely gone. The walls that were still standing looked like they could fall down at any moment. There was nothing left here at all, save for the trail. Around the ground was a lot of blood soaked earth, a red mud. In this mud we found drag marks and boot prints that were going the way the others had come. Some of the boot prints were half dragged and laying in the mud I found a fired Flint Lock pistol, then a few feet further, a large bowie that I recognized instantly as Musket's. I knew the blade because I had given it to my brother as a gift. I picked up the heavy knife and turned it around in my hand. It had blood and mud on it. He was here.

In my mind's eye, I could see him being dragged in the direction the zombie horde had come from, carried and dragged bodily by two oversized zombies, Red Eyes. The two zombies were wearing what looked like Russian Military uniforms, but the clothes were too torn up to be sure. But considering the source of the mines we had seen, there was a connection.

We followed the trail for days and crossed the border from Germany into the Czech Republic. I sent the majority of our forces to take the CZ Factory and Facilities. Some new weapons and ammunition sources would be a nice start. While they went that way, I continued to follow the trail. Zombies didn't seem to have cared about tracking and it took little skill to follow the wide swath they had cut in the earth through the foliage. It reminded me of the trails that buffalo used to make in the Western States when thousands and thousands of them ran together before they had been wiped out. The trail at least cut through good country and we went hundreds of miles. We came to a farm house near the Polish border.

## Musket's Tatoo

The small farm house was made with simple split-log construction. Most of the logs were shredded with hundreds of thousands of claw marks. Planks surrounding the windows had been ripped away and the glass shattered. Large scorch marks punctuated the damage. I approached the front door slowly, with my shotgun held at ready, just below my line of sight. It was hot, loaded, safety off and my trigger finger was up just along the frame. Sinead was following close, with her weapon at a low ready, muzzle pointing at the ground and behind her, Miko was moving like a ghost with her weapon also in a low ready.

Kilo and Caroline came out of the barn. He shook his head, "no", and from a hundred yards away I could see frustration and anger on his face. Musket wasn't in the barn.

I heard rustling inside the farm house just before I made my entrance. I went through the door quickly with my weapon coming up. A figure darted from the shadows, and since I knew we had no friendlies inside and the figure was not shaped like Musket, I took a snap shot. #4 Buckshot shredded the lower legs and the person fell to the ground. As I moved forward I took a second shot, better aimed, and removed a foot of the person that was now laying on the ground, trying to crawl away. "Don't Move or the next one goes to the head!"

Sinead and Miko swept past me on either side, clearing the rest of the room and the small bathroom. No one else was here.

The figure on the floor slowly rolled over. Hate-filled red eyes looked at me and screamed. "You are too late!"

"Where is he?"

The Red Eye just laughed. I lowered my shotgun and aimed at the knee. Wham. There was no more knee. The Red Eye screamed again, but not in pain. They don't feel pain, but they don't like being crippled.

"Tell me!" The Red Eye hesitated, and I shot off its other foot.

It hissed at me, "this will do you no good, he is ours now."

"Where is he? Don't make me ask you again."

"Do you think you can make me tell you?"

I answered by blowing off the other knee. "You might as well. You tell me, and I'll blow your head off nice and clean. You dick with me, and I'll take your arms off and tie you to a tree outside, nice and high up. You will be very bored and it will take the birds a long time to eat enough meat out of you to kill you... I know how you bastards hate being bored."

The Red Eye twisted and turned. "He was taken..."

"Where was he taken?"

"East, into Russia! He's in Russia now... Our ground! You can't get him, you're too late! Even if you could find him. It won't matter now, he's ours!" The Red Eye laughed hysterically.

Miko came out of the bathroom, her face was white as a sheet and I knew something was wrong. Miko has strong will and doesn't let things visibly effect her. Something affected her.

"Father." She was shaking.

"What did you find?"

She closed her eyes tight and pointed to the bathroom with her rifle.

Oh no, I thought. I turned to the Red Eye and blasted off each hand so it couldn't grab anything. "Watch it." I barked to Sinead who turned her rifle to the Red Eye.

I took the few steps over to Miko and put a hand on her. I could feel her trembling. "Be calm, my chosen daughter."

"Musket." She said. My blood ran cold. Before I went into the bathroom, I finished off the Red Eye with one final shot. I walked the few steps to the bathroom slowly and looked around. Blood splattering and little flecks of meat were on the walls. In the sink was a razor and blood soaked brush. Then I looked in the bathtub. It took me a moment to recognize what I was seeing, because I didn't want to see it.

Stretched out in the bottom of the bathtub was a thick layer of skin. The tattoo on the skin. It was the insignia of the $26^{th}$ Marine Expeditionary Unit. It was Musket's tattoo from the back of his shoulder. The skin was from the shoulders down to the small of the back. The scars were also recognizable. They had peeled my brother. I almost dropped my shotgun. I felt sick. Then I saw them. The demonic symbols, cut through the skin. Each symbol was a sign of a curse, and in the center of the skin was the symbol of the demon's name. This was one I knew too well. Abaddon. His plan was to use my brother's body as a vessel for possession. This was left for us to find. This was left for me. It was a message.

I felt dizzy. I staggered out of the bathroom and out of the cabin. My shotgun hung limp in my hands. My brother! I couldn't even think straight. "Father?" Miko asked, following. She knew what the symbols were, and who's tattoo, whose skin she had found.

"Dad?" Kilo came running up. "What is it?"

"Musket." Was all I could say.

A moment later, my frustration and fear changed and turned. Anger welled up inside me, and all worry doubt and fatigue left me. I picked up my weapon and looked east out across Polish fields. The zombie's trail went straight east. Into Russia.

"What now?" Kilo asked.

I turned and looked at everyone with me. "We're going to Russia."

About the Author

George Hill, a.k.a. "Ogre" a.k.a. "The Blogfather" a.k.a. "Dad", is obviously a man of many hats. As The Mad Ogre of MadOgre.com he says what he wants and says it like it is. He has been blogging about the gun industry, politics, and life since 1998 earning him the title "The Blogfather". George writes for *Concealed Carry Magazine* and is a frequent guest and occasional Co-Host on Armed American Radio. He is a Co-Owner and Chief Instructor for Crusader Weaponry. As the father of six boys he spends his free time shooting prairie dogs on Ogre Ranch, eating too much Tabasco sauce, drinking Gator-Bull and preparing for the Zombie Apocalypse.

Coming in 2012 !

Don't miss the continuation of
George Hill's exciting series in:

# *Uprising Russia*

Turn the page for a
special sneak preview!

Vasili watched the small jeep-like UAZ through his rifle scope. The UAZ-469 kicked up dust as it bounced and careened around the curves of the trail that someone back in Moscow labeled a road, and someone else labeled it important. In reality it was little more than an over developed goat-trail that farmers used to move livestock to and from marked. "One driver, no passengers."

"Someone is in a hurry." Dmitry said.

"It's none of our fucking business." Kievien announced.

The small Spetznas team was high up on a ridgeline, overlooking the trail, and past that they could look deep into Chinese territory . Each man carried his own pack, his own gear, and was responsible for his own weapons. The mission they were on was a simple training mission. There task was to escape and evade searchers that were after them since they ambushed a supply convoy. All they had to do now was remain hidden and wait for extraction.

"If he spotted us, he could radio it in. We'd best be moving."

"Relax. He didn't spot us. Besides, he could call it in to anyone if he had seen us."

"How do you know that? Smartass. You are willing to bet your life on that?"

"No antenna on the vehicle. That means no radio. And," he held up his little Motorola cellphone. "We have no signal here, how could he have signal down there amid the rocks?"

Dmitry nodded. "What if he drives to a place that has signal?"

"There is no way he saw us, relax."

Starshina Alexander Nevsky sat back and considered everything, "He did seem too preoccupied to be looking for people hiding behind stones. He was barely able to keep the truck on the road."

Just then they heard a crash and went to investigate by crawling up to the crest and slowly peeking over to see the trail that passed them and wrapped around the ridge before heading due south to the small village there.

They saw the UAZ had failed to negotiate a turn and was laying on its side, nose first in a ditch.

"Come on!" Dmitry stood up.

"You are breaking protocol, Dmitry!"

We can't let him suffer. Maybe he needs help."

"It's not our mission."

"There is no one else around for miles save for the goats and sheep."

"If we get caught we fail our mission."

"What is more important here? Someone's life a training op? Maybe this is part of the scenario."

The Starshina stood up and picked up his rifle. "I do not want to be responsible for an unnecessary death. We go and will render what aide is needed."

The nine men followed their Starshina single file, making their way down from the high ridge, picking their way slowly and carefully. A twisted ankle out here could be a death sentence.

As they approached the small truck, one of the Mule Brothers noticed something. "It is not Russian. That is Chinese, look." Dmitry Donskoy said. His brother Vasili Donskoy nodded his head. "For the first time in your miserable life, you might be right."

The team spread out as they got closer, maintaining their intervals and making sure they had clear fields of fire. They could see someone moving inside and they could hear a low moaning.

Serzhánt Ivan Kulkovo called over to Kievien Rus, the team Medic. "See if he is okay."

Kievien didn't say anything, just nodded and ran to the UAZ as the team behind him raised their empty weapons and found firing angles. The UAZ's door was jammed but a couple solid tugs pulled it open enough to get to the man trapped inside. "Are you injured?" He said in Russian since he didn't know Chinese. But most of the Chinese in this area could speak some Russian.

The person in the UAZ only moaned. Kievien crouched low and looked in. The man was bleeding from a number of cuts, too many to have come from just rolling the little truck. "Come on, let's get you out of there." He looked over at one of the Mules. "Vasili, get over here. Help me open this door wider."

Vasili slung his AS VAL rifle and jogged over. With a couple grunts the two Spetznas got the UAZ's door open wide enough to pull the man from the vehicle. He was covered in blood and moaning, and he was Chinese Military. His uniform was that of Shang Wei, a Captain. On his belt was an empty holster.

"What is he doing here?"

The Chinese officer moaned and started thrashing. "Look at his eyes!" Vasili said as he backed away. "They look like the eyes of a dead fish!"

"Hold him down!" Kievien cried as the Chinese officer twisted around and started grabbing him.

The man's uniform was torn in several places and stained in blood. He screamed and moaned incoherently. Vasili and two others jumped on the man, pinning him back to the ground. Andrei Kurbzky reached across the officer to hold his arm and shoulder when the Chinese Officer's head turned and bit his arm. "Ayyyeee! He's bitting me!"

"Sedate him!"

Andrei screamed as the Chinese man's teeth sunk deeper into his arm. "Get him off me!"

The Chinese officer opened his mouth and tried to yell, but it came out like a breathless hiss. Andrei rolled away, cussing and holding his arm.

Kievien scrambled out of his backpack to retrieve his medical kit. He had everything he would need to handle trauma, but not a lot of it. His experienced hands quickly found what he needed, tranquilizers and pain medication. "This should do it, just hold him still!"

As Kievien pulled up on the sleeve of the bloody uniform, he saw the chunk of flesh torn from Chinese Officer's arm. It was a deep wound, exposing bare bone. The wound had festered and the flesh around it had blackened. Dark streaks ran from the wound, up his arm. In spite of the missing muscle tissue, the man was still strong. "Hold him still!"

Kievien plunged the needle into the arm and injected the drug. The Chinese Officer didn't seem to be effected in the slightest and continued to moan and thrash.

Andrei Kurbzky staggered back up to his feet. "The man is insane!" He looked at it and saw his arm was bleeding from the teeth marks, but the damage wasn't nearly as bad as the pain. "He has sharp teeth!"

"You act as if you had been bitten by a wolf. Pick your vagina up and try to act like a man, Andrei." Ivan said with a shake of his head. Andrei grimaced at his arm. "He must be rabid, like a wild dog. We should shoot him."

"No one is shooting anyone. Even if we wanted to. Do you have a bullet?" Starshina Alexander Nevsky said quietly. "We should call this in. Ivan, you and Peter call this in and request a medical helicopter." Ivan nodded and turned to Peter started to pull off his rucksack to retrieve the satellite phone he carried.

After a few minutes the Chinese Officer laid still and only let out a soft moaning from the back of his throat. Kievien started working on the officer's wounds, cleaning and dressing them as best as he could. He used three times the amount it would have normally taken to sedate a man. This worried Kievien, but he said nothing. The other men, no longer needed to hold the officer down, had started trying to turn the UAZ back onto it's wheels. It took most of the team to do it, but soon the matte green truck crashed down on it's tires. It's roof was caved in, but it was in good shape otherwise.

"Alex." Kievien said. "Come here. Look at this." When the Master Sargent stood over the officer, the team medic pointed to one of the wounds. "This looks like human teeth here and here. And this looks like from a human hand clawing." Kievien held his hand over the wound, showing the spacing of the four lines torn into the officer's flesh.

"So he was attacked by someone."

"Several someones. Not all these teeth marks are from the same person biting him." Kievien pointed to other marks. "See the differences? At least three people were biting him."

"Are you trying to make me hungry, Kievien?"

"No, Alex. I am trying to figure out what happened to this man. He has deep wounds and has lost a great deal of blood. These... " Kievien pointed to some of the deeper tears, "these should still be bleeding, but they are not." He pushed in on a deeper wound to force out some blood, it was dark and thick, more like old motor oil than human blood. "See how it is coagulated? In the veins, it's coagulated... this isn't good. His heart beat is so faint, I can't even feel it. This man should be dead." Kievien looked up at Alex. "If I was in a hospital back in Moscow, I would say that he was. Yet he fought like a bear."

Alexander looked down at the Chinese Officer. The skin was pale with darkened lips and dead-like eyes. He had seen eyes like that before, on a woman that had been blinded years ago while working in a factory. Caustic chemicals had splashed her in the face and killed her eyes. Yet this man was able to drive all the way out here. He couldn't have done this blind. He couldn't have been an Officer, blind. This didn't make any sense.

"Starshina." Ivan called over. "We can't reach anyone." He held up the Sat-Phone and shook it. "No one is answering."

"Raise the long antenna then. We need to get a helicopter here quickly."

Peter had been expecting that and already pulled out the long antenna. This was a simple system that used a large helium balloon to pull an antenna and wire high into the air. The balloon inflated in a matter of seconds and started pulling wire off the spool quickly. Ivan connected the line to a radio set and tuned in to the proper frequency.

Ivan keyed the radio and called his codes, then let go of the transmit button and turned up the volume. Over the radio they could hear screams and shouting. "What the hell is going on?" Ivan looked up at Peter.

"You have the wrong frequency, you idiot." Peter pushed Ivan out of the way and checked the dials and compared them to the frequencies he had written down. It was correct. Peter then changed to an alternative and before he could key the microphone, the sound of chaos came over the set. Peter looked at Ivan. "What the hell is this?"

"Have you made contact yet?" Alexander called over to them.

"Negative, Starshina. No one is responding on any channel."

"Is the radio damaged?"

"No, it's fine... it's just..." Peter didn't know what to say. He just turned the radio on and cranked up the volume. The sounds of screaming carried out and the whole team heard it. Everyone stopped what they were doing.

Starshina Alexander Nevsky stood up straight and looked around. "This training exercise is over, right now. We need to get back to base."

"But we can't get a helicopter." Ivan started to object.

"We can use that." Alex pointed at the wrecked UAZ. "Cut the top off of it and it will serve."

Just outside of Ramstein Air Force Base, Uncle Musket was just putting the finishing touches on the brand new pub that he was calling "Fosters & Brenneke". He had already hired on his first Tavern Wench, a busty blond haired German local girl that was pretty enough and randy enough to be Musket's type. He especially liked the way she smiled out him.

She said something flirty to him in her own language, one which Musket didn't understand in the slightest, but enjoyed the sound of. It reminded him of father, but the way she spoke, made it seem all the more naughty. Musket looked up at her from wiping off the newly varnished bar counter. He smiled back at her, and he didn't know why, but he liked her more than the other Tavern Wenches.

The sound from just outside the door startled both of them. It was loud deep moan that turned into a roar. Suddenly there was a hard bang against the side of the building. Bottles of brandy, rum, and whiskey shook and some fell to the floor, shattering and wasting Musket's hand chosen selection.

"Crap." Musket reached for his Howda, a single shot pistol of an unreasonably large caliber. There was another crashing against the wall. This time, the wall caved in several feet and the walls timbers were splintering. Time seemed to slow down. Everything was in slow motion. A huge mutated zombie crashed through the wall with an animal-like roar. Splinters of wood slowly rotated through the air. The zombie was the largest he had ever seen, like a professional body builder, but much bigger, to the point of deformity. It stumbled into the room huffing like a bull, splattering blood and spittle as it breathed. It looked around the room with dead white eyes glaring. It turned it's massive neck-less head to Musket and roared again. The heavy oaken table between them gave it only a moment of pause before it raised a pair of fists and smashed the table in half as if it was made of balsa wood. The Wench screamed. The zombie wasn't just massive in size, but it looked as if it had been created, sewn together from tissues and muscles from other zombies. "Well arn't you an ugly bastard!" Musket raised the Howda and fired. The report sounded like a big truck backfiring with two flashes, one from the side of the lock and the other from the muzzle. A big fat ball of hardened lead zipped out and struck the beast's chest, blowing a hole through meat and bone, but with no apparent effect. The huge zombie was only turned slightly. It looked down at the wound on its shoulder and then back at Musket and roared.

"Shit."

The beast flung half of the table across the room where it smashed into the wall. The slow motion sensation came to an abrupt end. The Wench cried out as wooded shrapnel struck her across the face. Musket let go of the Howda and reached behind his back with both hands for the cap and ball pistols. He drew them a split second before the Howda hit the ground. The monstrous zombie stepped forward as Musket cocked the hammers. The monster roared and jumped at Musket just has he fired. One ball caught the beast in the jaw, wrecking it and leaving it hanging from one side. The other ball struck the monster on the cheek bone and opened up the rotten flesh, exposing bone and gristle. The huge zombie was staggered but not stopped.

The Tavern Wench screamed and ran to Musket's side. "Woman, run to the base and raise the alarm!" Musket growled. "I'll hold this creature as long as I can!" He threw one of the pistols and drew out his large, crudely made bowie knife. "Come on, you filth! I'm tired of waiting for you!" Musket moved forward, as the Wench ran out the door and into the night. The mutant zombie paid her no attention at all and Musket knew they were here for him.

The mammoth sized zombie stepped forward and Musket buried his bowie knife into the monster's mouth as it brought his fists down on Musket's shoulders, sending musket crashing to the ground. As the huge beast staggered backwards with a huge portion of Bowie sticking up out of top of it's head, another huge mutant of a zombie crawled through the whole in the wall. Just like the first one, this one was also made of assorted parts and pieces.

Musket looked upwards as he pushed himself up off the floor. He was dizzy from the impact and at first he thought he was seeing double until he saw that one of the huge mutant zombies was holding the head of his Tavern Wench. Her body was someplace else. Musket's eyes went wide.

The second zombie was just as big as the first one, but wider and some of the patches of skin that covered it was different colors than the rest of it. Musket rolled and came up on his feet by his bar. He had no weapons but picked up a bottle of his personal favorite. He threw it at the first zombie, breaking the bottle on it's face. Musket had no other weapons, so he picked up another bottle and knocked it back. With a mouthful of high proof liquid, he grinned as he flicked open his stainless Zippo. The wet monster came forward as Musket spewed out a mouth full of the well aged adult beverage and sent a fireball into the creature's face. The fire spread over the beast, and then across the floor and over the bar.

"That didn't go as planned." he said as he dove away from the fire.

The huge flaming monster was roaring and it stood up straight, hitting its head on the ceiling as yet another gigantic beast crashed through the door. The monster flung something at Musket. It was the head it had pulled off the Tavern Wench. The base would get no warning.

Half the tavern was engulfed in flame and for the first time in his life, Musket was thinking about running away. He was about to bolt for door, when he heard someone laughing. Through the door, a tall thin person walked through casually. He was smiling with a broad tooth filled grin. His red eyes reflected the fire. "What a great place you have here, Musket." The Litch's voice was dry and cold, like metal being dragged over gravel. "Feels very warm. Reminds me of home."

Just as Musket was about to retort, one of the massive zombies backhanded him. Musket flew across the room hit the wall and everything went black.

When he opened his eyes again he was being dragged by his arms between the two huge mutant zombies.

Dmitri had to wrestle the steering wheel to keep the UAZ on the road. Something in the front end must have been bent. If he let go of the wheel, the little truck would want to turn hard to the right. It was hard enough to stay on the road as his brother was riding on the hood in front of him. "You drive like you had just drank a whole bottle of Vodka!" Vasili said.

"I could drive better if I did."

"If I had some, I would think you drove better."

"I could also drive better if I didn't have to try to look around your fat ass. How can one so large be a Spetznas?"

"I'm smaller than you are..." Vasili was winding up for a good insult when Alex interrupted him.

"Would you two please the hell shut up? You are both giving me a headache. You sound like a couple of bitches."

The Spetznas team was piled in and on the little UAZ. The Chinese officer was laying on a makeshift litter that was across the UAZ's hood. Two Spetznas were riding on the hood with him, the others were sitting on the seats, on the backs of the seats and piled on wherever they could. The little truck had to struggle to get moving, but it was running just fine. The only problem was the fuel gauge was not as optimistic as Alex would have liked.

"I think I am going to be sick." Andrei Kurbzky said, he was sitting on top of the back seat, with his legs dangling off the back.

Peter patted Dmitry on the shoulder, "Good job, Donkey. You've now made half the team ill."

Andrei shook his head then suddenly bent over in half and started vomiting like a fire hose. The spew was bright red. The UAZ hit a small bump in the rocky trail and suddenly Andrei was no longer on the truck.

"Stop the truck!" Peter called out. "Stop now!"

Dmitry hit the brakes and the UAZ skidded to a stop. The team jumped off and out and ran back to where Andrei was laying in the dirt and rocks. He was curled up in a ball and his body was convulsing.

"This isn't from Donkey's bad driving." Kievian said. He rolled Andrei over. The man was as pale as a ghost and his mouth was filled with blood. "He's burning up with fever." Kievian knelt down and started checking Andrei's vital signs. "His heart is beating like a machine gun, but it's weak." The Medic said to no one in particular. "Andrei. Andrei, can you hear me?"

Andrei turned his face to the sound of the voice and opened his eyes. They were cloudy and unfocused. "Rrrrrrrraaaaaahhh. Heeelp m, m, meee.. Aaaauughh!" Andrei moaned in pain and started convulsing harder. He threw up more blood, but this time the blood was dark, almost black.

Kievian started to set up an IV. He was about to push in a needle when Andrei started to thrash around then went completely still. Kievian stopped.

"Andrei?" Kievian slapped the man's face, lightly at first, then harder. "Andrei?" But Andrei was unresponsive. The medic checked vitals and slowly put the IV kit back into the bag.

Some of the men in the team pulled off their hats and looked down at the ground. Starshina Alexander Nevsky wasn't a religious man, but his parents had been Orthodox. He crossed himself in the moment of silence.

Andrei had been with the team for almost a decade, which was a rare thing for a group with such a high attrition rate.

Everyone turned when they heard the loud moaning. It was unbelievable that the Chinese Officer was standing up at the front of the UAZ. When everyone turned to look, some of the men raised their weapons before they remembered they had no live rounds. The Chinese man turned and looked at the group of soldiers. Blackened lips curled up from discolored teeth. It hissed and growled like an animal as it took a step in their direction. The man looked worse than he had before. More cadaverous. His skin was pulled tight around his face. The worst was the eyes. Completely white and dead, yet the eyes looked at the Russian Special Forces soldiers, seeing them and seeing into them. Alex felt a chill and inside, he knew this wasn't right. There was something deeply wrong here. Evil. True, seething evil.

The Chinese Officer broke into a run, straight for the Soldiers, hands out in front of him like the talons of an eagle.

Leo Kalita was standing closest. As the zombie threw its self at Leo, he instinctively reacted and turned stepped to the side. His VSS rifle came up and smashed the zombie in the face as it dove past him.

The zombie picked its self back up and turned its head back to Leo. The rifle had torn the zombie's face wide open. Bone was visible from jaw to temple, but the zombie was unfazed. It screamed at Leo and was about to charge when Vasili swung his wooden handled shovel. The shovel's wide blade sunk deep into the back of the zombie's neck, causing the creature to collapse. Vasili jerked the shovel out and swung again, and again, the shovel chopping open the zombie's head.

Alex put a hand on Vasili's shoulder, "Easy, comrade, it's dead."

"So is Andrei!" Vasili brought the shovel down again on the zombie's corpse one last time and stood back. "It killed Andrei!"

Just then Andrei's corpse twitched. "Andrei! You are alive!" Kievien shouted. "Andrei!"

The body of Andrei moved, but not in a normal human way. It twisted and shrugged and moved strangely. Then suddenly its eyes opened. They were dead and white like the Chinese Officer's. Suddenly the Andrei zombie lurched and lunged at Kievien. The zombie grabbed the medic and went for his throat. Kievien screamed and tried to push his old friend away. The zombie bit into the medic's neck as he screamed.

Everyone was yelling and some tried to pull Andrie away. Everyone was disturbed except their Starshina. Alex calmly pulled out his own shovel and let it fall in his hand to the end of the handle. The Russians had dealt with this sort of thing in the past. Old stories came to his mind. He had thought them to be just that, stories. Tall tales to scare kids. He remembered his grandfather telling him and his brother of the mass grave, filled with dead Nazis outside of Stalingrad, the night after the grave had been covered with dirt, the Nazis crawled back out. Alex didn't sleep for days after that story. Now he knew that it wasn't just a story. He did what his Grandfather did. He swung his shovel.

www.ingramcontent.com/pod-product-compliance
Lightning Source LLC
Chambersburg PA
CBHW020614260626
47157CB00003B/1007

* 9 7 8 1 6 1 8 0 8 0 2 5 7 *